Pacys kicked and rose
scious of the myriad battle
riors died by the dozens between heartbeats. There was no
way the defenders of the Sharksbane Wall could hold their
positions. The old bard was watching history in the making
and he knew it.

The Taker

"My time will come again, little malenti," Iakhovas said.
"For now I conserve my strength and mask my presence.
We have enemies who know of me. The high mages and the
Taleweaver have learned about me. Perhaps they know
more than they should have ever known—but we will see.
Despite everything they have heard about me, I am more
powerful than they can possibly imagine."

The Taker's Bane

"Boy, if something powerful enough to stop the winds
and control the waters wanted you dead, it would have
drank down the ship and you with it," the captain said.
"You're still alive, so I have to ask why."

"I don't know," Jherek said with grim determination,
"but whatever it is that calls me, it will regret it."

THE THREAT FROM THE SEA

RISING TIDE
THE THREAT FROM THE SEA: BOOK I

MEL ODOM

UNDER FALLEN STARS
THE THREAT FROM THE SEA: BOOK II

MEL ODOM

REALMS OF THE DEEP
THE THREAT FROM THE SEA

EDITED BY PHILIP ATHANS

THE SEA DEVIL'S EYE
THE THREAT FROM THE SEA: BOOK III

MEL ODOM

FORGOTTEN REALMS

THE THREAT FROM THE SEA

BOOK III

The Sea Devil's Eye

MEL ODOM

THE SEA DEVIL'S EYE
The Threat from the Sea, Book III

©2000 Wizards of the Coast, Inc.
All Rights Reserved.

Distributed in the United States by St. Martin's Press. Distributed in Canada by Fenn Ltd.

Distributed to the hobby, toy, and comic trade in the United States and Canada by regional distributors.

Distributed worldwide by Wizards of the Coast, Inc. and regional distributors.

Cover art by Don Maitz
Interior art by Sam Wood
Map by Rob Lazzaretti
First Printing: May 2000
Library of Congress Catalog Card Number: 99-69833

9 8 7 6 5 4 3 2 1

ISBN: 0-7869-1638-9
TSR 21638-620

U.S., CANADA,   EUROPEAN HEADQUARTERS
ASIA, PACIFIC, & LATIN AMERICA   Wizards of the Coast, Belgium
Wizards of the Coast, Inc.   P.B. 2031
P.O. Box 707   2600 Berchem
Renton, WA 98057-0707   Belgium
+1-800-324-6496   +32-70-23-32-77

Visit our web site at **www.wizards.com**

**This book is dedicated to
Ethan Ellenberg**

My friend and agent, who has stood with me during the darkest hours, given me his belief in me when my own flagged, and has helped me reach for dreams that I might have once thought out of my grasp..

Thank you.

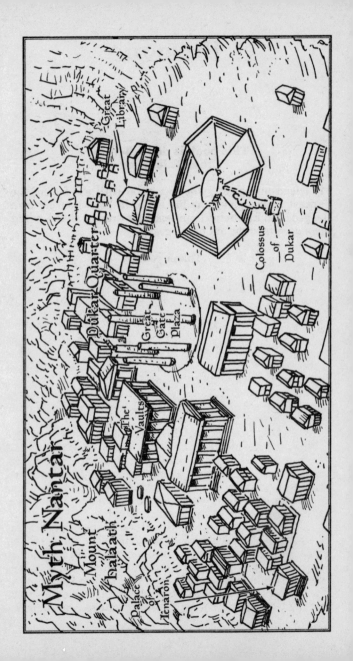

Prologue

The Alamber Sea, Sea of Fallen Stars
4 Flamerule, the Year of the Gauntlet

A man's dying scream drew Pacys's attention. To his right, the Sharksbane Wall extended across the sea floor until it disappeared in the gloom. Below and to the left, for as far as Pacys could see, the wall lay in ruins. Chunks of stone and coral lay in a fan shape, as if a huge hammer had shattered the wall.

"Marthammor Duin," Khlinat breathed somewhere above and behind the old bard, "watch over them what wander far and foolishly." The dwarf was thick and broad. Unruly gray whiskers stuck out around his wide face and his hands caressed the hafts of the two hand axes at his waist. He kicked out with his good foot. A gray-green coral peg took the place of his lower right leg.

Elf, merman, and sahuagin all warred below. From this distance, they looked tiny against the wall, but Pacys felt their terror and courage. Those emotions transmuted to musical notes in his mind. He carefully braided and twined them, piecing together the songs that haunted him.

The hum of sahuagin crossbow strings rolled over the sharp clash of coral tridents against stolen or salvaged spears.

Even the whisk of the sea devils' barbed nets echoed across the terrain, picked up by the old bard's heightened senses.

For the moment, Pacys *was* the battle. He was the life and death of every one of the hundreds of warriors at the Sharksbane Wall. He wore only a sea elf's diaphanous gown of misty blue. The magic of the emerald bracelet on his wrist allowed him to breathe underwater and kept him comfortable even from the occasional chill. Though he kept his head and jaw shaved, his silver eyebrows hinted at his age. The bard was seventy-six years old, still vigorous but in his waning years.

> *"Hallowed wall, prized from death,*
> *Built on blood and mortised by fear,*
> *Stood broken, shattered, crumbled,*
> *No longer protecting those here.*
> *The loyal warriors warred, sinew against sinew.*
> *They fought, and they died,*
> *Clamped tight between unforgiving fangs*
> *Of those who followed the Taker's dark stride."*

It wasn't a song of victory. Despite the excitement at having found another piece of the song he'd searched for, the old bard's heart grew cold and heavy.

His trained eye noted the whitish colors of the rock, nearly a dozen hues that he could pick out at a glance, all colored by pearled iridescence from the millennia the wall had stood. The blue sea had texture, the color of a sky rent by gentle summer rains. The uneven terrain at the foot of the Sharksbane Wall spilled in dozens of cliffs and gullies where schools of brightly colored fish cowered.

Through it all, clouds of blood twisted and spun, caught by the shifting ocean currents and the movements of those who fought and died. Even though the bracelet gave him the ability to breathe underwater, it didn't remove the harsh metallic taste of iron.

In the land engagements he'd witnessed, Pacys had smelled the stench of battle, spiced by the fear and anger of the men and women who sold and bought lives with a sword stroke. But here, in the underwater realm of Serôs, the kingdoms scattered across the bottom of the Sea of Fallen Stars, death had flavor.

Pacys steeled himself, gaining control over his lurching stomach. Bright blue light flared like a dying star to Pacys's left. The old bard turned and spotted Taranath Reefglamor, Senior High Mage among the High Mages at Sylkiir. The old elf mage wore his silver hair loose. Blade thin, his blue and white flecked skin hung loose on him. The pointed chin and pointed ears made his face seem harsh and angular. He thrust a hand out at a knot of a dozen nearby sahuagin that swam toward them.

In the blink of an eye, shark's teeth seemed to form in that part of the water. The teeth were etched in silvery gleams, bare sketches that still left no doubt as to what they were.

The cone of shark's teeth grew to twice Pacys's height in width and nearly five times that in length. The sorcery ripped through the sahuagin, shredding flesh and breaking bone. Severed limbs and heads exploded out from the corpses, and mutilated torsos came apart in chunks.

Surviving sahuagin swam at them, clutching their tridents to their chests. Fangs filled their broad mouths to overflowing, showing bone-white and ivory against the teal and pale green of their skins. Fins stuck out from their arms and legs, sharp-edged appendages they used to slice open their prey.

Built broad and squat, hammered into near indestructibility by the pressure of the uncaring ocean, the sahuagin moved gracefully through the water. Webbed feet and hands pulled at the sea. Their magnetic black eyes sucked the light from the depths, black holes that held no mercy.

Pacys brought his staff up. There wasn't time to run.

"Die hu-maan!" the lead sahuagin snarled.

"Friend Pacys!" Khlinat cried.

From the corner of his eye, Pacys watched the dwarf struggling to swim through the water to reach his side. They'd met in Baldur's Gate, at the time of the attack that destroyed the city's harbor, and they'd remained together since.

Pacys struck with the staff, lodging it in the tines of the trident his opponent carried. The old bard pushed away from the attack.

The sahuagin flew past him, streaking toward the dwarf

who was clawing up to an even keel.

Pacys reached into the bag of holding at his waist, took out a piece of slate and a fingernail clipping, and held them in his fist.

Pointing with the forefinger of the fist that held the ingredients to his spell, Pacys scribed a powerful symbol in the water that flared pale violet for a moment. He mouthed half a dozen words, then felt the explosion in his fist as the spell claimed the materials in his hand.

Gray ash spilled from his hand as a shimmering wall formed in the water before him. A dull roar blasted out from the other side of the shimmering wall.

The sahuagin trapped there writhed in agony. The sahuagin, like many sea creatures, had lateral lines that ran the length of their bodies. Those lines sensed vibrations in the water, and the roar was agony to them.

Pacys swam for Khlinat.

"Foul devilspawn," Khlinat roared in a voice only a dwarf in full battle frenzy could muster. "I'll keelhaul ye and have yer guts for garters, I will. I'm one of the Iron-eater clan, one of the fiercest, fightingest dwarven clans ever blessed by Marthammor Duin!"

"Die!" the sahuagin replied in its raspy voice.

The bard gripped his staff in the middle and twisted. Foot-long, razor-edged blades shot from both ends.

The sahuagin released its hold on Khlinat's hand axe, then ran its talons down the dwarf's arm.

Yelping with pain and surprise, Khlinat brought his knees up, then shoved his claw coral peg into the sahuagin's chest. The peg burst through the sahuagin's back. Blood roiled out and settled in a cloud around the creature's upper body.

"I done for ye," Khlinat declared, putting his other foot on the sahuagin's face and kicking out. "Behind ye, songsmith, and be right quick about it, too."

Moving with the fluid grace of a dancer, Pacys whipped the staff around. The razor-edged blade sank into the sahuagin's shoulder next to its thick neck.

The creature's momentum and speed shoved Pacys back and down as he held onto the staff. The old bard ripped the staff free, and let his momentum carry him around. The staff flashed as the sahuagin swam over his head. The keen blade ripped across the creature's stomach, spilling its entrails in a loose tangle.

Two sahuagin who'd been close to the one Pacys disemboweled were overcome by the bloodlust that fired their species. Their predatory instincts sent them after the easier prey of their own kind rather than the bard. Their jaws snapped and clicked, biting into the tender flesh released into the sea. They followed their dying comrade toward the seabed below.

Pacys moved the staff in his hands, keeping himself loose, but his head played the song that would be part of the fall of the Sharksbane Wall. It was not a song of victory. The music was a dirge, a song of defeat and death.

A dozen sahuagin surrounded the bard and the dwarf. Pacys swam toward Khlinat, putting his back to the dwarf's.

One of the sahuagin in front of the bard lunged forward.

"I've got 'im, songsmith," Khlinat said. "Mind you watch yerself."

The dwarf sliced his right axe across, shearing off two of the sahuagin's fingers. Before Khlinat could recover his balance, another sahuagin threw one of the barbed nets over him.

Khlinat bawled in rage and pain. He slid his fingers through the openings in the net and tried to pull it away, but succeeded only in sinking a dozen or more of the bone hooks into his own flesh.

Pacys ripped free the keen-edged, dark gray coral knife from his belt and raked the blade at the net strands, parting a handful of them.

A sahuagin swam across the top of the net, grabbed the loose line floating at the top of the seaweed hemp, and dragged Khlinat easily after it.

Another sahuagin swam up from under the net and rammed its trident into the old bard's right thigh. The sahuagin swam backward and yanked hard on the cord. The pain hit Pacys with blinding intensity.

Suddenly, a fan-shaped spray of bright red, gold, green, and red-violet lanced through the water. Pacys experienced a sudden vertigo, then the feeling passed and he only felt slightly dizzy. The sahuagin pulling him lost its bearing and started flailing helplessly in the water.

"Easy, Taleweaver."

The old bard recognized Reefglamor's voice and turned in time to see the Senior High Mage swim toward him. A group of mermen and sea elves were with him. They moved among the disoriented sahuagin and stabbed their swords and knives through the creatures' gill slits, then ripped all the way through, bleeding them out.

Reefglamor laid his hand on the trident that impaled Pacys's leg. He spoke a few words, and a pale green fire leaped from the High Mage's fingers and quickly enveloped the offending trident. In the next heartbeat, the trident was gone, leaving only gray-black ash to drift along the ocean's currents. Two mermen freed Khlinat from the net.

Further down below, the battle raging across the fallen section of the Sharksbane Wall continued.

"We are losing this fight," Reefglamor stated in a low voice.

"Yes," Pacys agreed reluctantly.

"Senior," Pharom Ildacer called. His fondness for food and drink made him more round than most sea elves. Black strands still stained his silver hair and he wore a deep purple weave. Anxiety colored his features. "We can't stay. The guards here can't hold their positions."

"I know," Reefglamor said. "Gather who we can, and let's save as many of them as we are able."

Ildacer nodded and swam away.

The music inside Pacys's head continued, mournful and hollow. He was certain the song would stand in the memories of its listeners as strongly as the fall of Cormanthyr and the flight of the elves.

"There! Do you see it then?" one of the nearby mermen asked, pointing with the trident he held. "That's the Taker's ship."

Pacys spotted the great galley cutting through the water. It was strange to see the big ship completely submerged, yet moving like a great black shadow.

And somewhere aboard her, Pacys knew, the Taker savored his victory. The threat from the sea was a threat no longer, and death now traveled through the world of Serôs, powered by sharp fins and devouring fangs.

I

4 Flamerule, the Year of the Gauntlet

"What you want here, boy? Is it enough for ye to take a man's rightful belongings, or are ye gonna cut an honest man's throat too?"

Jherek pressed the older man up against the back wall of the Bare Bosom and held a scaling knife hard against the man's bewhiskered throat.

The man was in his early forties and his breath stank of beer. A skull and crossbones tattooed over his heart advertised his chosen profession.

Jherek breathed hard, and struggled to keep his hand from shaking. Full night had descended over the pirate city of Immurk's Hold hours ago. Clouds covered all but a handful of blue-white stars. Shadows filled the narrow alley behind the tavern.

Even at nineteen, Jherek was bigger and broader than the pirate, his muscles made hard from years of working as both shipwright and sailor. His light brown hair caught the silver gleam of the stars in the highlights bleached by the sun, and hung past his shoulders now. His pale gray eyes belonged to a wolf living in the wild. He wore leather armor under a dark blue cloak that reached to the tops of his boots. A cutlass hung at his side.

"If it's me purse ye want," the pirate offered, swallowing hard, "yer gonna find it light tonight. I been swilling old Kascher's homemade beer and dallying with them women what he keeps upstairs."

"I'm not after your purse," Jherek whispered. The very idea of robbing the man turned his stomach.

"Slice his damned throat."

Jherek cut his gaze over to the left, startled by the harshness of the words.

Talif stood near the building, fitting in neatly with the shadows. A sharp short sword was in his fist. He was one of Captain Azla's pirate crew. The ship's hand had stringy black hair and a triangular face covered with stubble.

"He lives—or we live. Which is it going to be?" Talif sneered.

* * * * *

Sabyna Truesail sat at a table in a hostel across the cobblestone street from the Bare Bosom and tried to relax. Nothing worked; she still worried.

The hostel was small, and at this time of night most of the guests meandered over to the Bare Bosom for more ribald festivities. The rest had called it a night in favor of an early morning. Sabyna, Captain Azla of *Black Champion,* and Sir Glawinn—a paladin in the service of Lathander—were half the crowd in the common room of the hostel. The scents of spiced meat and smoked fish warred against the stench of pipeweed and bitter ale. The tavern crowd could be heard easily from across the street, screamed curses mixed in with shouts of glee.

"I believe your attention would be better served elsewhere," Glawinn stated softly.

The paladin was middle aged but only a couple inches taller than Sabyna. He possessed a medium build, but carried himself with confidence, every inch a soldier. His black beard was short-cropped. Tonight he wore leather armor with a dark gray cloak over it. He used a brooch with Lathander's morning sun colors to hold the cloak around his shoulders.

"Where should I look?" Sabyna asked.

She stood a little more than five and a half feet tall, with copper-colored curls shorn well short of her shoulders. Seasons spent with the sun and sea had darkened her skin, but a spattering of freckles still crossed the bridge of her nose and her cheeks. Light from the big stone fireplace that warmed the hostel against the wet chill of the sea ignited reddish brown flames in her eyes. Her clothing was loose and baggy, worn that way so it wouldn't draw attention to her femininity.

Beside them, Azla wrinkled her nose in distaste. She held a half-drunk schooner of ale curled neatly in one gloved hand.

"He means you need to stop looking out that window so much," the pirate captain stated. "You're going to draw attention." Azla was a half-elf, bearing the characteristic pointed ears and slender build of her elf parent. Her features were beautiful and dusky, made even darker by a dozen years and more in the sun and wind. Silky black hair hung just to her shoulders, cut straight across. She wore a green blouse so dark it was almost black, and leather breeches dyed dark blue.

"The thing that worries me," Sabyna said, "is that he doesn't seem to be himself."

"No," the paladin said, "our young warrior is torn."

"By what?" Sabyna asked.

She risked another glance at the Bare Bosom, watching a sailor stride drunkenly from the establishment in the company of a serving wench doing her best to prop him up. The girl's fingers found the man's coin purse.

"There are things I feel a man should be willing to discuss on his own without having others discuss them for him," Glawinn answered.

"He could get killed over there tonight," Azla warned coldly.

"True enough," Glawinn replied, "but sometimes you have to rely on faith."

Azla snorted. "Faith isn't as certain as cold steel."

"It is for some." Glawinn's words were soft, but strong.

"Faith has never done well by me," Azla went on. A trace of bitterness threaded through her words.

Sabyna knew the captain hadn't always been a pirate. Azla had grown up in the Dalelands, but events and her own guilt forced her down to the Sea of Fallen Stars and into a pirate's life. Glawinn had no way of knowing that.

"The problem could be that you're not supposed to expect faith to do well by you," the paladin said. "You're supposed to do well by your faith."

"I am a mage," Sabyna said. "My faith is strong enough, but I'm no cleric to be led around by looking at a chicken's entrails to figure out what my chosen god wants me to do. I believe in knowledge. Our gods choose what knowledge to put in our paths, but it's up to us to learn it and choose what to do with it."

"My faith is not that way," Glawinn said. "I choose to let Lathander set me upon a path, trusting in the Morninglord that I will know what to do when the time comes."

"More men have died from conflicting beliefs than over gold and silver," Azla said. "Trusting a god is a very dangerous thing."

"On that issue, Captain," Glawinn said gravely, "I fear we'll have to disagree."

Sabyna pulled her cloak more tightly around her against the night's chill. More than anything she wanted to be up and around, doing something but not knowing what. "He's changed so much since I first met him," she whispered.

"How so?" Glawinn asked.

Across the street, a handful of cargo handlers deep in conversation walked across the uneven boardwalk in front of the Bare Bosom. One of them carried a shielded candle hanging from a crooked stick that barely beat back the night.

"When he first came aboard *Breezerunner*, there was a quiet desperation in him," Sabyna said. "I didn't understand that, now I understand his feelings even less after seeing how he handled himself aboard *Breezerunner*. He stood up against Vurgrom and his pirate crew in the middle of a maelstrom and never faltered. Now he seems . . ."

"Afraid?" A faint smile twisted Glawinn's lips. "He's a warrior, lady."

"Then why should he be afraid?"

"So that he might live, of course." Glawinn sipped his drink. "Warriors live with fear as they might a lover. They never forget that fear, else they step closer to Cyric's cold embrace."

The ship's mage wrapped her arms even tighter around herself, losing the battle against the night's chill creeping in against the banked coals filling the hostel's fireplace.

"Then where does that leave him?" she asked.

"He's dangerous," Azla commented. "He's dangerous to himself and to us."

"I don't think that's entirely true," Glawinn said.

The pirate captain shook her head. "I don't mean to disparage your beliefs, Sir Glawinn, but men believe what they want to believe. Sometimes purely because they have nothing else to believe in."

"And to live a life with nothing to believe in?" The paladin looked directly at her and asked, "What kind of life is that?"

Azla broke the eye contact, put on a deprecating smile, and said, "A very profitable one. If you're a pirate."

"Gold and silver assuages a wounded heart?"

Azla's eyes turned cold and hard. "You step over lines here, paladin."

"Forgive me, lady," Glawinn replied, though he showed no remorse, "I do indeed."

Sabyna watched the exchange in silence. She didn't know how Glawinn knew so much about the pirate captain, but she was aware how close he was to the truth. Azla's own life was filled with tragedy. The ship's mage reached for the hot tea she'd ordered and sipped it only to find that it was now cold.

"The thing that most concerns me is that your young friend didn't come here to take that pearl disk back from Vurgrom," Azla said.

"Then what?" Sabyna asked.

Azla kept her voice quiet and still. "I think it's very possible that your young friend came here to die as nobly as he can."

* * * * *

"I can't kill him," Jherek said. He stood in the alley, his body pressed up against the man, and silently damned all the events and the false pride that led to the point of holding a man's life at the edge of his knife.

11

"Then let me." Talif stepped forward and lifted the short sword.

The man in Jherek's grip tensed, on the verge of fleeing and taking his chances.

Jherek swung his empty hand, balling it into a fist and rolling his shoulder to get most of his weight behind the blow. His fist caught the pirate on the point of his chin and dropped him.

Talif knelt and grabbed the man by the hair. He swung his short sword toward the man's exposed throat.

Jherek kicked Talif in the chest, knocking him back across the hard-packed earth of the alley. Talif rolled instantly, coming up from the ground like a trained acrobat. His triangular face was a mask of rage. The short sword came around in a glittering arc.

The young sailor stepped in close and brought up his left arm. His open hand smacked into Talif's wrist and blocked the sword strike. Talif grunted in pain and anger. Before the mate could recover, Jherek slipped his free arm under the man's outstretched one and flipped him over his shoulder.

Carried by his own weight and momentum, pulled by Jherek's strength, Talif landed hard on the ground on his back. Murderous rage gleamed in his black eyes. "You're a fool," Talif snarled.

"That remains to be seen," Jherek said, "but I do know I am no murderer."

Talif struggled a moment to get free but couldn't.

"You knocked that man out, boy, but I've seen men knocked cold like that before. Sometimes they come around in just minutes, none the worse for it. He could still come into the tavern after us and let them all know we're among them."

"He doesn't know who we are," Jherek said quietly.

"By Leira's razor kiss, you fool, that man has seen me. He'll know I sail with Cap'n Azla."

"So you say." Jherek shook his head. "Maybe that's just your pride talking. We'll take our chances."

Talif cursed him soundly, using invective that would have shamed even most sailors.

Jherek maintained his grip even though Talif sought to shake out of it. "You think me a fool for letting this man live, but keep in mind that should a man attack me willingly with a sword in his fist, I'll not be so generous."

"A man doesn't always see the sword that cleaves him, boy," Talif threatened.

Jherek nodded. "But Glawinn would know." Azla's pirates walked lightly around the paladin.

"Umberlee take you both," Talif snarled. "The two of you think you're so high and mighty."

Jherek felt even more embarrassed. Glawinn was a paladin, a noble and courageous man who lived for honor and served a god who put quests and challenges before him. The young sailor knew he didn't belong in such company. He was only a foolish boy with misbegotten pride and an ill luck that followed him all his life as a birthright from his pirate father.

"Standing among men such as yourself," Jherek said in a harsh voice, "Sir Glawinn has no choice but to shine. I'd keep a civil tongue in your head, otherwise I'm going to feel that you're questioning his honor. That's something I won't allow."

Talif started to say something, but he glanced into Jherek's eyes, swallowed his words, and looked away.

Jherek released the man and stood with easy grace. He slipped the scaling knife back into his boot, then turned and walked toward the tavern's back door. He knew Talif thought about attacking him, but he counted on his own hearing and the dim shadows that moved on the alley wall to warn him if the man tried. And, truth to tell, maybe he didn't care.

Talif straightened his clothing and followed him a heartbeat later.

A short flight of steps led up to the tavern's back door. The door was narrow and made of scarred hardwood that showed years of abuse by guests and thieves and the neglect of uncaring employees.

Azla proved most resourceful as a pirate captain, though, and had provided Jherek a key that let him pass. He opened the door and stepped inside. A mixture of spicy odors tweaked his nose, almost drawing a sneeze. The aroma filling the room also held the scent of jerked beef and the strong odor of seafood. The stink of smoky grease overlaid everything.

13

Sand covered grease spills on the stained wooden floor. Grit rolled and crunched under Jherek's boots as he walked toward the narrow door on the east wall. He found the latch with his fingers and slipped it open with a tiny screech that he knew wasn't heard over the uproar in the tavern's main serving area.

Quietly, he went up the narrow and winding staircase, making himself go when every thought in his mind was to turn and leave. Kascher, Azla had assured him, used the hidden passageway to serve meals to guests who preferred to remain incognito. The man the young sailor was after was such a man.

Kascher's Bare Bosom tavern stood three stories tall, shouldered between the warehouses along the natural harbor at the center of Immurk's Hold.

On the top floor, Jherek paused at the door, listening. Muted voices echoed in the hall as footsteps passed.

The young sailor let himself out into the passageway. His eyes narrowed briefly even against the dim brightness of the small oil lamps hanging on the walls.

He glanced at the door on the right, reading the numbers. According to the information Azla gave him, the room he wanted was at the end.

The door at the end of the corridor was heavy oak, reinforced with bands of beaten iron.

"One side, pup," Talif said arrogantly. "Let a man do his job."

Grudgingly, Jherek stepped aside, leaving the door open to Talif. The thief moved to the door with a small smile curling his thin lips.

"Ah, pup," he whispered, "there's nothing like the sensation of being someplace you ought not be." Thin pieces of metal glinted briefly in his gloved hands. "Gladdens a man's heart, it does. The chance to prowl through another's secrets, steal kisses from another man's woman . . . there's nothing more sweet."

Shamed and furious, Jherek turned away. He heard the thin scratches of metal and tried to ignore them. The subtle arts Talif practiced went against everything Jherek believed in. Yet here he was, depending and hoping on the man's skills that he might set a greater wrong right.

The young sailor glanced out a window at the city.

Torches gleamed brightly along the wharf. From the tavern room, Jherek saw ships at anchor, men scurrying about aboard them, carrying crates and other prizes they'd no doubt taken from some luckless merchanter. His father, he knew, would have been perfectly at home here.

Farther into the interior of the city, fewer torches gleamed. The houses were ramshackle affairs for the most part, places cast together by seafaring men for families formed more by desperation than any emotion.

The men who worked the night were down by the harbor and the others lay abed or in the dozens of taverns throughout the city. Shadowy figures crossed the narrow, twisting streets below, some of them in groups but most of them alone. Thin wails of bawdy pirate chanteys drifted over the rooftops. The only thing that seemed normal to Jherek was the salt smell that lingered in the air.

"I'm done, pup. Do you want to join me?" Talif's whisper barely carried to Jherek's ears.

"Aye."

The young sailor drew his cutlass, the razor edge sliding free of the sash he used to bind it to his waist. He filled his other hand with the wickedly curved boat hook.

Pausing, Jherek nudged up the thin glass protecting the oil lamp's wick and flame. He blew it out, then replaced the glass cover. That end of the room darkened immediately.

"You have more skills at this kind of skullduggery than you'd think, pup," Talif said as he eased the door open. "Maybe you're not so honest as I thought, or you'd like to believe."

Jherek didn't argue, but he felt a sick lurching inside his stomach. Pirate's get and thief—he didn't really deserve any other label. Except maybe fool.

Talif led the way into the room, and Jherek covered his back. The young sailor heard the hoarse rasp of deep breathing as he gently closed the door.

Reaching back, Talif pressed a finger against Jherek's chest. "Wait," the man hissed.

Jherek breathed shallowly, taking in the sour odor of unwashed flesh and old rotgut whiskey. The stench of pipeweed clung to the room, salted with the flavor of cheap perfume.

"Not alone," Talif whispered. "I smell a woman."

For a moment, Jherek considered leaving the room. Catching the man they were after, even with everything Azla had ferreted out, had been difficult and risky enough. Endangering an innocent wasn't something he was prepared to do.

Talif's finger left his chest and the man glided silently across the room, a swiftly moving shadow.

Jherek moved immediately. His own vision quickly adjusted to the dark. The room was spacious but held only a couple trunks, an armoire that listed badly to one side, and a four-poster bed shrouded in mosquito netting.

"Alive," Jherek warned.

Reluctantly, Talif nodded. He moved to the left of the bed, while Jherek moved to the right.

Jherek put the hook back in his sash, then reached for the sleeping figure, brushing aside the mosquito netting with the blade of the cutlass. He clamped his hand on a face that he suddenly realized was too small, too smooth, and without whiskers.

At the other end of his arm, the young woman he'd grabbed by mistake opened her eyes wide in fear. She tried to sit up in bed. Jherek was so surprised by the turn of events that he didn't resist, watching in horror and embarrassment as the sheets fell away from her bare breasts.

The other form in the bed lurched up, a wickedly curved scimitar sliding free of the space between the feather-filled mattress and the carved headboard. Jorn Frennik was a large man, broad shouldered and beefy from a dozen years and more of living the savage life of a pirate.

Like the woman, he was naked, but he wore his calf-high boots. Bed covers flew as the pirate forced himself to his feet in the middle of the bed, yelling in rage and fear. He drew his scimitar back to swing.

II

4 Flamerule, the Year of the Gauntlet

Jorn Frennick's scimitar cleaved the air sharply, and
Jherek met the yelling pirate's steel with his own. Sparks
flared from the blades.

Despite the shadows and darkness filling the room,
Jherek read the pirate's moves. Keeping track of the
woman on the bed was harder, but he managed.

"Kill him!" Talif croaked hoarsely as he jockeyed for
position.

"No," Jherek ordered. "We need him alive."

Frennick shifted on the bed, kicking at the frightened
woman and forcing her away from him. She screamed in
pain and covered her head with her hands.

Moving swiftly, Jherek raised a booted foot and slammed
it into the center of the man's chest as hard as he could,
getting his weight behind the thrust.

Frennick flew backward off the bed and crashed against
the wall. Plaster shattered as he burst the inner wall and
dust roiled up in a great cloud.

Jherek pursued the man, striding across the bed and
barely avoiding the naked woman cowering in the twisted
bedding. He slipped through the mosquito netting.

Wheezing, his face a mask of rage, Frennick struggled desperately to push himself up from the wreckage of the wall.

The young sailor feinted, drawing out Frennick's attack. Jherek stepped back just enough to let the wickedly curved blade pass by him. He slammed his cutlass broadside against the pirate's scimitar, trapping it against the left side of Frennick's body.

"I'm gonna kill you, whelp!" the pirate roared. "Gonna have your guts for garters, I am!"

The young sailor ducked his head forward, slamming the top of his skull into Frennick's face. The pirate's nose broke with a snap. Blood gushed over his beard. Before Frennick could recover, Jherek drew back his left hand, balled it into a fist, and slammed it against the man's jaw twice. Frennick staggered. Still in motion, the young sailor grabbed a handful of Frennick's beard and slammed the man's head up against the wall. He lifted his knee three times in quick succession, driving it into Frennick's stomach.

Vomit streamed suddenly from Frennick's mouth, a gush of noxious liquid that spilled down his chest and stomach. The stench of soured hops almost gagged Jherek, but the young sailor breathed shallowly through his mouth.

The strength drained from Frennick in a rush as he struggled to regain his breath. Jherek kicked the scimitar from the man's hand. He placed a foot on the back of Frennick's head to hold the pirate in place, then turned back to the woman on the bed.

Talif leaned over her, holding a pillow over her face. The woman struggled, kicking her feet and scratching with her fingernails. Talif cursed her in a quiet voice.

Jherek slipped the knife from his boot and threw it. The effort wasn't hidden by his body as Malorrie and Glawinn had coached.

The knife spun and cut the air.

Cursing, Talif leaped to one side so it wouldn't spear his face. "Umberlee take you," he snarled.

The woman on the bed sucked in her breath in ragged gasps. She peered at the young sailor with rolling, frightened eyes, not bothering to cover her nakedness at all. Tears tracked down her face, and she shivered.

18

Still cursing him, Talif turned his attention to the small chest at the foot of the bed. "If she leaves the room, she'll warn the tavern—maybe call his mates up here on us."

Jherek gazed at the woman. "Lady," he said softly enough only to be heard over the noise coming from the tavern below, "I ask that you not leave this room."

Slowly, the woman sank more deeply into the bedding. She shook her head in a small motion that stirred her dark curls and said, "No, sir. No, I won't try to leave."

The term of respect, applied in such a situation, stung Jherek. He dropped his eyes from the woman's in shame. To have come so far pursuing what he hoped would have been a clue to his destiny, only to end up like this, making prisoners of frightened women, it was almost too much. If it were up to him, he would have left then, but the pearl disk Vurgrom took was not Jherek's to leave.

Talif ransacked the room with quick, knowing movements. Small drawers came out of the chest at the foot of the bed. Each was checked, inside and under, before being discarded. The thief even went on to disassemble some of the bigger pieces, checking for hiding places within them.

Frennick remained dazed, sick drool oozing occasionally from the corner of his mouth.

Jherek bound the man's hand behind his back with strips torn from the stained and faded sheets. He yanked the man to his feet. Frennick swayed drunkenly, like a storm-tossed cog riding out a stiff crosswind.

"Lady," the young sailor said, "I have one more task to ask of you."

"Yes, sir." She looked at him in bright fear.

"Could you dress him, please?"

Talif's derisive snort filled the room.

Cautiously, the woman climbed from the bed. She left the bedding behind and stood naked, embarrassing Jherek further. She took the pirate's clothing from a pile beside the bed, choosing the breeches first.

"At least have the common sense to go through his clothing first," Talif called out as he helped himself to the coins inside Frennick's duffel.

"Search his clothing then," Jherek told the woman. "Leave his personal effects. I'm looking for a gold disk that

19

looks very old. At its center is a pearl with a carved trident overlying a conch shell."

The woman knelt and began searching the pirate's clothing with experienced fingers, easily finding hidden pockets sewn into the material. Coins and small gems scattered on the floor before her, barely catching the dim light. Two small, very sharp blades that couldn't be properly called knives slid across the floor as well.

Frennick stood straighter, growling under his breath. "You've signed your own death warrant, boy. You do know that?"

"My death," Jherek told the pirate, looking him calmly in the eye, "was guaranteed the day of my birth. The only thing that remains to be seen is the how of it."

"At the end of my sword," Frennick promised, "with your guts spilled before you."

The young sailor glanced down at the woman, who was busy making some of the coins and gems disappear.

"No, lady," he said gently. "Don't rob him. You don't want him looking for you later."

The woman looked up and said, "He owes me a night's wages."

Embarrassed, knowing what the wages covered, Jherek gave her a tight nod. "As you will," he said.

"The night's not over," Frennick grumbled. "She didn't earn all her wages."

"The night was over for you," the woman rasped. "Once you've gotten so deeply into your cups and sated yourself like some rutting goat, you never wake again until well after morningfeast."

Frennick snuffled, drawing in phlegm and saliva, preparing to spit.

Jherek yanked the pirate's head back as he spat. Frennick succeeded only in spitting into his own face.

"No," he told Frennick softly, hating that he was taking part in any of the night's events.

The pirate growled in rage.

"Take a fair price, lady," Jherek said. "No more, no less."

Jherek watched as the woman hesitated, then dropped most of the coins and gems back to the floor.

"I can't find a disk like the one you described, sir," the woman said.

"Please dress him," Jherek replied.

Frennick kicked at her, but the woman quickly dodged away. Jherek rapped the man's ear with the flat of the cutlass blade, splitting the skin.

"Conscious, or dead weight," the young sailor promised, "I'm getting you out of here tonight. How things go after that will depend on how you act now."

Reluctantly, Frennick stood, then stepped into the breeches the woman held ready for him.

"Watch her," Talif advised from the other side of the room. He pried at the facing along the bottom of the wall, searching for hidden places. The wood pulled out easily. "She may act like she hates that bastard, but she may try to slip him a knife all the same."

Jherek didn't respond. He was already aware of that possibility. He watched carefully, trying to ignore the embarrassment he felt at watching the smooth, rolling nakedness the woman presented.

"Put back everything you've taken," the young sailor said.

"What?" Talif demanded.

Jherek spared the man a hard glance and said, "I won't be party to robbery."

"What do you think we're doing here tonight?"

"Taking something back that Frennick has no right to," Jherek answered.

Talif glared at the young sailor, trying to intimidate him. Jherek met the other man's gaze.

"I mean what I say," the young sailor said, "and I'll know if you lie and try to take something."

Despite his own show of will, Talif melted before the younger man's gaze. "Cyric take you," he said. "Are you afraid for your soul?"

"No," Jherek answered, knowing that the birthright passed on by his father already doomed him, "but I will stand accountable for my actions."

"These are *my* actions."

"You wouldn't be here if it weren't for me."

"Foolish, prideful stubbornness."

"Aye," Jherek responded without rancor. "Call it as you will, but you will not leave here with any stolen goods."

"Others will steal it in our stead," Talif protested.

"But we won't."

Uttering venomous curses, Talif emptied his pockets of coins, gems, and pieces of jewelry.

"I've not found your precious disk, boy, and I've searched every inch of this room."

"That disk is not here," Frennick said. He stood dressed in boots and breeches. With his hands behind his back, the woman hadn't been able to get a blouse on him. "Vurgrom has it."

Jherek faced the pirate more squarely and asked, "Where can we find Vurgrom?"

"If I tell you, Vurgrom will kill me."

Talif stepped closer, a wickedly curved blade in his hand, and said, "At least the death he hands out won't come as soon as the one we'll give you."

"There are things worse than death," Frennick said. "Vurgrom knows many of them."

Jherek grabbed a cloak from the foot of the bed. He checked through it quickly for weapons, turning up three knives, a sap, and a set of brass knuckles. He dropped the collection to the bed and draped the cloak over Frennick's shoulders, securing it with a brooch at the throat. Unless someone looked closely, they'd never know he went blouse-less beneath it.

"You're even more of a fool than I believed to think you can simply walk this man through the tavern and out the building," Talif stated.

"He knows about Lathander's disk," Jherek replied. "I need to know what he knows of it, and Captain Azla wishes to know about Vurgrom's movements."

The young sailor placed a hand on his prisoner's shoulders and shoved him forward.

"You can't just leave my valuables out for anyone to take," Frennick protested.

Jherek kept the man moving forward. "I won't be taking them," he said.

The noise from the pirates gathered downstairs filled the hallway, echoing up the stairwells that led down to the tavern. They were noisy and they were drunk, but the young sailor knew every sword in the place would be turned against him if they figured out what he was doing.

* * * * *

Over thirty pirates crowded into the Bare Bosom tavern, seated on the long, rough-hewn benches on two sides of the uneven rectangular tables in the center of the large room. The wooden walls held scars that were obscene pictographs, fake treasure maps, and touchstones for tall tales told over tankards of ale when storms kept men from the sea. A fireplace built into the far wall held caldrons of fish stew and clam chowder.

Booming, drunken voices raised in song and tale-telling made a cacophony of noise. The soot-stained windows at the front of the tavern faced the empty, dark street outside.

Three serving wenches made the rounds of the tables, ale-headed enough now that they no longer avoided the groping hands of the pirates. Only one of the serving girls seemed determined to stay out of their grasps. She was thin and short, looking barely into her teens if the rosy glow on her cheeks was any indication.

Behind the bar, amid the clutter of shelves that held glasses and bottles, was the tavern's centerpiece. It looked as if the prow of a ship had smashed through the wall, leaving ripped timbers in its wake. The prow held a mermaid whose carved auburn hair flowed back to become part of the ship. Her proud breasts stood out above the narrow waist that turned to scales.

Frennick hesitated for a moment, and Jherek tightened his grip on the man's arm.

The young sailor kept his prisoner moving, using his body to press the man toward the broad oak door. Jherek and his prisoner were at the door when the girl screamed behind them.

At first Jherek thought it was the woman they'd left in the room above. He turned swiftly, stepping back and away from Frennick so the pirate couldn't turn on him.

A pair of the pirates caught up the young serving girl. Her long skirt and sleeveless blouse looked incongruous compared to the scanty clothes of the other wenches. Her blond hair fanned out over her shoulders as one of the pirates ripped her scarf from her head. She struggled in the powerful grip of the man who held her.

"Let's see what you look like when you let your hair down, you little vixen," the pirate said. "Old Tharyg believes you're a pretty little peach."

The girl tried to batter the old pirate with her fists but Tharyg seized them effortlessly. She shrilled in frustration and fear.

The bartender and bodyguards stayed back, thin, wolfish grins on their faces.

"Clear the room," Tharyg entreated. "Give a sailing man room to work."

The pirates pushed themselves up and staggered into motion. Bets were placed on Tharyg's ability after imbibing so much ale. " 'E'll never get the old Jolly Roger unfurled!" one man cried out.

The girl continued to scream and fight, but it was no use. She was outnumbered and overpowered. They held her at wrist and ankle, pinning her to one of the rectangular tables.

Jherek paused, knowing these events weren't uncommon in such a place as the Bare Bosom.

"No." Talif came up behind the young sailor and shoved him forward, adding, "Leave her to the jackals."

"I can't," Jherek said.

"You're a fool," Talif told him, his eyes hard. "Get him to Captain Azla."

"Aye. Good-bye and good riddance," Talif grumbled as he prodded Frennick through the door.

Coldly calm, Jherek approached the group of pirates. He caught up a chair in his free hand and never broke his purposeful stride.

* * * * *

Laaqueel luxuriated in the swim to the mudship *Tarjana*. The water off the coast of Turmish was dirtier than she was accustomed to, but the brine was sweet relief after all the hours of overland travel.

She was malenti, a sahuagin trapped by the appearance of a hated sea elf. The dreaded mutation happened to sahuagin born too close to sea elves. Her life had been further cursed by the fact that her skin was the pink of a surface world elf, not the blue or green of a true sea elf.

Somewhat less than six feet tall, slender and supple, she looked weak.

She wore her night-black hair pulled back, bound with

fish bones and bits of coral. Her clothing consisted only of the war harness worn by the sahuagin, straps around her waist, thighs, and arms that allowed her to tie weapons and nets so she could keep her hands free.

Iakhovas's mystical ship lay at anchor half a mile from shore, only a short distance for one born to wander the sea. *Tarjana* was one hundred thirty feet long and twenty feet wide, and took one hundred forty rowers, seventy to a side. There was enough room aboard to comfortably fit another one hundred fifty men. Huge crossbows with harpoon-sized quarrels lined the port and starboard sides. Purple and yellow sails lay furled around the three tall masts. Sahuagin warriors filled the deck as well as the water around the ship.

Laaqueel swam among the sahuagin without comment. As senior high priestess to the king, she demanded respect. She grabbed the net hung over the vessel's side and pulled herself up, regretting the need to leave the sea. She crossed to the stern castle and knocked on the door to the captain's quarters.

"Enter," Iakhovas's great voice boomed from inside the room.

The malenti priestess felt a momentary tingle when she touched the door latch and knew that Iakhovas had heavily warded the entrance. She stepped through into the large room and blinked, adjusting her vision against the darkness within.

"Did you find the item I sent you for?" Iakhovas asked.

"Yes, Most Exalted One, but I lost all the warriors under my command."

Laaqueel stood, waiting to be chastised.

"The druids are a cunning and vicious lot. Don't worry, Most Favored One, the Shark God smiles down on you without respite."

Iakhovas sat in a large whalebone chair that could have doubled as a throne. Though other sahuagin aboard *Tarjana* only saw him as one of their own, the malenti priestess saw him as human, though she wasn't sure if even that was his real form.

Iakhovas stood over seven feet tall, an axe handle wide at the shoulders and thick-chested. Black hair spilled over his shoulders, framing a face that would have been handsome if not for the ancient scarring that twisted his features. He wore a short beard and mustache. A black eye patch covered the empty socket. He was dressed in black breeches and a dark green shirt. A flowing black cloak hung over his shoulders.

The table before him was nailed to the ship's floor so it wouldn't move in rough seas. Dozens of objects littered the tabletop.

Laaqueel recognized some of them from the hunts Iakhovas had engineered over the years. Others were from recent finds made by Vurgrom and the other Inner Sea pirates. Sea elves and other creatures, as well as many sahuagin warriors, had died in the gathering of those things. Just as the sahuagin warriors that accompanied her that day had died.

Iakhovas worked diligently at his task. He picked up a curved instrument set with five green gems, each of a different hue. In his hands, the instrument grew steadily smaller, until it was a tiny thing almost lost between his thumb and forefinger. Satisfied with his efforts, he fitted the piece into a small golden globe in the palm of his hand. A distinct, high-pitched note sounded when the instrument fit into place.

"Give me the item I sent you for," he commanded.

The malenti reached into the net at her side and brought forth the slim rod she'd found in the druid's wooden altar. It was scarcely as long as her forearm and as thin as a finger. Carved runes glowed beneath the surface but none of them were familiar to her.

Iakhovas took the rod from her, running it through his fingers with familiarity. The rod glowed dull orange for a moment, then faded. He closed his hands over it and it shrank. With practiced ease, he slid the small version of the rod into the golden globe. It clicked home.

A thousand questions ran through Laaqueel's mind, but they were all prompted by her doubts about him. She forced them away as she'd done for months. Even if Iakhovas's motives and methods were questionable, he still followed the edicts set forth by Sekolah, strengthening and improving the sahuagin condition across the seas of Toril.

Iakhovas finished a final adjustment on the golden

globe in his hand, then popped it into the empty socket where his eye had been. The orb gleamed. He stood, and his appearance seemed to shimmer.

A knock sounded on the wall and Laaqueel glanced at the spot. She knew the draft of the mudship put the knock below water but the sharp raps didn't sound hollowed out the way the sea would make them.

"Follow me," Iakhovas said, and walked toward the bulkhead without hesitation.

He reached back and captured one of her hands, then stepped through the bulkhead.

III

4 Flamerule, the Year of the Gauntlet

"Unhand the girl."

Jherek spoke softly, but his words interrupted the raucous voices of the pirates as they terrorized the frightened young woman. The closest pirates noticed him first. They stepped drunkenly backward, stumbling against chairs and tables. Snarled curses reached Jherek's ears.

The girl's rolling eyes met the young sailor's, and for a moment he felt her fear and weakness.

"Mind your own business," one of the sailors said. He took a threatening step forward, drawing a short sword from his hip.

Jherek hesitated only a moment. The man before him was drunk, as were most of the men in the room. Still, they remained fully capable of hurting the girl on the table, and they were just as capable of killing him.

"Help me," she cried softly.

Sparked by his own sense of justice, Jherek spun into battle. He whirled quickly, smashing the flat of his blade into the nearest pirate's face.

The man's nose broke in a bloody rush and an audible crack. He stumbled backward, cursing Jherek in Umberlee's name. His size and the drunkenness of his companions sent a small group of them reeling back for the short bar.

Pressing his advantage as the other pirates fell back and tried to bring their weapons into play, Jherek stepped forward. He swung the chair he'd picked up as he'd approached the group, breaking it across Tharyg's back.

The big man roared in pain and anger as he dropped to his knees on the floor. He turned his baleful gaze toward Jherek and reached for his sword.

Jherek focused on the two men who lunged at him from the left. He met their swords with his own, slamming the blades aside. He twisted the cutlass, wounding one of the men deeply across the forearm. Blood spurted on the man and his nearest fellows.

"Make way, you damned sot-heads!" one of the bouncers standing watch at the tavern called.

Turning to the right, Jherek overturned a table, then kicked it at the three armed men coming at him. The table skidded across the sawdust-covered floor and slammed into their legs. If they hadn't been so impaired by their drinking, maybe they'd have remained standing. As it was all three of them tumbled across the table.

Still in motion, Jherek set himself and met the blade of the man who came at him from the front. The young sailor was already aware that pirates were circling behind him, closing off his escape route to the front door.

"Kill him!" Tharyg ordered. "A gold piece to the man who takes that bastard's head!"

Jherek hardened himself, driving out all merciful feelings that remained within him. Despite their drunkenness, the men were all killers, skilled and experienced at their profession.

His cutlass leaped out like a thing alive, sliding along the man's sword and opening his throat in a tight riposte. Gurgling, dying, the man fell backward, clawing at his mates to help him.

Two men rushed at Jherek with long knives. The young sailor dropped almost to his knees and caught himself on his empty hand. He pushed forward, catching the man on the right just above the knees with his shoulder. Jherek drove the man backward, lifting him off his feet and hurling him into the pirates behind him. They collapsed in a staggering melee.

Recovering, Jherek ripped his cutlass up in time to block the overhand blow Tharyg directed at his head. The young sailor shifted his footing, parrying two more blows from the bigger man, then pushing the cutlass's point through the pirate's heart.

"Bloody hell!" Tharyg gasped, staring down at the steel blade thrust into his chest. "You've done killed me!"

Jherek pulled his sword free, feeling the steel grate along bone. The young sailor gave himself over to his training and to the blade. The cutlass whirled before him, striking sparks from the other blades that reached out for him, creating a rhythm of metal rasping against metal.

He sliced a man across the stomach, spilling the pirate's entrails onto the floor. The other pirates shouted in horror and disgust while the wounded man screamed in fear and struggled to hold himself together. Jherek whirled again, bringing the cutlass around in a flat arc that all but decapitated another pirate.

Seizing the moment when the area briefly cleared around him, Jherek reached the side of the young woman. He sliced the hand from a man who'd been slow in releasing his grip on the girl. With his free hand, the young sailor grabbed the girl's arm and pulled her from the table. The floor around them was slippery with blood in spite of the sawdust. The girl remained wild-eyed, trying desperately to hold onto the young sailor.

"No, lady," Jherek told her in a calm voice as his eyes raked the hellish destruction he'd wrought. "I need my arm."

He had to force her from him, hoping he didn't hurt her or accidentally steer her into an opponent's blade.

A pirate came up behind Jherek, blindsiding him by standing behind the young girl. He didn't see the pirate until the man almost ran him through, but a preternatural sense warned him. Unable to bring the cutlass into play, Jherek let the short sword skim past him when he took a step back. He locked his free hand in the pirate's blouse, then stepped in and pulled as hard as he could.

The pirate spun over Jherek's shoulder and crashed into another group of men, bowling them all down.

Jherek gazed around the tavern room, unwilling to believe he was somehow still alive. Over a dozen sailors were down, most of them never to rise again.

A blade drew in close before he could dodge. The edge kissed the flesh of his upper left arm, ripping through easily. Hot blood spilled down his arm and drenched his blouse and cloak. He managed to keep the few sword thrusts at the girl turned aside.

Whirling again, aware that the drunken pirates were starting to get organized, Jherek glanced up at the heavy wooden wheel depending from the ceiling. Glass-encased candles, most of them still lit, stood proudly around the wheel.

Tracking the line of rope that held the wheel in place near the ceiling, Jherek spied the support post the rope was tied to near the front windows of the tavern. He planted a hand in the girl's back, helping steady her over a broken table and scattered chairs.

"Run," he told her. "Don't look back."

The girl ran, staying low, both hands wrapped protectively over her head.

Jherek picked up a chair and hurled it at a pirate who moved after the girl. The chair smacked into the pirate from behind, two of the legs shooting by his side while the other two slammed into his back. Chair and pirate plummeted toward the floor.

"Get him!" one of the tavern's bouncers shouted, shoving the pirates before him like an incoming tide pushing flotsam.

Taking two quick steps, Jherek swung the cutlass hard into the support pole where the chandelier was tied. The rope parted at once and the wheel plummeted from the ceiling like a rock. The wheel was almost as wide across as a man was tall. When it hit, it carried half a dozen pirates to the ground, burying them under its weight.

Another pirate swung his sword at Jherek's knees. The young sailor vaulted the man easily, placing a hand on the back of the bent pirate's head and pushing off. The pirate skidded face first into the floor.

Jherek leaped to the next table, feeling it skid uncertainly for a moment before snagging on the rough-hewn floor. As it started to tip, he vaulted to the next table near the bay window, then folded his arms over his face and threw himself through the latticework and panes.

Glass shattered and wood splintered around Jherek as he plunged through the window. He landed on his feet, bending his knees slightly to keep his balance. As he stood, he saw Glawinn, Sabyna, and Azla run from the inn across the street.

"This way, young warrior!" Glawinn roared, waving his sword.

Before Jherek could get started, a pirate leaped through the broken window after him and landed on his back. Only a swift move of the cutlass prevented the pirate from raking his dagger across Jherek's throat. Grabbing the man's loose shirt with his free hand, the young sailor bent and pulled, yanking the man from his back. He ran, spotting Talif and Frennick moving quickly through the shadows toward the paladin.

A crowd boiled out of the Bare Bosom. Two of them had lanterns, filched from the tavern's walls. "This way!" someone yelled. Booted feet beat a rapid tattoo against the wooden slats in front of the tavern.

Jherek caught up with the thief and his prisoner easily. He grabbed Frennick by the arm and hurried him after Glawinn.

The paladin raced into an alley beside the tavern where they'd been waiting, Sabyna and Azla close at his heels. Jherek swung around the corner, still pulling on Frennick, who was yelling encouragement to their pursuers.

Glawinn pulled himself up into the bench seat of the freight wagon waiting in the alley. The rear deck of the wagon contained barrels, kegs, crates, and sacks of foodstuffs and other supplies.

"Get in!" the paladin yelled. "Pirate stronghold though this may be, they take care of their own. We've worn thin our welcome here."

Jherek wholeheartedly agreed. Azla and Sabyna easily vaulted into the back of the wagon. The half-elf pirate captain set herself to work at once, smashing open a keg of spirits with her sword hilt.

Glawinn had the wagon going before Frennick was up in the back. The pirate dropped to his knees in an effort to keep from being forced on.

"Leave him," Talif snarled, hauling himself aboard the wagon.

"No," Jherek said.

He sheathed the cutlass in the sash at his waist and hooked his hand under the pirate's wide belt. He heard the yelling approach of the tavern crowd and saw the yellow glow of the lanterns paint long shadows on the wall to his left as they rounded the corner.

"There they are!"

"Kill that salty young pup—and his friends!"

The wagon started out slowly. Old horses and a heavy load held them back.

Holding Frennick's belt and the back of the pirate's hair, Jherek lifted his prisoner to his feet and rushed toward the fleeing wagon. In three great steps, he covered the distance. He pulled Frennick over his hip and threw him into the wagon bed.

"They've got Frennick!" someone yelled.

"Or he's with them!" another said. "I never trusted him."

Jherek ran to the wagon and vaulted up. He turned immediately, seeing that the tavern mob was closing the distance. Desperately, he grabbed a nearby five-gallon keg in both hands and heaved it at the lead man.

The keg broke against the man's chest, scattering salted pork across the alley and knocking the pirate back. Four more men went down with him, breaking the pursuit for just a moment.

"Everything goes off," Jherek ordered.

He remained on his knees and tossed the wagon's load over the back as quickly as he could. Sabyna and Talif helped him, shoving things over the end of the wagon.

Sacks of flour burst and spilled filmy white clouds into the alley, soaking into the potholes of the uneven cobblestones. Nail kegs, broken bottles, and shattered jars created more obstacles in the path of the tavern crowd. Potatoes and beans rolled across the stones.

As the load lightened, the horses pulled more strongly. The ironbound wheels rang against the cobblestones, knocking off accumulated rust and striking occasional sparks.

Glawinn yelled to the horses and pulled them hard to the left as they bounded out onto the street at the end of the alley. The new street plunged down and twisted crazily on its way to the harbor.

The crowd from the tavern made the next turn much tighter than the wagon. They were gaining. Other men walking along the new street joined in the chase. Jherek stared at the wolf's pack in dismay. Anything like a quiet escape was totally out of the question now. Flame suddenly flared at his side. He turned and watched Azla fit an arrow to the short bow she'd carried into town.

The pirate captain pulled the string back to her cheek and fired from a kneeling position. The arrow sped true, shedding sparks from the cloth tied just behind the barbed head. The missile found a home in a man's chest. Blue and yellow flames twisted up and caught his beard on fire, wreathing his face in flames. He fell back among his companions.

Azla picked up another arrow that held a scrap of cloth tied to it and drenched it in the keg of spirits she'd broken open.

"Talif," she called calmly, her black eyes searching the street for targets.

The thief held a green flame between his cupped palms. The strange fire emanated from a coin. Azla lit her second arrow from the enchanted coin and fired it into the thatched roof of a nearby warehouse. The flame spread quickly across the wooden shingles.

A cry of alarm sounded from the pirates. More than half of them peeled off and ran for the building. As tightly packed as Immurk's Hold was, and being constructed of wood, Jherek knew there was a real danger of the town burning down if a fire was left untended. He balanced on his knees, his fist curled tight around the cutlass hilt, rocking as the bumpy ride continued.

Azla shot two more fire arrows into buildings they passed, creating even more of a diversion. By then the horses were hitting their pace and the wheels rattled across the uneven cobblestones.

* * * * *

Laaqueel felt a moment of heated resistance, then she slipped through the wooden timber of the bulkhead behind

Iakhovas. In the next instant, harsh sunlight and the unsteady deck of a ship lunging at sea greeted her. Iakhovas had set up gates in the sahuagin castle as well that let him travel immediately to different areas along the Sword Coast.

"Lord Iakhovas!" a loud voice boomed. "Welcome aboard!"

Turning, the malenti priestess spied the tall, big-bellied form of Vurgrom the Mighty. The pirate captain came down the stern castle stairs like a flesh and blood avalanche.

Vurgrom was a mountain of a man, no taller than Iakhovas but easily twice as broad. He had flaming red hair on the sides of his head but none on top, and long chin whiskers that thrust out defiantly. He wore scarred leather breeches and a sleeveless leather vest.

"You called me," Iakhovas stated.

The big pirate captain grinned, swaying slightly as the ship thundered across the ocean waves, pushed by a strong wind.

"Aye," Vurgrom said, "and it's because I've got some news you might be interested in."

The crew tried to get closer to him, but he waved them all away.

"What is your location?" Iakhovas asked.

Vurgrom shrugged and said, "A few days from the Whamite Isles."

"You will be there." Iakhovas's tone left no margin for misunderstanding.

The big man flushed a little. "Aye," he said, "and I won't let you down, Lord Iakhovas, but I have something else to show you—something you need to know about."

Vurgrom dug in a pouch belted at his prodigious waist and produced an oval pearl encased in a golden disk. Laaqueel watched sudden interest dawn on Iakhovas's face. He studied the disk in the pirate captain's fat palm.

"I hired a diviner to look at it," Vurgrom said. "She told me it would lead me to a weapon."

Iakhovas studied the disk. "So it will."

"I've been trying to get in touch with you," Vurgrom said. "The device you gave me wasn't working."

"It worked when it was supposed to," Iakhovas said sharply.

Vurgrom's face blanched. "Of course, Lord Iakhovas," he

said. "I only meant that I would have spoken with you earlier if I had been able."

"It's a powerful piece," Iakhovas said.

"It guides us, lord. Place this trinket into a bowl of water and it floats like a lodestone seeking the north."

"The weapon," Iakhovas said, "lies on the Whamite Isles."

Surprise gleamed in the pirate captain's eyes. "You know this?"

"Yes."

Vurgrom laughed and said, "I should have come to you, lord, instead of paying the diviner."

"You took two days' travel from my schedule," Iakhovas said in a hard voice. "If it weren't for the wind that pushes you now, you wouldn't make your assigned destination on time."

With a shrug, Vurgrom said, "I've been fortunate."

Iakhovas held a hand up. The wind died suddenly and the sails hung limply from the lanyards. Laaqueel shifted her footing. The ship felt as though it had become mired in mud.

"It was more than fortune's good graces," Iakhovas said. "I am seeing to it that you arrive on time in spite of your bad decisions."

Iakhovas clenched his raised hand into a fist. The blast of wind that hit the ship staggered it, almost rolled it over on the cresting wave. The sails popped and cracked, sounding as if they were going to be ripped free. Some of the ship's crew went rolling across the deck, unable to balance themselves quickly enough. At least three men went over the side, screaming until they hit the water. The ship sailed on, having no way to come around for those overboard.

Iakhovas stood as if rooted to the pitching deck.

Vurgrom grabbed the rearmost mast only a few feet away, unable to maintain his stance. He roared and knocked away other pirates nearby. The ship continued to pitch and twist.

"You're going to tear her apart!" the captain shouted.

"The ship will hold," Iakhovas declared. "I won't allow you to be late, Captain Vurgrom."

"I won't be late, my lord." Vurgrom had to yell to make himself heard over the gale force winds. "I won't be late."

"See to it then," Iakhovas threatened. "If you are late, Vurgrom, after everything I've invested in you, you won't 'be' at all."

He gestured and the golden orb in his eye flared. The world seemed to ripple at his side, like a pool disturbed by a tossed pebble. He stuck his arm into the ripples and it disappeared up to the elbow.

The pirates looked on in superstitious awe. Magic was known to them, of course, but not so familiar. Many of them, Laaqueel knew, had seen more this day than they would in their whole lives.

"Get this weapon if you want, Vurgrom," Iakhovas said, "but I'll want it when you do. You belong to me until such a time as I release you."

Vurgrom held tight to the mast and said nothing.

Iakhovas held out a hand to Laaqueel. The malenti priestess was barely able to maintain her own stance as the ship pitched again and the canvas cracked overhead. Even during her spying days, she'd hated ships. She reached for Iakhovas and felt him take her hand. Her balance steadied at once and she stepped through the gate back into the captain's quarters aboard *Tarjana*.

"I sense conflict within you, little malenti," Iakhovas said flatly.

He moved behind the table again and resumed his seat. The king of the sahuagin studied her with his one good eye and the golden one, and the malenti priestess felt as though he could see her clearly with both.

"When we arrived here and you saw that things were as I promised regarding the imprisonment of the Serôsian sahuagin, your faith seemed to return to you, stronger than before. Now I feel that you are questioning yourself again."

"Faith," she replied, "lies in the ability to answer those questions."

"You are my senior high priestess, and you serve the will of Sekolah. There should be no questions."

"I am weak." The admission was as much to herself as to him.

"I need you strong."

"I will be," she promised. "Have I ever failed you? I returned from the dead at your call."

Not so many days ago in Coryselmal while searching for the talisman Iakhovas had used to sunder the Sharksbane Wall, Laaqueel was certain she'd died at the hands of a vodyanoi, or come as close to it as the living could without fully crossing over.

Iakhovas had been as close to panic as the malenti priestess had ever seen him. He'd worked to save her, using a black skull with ruby eyes he'd gotten from his artificial eye. Laaqueel still felt certain somehow that it hadn't been Iakhovas's efforts that turned her back from death. It had been another, someone with a soft, sweet, feminine voice.

Go back, the voice told her. You are yet undone.

Iakhovas raked her with his gaze. She felt the quill quiver tentatively inside her.

"Go then, little malenti," he said, "and attend to your faith. Answer your questions as best as you are able, but in the end you'll find that the truest belief you have is in me. You may have rescued me from the prison I was in, but I have made you more than you have ever imagined you would be."

Stung by the dismissal and the knowledge of her own uncertainty, Laaqueel left the room and strode back out onto *Tarjana*'s main deck. She walked to the starboard railing and peered over into the sea. For a moment she wished she could just leap in and swim away to leave all the confusion behind her.

Farther along the railing, a group of sahuagin hauled on a length of heavy anchor chain hanging in the water. Bodies—some of them sahuagin of the inner and outer seas, others sea elves—were hooked to the chain. All of them were relatively fresh kills.

Three of the sahuagin group doing the hauling reached down and began plucking off bodies, harvesting them for meals. Razor-sharp talons sliced through flesh and brute strength snapped joints. Gobbets of flesh were torn free and passed around. Crabs and other sea creatures that had taken up brief residence within some of the corpses, and they became part of the meal.

One of the sahuagin warriors turned to face Laaqueel, regarding her with his black gaze. "Join, Most Favored One," he said. "There is plenty for all."

He held out a forearm, not a choice section, but not food to be turned away either.

"I am not hungry," she declared.

The warrior looked at her with consternation. No true sahuagin passed up a meal. A warrior needed to consume huge quantities of flesh to give him the strength to make it through a day.

"I ate the fallen on my return," Laaqueel said.

She knew the warrior probably wasn't listening and didn't care, but she made the excuse so that she might hear it herself. In truth, she was nearly starving. Since her arrival, days ago, in the Sea of Fallen Stars, she hadn't eaten from either dead sahuagin or enemy. The thought repulsed her, made her stomach twist violently within her.

There was no reason that she could think of for that to be so, no malady that she'd heard of that so plagued her people. Sahuagin, even ill-born malenti, were born to eat.

She watched as the warriors who made up *Tarjana*'s crew ripped at the dead bodies and ate what they wanted. She sighed, trying not to think about what Iakhovas had told her, trying not to succumb to the doubts that filled her. Her faith was more fragile than ever, a hollow shell she wrapped around Iakhovas.

She leaped overboard, longing to find solace in the sea.

* * * * *

Black Champion sat at anchor in the harbor. Jherek stood on the ship's deck and looked up at the Earthspur. The huge tower of rock and windswept land stabbed more than a mile above sea level in the center of the Dragonisle, the island where Immurk's Hold was located. Even in the night, the mountain left a shadow across the black water.

Azla was below with the others, questioning Frennick. The pirate captain laid out torturer's tools on a small table, the metal gleaming from the lantern light.

Jherek hadn't been able to stay, nor did Azla permit it.

He struggled with his conscience, telling himself that Frennick deserved all that Azla could think to give him, but it was no use. Through it all, the young sailor remembered that it was his doing that placed Frennick in her hands.

"Young warrior."

Turning, Jherek saw Glawinn approaching him, two steaming cups in his hands.

"I brought you some soup," the paladin said. "I thought it might serve to warm you some."

Jherek didn't want the soup, didn't want to pretend that everything was normal. A man he'd captured was being tortured down in the hold. He couldn't help but listen for the screams he knew must come. Thankfully, the crash of the sea's waves was too loud.

He accepted the cup anyway and said, "Thank you."

"What an awful place this is," Glawinn commented quietly.

"There are people in Immurk's Hold who still maintain an innocence," Jherek stated, thinking of the girl he'd rescued in the tavern.

"That was a brave and good thing you did back there, young warrior."

"It was foolish," Jherek grumbled, then shook his head. "Come morning, the girl will still be on the island."

"You saved her from a bad night."

"Delayed, is more correct, I think." Jherek turned the cup in his hands, absorbing the heat. The soup smelled delicious, full of spices.

"You've got a headful of dark thoughts," the paladin said.

"I look out there, and I wonder how different I am from those men," Jherek said. "Did I ever tell you how I came to Velen from my father's ship?"

IV

5 Flamerule, the Year of the Gauntlet

"I was twelve," Jherek said. "My father spotted a merchant ship, heavily laden so she was sitting low in the water and dragging down the wind. That night he announced to the ship's crew that we would claim it as a prize the next morning."

Glawinn listened in silence.

"My father is a hard man," Jherek said. "You know the stories they tell along the Sword Coast of Bloody Falkane, and you know that nearly all of them are true. He's unforgiving and merciless, as able to cut down an unarmed man as he is to fight to the death. There is no right or wrong in his world, only what he is strong enough to take."

The rattling of the rigging on the lanyards sounded hollow, echoing the way Jherek felt. Glawinn waited silently.

As he spoke, Jherek felt the heat of unshed tears burning his eyes. Still, even though his voice was so tight it pained him to speak, he had to.

"I loved my father."

"As a child should," Glawinn said.

"I remember how he laughed. It was a huge, boisterous

41

sound. Even though I didn't understand much of what made him laugh, I laughed with him. As I grew older, I stopped laughing and learned to fear him. Then, one day, he saw that in me. My father told me that I had to learn to be hard, that the world was cold and would eat the weak. I believed him, and I believed I was weak."

"That's not true."

Jherek didn't bother to argue. "He had me taken from the small room off his cabin where he'd kept me all that time and put in with the men. They weren't any more gentle than he'd been, though they were careful not to leave any marks that he could see."

In the distance, another longboat drew up to a cog and lanterns moved along its length as the passengers prepared to board.

"For the next eight years, I lived in the shadows of my father's rage. There was never a day I felt peace between us, nor anything even close to love."

"To be the son Bloody Falkane wanted," the paladin said, "you'd have to have been born heartless and with ice water in your veins. Where was your mother?"

"I never knew her."

"Your father never spoke of her?"

"Not once," the young sailor replied. "Nor did the ship's crew."

He stared up at the dark sky and refused to let the tears come. How much of it came from what he remembered, and how much because he knew Frennick was down in the hold, he couldn't say.

"The night I chose to leave," Jherek continued, "my father visited me in the hold. He brought a cutlass and placed it in my hand and told me I would take a place in the boarding party in the morning."

"At twelve?"

"Aye. He told me I'd kill or be killed, and in the doing of that, I'd be dead or I'd take my first steps toward becoming his son."

"Lathander's mercy," the paladin whispered.

"I stayed up most of the night," Jherek continued. "I knew I couldn't be part of that boarding party."

"Because you knew it was the wrong thing to do."

His throat hurting too much to speak right away, Jherek

shook his head. "No. I only knew I was afraid," he said hoarsely. "I was afraid I would be killed, but mostly I was afraid of what my father would do to me if I froze and could not move, could not make it onto that other ship. I was certain he would kill me himself. So I walked out onto the deck when no one was looking, threw the cutlass into the sea, and jumped in after it. *Bunyip* sailed on, leaving me in the ocean. I wanted to die, but I started to swim, not even knowing where I was heading. I don't know how long I swam, but I know it was well into the next day before I washed up on Velen's shores."

They were silent for a time and Jherek struggled to ease his thoughts back into the dark places of his mind where he kept them.

"Why are you telling me this?" Glawinn asked.

"Because you seem to see something good in me," Jherek said, "and I wanted you to know it was false. I ran from my father's ship that night."

"You didn't want to kill innocent people," Glawinn objected.

Anger stirred in the coldness that filled Jherek. "Am I any better now? I took a man prisoner tonight only so he could be tortured."

"It's not what you think."

"Isn't it?" Jherek demanded. "I am my father's son. When it came time to take Frennick, I took him and I brought him here."

"No, young warrior, you judge yourself too harshly. You did only what you had to do. You are meant for more than being a pirate's son, Jherek."

"How can you believe that?"

"That's the wrong question." A small, sad smile twisted Glawinn's lips. "After having heard everything I have from you, the question is how could I not believe that."

"I just want out," Jherek said tiredly. "I don't want any more false hope, no more dreams, and I'm sick of the fear that has filled me all my life."

"A way will be made," Glawinn whispered. "You must believe."

Jherek couldn't, and he knew it. He looked out over the black water, taking in all the emptiness that made up the Sea of Fallen Stars.

"It's done."

Almost asleep, Jherek blinked and looked up at Azla as she strode across the deck.

More than an hour had passed since Azla had gone below with Frennick. The young sailor pushed himself up from his seated position against the prow railing.

"And Frennick?" Jherek asked.

"Relax," Azla told him. "Frennick is alive and of one piece still."

Images of how the man must have been tortured ran rampant through Jherek's mind. The instruments the pirate captain had laid out with such familiarity looked vicious enough to come straight from Cyric's darkest hells.

"Nor have I harmed him," Azla went on, "so your precious honor and integrity yet remain whole."

Jherek shook his head. "I don't understand."

"Glawinn asked that no harm come to Frennick when we returned to the ship," Azla said.

"Glawinn didn't tell me he'd asked that," Jherek told her, confused.

"No, nor did he want you to know until it was over."

Jherek grew angry but pushed it away. That lack of knowledge was something he intended to deal with the paladin about. He should have been told instead of spending time worrying over it.

"Pirates are a superstitious lot," Azla commented. "Despite all his blustering and bravado, Frennick is not a brave man. My ship's mage bewitched him, making him think we'd immersed his hand in a pot of acid till the flesh melted from his bones. Actually, it was a pot of water."

Two of the ship's crew marched Frennick up from the hold. The pirate captain swore venomously, calling down the spiteful rage of Umberlee on Azla, her ship, and her crew. When the crewmen threw him over the side, both the splash and Frennick's curses echoed around the ship. Relief filled Jherek, but it didn't take away the anger he felt toward Glawinn.

"Where is the disk?" the young sailor asked.

"Vurgrom has it."

"Does Frennick know where Vurgrom is?"

Azla shook her head. "But he did know that Vurgrom used a diviner to learn what he could of the disk."

Jherek's heart sped up. "What did he learn?"

"Frennick wasn't allowed in the room. Only the diviner and Vurgrom were there. However, Frennick gave us the location of the diviner. She lives off the northeastern harbor of the Dragonisle."

"If we are not sailing there," Jherek said, "I need to know so I can make other arrangements."

Azla looked at him, her dark eyes flashing, and asked, "You would, wouldn't you?"

"Aye, Captain. I've no choice."

"You won't have to walk," she replied. "We're going to weigh anchor in a short while."

* * * * *

"Enter, young warrior."

Jherek slipped the lock on the door and let himself into the room.

Glawinn sat on the lowest of the bunk beds, crouched over so his head wouldn't bang against the upper berth as the ship gently pitched at anchor. An oil lantern hung from the ceiling over the small desk in the corner. The paladin was cleaning his armor, a task he tended to every day.

"You lied to me."

"No." Glawinn's eyes narrowed and became hard. Steel filled his voice. "You never accuse another man of lying unless you know that for a fact. Especially not a man of honor."

Shame burned Jherek's cheeks and ears. "My apologies." He tried to maintain his level gaze but had to drop it to the floor. "You didn't tell me that they weren't torturing Frennick."

"No."

"You let me believe they were."

"Yes."

"Why?"

"You were comparing yourself to the wretches and scoundrels that populate that island like that was your destiny. Suddenly you were seeing yourself as no better than they are, doomed somehow to follow in your father's footsteps."

"They say the apple never falls far from the tree."

"Then looking forward to a life as a pirate or a thief is something you deserve?"

"I never said that."

"Yes you did. You were pulling penance for Frennick. You looked out over Immurk's Hold and told me you couldn't see the difference between yourself and those men. Can you now?"

"Aye," Jherek said, his voice tight, "but I also see the difference between you and me."

"Do you believe that difference to be so great, young warrior?" Glawinn stood. Without his armor, he looked like only a man. Lantern light gleamed against the dark black of his hair and short-cropped beard.

"You're a paladin, chosen by a god to represent the covenants of his faith."

"Was I anything before I became a warrior for Lathander? Or was it Lathander who made me the man I am today?"

"I don't know."

"Tell me what is in your heart, young warrior," Glawinn said softly, his voice barely carrying across the small room. The waves slapping against the side of the ship outside the room underscored his words. "Tell me what you believe me to have been before I followed Lathander's teachings."

"You were a good man."

After a moment, Glawinn nodded. "My father was a knight before me, and my mother a good woman who learned the art of cheese making from her father. I am their get, and I wear Lathander's colors and fight the battles the Morninglord sets before me."

Jherek stared into the paladin's eyes, wondering for just a heartbeat if Glawinn was telling him this to make him feel worse.

"I was born one of twins," Glawinn said. "I have a sister. She was never a gentle child, and never easy on my parents. When she was seventeen, she left our home in Daggerdale and joined the Zhentarim."

Astonishment trailed cold fingers across Jherek's back. Even on the Sword Coast people knew the Zhentarim to be an organization of great evil.

"I was a boy when I fought at my father's side under

Randall Morn against Malyk," Glawinn went on in a steady voice. "My sister, like many other Daggerdale citizens, felt that the Zhentarim would continue to hold the lands after the battles. Some thought only to hold onto their property, not caring who ruled them as long as they were allowed to follow their own lives. Cellayne—my sister—saw joining the Zhentarim as a chance to follow the dark nature that possessed her."

Footsteps passed beyond the door. Men's voices talked quietly. Eyes reddened with pain and glazed with memory, Glawinn turned to peer at the armor lying on the small bed.

"I've seen Cellayne twice in all these years," he said. "The last time she tried her best to kill me. Only by Lathander's grace was I spared. I lost two dear friends. Cellayne has immersed herself in the dark arts and become a necromancer. She's very powerful." The paladin tried to clear his thick voice but was unsuccessful. "As penance for daring to attack her in her stronghold near Darkhold, Cellayne . . . did something to my two fallen companions . . . set them on my trail. I destroyed the walking corpses of my friends. I know not what happened to their souls, though priests I've talked to since tell me that the good part of them knows peace."

"I'm sorry," Jherek whispered, knowing how feeble those words were.

"Lathander keeps me strong." Glawinn bowed his head for a moment, then turned to Jherek. "You need only believe, young warrior. Let your faith and your heart guide you, not your birth, not everything you've seen. Pursue that which you want, and a way of living that pleases and rewards you."

"There is nothing to believe in."

"So, for now at least, that is what you believe, young warrior, but to believe that there is nothing to believe in, is a belief itself." Glawinn smiled at his own circular logic. "Don't you see? If there was no belief in you, you would be like a piece of driftwood tossed out on the sea."

"Even driftwood finds a shore sooner or later," Jherek said.

A smile crossed Glawinn's face. "How much you know yet refuse to see. Truly, your stubbornness is as great as

47

any I've ever witnessed." He crossed the room to stand in front of Jherek, then put his hands on the young sailor's shoulders and said, "When I look at you, I see a good man."

Unable to maintain eye contact, Jherek dropped his gaze to his boots.

"I only wish that you could see yourself through my eyes." Glawinn paused. "Or Sabyna's."

"I've got to go." Jherek couldn't stand there any more. It hurt too much.

The paladin pulled his hands away and said, "You won't be able to escape the doubts that fill you, young warrior. They only sound the emptiness that is within you. Belief is the only thing that will make you whole again."

Jherek held back hot tears. "If there was just something to hold to, I could," he said, "but there is nothing."

"Sabyna loves you, young warrior."

That single declaration scared Jherek more than anything else in his life.

"Even if that were true," he said hotly, "my father murdered her brother. She could never forgive me."

"For your father's sin?"

"A father's sins are visited on the son."

"Not everyone thinks so."

"I'd rather not talk about this."

"I told you I'd teach you to believe again, young warrior," Glawinn said, his voice carrying steel again, "and I will."

"You weren't able to rescue your sister."

As soon as the words were out of his mouth, Jherek regretted it. Pain flashed in Glawinn's eyes.

"Now is not the time to speak of this," Glawinn said. "I see that." He turned and walked back to his bunk, sitting and taking up his armor again. "Good night, young warrior."

Hesitating, Jherek tried desperately to find something to say, but couldn't. He had no head for it, and he didn't trust his tongue. His heart felt like bursting.

The sound of the scrubbing brush filled the room, drowning out the echo of the waves lapping at the ship's hull.

With a trembling hand, Jherek opened the door and left. There was nothing else to do.

V

6 Flamerule, the Year of the Gauntlet

Seated midway up *Black Champion*'s rigging, Jherek stared hard out at the sunlight-kissed emerald green waters to the west. The Dragonisle maintained a steady distance to the southeast as the ship sailed north over slightly choppy waves, but the Earthspur towered over all. Below Jherek's position, the pirate crew worked steadily under Azla's watchful eye.

Reluctantly, he returned his attention to the wooden plate he held. Over half of the steamed fish and boiled potato chunks yet remained of his meal, long grown cold. He picked at the morsels with his fingers but found no interest. The worry and the headache that settled into the base of his skull and across his shoulders left him with no appetite.

Giving up on the meal, he gripped the edge of the plate and flung the contents into the wind, watching them fall the long distance down to the sea. An albatross wheeled and dived after them, managing to seize one of the chunks before it hit the water.

The rigging vibrated, drawing his attention. When he peered down, he saw Sabyna climbing up the rigging toward him.

"I didn't expect to find you up here," she said. "You're usually laboring about the ship."

"I wasn't feeling well."

Sabyna huddled expertly within the rigging, hooking her feet and leaning back so that her elbows held her as well. She gazed at him with concern and said, "Perhaps you should have stayed in bed."

Jherek shook his head.

"I'm worried about you." Sabyna regarded him sternly with those frank, reddish-brown eyes.

Sabyna loves you, young warrior. Glawinn's words spun through Jherek's mind as soft as silk and as unforgiving as steel.

"I worry about you. Perhaps it is time you make your way back to the Sword Coast."

"Do you think I'm some kind of ballast you can just heave overboard?" Sabyna's voice turned icy.

Jherek felt as though his thoughts were winding through mush.

"No, lady," he said. "I worry only about your safety. This is not your fight, and I fear that things are going to get even harder from this point on. Last night has proven that."

"I remember a time when you spoke pretty words to me, and enjoyed my companionship," she told him in a cold voice.

"Lady, I have no hand with pretty words. My skills are with the sea, and with raising the ships that sail on it."

"Then you're telling me I heard wrong?"

Jherek felt as though he was being mercilessly pummeled. "No," he said, "I wouldn't tell you that."

"Then tell me what you feel."

Jherek hung his head. "I can't." He hated the silence that followed.

"Perhaps," Sabyna said in a softer voice, "I did hear wrong. Maybe I was wanting to hear something that wasn't there, nor ever offered."

She reached into the bag of holding at her hip and brought out two books. "I spoke with Glawinn this morning. He asked me to give you these."

Heart still hurting, Jherek took to the books, meeting her eyes and never even glancing at the titles. Normally books were a fascination to him, a promise of adventure and other lives he could share.

"Has something happened between you two?"

"Please," Jherek said, "I don't wish to speak of it."

"I'm sorry. I didn't mean to intrude. It's just hard watching the two of you have trouble when it's obvious you're so much alike."

"Alike?"

The comparison stunned the young sailor. He saw no way in which he and the paladin were alike.

"You're both proud, strong men. You're brave enough to face your fears, and you're a good friend."

"If I was such a good friend, Glawinn wouldn't be angry with me, and you wouldn't be so uncomfortable around me."

"I have no doubt that you and Glawinn will work things out," Sabyna told him. "That is the nature of men. And you're not responsible for my discomfort." Unshed tears glistened in her eyes. "That is caused by my own folly and foolishness. You have worries enough of your own. I only wish I could help you."

Without another word, the ship's mage turned lithely in the rigging and glided down the ropes, hard muscles playing in her arms, shoulders, and the small of her back.

Jherek almost went after her. It was only when he realized that he'd have to say something, but had no idea what, that he stopped. He watched her, though, as she dropped to the deck and strode to the stern to join Azla. They looked up at him together, then they turned and walked behind the stern castle.

The young sailor felt shamed to have been caught watching after them and quickly turned his head. He'd never felt so alone or unhappy in his life. He glanced at the two books he held, wondering what Glawinn would have thought to send him—and why.

Both books showed signs of stress, as if they had been read a number of times. The first was a thick volume called *The Rider and the Lost Lady of Grave Hollow*. Jherek carefully opened the front cover and read the frontispiece, discovering the work to be a romance about a Ridesman of Archendale. He flipped through the pages, smelling the scent of the parchment and the ink and remembering all the hours of pleasure he'd received from the books Malorrie had let him borrow.

The second tome was *Way of War, Way of Peace* by Sir Edard Valins. The book was much slimmer and promised to be a treatise on the art and thinking of combat.

Jherek closed the books, wondering why Glawinn would have sent them to him. He secured the book on the strategies of war in the rigging and opened the romance. A few hours of sailing yet remained before *Black Champion* reached her destination and he felt it would be best if he could stay away from other people in the meantime.

* * * * *

Standing at *Black Champion*'s starboard rail, Jherek gazed out at the grotto of sea caves that made up the Dragonisle's northeastern harbor. The harbor sat back in the curvature of the rocky shoreline below and around the caves, creating a crescent of calm water scarcely able to shelter a dozen ships. Nesting pelicans and seagulls lined the craggy surface.

"These waters are filled with treacherous rocks and reefs," Azla said as she belted her scimitar around her slim hips. She tucked a fighting dagger down inside the rolled top of her left boot, then pulled on a cloak against the chill of the bitter wind. "I won't take my ship in there. We'd only be a target if two or three of the other ship's crews decided to take us as a prize. Out here, *Champion* can maneuver."

Glawinn gave a quick nod, accepting her judgment. He offered his hand to her at the ship's rail and said, "Lady, if I may."

The half-elf pirate captain seemed a little surprised at the offer, but she took his hand and said, "My thanks, but I am *captain*, not lady."

"Of course, Captain."

Azla made her way down the rope ladder hanging over the ship's side to the waiting longboat, and Glawinn followed.

Jherek hadn't noticed the change in temperature until they'd come closer to the harbor. The sun hung low on the horizon behind them, drawing long shadows over the emerald waters. He pulled his cloak more tightly around him.

Without a backward glance at him, Sabyna strode to the side and quickly descended the rope ladder. Jherek shifted hands with his wrapped bow and followed. He quietly made his way to one of the rowing stations and sat. No one seemed inclined to speak to him and that fact gladdened him at the same time it made him feel disappointed.

No one came to meet them when they reached the uneven shoreline, but there were plenty of eyes watching. Five ships sat at anchor inside the harbor proper. Pirates lined the railings and hung in hammocks beneath the yardarms. Others cooked fish over slow fires on the rocky beach. The beach butted up against the gray rock of the cliff face where the caves were.

They ran the longboat aground, then shipped oars. Jherek and three pirates leaped out onto the beach and grabbed the longboat's sides, pulling it easily onto the rocky sand. The wind ripped low howls from the caves as the breeze traveled across the mouths. Jherek looked up at the towering cliff face while the others stepped from the longboat. A few of the seagulls took wing curiously, swooping down within a few feet of him.

"Look at 'em," one pirate growled. "You'd think they was watchdogs close as they eyeball a body."

Azla assigned four of the ten men in the crew to guard the longboat. She took the lead with long strides, crossing the shoreline to the nearest group of men frying fish.

"I need some information," Azla told the strangers.

A hulking brute of a man standing nearby gave her an evil, gap-toothed grin. "Ain't nothing free here, wench. Mayhap you show me a little kindness—"

Before the man even knew what was going on, Azla ripped her scimitar free and touched the blade to his throat.

"How much," she asked coldly, "would you be willing to pay for your next breath?"

Color drained from the big man's features. "What was it you'd be wanting?" he asked.

Azla kept the scimitar at the big man's throat. "There's a diviner who lives here. Do you know her?"

"I know *of* her, Cap'n." The big man's Adam's apple slid

across the blade's edge. "Name's Dehnee. She gives readings and such for them what want 'em."

"Where can I find her?"

The man pointed up the narrow ledge that wandered back and forth across the cliff face. Other branches led off to other caves, giving each a portion of privacy. The diviner's cave was halfway up and on the right.

"Take us there," Azla commanded.

"Cap'n, I'd rather not. The woman lives with a ghost."

"You'd rather not more than you'd rather try breathing through your neck?"

The man started walking, glancing in cold rebuke at his companions who sat without comment. Azla kept the scimitar's point at the back of the man's neck.

Jherek kept a ready hand on his cutlass hilt as he brought up the party's rear. They marched up the narrow, inclined path to the cave the big man indicated.

A handmade sign hung beside the cave mouth that simply proclaimed DIVINER. A thick carpet of sea lion hides stretched across the cave mouth, hung from a length of rope. The hides possessed the maned heads and forelegs of great lions, but the body and tail of a fish. The bottom of the carpet of stitched hides was rolled up and sewn around rocks that weighted it to the ground.

Azla dismissed the big man with a turn of her head. He went quickly, muttering beneath his breath.

"Dehnee," the half-elf captain called out. "I've got coin if you've a mind and skills enough to earn it."

The hides slid to the side, revealing the torchlit interior of the cave. A woman no older than her late twenties stood at the entrance. Her hair was mousy brown, long and pulled back in a ponytail. Gold eyes regarded the party and showed no fear, set deeply in a face that was chiseled and translucent as if she seldom saw the sun. She wore a gown of good material that showed age as well as care.

"I've always got a ready use for coin," she said, smiling, "but I'm not a desperate woman."

"I don't particularly care for the desperate," Azla said. "They have a tendency to tell you what you want to hear."

"It's the truth you're after then?"

"Aye, and we've come a far way to get it."

Jherek watched the woman, remembering the times

he'd seen Madame Iitaar work at home in Velen over a man's hand or an object yanked up from the sea in a fisherman's net.

Diviners could tell of things yet to come upon occasion, as well as the past of objects that were brought to them. Those who lived on the sea, depending on the gracious bounty of the waters, learned to respect people like that.

Dehnee looked at them coolly and said, "My home is small, and I like my privacy."

"Only four of us." Azla pointed out Sabyna, Glawinn, and Jherek.

The diviner's eyes raked casually across the ship's mage and the paladin, but came to rest on the young sailor.

"Yes," she said softly. "I can see that the four of you are tied. Some in more ways than the one you came to see me about."

The announcement surprised Jherek, but he said nothing.

"Enter." Dehnee stepped back and held the folds of sea lion skins back.

Jherek entered last, his mind and eyes seeking danger everywhere. He hadn't forgotten the story about the diviner sharing her cave with a ghost.

The cave evidently divided into three or more rooms. Some of the division was natural but the young sailor could also detect scars and markings from tools and stone cutters.

More hides taken from sea creatures decorated the walls along with mounted fish on lacquered wooden plaques. Shells and bits of coral of different sizes and colors strung on sections of net in designs and patterns hung from the uneven ceiling. Red, blue, and green lichens clung to the walls in whirlpool patterns, evidently carefully directed in their growth.

Two clam shells more than a foot across hung upside down from more nets. They were filled with blubber and burning wicks to fill the cave with light.

Dehnee passed her hand over a small net with silver bells and shells that tinkled and rattled. The sensation of clawed feet crawled over Jherek, causing him to shift his shoulders.

"It's all right," Sabyna said in a soft voice. "The spell was intended as protection only."

"I have been hunted before," the diviner said. "I like to make sure that no one enters my home while bewitched by a charm, and that I have no unseen guests."

She sat cross-legged on a sea lion hide that had the creature's head still intact.

Jherek's hand tightened as he stared at the maned head. The itching sensation grew even stronger. Dehnee turned a hand palm up and offered seating on the piles of hides in the center of the cave.

"If you don't mind, lady," Glawinn said, "I'll stand. The armor becomes rather cumbersome."

"Of course, Sir Knight. I know merely being here must be troublesome to you. Some of the objects I use in my divinations would not be comfortable to you, but they are necessary in what I do."

"Thank you, lady."

Gazing at the paladin, Jherek saw that Glawinn was a little paler than normal and held his lips tightly as a man at rough sea might. The young sailor didn't feel well himself and was experiencing a throbbing behind his eyes.

Sabyna and Azla sat in front of the diviner.

Dehnee looked up at Jherek with dark, liquid eyes. "I can attempt this without you," she told him, "but my best chance of success will be with your assistance."

"I don't understand," Jherek said.

"You come here seeking an object," Dehnee told him. "Of all, you are the most closely tied to it."

Jherek hesitated only a moment, wishing there were some other way. "What do I need to do?"

"Sit."

Dehnee pointed to a place before her. The young sailor pulled his cutlass from the sash at his waist so that he could sit in comfort. As soon as the blade came free, the sea lion's eyes glinted with unholy light and tracked his movement. The massive jaws unhinged and loosed a coughing roar of warning. Skin prickling and heart hammering in fear, Jherek stepped back.

The sea lion's body rose from the carpet, magically transforming and coming fully to life.

VI

6 Flamerule, the Year of the Gauntlet

Half formed from the diviner's carpet, the sea lion glared at Jherek with hot hatred in its emerald green eyes. In life the creature had been easily a dozen feet long. Light danced on the shiny scales that began just behind its forelegs as it slithered protectively in front of Dehnee.

"Narik!" Dehnee cried, tugging on the fierce mane. "No!"

Slowly, the sea lion shifted its attention from Jherek to the diviner. The coughing growls subsided and changed to a plaintive whining that filled the whole cavern.

"He means no harm," Dehnee stated, continuing to pull on the ensorcelled beast. "He thought you were going to hurt me. He's not been around many such as you."

As if in grudging obedience, the sea lion glided back to the cave's stone floor and became inert. The green eyes continued to follow Jherek's movements.

The young sailor swallowed hard, discovering he had a death grip on the cutlass.

"This is an uneasy place for us, young warrior," Glawinn said softly. "As you sense danger about this cave, so it senses danger from you. Trust the lady to hold the balance."

Jherek let out a tense breath, reminding himself why they were there. He sat slowly, offering no threat, watching the green eyes that watched him. He sat with crossed legs, his cutlass across his knees.

"Believe in me," Dehnee told him, offering her hands.

"Lady," Jherek said in a tight voice, "as much as I am able."

He held his hands out and she took them. Her touch felt almost too warm, too exciting. Emotions and desires that he kept carefully bottled up slapped at the sides of his restraint, threatening to explode. He tried to yank his hands away, feeling shamed.

Dehnee tightened her grip, but he pulled hard enough to bring her to her knees before him. He gazed into her gold eyes.

"It's all right," she told him. "Your feelings are natural."

"No." Jherek shook his head and kept pulling at his hands. Nothing that strong and heady could ever be natural.

"An innocent," Dehnee breathed in quiet wonder. "By Umberlee's favored sight, I've not touched an innocent in decades."

"Have a care with him, lady," Glawinn warned softly. "I'll not have him hurt in any way."

"I know what I'm doing, Sir Knight."

All Jherek's ability to struggle deserted him in a powerful surge that left him weak. He still felt the woman's hands on his, still felt the unaccustomed and unacceptable desire that flamed him, but he couldn't move.

Then Glawinn's strong hand dropped to his shoulder, anchoring him and putting some of the feeling at bay. "Patience, lady," the paladin said. "He's never been around one such as you."

"What did you come here seeking?" Dehnee asked, her eyes totally focused on Jherek's.

Jherek's thoughts ran rampant. It was hard to concentrate. "Lathander's disk," he said.

"Picture it in your mind."

Unbidden, Jherek's thoughts ranged only on the woman before him. He saw her naked, her body trim and gently rounded, her small breasts heavy with desire. He closed his eyes tightly against the vision and whispered, "No."

"What you're feeling is normal," Dehnee said.

Jherek didn't believe her. Nothing like this could ever be normal—or acceptable.

"Picture the disk."

Calming himself as much as he was able, Jherek built the image of the disk inside his head.

"Good," Dehnee whispered. "I can see it as well. What do you wish to know?"

"Vurgrom took it," Azla said beside Jherek. "We want to know if he still has it."

Lathander's disk tumbled in Jherek's mind.

"Yes," the diviner said. "It is still in Vurgrom's possession."

"Where?"

Filmy black patterns ghosted over Jherek's vision, like rotten spots on fruit. They cleared momentarily, revealing a glimpse of a ship. He managed to peer closer and see her name, then the image slipped away. He recognized the ship from the confrontation at the Ship of the Gods.

"*Maelstrom*," he gasped.

"Do you know where she is?" Azla asked.

Jherek shook his head, too weak to say anything.

"It is far from here," Dehnee replied.

"We want to find it," Azla told her.

"Of course you do. And you will. It is meant for this boy to find."

The diviner released one of Jherek's hands but not the other. The young sailor watched as she reached into the sea lion's open mouth and pulled out a complex device.

"An astrolabe. It's used by a ship's navigator," Azla said. "With it a captain or anyone learned enough to take readings from the azimuth of the sun, the moon, or certain stars can determine where a ship is on the sea."

"This is no ordinary astrolabe," Dehnee told them. She cradled the instrument in her lap with one hand. "This device is ages old, and its origin is almost completely unknown to me."

The whale oil light glistened off the astrolabe's surface. Only then did Jherek realize it was cut from some kind of yellowed crystal that held only minute fractures.

"I was given this by a sea elf in exchange for information," the diviner continued. "I can enspell it to track Vurgrom's ship for you."

"At what cost?" Azla demanded.

"Only that you bring it back when you're finished," Dehnee replied. "And I would ask a favor."

Azla's eyes narrowed. "What favor?"

"Not from you, Captain." Dehnee's eyes locked with Jherek's. "From this boy."

Glawinn interrupted before Azla could respond. "He is only a boy."

The diviner nodded. "And what he faces will make a man of him." She glanced at the paladin. "You know this as well as I. That's part of the reason you're here. I won't ask a favor of the boy. I will want a favor from the man."

"He's too young to know what you ask," Glawinn interrupted. "A promise from him—"

"Is all that I will settle for," Dehnee said. "Otherwise, you are on your own."

"You know of the portents and magic that surround the Sea of Fallen Stars," Azla said. "Some are saying that ancient prophecies are being fulfilled, that an old evil is descending upon us."

"That's not my concern." The diviner stared at Jherek and he felt the pull of her gaze. "What is your answer?"

"Young warrior," Glawinn said gently, "don't agree to these terms. Wait until a more proper time."

"Time is against us." Jherek spoke clearly, but his words sounded distant.

"There is much for you to learn," Glawinn persisted.

"It's only a favor," Jherek said. "I owe a debt to the temple of Lathander . . ."

"Do you accept?" Dehnee asked.

Dehnee took his hand back in hers, holding both of them again. "Swear to me that you will honor my request, and that you will never lift your hand against me."

In the periphery of his vision, Jherek saw Glawinn's stony face and knew that the paladin didn't approve.

"Lady," the young sailor said, "I swear that I will honor your request and will never lift a hand against you."

"Swear by your god."

Jherek's throat tightened. "Lady, I'm sorry. I recognize no gods. I am adrift in my beliefs and hold no anchor."

The diviner's eyes studied his face, searching.

"He speaks the truth," Glawinn stated coldly.

"I can see that. Yet he's no stranger to falsehood."

Shame burned Jherek's cheeks. The only things he'd never been completely forthright about concerned his heritage and his true name—and those he'd hidden primarily from Sabyna.

"Not in this matter," Glawinn said.

"It's strange to think of one such as him without strong beliefs."

"As may be, lady," the paladin said, "but so it is."

Dehnee tightened her grip on his hands and said, "Then name something you believe in, boy."

An incredible weight seemed to descend on Jherek's chest. It felt impossible to breathe. He had confessed to Glawinn that he believed in nothing. The paladin swore to teach him to believe again, but hadn't told the young sailor what he was supposed to believe in. Only now there was a huge gaping emptiness where his faith in the gods had once been.

"My eye and my sword arm," he croaked in a tight voice, remembering what Glawinn told him he would believe in first. "I believe in those."

"No," the diviner said. "Those things you *trust* in, but that is no real belief. Search yourself, boy, tell me what you believe in."

Jherek thought furiously, trying to find some quote, some philosophy Malorrie had taught him that he could cling to in that moment. Memories piled in on him, breakfasts shared with Madame Iitaar, battle sessions with Malorrie, sunsets he'd seen sink into the waters off the western coast of Velen.

He recalled the smell of the blueberry pies Madame Iitaar made for him, the feel of the paper of the books Malorrie loaned him, the satisfaction he got the day he first finished mending Madame Iitaar's roof, already knowing the woman had more work for him and a bed as well.

He remembered the cake he'd gotten from Hukkler's Bakery to celebrate Madame Iitaar's first birthday since he'd gone there to live. An image of Madame Iitaar at her husband's grave filled his mind. The old woman had grown a special flowering plant, then planted it on the grave in remembrance. Her smile that day, both sad and joyous, was something he'd known he'd never forget.

And he remembered the first day he'd seen Sabyna. He avoided talking to the pretty ship's mage then, fearing himself too backward and too entrenched in lies about his own identity. He'd admired her from afar, watching how she managed *Breezerunner*'s crew so efficiently and effortlessly, the easy way she smiled and the graceful way she moved with the ship's roll.

"What do you believe in?" Dehnee asked again.

"These are troubling times for him," Glawinn said.

"He knows what he believes," the diviner replied. "All he has to do is give voice to it."

Jherek faced the woman, feeling scared and alone, but his thoughts kept focusing on the same images. Madame Iitaar hadn't been forced to take on an orphaned boy and make a home for him. Whatever drew Malorrie to him hadn't ensured the bond that grew between the phantom and the boy. He didn't doubt the way he felt about Sabyna. When he'd met her again in Baldur's Gate, his spirits soared. Even though he knew he could never be good enough for her, he knew how he felt about her.

"Tell me what you believe in," the diviner said in a softer voice.

"Love," Jherek whispered, knowing it was true. "I believe in love."

The diviner's hands suddenly shook as if palsied. Her eyes went wide. The sea lion beside her snarled irritably, one forepaw flexing, then drawing back.

"By the gods," the woman said in hoarse surprise.

Embarrassed, the young sailor risked a glance at Sabyna, not knowing what she might make of his answer. Her gaze didn't meet his, but unshed tears glittered in her eyes.

Jherek felt like a giant hand reached inside of him and tried to yank his heart from his chest. He sat up straighter, knocking the cutlass from his knees, his chest suddenly too tight to breathe.

The feeling of being yanked out of his own body passed as suddenly as it came, dropping Jherek back to the floor. He gasped, then his breath came back to him in a rush. Awareness returned to him, making him feel as though a part of him was gone, but he couldn't name which part.

"Your promise," the diviner stated in a strained voice, "is accepted."

"Lathander help you, young warrior," Glawinn said gravely, "as I will if I am able."

Jherek sat, stunned, unable to explain what had passed between the woman and him. He had no doubt that it would have consequences.

Dehnee took her hands from his and lifted the astrolabe from her lap. She spoke over the device, calling out in a language Jherek couldn't understand. A purple flame filled the yellowed crystal and threw a lambent glow over the room. A moment later and the light shrank back inside the astrolabe.

"It's finished," the diviner said, and offered the instrument to Jherek.

The young sailor reached for the astrolabe, his limbs feeling like lead. When he touched the polished surface, an icy chill filled him.

"All the readings you take from that astrolabe will give you the position of Vurgrom's ship and not your own," Dehnee said.

"You took a reading from the disk for Vurgrom," Azla said.

The diviner didn't try to deny it. "Yes."

"What did you learn?"

The diviner shook her head. "Not much," she said. "The disk is protected from the small skills I have."

From what he'd been through in the last few minutes, Jherek doubted the diviner's skills were in any way small. He wondered what brought her to the Dragonisle, and why to that place's most desolate harbor. Had it been through choice, or need? How would that affect the promise he'd made her?

"But you learned something," Azla said.

"The disk is designed to lead its possessor to a weapon," Dehnee said.

"What weapon?"

"I couldn't see that much, but I know it lies somewhere off the coast of Turmish. In the vision, I was able to see that coastline and the druids that care for the place. In the past, I've been there."

"You're certain of this?" Glawinn asked.

"Yes."

The paladin faced Jherek and asked, "Did the talisman ever try to guide you?"

The young sailor thought back. He had possessed Lathander's disk for only minutes. "No."

"Maybe the disk isn't guiding Vurgrom either," Sabyna offered.

"It is," Jherek told her.

"How do you know this?" asked Azla.

"Because," the young sailor said, "I felt it come alive in my grasp."

VII

10 Flamerule, the Year of the Gauntlet

"You're keeping to yourself a lot these days."

Jherek looked down from his position in the rigging and spotted Sabyna. "Good evening, lady," he said, and immediately felt uncomfortable.

There had been much to do in the four days since they'd taken their leave of the Dragonisle. Jherek had taken care to stay involved in shipboard duties that the pretty ship's mage hadn't been assigned to oversee.

"I've gotten the impression you don't care much for present company," Sabyna said as she hauled herself up in the rigging and looked out over the curved horizon of the sea.

They were well away from land now, sailing by the mystic astrolabe. The canvas cracked and snapped as it held the wind.

"Not true," replied Jherek. He marked his place in the romance Glawinn had loaned him.

"I thought maybe I was the cause."

"Of course not," Jherek assured her. "Why would you think such a thing?"

"Because the last time we spoke I was so . . . forward."

"You merely said what was on your mind."

"Is that what you think?" she asked softly.

Despite the quietness of her words, barely heard over the crash of the waves below and the snap of canvas sails around them, Jherek suddenly felt as though he'd stepped into the jaws of a steel trap.

"Lady, I don't know what to think," he admitted. "These are very confusing times."

"For all of us." She held his gaze with her eyes and said, "When things get confusing, people who are together should be most truthful with each other."

"Aye."

Jherek's temples pounded. He hoped she wouldn't steer their conversation in a direction that would force him to lie.

"Your name isn't Malorrie."

"No. Malorrie is the name of a good friend and teacher."

"Your name is Jherek. I know you feel that you have reasons to conceal your identity. I promised you I'd never push you about it." Her eyes searched his and he saw the pain there. "But times have changed. I can no longer bide my own counsel. There are things I must know."

Jherek's stomach protested, wanting to purge its contents. Even though the wind raced over him to fill the sails, he felt like he'd come to dead calm inside, the last place a sailor wanted to find himself in an uncharted sea.

"Are you a wanted man, Jherek?"

"Aye."

Sabyna didn't bat an eye. She'd already been mostly certain of that, the young sailor knew.

"Is it for something you have done?"

"I've never done anything in my life to harm another soul out of greed or anger."

"I believe you," she said.

Relief flooded through Jherek.

"So your guilt, the price on your head, came from association with others?"

"Aye."

"So how did you come to be with these people that earned you the price on your head?"

"Through no fault of my own, lady," Jherek replied honestly. "It was ill luck."

"When did you leave them?"

"I was twelve," Jherek whispered.

"By the Lady's mercy," Sabyna said in a hushed voice, "you were only a boy."

Jherek remained silent, hoping she had probed enough. Every question she asked—skirting so closely to the truth he felt he needed to keep hidden—felt like a healer lancing an infected wound. Only in this there was no release from pressure and misery, only the promise of even more, sharper pain to come.

"What did they do?" Sabyna asked.

"Lady, please, I can't talk of it."

"Why? Jherek, don't you see that there doesn't have to be anything unsaid between us?"

Her question caught him by surprise. He shook his head, unable to voice what she wanted to hear.

"Lady, I would never have anything unsaid between us."

"But there is something?"

He couldn't answer.

"I told you before, when we first met on *Breezerunner*, that I could be very forward," Sabyna said. "Most men feel uncomfortable around a woman who knows her own mind. Sailors especially. They're not used to it."

"Aye, but that is not true of me. Sometimes," Jherek said quietly to give his words weight, "no matter how hard you struggle for something, it's not meant to be yours."

"Is that a threat?" Sabyna's voice hardened, but it was only a brittle shell over uncertainty.

The young sailor laughed when he wanted to cry. "No, lady. May Umberlee take me into her deep, dark embrace this very moment if ever there was a time I would intentionally hurt you."

"Back in the diviner's cave, she asked you what you believed in. You told her that you believed in love." Sabyna gazed deep into his eyes. "Did you mean that?"

Jherek hesitated, but in the end he knew she would know if he lied. "Aye," he said, "I believe in love. Perhaps, lady, it's the last thing I do believe in."

"So many things, evil as well as good, have been done in the name of love."

"There is no evil when the love is true," Jherek stated.

"How much do you believe that, Jherek?"

He shook his head. "Lady, with all that I am."

"Then how can you be so far from me? Surely you must know how I feel."

The question hammered Jherek like a fisherman's billy.

Tears trickled down Sabyna's face. "Never have I met a man," she said hoarsely, "that I've wanted as much as I want you. From the moment I saw you hanging onto *Breezerunner*'s side scraping barnacles, to the time we sit here together. Yet you don't acknowledge it."

Helplessly, Jherek watched her cry, not knowing what to do or what to say except, "I didn't know."

Her eyes remained steady on him and dark sadness clouded them, took away the merriment he always saw there.

"I know," she said finally, "and I think it's that bit of naivete that endears you to me even more. I look at you, Jherek, and I see a kind of man I've never known before. The puzzle of it all is that I don't know you."

"You know what you need to know, lady," Jherek told her.

"Do I?"

Jherek forced himself to speak, choosing his words carefully. "The other things you don't know, they are of no consequence."

"Then how is it we are apart? Unless I am wrong in your feelings about me."

Jherek tried to speak but couldn't. He dropped his gaze from hers, looking down into the deep waters below. How could his life be so twisted and so painful? What could he have ever done to deserve this?

"Tell me I'm wrong, Jherek," Sabyna said in a voice ragged with emotion. "Tell me I'm a fool."

"I would never call you a fool, lady," he told her.

"Tell me again how you believe in love, Jherek. Gods above, when I heard that timbre in your voice in the diviner's cave, I felt more confused than ever. The anger I'd been harboring toward you left me, and with it all of my defenses against these feelings. Tell me."

He raised his eyes to meet hers, seated across from her in the rigging. "As you wish, lady."

She gazed at him expectantly.

"I believe in love," Jherek said, "but I don't believe in

myself. If I've learned anything at all in my life, it's that a belief in himself is what makes a man. I haven't yet become one."

Sabyna shook her head. More tears cascaded down her face. "Mystra's wisdom, I wish I knew some way to let you see yourself as I see you, and as others see you."

"It wouldn't matter, lady," Jherek said gently. "It's how I see myself."

"Why?"

"Because I know the true me that no one sees," Jherek stated. "Even now, you're in danger here on these seas because of a mistake I made. That weakness of pride I felt in accepting Lathander's disk at the Rose Portal has brought us all here."

"And what if that was no mistake?" Sabyna asked. "What if that disk is truly supposed to be here?"

"It's in evil's hands, lady. There's no way to make that right."

"You are so stubborn, Jherek," the ship's mage said in a harsh voice. "I would change that if I could."

"I know of no other way to be," Jherek told her.

"I know, and changing you would be so dangerous. Everything in you builds on everything else. Were one small part removed, I think the whole would somehow be changed as well. You are one of the most complete men I have ever known." Sadness carved deep lines into her face, draining her of the vitality he loved about her. "I'm sorry. I shouldn't have pressed you like this, but I couldn't go any further without letting you know how I felt. Forgive me."

"Lady, there is nothing to forgive."

"There is. I should have handled my own emotions better. I am a ship's mage, trained to handle battle, dying men, and the ravages of an uncaring sea and a fickle wind. I am no young girl to have her head turned so prettily. I have a heart, though, Jherek, and I've learned to listen to it. Selûne forgive my weakness."

Sabyna stood in the rigging and turned to go.

"Lady." Jherek stood too, catching her hand in his. It felt so slim and warm, so right in his. "It is not you."

Tears sparkled like diamonds on her wind-burned cheeks. "I know. I only wish I could be brave enough and strong enough for both of us. I wish I could help you trust me."

69

Without warning she leaned in, too quickly for Jherek to move away. Her lips met his, and he felt the brand of her flesh, tasted the sweetness of her tears. His pulse roared, taking the strength from his knees. In all his life Jherek had never known such a feeling, so strong and so true. For the moment, all his fears and self doubts were nothing. He felt whole.

She pulled back, breathing rapidly. The wind swept her tears away, sipping them in quick gusts.

"I do trust you, lady," Jherek said in a thick voice. He still held her hand, pulling it to him and placing it against his chest. The heat of her flesh almost seared him. "I swear to you, if it came to it, I would give my life to save yours, and you would never have to ask."

"I don't doubt you," she replied. She clenched her hand against his chest, knotting up his shirt and pulling him toward her with surprising strength. "You would give me your life, but can you give me your heart?"

VIII

10 Flamerule, the Year of the Gauntlet

At Iakhovas's bidding, Laaqueel stepped through the wall of *Tarjana* and out into the ocean. She only felt a moment's sensation of passing through the wood. Though it was not uncomfortable, she noticed immediately that the water on the other side was cold. The depth also blocked the penetrating light from the sea, turning the craggy ledges and canyons of the ocean floor black. She floated easily, adjusting the pressure in her air bladder to make herself weightless.

"Where are we?" she asked Iakhovas.

Silently, Iakhovas replied, through the connection made between them by the quill near her heart. *There are others here.*

Picking up on the tension in Iakhovas's words, Laaqueel grasped her trident more tightly and peered into the shadows around them. Her lateral lines picked up the small movement of fish nearby, and the coil of an eel shifting in its hiding place.

Who are we meeting? she asked.

Allies, Iakhovas replied. *That is all you need trouble yourself to know, little malenti.*

Unease swept through Laaqueel. Over the last four days, she'd seen little of Iakhovas. He'd remained within *Tarjana*'s belly and hadn't allowed her to visit with him much. He watched over the princes in Vahaxtyl, and even though the malenti priestess told him they should return to the sahuagin city and change the currents that were passing through the minds of the populace as the princes spoke out against him, Iakhovas resisted. Clearly, he followed his own agenda.

She felt new movement. Something was slithering in from the left. The sensation pulsing through her lateral lines made her skin tighten in primitive fear. She turned to face it, dropping the trident's tines in front of her.

"Welcome," Iakhovas boomed.

He moved his arms and floated twenty feet down through the water to the sea floor. Puffs of sand rose up around his boots, then quickly settled again.

Three figures glided across the ocean floor from beneath a coral-encrusted arch. Laaqueel's senses told her more of them remained in hiding, but she could not tell how many more. She studied the figures, opening her eyes to their widest to use what little light the depths held.

They looked like surface dwellers, dressed in clothing rather than going naked as most races in Serôs did. There were three men, none of them possessing any remarkable features. They carried no apparent weapons, which surprised Laaqueel. The only surface dwellers the malenti priestess came in contact with who hadn't carried weapons were magic-users.

"Welcome," one of the men greeted. The word sounded foreign to his lips. "You have received word through Vurgrom of the Taker's Eye?"

"Yes," Iakhovas said. "I was told the eye resides in Myth Nantar."

"And so it does."

"I have brought gifts for the Grand Tor, a means of increasing his own armies," Iakhovas said.

He whirled the net above his head and it grew, increasing in size until it was as big as Iakhovas. He flung it away from him and still it grew. Something struggled within the strands.

When the net finished growing, it was huge. Tritons

moved against each other inside it, striving desperately against the hemp strands.

The tritons were humanoid in appearance. They had the pointed ears and beautiful features of elves, long manes of dark blue and dark green hair. From the waist up, they could be easily mistaken for sea elves. From the waist down they were covered in deep blue scales. Their finned legs ended in broad, webbed flippers.

"How many?" one of the strangers asked.

"Thirty-four," Iakhovas said. "Four above the agreed-upon price. A gesture of good will to Grand Tor Arcanaal."

"He will be most appreciative," one of the men said. He gestured and shadows swam from the darkness, moving through the water smoothly, their arms at their sides. Two men swam to the net and grabbed it, then towed it back toward the gloom.

The tritons cursed and called on their god Persana but it was to no avail. They were doomed to their fates at the hands of the men Iakhovas gave them to. In only minutes, they were gone from sight and no longer heard.

The man gestured again. Another man swam from the shadows bearing a gold chest inlaid with precious stones, marked with sigils of power. He handed it to Iakhovas. The man turned and swam away.

Come, Iakhovas commanded, gesturing at the water and opening the gate again. *We have much to do.*

Shaken and mystified by the encounter, Laaqueel propelled herself after Iakhovas.

Look back, priestess.

The serenity of the feminine voice was startling. Laaqueel glanced at Iakhovas as he summoned the gate.

He does not hear me, priestess, the serene voice went on. *My words are meant for your thoughts alone.*

Who are you? Laaqueel asked. The voice was the same one that she had heard in Coryselmal as she was turned back from death.

Patience. All will be explained. For now, turn back and see the lies that Iakhovas has woven for your eyes to see.

Almost unwillingly, Laaqueel finned around, sweeping a hand through the water with the webbing open. The men were still in sight, only they weren't men anymore.

The three figures had deep purple skin that darkened to

inky-black. Iridescent tips and lines marked the dorsal fin on their heads and backs. The heads were not oval like a human's or an elf's, but rather elongated and stretched out like that of a locathah. Their jaws formed cruel beaks.

Instead of two arms, they had four, all of them with humanlike appendages instead of the pincers or tentacles Laaqueel knew were also possible on the creatures. Their lower bodies ended in six tentacles.

Iakhovas lies, the serene voice said. *He's not as invincible as he would have you believe. You must watch yourself.* Then the voice was gone, a slight pop of pressure that faded from the inside of Laaqueel's skull.

* * * * *

"I am Myrym, chieftain of the Rolling Shell people, and I bid you welcome."

Pacys believed Myrym to be the oldest locathah he'd ever met. Cataracts clouded her eyes, but she gave no indication of missing anything around her.

The fin at the top of her head ran all the way down her back. Other fins underscored the forearms and the backs of her calves. The huge eyes were all black but were unable to both focus on the bard at the same time. The locathah turned her head from side to side. She wore a necklace made of threaded white and black pearls that would have been worth a fortune in the surface world, and a sash of netting that held a bag of different kinds of seaweed, coral, and shells. The old bard's own magical inclinations told him the net bag contained a number of items of power.

They sat at the bottom of the abyss in a grotto between a crevice of rock made easily defensible by stands of claw coral. Fist-sized chunks of glowcoral had been used to build cairns around them, punching holes in the darkness of the sea bottom. The tribe sat scattered about her, nearly three hundred strong, covering the ledges above them as well as smaller caves. The young in particular pooled together in schools, floating and watching with their big eyes.

Three days ago, the music had brought Pacys south and east of the sea elf city, drawing him toward Omalun and the Hmur Plateau at the base of Impiltur. The old bard couldn't lay name to what exactly pulled him, but he'd been insistent about going. Taranath Reefglamor had assigned guards to him and provisioned them well. The sea elf guard waited further up the Hmur Plateau with the seahorses they'd used as steeds.

Seated cross-legged only a few feet from the locathah chieftain, Pacys ran his hands over the saceddar, underscoring their conversation with a gentle melody that spoke of calm seas and the patience of her people, their willingness to sacrifice so they might live.

Khlinat sat only a little distance away, laughing at the antics of the foot-long locathah children as they swam close to him to investigate, then swam away with quick, darting movements.

"Thank you for your hospitality," Pacys said, listening to the music that crooned within him. "I didn't know what drew me out here, but I think I know now."

"We were drawn to each other," Myrym told him. "We've only been in this place two days. We have kept moving. The sahuagin have come into these waters, and the surface world has developed a strong distrust of anyone who calls the sea home. We have received word that our locathah brethren in the Shining Sea have allied with the Taker, an unfortunate choice that will affect us all."

"I know," Pacys replied.

Khlinat chuckled heartily as one of the small locathah children finally got the nerve up to touch his beard. The sudden explosive laughter sent the locathah child swimming for its life, threading under and between stands of rock thrusting up from the seabed.

"Oh, an' yer a quick lad, ain't ye?" the dwarf chuckled. "A-dartin' through them waters like that, it's a wonder ye didn't brain yerself."

The locathah child cowered behind the nearest adult, who laid a tender hand on the child's head. The other locathah laughed with the dwarf.

Even in that moment of levity, though, Pacys could sense the innate fear of the locathah tribe. They hadn't known peace and prosperity for generations, nor were there any reassurances now.

"What do you know of the Taker's beginnings?" Myrym asked.

75

"Nothing." Pacys paused his song. "All whom I have talked to have told me only that he was born long ago, when Toril was young. They didn't know if he was human or elf in the beginning, or what he would look like now."

Myrym nodded. "Someone once knew, but they have forgotten. However, that which others forget, the locathah hold close and treasure that it may someday benefit us. The other races have prophecies, parts they are to play in the coming battle."

Pacys changed tunes, finding one that played more slowly and conveyed menace. He recognized it as one of the Taker's alternate scores.

"Those thousands of years ago," Myrym said, "there existed a being unlike any that ever lived before. Some have said he was even the first man, the first to crawl from the sea and live upon the unforgiving dry. What made him crawl from the blessed sea, no one may know, but some say there was a longing within him to find another such as himself. The sea in those days was very green and had only recently given up space to the lands that rose from the fertile ocean bottom at the gods' behest."

Pacys listened intently, striking chords that would help his song paint the pictures of the tale.

"The Taker wandered the lands," Myrym said, "but of course, he found nothing there. The dry world was too new, and even the world of the sea was very young. While he was on the land, he talked with the gods. They were curious about him, you see, at this weak thing that dared talk to them and question the things that they did."

From the corner of his eye, Pacys saw that the locathah woman held the full attention of her tribe. The cadence of her voice pulled them in.

"With nothing to find on land, the Taker returned to the sea. It has been said that the Taker was there the day Sekolah set the first sahuagin free."

"Did he have a name?" Pacys asked.

"If he did, it has been forgotten," Myrym answered. "In those days, before people came to the sea, before some of them left the oceans and made their homes on dry land only later to return to the sea, names were not necessary. There was only one."

"Is he a man?" the old bard asked. "A wizard?"

"Not a true man, but again, not a creature of the sea either. He was himself, a thing unique."

"How did he come to be?"

"No one knows for sure, Loremaster. There are those who say his birth was an accident, created by the forces that first made Toril. Others say the god Bane crafted him to torture others. All agree that the Taker searched for love, for acceptance, for an end to the loneliness that filled him at being the one."

"But we all crave those things," Pacys said, not understanding. "How could this monster look for that which we all seek? I've been told the Taker is evil incarnate."

"He is," Myrym replied. "Are the wants and needs of good and evil so very different?"

"No," Pacys said. "Our stories are filled with those who fell from grace. Heroes and villains, only the merest whisper sometimes separates them."

"The Taker simply was," Myrym said. "His loneliness persisted till he drew the eye of Umberlee. The Bitch Queen in those days was softer. The gods had not yet begun to war over territories and the supplication of the thinking races that spread throughout the lands and seas of Toril. They existed in peace, each learning about their own powers, learning to dream their own dreams. Umberlee found the Taker, and she grew fascinated by him."

"Why?" Pacys asked.

"Because she had never known anything like him. He hurt and bled easily compared to her, weak in so many ways. Still, he held forth a joy and a zest for life that she had never envisioned. She grew to love him."

"And he grew to love her." Pacys's fingers sketched out a brief, sprightly tune that echoed in the grotto.

"As much as he could," Myrym admitted. "The concept of love, though credited to the gods, was a virtue of the elves, who knew loyalty and honor first. It was made bittersweet by the humans, whose lives ran by at a rapid pace and who could not maintain the attention and focus of the elves. In the beginning, an elf could love others, but only if he loved himself first. Humans, though, could love past themselves, love others more than themselves. They could love ideas, could love even the sound of laughter, which many thought was foolishness. No one, it is said, can love as a human can whose heart is pure and true."

* * * * *

Jherek gazed down into Sabyna's eyes and felt shamed. That she should have to ask him was his own failing. He held his hand in hers, feeling her fingers knotted up in the material of his shirt.

Her eyes searched his. "Can you promise me your heart, Jherek?" she asked again.

"Lady—"

"The answer can be so simple," Sabyna said. "Despite everything else you have on your mind, despite the other troubles that have your attention, there can be only two answers. Anything else would be no answer at all, and that wouldn't be fair to me after all I've revealed to you."

In the end, he knew what his answer must be, and why. He was not the man he needed or wanted to be, and she deserved far more than he ever could be.

"No."

Her fingers unknotted from his shirt and she pulled her hand back. Jherek made himself let go her hand, thinking he would never again have the opportunity to touch her.

"You tell me no, yet you made the diviner a promise not knowing what she might ask."

"There was no choice in that, lady."

"There's always a choice, Jherek. That's what life is about."

"Lady, I've never had the choices of others."

"No," Sabyna said. "I think maybe you've never been one to fight time or tide, Jherek. You gave your promise to the diviner even though that promise might take your life."

"Lady, I swore my life to you."

"Your life isn't what I wanted," Sabyna said. "A chance at a life with you is all that I asked."

She turned to go, tripping over a line in the rigging even though she'd been so surefooted earlier.

"Lady—" Jherek took a step forward, meaning to catch her, meaning to tell her—something.

The bag of holding at her side suddenly erupted and the raggamoffyn exploded from it. The bits and pieces of cloth wove themselves into a serpentine shape that struck like a cobra. The blow hammered Jherek's chest hard enough to knock him off balance.

"Skeins!" Sabyna cried, grabbing the raggamoffyn as it prepared to strike again. "No!"

Reluctantly, the familiar backed away, relaxing and floating easily on the wind.

Steadying himself, Jherek stared at the pretty ship's mage. Before he could find anything to say, a voice bawled out a warning from below.

"Slavers! Slavers off the port bow!"

IX

10 Flamerule, the Year of the Gauntlet

Jherek turned to face *Black Champion*'s port side. Below, the pirates ran across the deck, following orders Azla barked out on the run. The pirate captain grabbed the railing of the prow castle steps and hauled herself up.

"Malorrie!" Azla yelled. "Do you see the damned ship?"

"Aye," Jherek replied in full voice. "She's off to port about a thousand yards."

"Her heading?"

"For us, Captain."

There was no doubt about her heading. White-capped breakers smashed against her prow as she cut across the green sea. Her lanyards bloomed with full canvas, harnessing the wind as she rose and fell on the great hills of the Sea of Fallen Stars.

"Is she riding high?" Azla demanded. "Or wallowing like some fat-arsed duck?"

"She's riding low, Captain," Jherek bellowed back between his cupped hands, "but she's coming hard."

He turned to glance at Sabyna but found the ship's mage was already climbing rapidly down the rigging. The young sailor's heart hurt as he watched her go.

He grabbed the book Glawinn had loaned him and quickly shoved it into the leather pouch where he stowed his gear. He left the pouch tied to the rigging, hoping it would be there when he got back. Out of habit he took the bow and quiver of arrows he'd brought up with him.

Glancing back at the approaching ship, the young sailor noted that it had gained considerably, pulling to within eight hundred yards and still closing. *Black Champion* held a south-southwesterly course, headed for the coast of Turmish. The slaver ship drew on due east, running straight ahead of the breeze as it swooped upon them.

"Bring her about!" Azla thundered. "Take up a heading due east. She's got our scent, boys, but let's see if the bitch can run!"

Black Champion came about smartly, taking up the easterly course. Deck crews sprang into action, bringing around the sails and running up new canvas. The caravel jumped in response to the wind, diving forward through the rolling brine hills. She dived into a wave, miring down, sliding back and forth like a hound trying to run up a muddy incline, then—when she broke through—she surged forward, her prow coming out of the water.

Jherek abandoned his place. Azla already had a man up in the crow's nest acting as a spotter. He pulled the bow and quiver over his shoulder, then ran through the rigging toward the bowline that ran from the mainmast to the prow.

He crossed the rigging without a misstep, pulling his cutlass free of the sash around his waist. He paused long enough to hang his hook from one boot, making sure it was secure, then he unknotted the sash. Shaking out the sash's length, he steadied himself on the rigging, then used the tautness of the ropes to spring up high. With the way *Black Champion* fought her way through the sea, the move was risky, but he trusted himself.

Holding the cutlass in one hand, he flipped one end of the sash over the bowline, then caught it in his fingers while holding the other. Squeezing both ends of the sash tightly, he hung from the bowline for just an instant, then began the long slide down to the prow. The sash sang across the twisted hemp. He lifted his feet to clear the canvas belled out from the forward mast.

Sliding across the bowline, Jherek glanced at *Black Champion*'s decks and watched the pirates taking their battle stations. They brought the prow and stern heavy ballistae around and fitted them with the ten-foot-long bolts. Two men began winding the winch that drew the great bowstring back.

The bowline was tied off at the end of the bowsprit sticking out from *Black Champion*'s prow. Judging the distance and the caravel's pitch, Jherek released one end of the sash. It unfurled from the bowline, and he fell to the prow castle, landing only a few feet from the forward ballista crew.

The young sailor rolled to his feet gracefully. He looped the sash back around his hips and slid the cutlass home, adding the hook from his boot a moment later. Taking the bow from his shoulder, he placed one end against his boot, took the greased string from his pocket, and strung it quickly. He unbound the strap that kept the arrows tight in the quiver and slid four shafts free. He nocked one to the string, then held the other three clasped in his left hand on the bow.

Azla stood at the prow railing, her scimitar naked in her fist. The wind tangled her dark hair. She took her chain mail shirt from a crewman and quickly pulled it on. The ringing chains on leather barely sounded over the crack of the canvas and the smashing waves.

"Who is she?" Jherek asked.

"I don't know the ship," Azla answered, "but I know the flag."

Jherek concentrated on the flag atop the approaching ship's mainmast. A feathered snake curled across a field of quartered black and red, mouth open and fangs exposed.

"They're of the Blood Tide," Azla said, "a loose network of slavers who work for the Night Masks in Westgate."

The slaver vessel was within four hundred yards, its advance slowing as *Black Champion* seized the wind. Jherek rode out the rise and fall of the ship, his free hand resting on the railing while the other held the nocked bow.

"Unfurl the spinnaker!" Azla shouted.

Crewmen rushed to the ship's prow. An instant later, the white sail billowed out, blotting the sky from forward view.

"Cap'n!" a mate squalled from the crow's nest. "Something just leaped off from that ship's rigging, and it ain't falling. Some kind of bird."

Jherek peered into the cloudy blue sky. The sun setting behind them turned the cloud banks blood-mist red, but he could make out half a dozen black shapes boiling out from the ship's lanyards.

The creatures swiftly overtook *Black Champion*, cutting through the air. The bat-winged humanoids had wedge-shaped faces and fangs that ran nearly to their lower jaws. A single horn sprouted from their narrow foreheads, curling back slightly. Grayish-white skin looked like marble in the sunlight, glowing with a rosy hue from the setting sun. Besides the arms and crooked legs, the creatures had long, spiked tails.

"Gargoyles," Azla breathed.

The gargoyles screamed, a raucous noise that filled *Black Champion*'s deck. They attacked the two men in the crow's nest first, swooping in to rip bloody furrows across the sailors' faces, chests, and backs with curved talons. Their blows also splintered the wooden cupola.

Tracking the nearest gargoyle , Jherek drew the arrow's feathers back to his cheek, led the creature a little, then released. The arrow jumped from the bow and struck the creature in the thigh.

The gargoyle screamed in pain, breaking the rapid beat of its wings for just an instant. It unfurled its wings and stopped its downward momentum less than ten feet above the main deck.

Horrid red eyes burned with rage as it spied Jherek. Screeching again, the gargoyle flapped its wings and gained height, streaking for the prow castle.

Standing his ground, Jherek fitted another arrow to the string. The other gargoyles in the rigging slashed the sails and smashed smaller lanyard supports.

"Kill those things!" Azla ordered at Jherek's side.

The young sailor released the bowstring when the gargoyle cleared the prow castle railing before him, less than twenty feet away now. Even with the uncertain pitch and roll of the caravel, his arrow splintered the gargoyle's head.

Jherek sidestepped the flying corpse and watched the

gargoyle smash into the bow railing, shattering some of the thinner decorative spindles. He already had another arrow nocked, searching for a target.

Pirates scampered through the rigging with swords in their fists to take on the gargoyles rending the sails. One of the creatures clung to the side of the forward mast with both legs, tail, and one hand. It struck out with the other, cleaving a pirate's face from his skull. Shrieking, the pirate fell from the rigging and smashed into the deck below. The screams stopped abruptly.

Releasing the bowstring, Jherek watched his arrow go wide of the mark, catching the canvas beside the gargoyle and sinking to the fletching. The young sailor nocked another arrow and let fly again.

The arrow sank into the gargoyle's thin chest, driving it back and nailing it to the mast it clung to. The wings fluttered as it struggled to get away. Before it could, three more arrows from the deck crew feathered it. The ship pitched across a breaker and snapped Jherek's shaft. The gargoyle dropped, missing the deck and falling over the side.

Jherek took four more arrows from his quiver, nocked one and locked the other three in his fist. He searched for other targets, missing twice as the gargoyles scampered and glided among the sails..

The mainsail came loose in a rush, snapping and fluttering as it dropped to the deck where it covered a dozen pirates. The loss of the sail had an immediate effect on *Black Champion* as the wind blew through her instead of against her.

Sunlight gleamed against copper-colored armor, drawing Jherek's eye. He put another arrow to his string as he watched Glawinn stride on deck, his long sword in one hand and his shield on his other arm.

The temptation proved too much for the gargoyles. Two of them swooped down from the rigging, flying directly toward the paladin. Pirates on the deck around Glawinn scattered, running for cover.

Pride swelled in Jherek's heart even as he drew back the bowstring. Glawinn's stance never faltered.

"For Lathander!" the paladin roared in challenge.

The young sailor launched his arrow, missing his mark

by little more than a hand's width. The arrow thudded into the deck.

Glawinn stepped forward, striking the lead gargoyle in the face. Still in motion, he turned to the side, bringing his shield up and setting himself behind it as the second gargoyle hit him head on. The weight and speed of the creature staggered the paladin, but he held, turning the creature's momentum to one side.

The impact against the shield shattered bones in the gargoyle's arms and shoulders. It rolled across the deck, beating its wings futilely and howling in pain. As it tried to curl up and get to its feet, a nearby pirate ran at it and shoved a harpoon into the gargoyle's chest, driving it back against the starboard railing.

"They're going to overtake us," Azla said.

Jherek swung his attention back to the approaching ship. It was a hundred yards behind them, closing fast.

* * * * *

"Was Iakhovas immortal when Umberlee took him as her lover?" Pacys asked.

Myrym released the locathah child from her hands and smiled as it finned back among its brothers and sister. "Over the years they courted, the Bitch Queen gave him many gifts. Some merely of worth—gold and jewels and precious things—but many of them possessed powers that none but the gods had ever wielded before. When life began in the sea and took shape upon the dry lands, among the jungles and forests and swamps, Iakhovas was drawn to them. He wanted them to love him as Umberlee did."

"He was filled with his own conceits," Pacys said.

"Using Umberlee's gifts, he set about conquering the dry lands. There is a land where ferocious lizards still live till this day, unchanged for millions of years."

"Chult," the old bard said. "I know of the place." He had even visited there, seeing the dinosaurs for himself and carrying back tales of the adventurers who traveled there seeking fortunes.

"There Iakhovas caused to be built a huge palace," Myrym said. "They say it was more grand than any building on Faerûn. A man could walk it, I have been told, from one end to the other if he planned for a full day's travel. While Umberlee was away on other planes, Iakhovas warred incessantly, pitting one kingdom against another. He sent thieves out to take powerful items mages created, going there and taking them himself when no one else could do it. His greed knew no boundaries, no satisfaction. All he knew how to do was consume."

"And this was his true nature," Pacys said, understanding.

"Yes. The nature of the Taker is that he must take. His world was first the seas, remember, and those who live beneath the water have to move incessantly to feed. He was the chief predator among all the lesser species."

"What is he truly?" Pacys asked.

"Only the man who destroys him will know."

"Do you know this man's name?"

"No," Myrym said, shaking her narrow head, "but it is his destiny to become known to all through your songs."

"Can you tell me where to search for him?"

"No, but your path, his, and the Taker's will cross as surely as the limbs of a starfish have a common center. Learn what you need to."

Pacys nodded. "I have also heard it said that the Taker fell from grace with Umberlee."

"Twice," Myrym agreed. "The first time, it was over an elf woman the Taker took as his lover. By this time, his harems contained hundreds of women. Remember, gluttony was a way of life for him."

"Umberlee didn't know he had harems?" Pacys asked.

"The Bitch Queen knew," Myrym said, "but she didn't care. Physical relations were nothing to Umberlee, something to while away the time. What she wanted from the Taker was the way she felt when she saw her reflection in his eyes."

"Adoration."

"Yes. Nowhere else did she succumb to the draw of it. But she was gone too long to the other places she sought out for learning and conquering, and giving wasn't truly in the Taker's nature. His need was to take for himself. So he took this woman from his harem, and though he didn't truly care for her, he made it look like he did so that Umberlee would be jealous."

86

"Why?" Pacys asked. "Umberlee already loved him."

"But not as he wanted to be loved by her," Myrym said. "Her love for him was natural and good, as things are meant to be, but there was nothing natural and good about him. His appetites ruled his life. When she returned, she found this woman in the bed she shared with the Taker, not one of the harem rooms. The Taker pretended the woman put the shine in his eyes that he showed Umberlee. So great was the Bitch Queen's love for him that she did not see the truth."

Pacys listened to the story with sadness. He'd seen good love turn out badly as well.

"Umberlee killed the woman in a fit of rage," Myrym continued. "The Taker knew true joy as he saw in the Bitch Queen's face the pain and hurt her love for him caused. He thought he controlled her, then, and he mocked her for her weakness. Only he had no true accounting for how hurt Umberlee was. She'd never experienced pain like that before, and swore then that she would never experience it again. She lashed out at him, raking her claws across his face and ripping an eye from its socket, almost tearing the face from him."

Discordant music emanated from the saceddar as Pacys envisioned the fight, and words already came into his mind to paint the scene for his listeners.

"Umberlee left him there in his grand palace," Myrym said, "broken and ruined, no longer ever able to be what he once was. She did not suffer to kill him, but it was a near thing. The Taker brooded and banked his hatred for a thousand years and more.

"He began to build again," she continued, "to make himself stronger than ever before. He scoured all of Toril for powerful items, devices that he could use to control elements and men and magic. He scarred his body with sigils of power that allowed him to reach into other planes. In his mind, he was more than he had ever been or ever could be.

"He sought out Umberlee then, to take his vengeance."

* * * * *

Azla ran to the forecastle railing over the main deck and called, "Ship's crew, stand ready to repel boarders!"

Black Champion's crew numbered twenty-seven, Jherek knew, and a handful of them were involved in steering and trying to salvage what they could of the sails.

At least forty men lined the starboard side of the attack craft as it sped forward. They manned the fore and aft ballistae as well as the one on the main deck. The sound of running water filled the air.

A desperate smile played on Azla's lips, and Jherek recognized it as reckless determination.

"Ballista crews," she bellowed, "prepare your shots fore and aft! Make them count or I'll have the hide from your backs!"

"Aye, Cap'n!"

"Fire on my command!"

Jherek spied Sabyna making her way up behind Glawinn. Skeins drifted protectively over her shoulder.

"Ballista crews, ready."

"Ready, Cap'n."

"Fire!"

The two ballistae sang basso thrums as they released within a heartbeat of each other. The ten-foot shafts sliced through the air. One of them thudded into the slaver's wooden hull only a few feet from the railing, frightening the crew back. The other missile struck the foremast and broke it cleanly. The forward sails toppled, raining down on the crew below.

A ragged cheer burst from *Black Champion*'s crew.

"Belay that!" Azla roared as the caravel followed the next ocean rise down into a trough below the slaver's line of sight. "We've won no battle here yet. That remains for you to take it from their teeth!"

Jherek's heart beat rapidly. Here in this battle, there was no confusion.

"Archery crew," Azla called. "Stand ready!"

Black Champion's sails blew her forward, riding her up the next wave and pulling her back within sight of the slaver only fifty yards away.

"Fire arrows!" Azla commanded.

The crew fired, and Jherek bent his bow with theirs, aiming toward the knot of men standing in the slaver's amidships. Most of the arrows missed, striking the water or snapping into the canvas above. Jherek's own shot hit a

man in the shoulder and drove him back and down to his
knees.

The three ballistae aboard the slaver cut loose. One of
them shivered into the stern castle and punched through.
The second struck below the waterline, but the vibration
that ran through *Black Champion* let Jherek know the
shot struck home.

The third shot hit the railing near Glawinn. Splintered
wood flew into the air as the ten-foot shaft punched an
eighteen-inch hole dead center in a pirate's chest. Laden by
the corpse, the shaft careened on, knocking down pirates
like tenpins. It forced the body across the deck, then tore
through the railing on the other side.

Cries of fear and prayers to gods filled the air. For a
moment, the pirates' resolve seemed broken.

"Live or die, you damned brutes!" Azla yelled down. She
hurled herself over the forecastle railing and landed in a
crouch on the pitching deck. "The choice is in your hands
and in your blades. Do me proud!"

A ragged cheer rose with her scimitar. "For Captain
Azla! For *Black Champion!*"

The caravel dropped into another trough as Jherek
heaved himself over the forecastle railing and dropped to
the main deck.

"Young warrior," Glawinn called.

"Aye."

"If that's a slaving ship and she has a cargo in her hold,
it may be that our attackers are holding a blade to their
own throats. You understand?"

"Aye."

Jherek understood immediately. If the slaves were freed
and given a chance at their own freedom, many of them
would take it.

"I will stand with these men and lead them into the
battle," the paladin said. "If you are able, perhaps you can
raise us another army to even the odds."

"Aye," Jherek answered.

"Arthoris!" Azla roared.

The old ship's mage stepped forward. He was a gnarled
man with long gray hair and a groomed beard. He wore
robes with sigils and symbols on it and carried a staff. "Aye,
Cap'n."

"Give them something to remember us by."

Arthoris raised his staff and chanted in a strong, clear voice. The heavens above him darkened as if a storm were coming.

"Ballista crews," Azla called. "Ready . . ."

"Ready, Cap'n."

"Fire!"

One of the shafts gutted the boarding party along the slaver's starboard side, breaking their ranks. The second shaft hammered into the mainmast a good twenty feet from the deck. For a moment the missile's fluted edges held it embedded in the wood, then the mast gave way with a horrific crack. The top of the mast listed to the side, bringing down more canvas and pulling the slaver hard over to port.

Black Champion's crew cheered again, calling out vile oaths at their attackers. The slaver crew shouted out in anger. Before they could recover, Arthoris launched his attack.

Three lightning balls leaped from the old ship's mage's staff and struck the slaver. Peals of thunder split the air. The lightning balls struck the boarding crew, burning them and knocking them from their feet, but only incapacitated a couple of them.

The slaver vessel pulled away, disengaging from the attack. With the two broken masts and only one remaining, she wasn't any faster than *Black Champion*.

"Cap'n!"

Azla turned, spotting one of her officers near the ship's hold.

"Come quickly!" the mate called.

All his arrows gone now, Jherek joined the ship's captain at the hold. Another man stood below with a lantern. The pale yellow light played uncertainly in the darkness as the ship yawed across the waves and reacted badly to the wind due to the tattered sails. There was no mistaking the heavy shaft that had broken through *Black Champion*'s side.

X

10 Flamerule, the Year of the Gauntlet

"The Taker thought he could defeat Umberlee?" The prospect astonished Pacys.

Myrym gazed at the old bard with her luminescent eyes and said, "Yes. She stripped his weapons from him, yanked the magic eye from his head and scattered it into its many parts, then caused storms to drive the weapons inland to the heart of Faerûn. The elves had only just abandoned Eiellur and Syorpiir during the War of Three Leaves to settle in the Selmal Basin.

"Then Umberlee reached into the heavens and caused stars to fall, crashing into the land and altering coastlines. It was almost enough, it is said, to drive the sea elves back to the surface, but they stayed. They became part of those whose destiny it was to cross paths with the Taker."

"In Myth Nantar?"

Myrym nodded. "All things above and below once passed through Myth Nantar. The elves named it City of Destinies because of the stories they'd been told about the Taker, but already they'd begun to forget some things."

"What is in Myth Nantar?"

"That I cannot answer, Loremaster. There are some

events foretold that must be lived through."

"You never said what Umberlee did with the Taker."

"In her rage, the Bitch Queen thought she killed him. Umberlee broke her lover, shattered his bones, and spilled his blood."

"I was told the Taker's eye is in Myth Nantar."

"Only part of the Taker's eye is there," Myrym answered. "It is a key piece that the Taker will need to make his weapon complete again. No one knows where in the city it is. The Dukars took charge of the eye fragment when the Coronal at Coryselmal gave it to them after the birth of Myth Nantar."

"The Dukars?" Pacys repeated. "I thought they were only legends."

"No, Loremaster." Myrym's rebuttal was gentle. "Despite all your travels, there is much you have yet to learn. Tell me what you know of the Dukars."

"They were wizards," Pacys said, recalling the few, seldom heard stories he'd been told over the years. "At first they were brought together in Aryselmalyr. Some believe they were historians, and others thought they were warriors seeking to take all of Serôs as their own territory. It's been said that Dukars could speak to the sea and have it listen, and grow weapons from their own bodies. I always thought them to be purely myth."

Myrym shook her head in disbelief. "Ah, the tales of gods-struck humans and jealous elves. The Dukars are real."

* * * * *

Jherek watched helplessly as the sea cascaded into the hold around the ballista shaft stuck through *Black Champion*'s hull. Already the water was up to their ankles, swirling around the stores and crates in the cargo area.

"Damn," Azla swore at his side. "Umberlee is getting her tithing today." She raised her voice so the pirates in the hold could hear her. "Tear off your shirts and breeches, use them to plug up the hole around that damned shaft."

"What are you going to do?" the young sailor asked.

"I'm going after that ship," Azla declared.

"You could rip out *Black Champion*'s bottom in the chase," Jherek protested. "The currents are already gnawing at her."

Azla's eyes blazed. "Unless you can pull a chunk of earwax from your head, cast it into the water and grow an island out of it, I don't see that we have much choice." She marched from the hold to the boarding party.

"She's tucked her tail between her legs and run," one of the pirates yelled.

Jherek saw the slaver vessel limping away to the south, evidently trying to leave the area with no further confrontation.

"They're not going to get away," Azla said in a stern voice. "They've holed our ship and we're sinking. So we're taking theirs in turn."

Her crew turned to look at her in amazement, clearly not wanting to believe it.

"Bring us around," Azla ordered.

The pirates sprang into action, shifting what sailcloth was left after the gargoyles' attack and cutting free other canvas that only impeded their progress.

As he stood on the deck, Jherek could feel the sluggishness of *Black Champion*'s response as she came about.

Sabyna approached. No tears showed in her eyes now, and she acted as if what passed between them only a few moments ago had never happened. "What's wrong with the ship?" she asked.

"The hull's holed," Jherek told her in a low voice. "Taking that slaver is the only hope we have."

* * * * *

"As you say," Myrym told Pacys, "the Dukars were wizards. They found their beginning almost nine thousand years ago, in a small town then called simply Nantar. Nantar was located on the Lower Hmur Plateau, its population made up exclusively of sea elves. At first, the Dukars were lorekeepers only. There were four of them who joined together after being taught by their master, Dukar, from whom they took the name of their order. These were Jhimar, the triton warrior maiden; Kupav, the sea elf; Maalirn, also a triton; and Numos, the female morkoth."

"A morkoth?" Pacys shook his head. "Chieftain Myrym, in the outer seas, the only morkoth that have been encountered are solitary creatures who dwell in caves and set traps for humans and elves, which they consider delicacies."

"You've heard of the Arcanum of Olleth?"

"Yes," the bard replied. "An empire of morkoth is something I'd have to see believe, though, and to accept the idea of a city of benevolent morkoth is harder still."

"The city is called Qatoris," Myrym said. "It is magically hidden by the Dukars who live there."

"How can this be?" the old bard asked.

"In the beginning, the Dukars recognized no oaths of fealty to the elven empire though pressure was put on them. Instead, they devoted their time to the development of their schools. Over the next three thousand years Serôs knew peace. More years passed, and more wars to go with them, and still the Dukars tried to serve the sea. They were captured and imprisoned many times in the struggles for power among the elves and other races. By the Year of the Druid's Wrath—six hundred and fifty-two years ago—the Dukars had pulled away from Myth Nantar, not wanting to take part in any of the Hmurran civil wars."

"What of the Taker's Eye?" Pacys asked the locathah.

"When Myth Nantar was built," Myrym said, "as I have said, the Coronal gave the eye to the Dukars for safe keeping. They hid it somewhere in the city."

"But Myth Nantar was lost," Pacys said. "That I remember."

Myrym nodded and said, "After the Dukars left, sahuagin warriors stole into the city and murdered the sea elves and merfolk who remained to stand guard. The sea devils destroyed much of the city, but could not stay. The mythal was designed to keep creatures like them out. They soon fled, but in later years, the magical shields around the Academy of the Dukars started growing till they encompassed all of fallen Myth Nantar. The water around the city became impenetrable even to those who built it. Some say it is haunted."

"And what do you say?" Pacys asked.

"Only that the city was properly named, Loremaster. It is the City of Destinies. For the Taker, for you, and for the

94

young warrior you seek. Somewhere in that wreckage is the Taker's Eye, and it holds the key to all your destinies. I have one final gift for you if you will accept it."

"What is that?"

"You asked me in what direction the young warrior you seek lies. These water lilies may hold an answer of sorts for you." The aged locathah held the leaves out to him. "Simply put them under your tongue and think of him."

The bard opened his mouth and put the leaves under his tongue. He pushed the seawater from his mouth and waited. A pleasant tingling sensation numbed the underside of his tongue and his lips.

All at once it felt as if the top of his head exploded, and he was swept away on a cold, black tide.

* * * * *

Black Champion bucked and fought the ocean like a horse trying to keep its head above the waterline. Jherek peered down at the dark, green-black water little more than an arm's reach from the railing. Perhaps only minutes remained before forward progress became impossible for the caravel. Despite the slave ship's loss of two masts, *Black Champion* was barely closing the last hundred yards to her.

The caravel smashed through another wave. This time the cold seawater swept over *Black Champion*'s deck, drenching the assembled crew in spray. They didn't look hopeful even after the ship surged forward again.

The slaver tried to cut away as *Black Champion* came abreast, tacking into the wind. If the slaver had flown another sail, Jherek knew the maneuver would have cost them their last chance at overtaking their quarry. As it was, the single remaining sail only offered a token attempt at quickly changing their course.

"Come hard to starboard!" Azla ordered from the forecastle.

Jherek looked up at the half-elf pirate captain with respect. She stood there knowing she was losing her ship, yet she remained inviolate, totally in command.

"What are you thinking, young warrior?" Glawinn asked.

"Look at her," Jherek said. "Aboard a dying ship, about to take on a crew twice the size of hers, yet she knows no fear."

"You don't think she's afraid?"

"Maybe she is," he conceded, "but she overcomes it well."

"Fear isn't necessarily a bad thing, young warrior. It's meant to warn of uncertain situations and concentrate resolve, to give strength to flagging muscles and wings to thoughts. In the end it must be embraced and accepted, not conquered like an enemy blade. Aren't you afraid now?"

"Aye," Jherek said, continuing to watch the pirate captain as she ordered the grappling crew to the railing, "and it shames me."

"I'd rather see you afraid," Glawinn said, "and know that you are truly alive, than to see you the way I have seen you in the past days."

"I have done so many wrong things, made so many mistakes." He glanced at Sabyna, who stood on the forecastle deck with Arthoris and Azla. "I've hurt someone I would never have offered any injury." He turned his attention to the paladin and added, "I've even offended you, who have done nothing but try to help me."

Glawinn smiled, his eyes twinkling, and dropped his mailed hand on Jherek's shoulder. "Young warrior," he said, "if you made no trespasses, who would there be to say you'd ever been by?"

Black Champion smashed through another wave and took a while to right herself. Jherek held onto the railing, balancing himself easily while Glawinn struggled slightly with all his armor on.

"Keep something in mind, young warrior. A hero who has never known fear or want, uncertainty or anger, hunger or loneliness, is no real hero. It isn't their bravery that should impress you. That turns on a moment, marking an event that most people choose to recognize as heroic. It is in the journey that leads up to that moment, the persistence of vision, that makes a man or woman truly heroic. Do you understand?"

"Some of it."

Glawinn patted him on the shoulder. "The rest will come in time. For now we have a ship to take."

Jherek watched as the slave ship drew closer and closer.

The slaver's stern ballista crew swung the large weapon around. Even as they started locking the ballista down and getting ready to fire at *Black Champion*—a target scarcely more than seventy feet distant—a mass of writhing black tentacles suddenly sprouted from the deck.

The ballista crew turned and tried to flee, but the black tentacles whipped out blindly and wrapped the slavers up, snapping bones and squeezing the life from them. Their screams were lost in the rush of water and wind. The tentacles ripped the ballista from the deck and smashed it into a thousand pieces.

"Azla's mage," Glawinn said.

Jherek nodded and watched as the slaver crew attacked the tentacles with harpoons and swords.

Twisting tongues of flame suddenly ignited in the slaver's amidships. For a moment, Jherek believed the vessel was afire, then the flame blossomed hotter and brighter and shot toward *Black Champion.*

"Fireball!" one of the pirates squalled. As a man, the boarding crew ducked under the huge mass of roiling flames.

The wizard's casting was slightly off, and the fireball sizzled as it touched the water beside the pirate ship, then exploded into a wall of flames that rushed across *Black Champion*'s deck. Rigging and sailcloth caught fire. Only the water washing over the deck kept it from burning as well.

Arthoris stepped to the edge of the forecastle railing above and extended his hands to the heavens, the sleeves of his robes falling back down his skinny arms. He cried out in a language Jherek didn't understand, his tone at once commanding and beseeching.

Dark clouds spiraled into the sky above the ships, spreading out for miles in all directions. The wind lifted and came howling across the choppy ocean surface. Rigging creaked above, and lanyards that were cracked but not broken through now gave way. A heavy, stinging rain smacked into *Black Champion* and her crew.

The flames atop the rigging were quickly snuffed.

"Grappling crew!" Azla yelled above the roar of the storm. "Ready on the line!"

The pirates surged forward to the railing again. Jherek

stooped and picked up a grappling line, running the rough hemp through his hands. He measured back from the big, three-pronged hook and readied himself to cast.

A giant shape surged out of the water between the two ships. A webbed green foot with great claws slapped against the starboard railing. A huge head at least eight feet across, cut with a grim maw and gold-webbed spines along the back of its neck, followed the foot. Malevolent red eyes glared at the surprised crew. Another foot followed the first, and the great creature tried to drag itself aboard. The neck strained up from the dark green shell on its back.

"Dragon turtle!" a man screamed.

The grappling line crew surged back, breaking away from the deadly creature.

* * * * *

Pacys woke in black waters. Panicked, he struggled to get free of the ocean. He tried to find a way back to his own body.

Taleweaver.

The call wasn't from anything human. Pacys heard it in his mind, but the syllables were long and drawn out.

Do not be in such a hurry, the voice went on. *There is much to learn.*

Basso booming filled the water, stretching out into squeaks and squeals, turning again to a deep moaning sound like wind blowing over the neck of a bottle. The old bard listened to the sound carefully, drawn to its melodic nature.

Where am I? Pacys asked.

We call this the dreaming time.

Who are you?

Enemies of the Taker and his sahuagin.

What do you want with me?

We did not summon you. You came to us as it was foretold in our songs.

With surprise, Pacys realized that the booming squeals and squeaks were whale songs. *Are you here with me?*

In the only way that we can be.

I can't see you.

Open your mind, Taleweaver. All that we may tell you will be revealed.

Letting go the panic that vibrated inside him, Pacys immersed himself in the whale song. There weren't words or even tones especially. The sounds played upon the ear, but they touched the heart. He closed his eyes, and when he opened them again, the black water was sapphire blue.

He peered below, seeing the pale white-gray of the ocean floor a hundred feet or more below. Above him, sunlight kissed the surface of the water and turned it to too-bright silver. He glanced away, trying to peer through the blue-gray cloud that settled in the water before him.

Where are you? the old bard asked.

I am here, the slow voice replied. *Reach out and you will touch me.*

Tentatively, Pacys stretched out his arm toward the gray-blue fog. Only instead of penetrating it as he'd expected, the fog felt rough and solid. With that single touch, the bard's perceptions changed.

A great whale floated in the water in front of him. The gray-blue color partially masked it in the water, and his closeness prevented him from seeing all of it even now. Pacys knew some of the great whales grew to be four hundred feet long. This one was so long its tail flukes disappeared in the distance.

Who are you? Pacys asked.

In your language, I am called Song Who Brings Bright Rains. My mother gave birth to me after a storm, when a rainbow stretched across the sky.

By looking up, then down, Pacys could make out the familiar wedge-shaped head of the massive cetacean. He knew this was a humpback whale. The bard trailed his fingers along the pebbly skin as he swam down the length of its body. He found the creature's eye only a little later.

The eye was dark and bigger around than Pacys was tall. Instinctively, the bard swam away from the eye, wondering if the creature could see him from this close.

I see you, Taleweaver, the whale boomed.

* * * * *

Jherek stared at the huge beast clinging to *Black Champion*'s starboard side.

"It's not real, young warrior," Glawinn said, starting forward.

Jherek wanted to reach out and hold the paladin back, even put a hand on his shoulder. "Wait," he said.

Glawinn turned on him, his beard wet with gleaming diamonds from the salt spray and the rain. "Look at it. Look hard at it and you will know it's not real. It's just more magery, and a weak spell at best, not one that will hurt a man. Where is that thing's battle cry? Where is the sound of those claws rasping against the wood? How is it that the creature's weight doesn't tear the railing free?"

Pirates screamed at Glawinn to get back as the dragon turtle sighted him. The neck elongated and stretched forward. The mouth opened into a cavernous gullet that could swallow a man whole. The paladin stretched his arms out and smiled.

The dragon turtle struck, snapping its jaws closed over the paladin. Only instead of tearing flesh and breaking bone, the edged beak passed through the paladin. The illusion faded, leaving Glawinn standing untouched on the rolling deck.

"Magery," Glawinn shouted. "A child's trick meant to give them enough time to get away."

Jherek lifted the grappling hook again and raced to the starboard railing. The slave ship had gained twenty feet in distance, too far to make the cast good.

"Boarding party," Jherek shouted. "Make ready."

Snarling curses, the pirates gathered again and took up the grappling hooks. *Black Champion* came about at a crawl, the waterline no more than two feet below her deck. She moved forward slowly, overtaking the slave ship with flagging strength.

The distance closed as the pirate ship came abreast the slaver. The pirates jeered the slaver crew as they overtook them, then came alongside. Aboard the slave ship, crewmen stood ready with hatchets and axes to chop any lines that succeeded in grabbing hold.

"Steady, men," Azla ordered. "On my orders."

The slaver crew consisted mostly of humans, but there were a few half-ogres among them. The half-ogres towered above the human crew, standing eight and nine feet tall, dressed in bear skins and sahuagin hides.

"Arthoris," Azla barked.

"Aye, Cap'n," the old ship's mage responded.

"Ready the men."

Jherek felt a tingle pass through him and knew that the old man's spell had affected him. He felt curiously light, as if he weighed nothing. Understanding what was about to happen, he quickly wrapped the grappling line around his left forearm, holding the hook itself in his hand.

The ships closed to within twenty feet. Over-eager crewmen on both sides threw daggers, but none of them did any real harm.

A robed man dashed atop the stern castle and spoke harsh syllables. He gestured at the writhing black tentacles still holding onto the corpses of its victims and the tentacles disappeared in an explosion of crimson powder, the spell broken. He turned and pointed a wand at the crew aboard *Black Champion*.

As the slaver mage spoke, Jherek felt the hair on his head start to stand while energies gathered in the air above him. A lightning bolt from the wand cracked like a beastmaster's whip between the ships, and struck a pirate full in the chest.

The bolt lifted the man from his feet and held him in the air for a moment before ripping the flesh from his bones in bloody chunks that showered down over the crew. The charred corpse, white bones showing through burned meat, dropped to the deck. When a wave lapped over the side of the ship and rolled over the dead man, smoke rose from the body.

The slaver mage pointed again.

A flutter of movement speeding across the rain-streaked sky caught Jherek's attention. It took the young sailor a moment to recognize the bits and pieces of material as Skeins, Sabyna's familiar. Before the mage could unleash the power of the wand again, the raggamoffyn attacked. The living cloth plastered the man, sticking to him and covering him from head to toe in an instant, as tightly as a second skin.

The mage tried to fight the raggamoffyn, beating against his own breast and shouting in fear as the pieces wrapped over his face. His voice became muffled, then ended abruptly. The mage jerked frantically as he tried to escape, then even that stopped. Totally under the raggamoffyn's control, the mage ran for the side of the ship and threw himself over. He disappeared at once into the black water between the ships.

"Boarding crew, advance!" Azla shouted.

Stunned by the events of the last few seconds, *Black Champion*'s crew leaped across the twenty-foot span between the ships. The slaver rode the ocean a good eight feet higher than the pirate ship's deck. Though Arthoris's magic allowed them to leap the distance between the ships, most men only rose four or five feet.

Two pirates slammed into the bulwark and fell into the sea. Three others used their grappling lines to catch onto the slaver's railing. Jherek and the others managed to grab the railing and started hoisting themselves up.

A half-ogre stepped up to the railing as the young sailor started his climb. His eyes showed the white pupils of a true ogre. Scars tracked his ugly, pointed face bearing a nose that was too long and too broad for the rest of his features. The pockmarked skin was the color of butter gone bad. A single braid held his long black hair from his face, revealing pointed ears.

"Throg kill you, puny man," the half-ogre growled. He shoved his harpoon down toward Jherek.

The young sailor hooked an arm inside the railing, aware of the roiling sea below him and the waves crashing against the side of the slave ship. Even as well as he could swim, dropping into the ocean would probably mean death. He let go with his free hand, pushing himself against the ship in a half-roll. The ship's pitching hammered him against the side with bruising force.

Snarling in rage, the half-ogre drew the harpoon up to thrust again.

Swinging back into position, Jherek reached through the railing and caught the back of the half-ogre's foot. The young sailor yanked as hard as he could, counting on the unsteady deck to aid him. Slipping across the wet deck, the half-ogre's foot came forward and smashed through the railing.

Even as his opponent fell backward, Jherek planted his boots against the slave ship's side and leaped again, using what remained of Arthoris's spell. He flew ten feet into the air, over the heads of the slaver crew, his fist still tight around the grappling hook and line he carried. He landed, drew the cutlass from the sash, and turned to face his adversaries.

He swung the big grappling hook into the face of the first man who reached him, knocking the man to one side. Giving ground immediately, the young sailor retreated toward the broken stump that remained of the ship's mainmast. Moving lithely, he dodged around the mast, slammed a slaver's blade aside, then slashed the cutlass through the slaver's stomach, cracking ribs and ripping the man open.

Other pirates from *Black Champion* landed on the deck as well, and the brawl quickly turned bloody. Crimson stained the wet decks, sluicing through the rainwater pools that collected on the warped deck.

"Secure the lines!" Jherek yelled.

He beat aside another slaver's sword thrust with the flat of the cutlass, then stepped into the man and slammed his shoulder into his chest, knocking him back. The young sailor kept going forward, staying in close and using his elbows and knees to beat his opponents back as Malorrie had taught him. He slapped a knife stroke down, captured the wrist in his same hand, and buried the blade in another slaver's chest.

Taking advantage of the confusion and the tangle of arms and legs around him, Jherek ran to the slaver's port railing. He shook the line free of his forearm, thrust the cutlass point down into the deck, and readied the grappling hook.

A man charged at him from the crowd of slavers with an upraised sword. Jherek ducked under the angled sword stroke, then slammed the grappling hook into the man's chest, hooking the belt that crossed him from shoulder to hip. He yanked and twisted, putting all his strength and all the leverage he could muster into the move.

Instead of merely going over the side of the ship as Jherek intended, the ship pitched suddenly and aided in the throw, making the slaver go high into the air. As he came down, *Black Champion* surged into the side of the slave ship, crunching the man between the two massive wooden hulls.

The impact nearly drove Jherek from his feet. He stumbled and caught himself against the railing, staring down at the pulped smear that remained of the slaver trapped between the two ships. A wave crashed against the ships, and even that was gone.

Horror filled Jherek and he pushed nausea from his mind. He stood on the lurching deck and watched as *Black Champion* went up broadside against the slave ship again. He cast the grappling hook and watched as Glawinn made it fast. Dressed in his armor, the paladin would never have made the jump even with the magic spell Arthoris had woven.

The young sailor pulled the line taut when the two ships closed again, then wrapped it around the slaver's railing. Wood creaked ominously as the two ships started to slide apart, but the line and the railings held. The drag created by *Black Champion*'s flooded hold was immediately noticeable, pulling at the slave ship like a drowning man.

Jherek turned at the sound of footsteps behind him, catching sight of the half-ogre charging at him. The young sailor plucked his cutlass from the deck, wrapping his fingers around the hilt. He met the half-ogre's bastard sword as it descended. Steel clanged, and the impact shivered down Jherek's arm.

Parrying the half-ogre's next attack, the young sailor attempted a riposte, only to find that the creature was faster than his bulk implied. Jherek parried again to keep his head on his shoulders. Another slaver attacked from the young sailor's side, trying to drive a spear through his guts.

Jherek stepped back, letting the spear go by, then catching the haft in one hand. He jerked at the man, using momentum against him and easily pulling him off-balance. Throg swung again, but the young sailor stepped behind the slaver crewman. The half-ogre's weapon sliced into the man's chest, killing him instantly.

Shoving the corpse at the half-ogre, Jherek turned and sprinted for the main hold in the middle of the ship's deck. Water and blood made the deck slippery as the ship lurched and fought against *Black Champion*'s dead weight.

A slaver rushed at Jherek as the half-ogre screamed curses behind him. The young sailor dropped to the deck just ahead of the slaver's sword and skidded on his side.

Jherek kicked and took the slaver's feet out from under him, knocking him backward. By the time the man stopped sliding, Jherek got to his feet and followed the steps down into the main hold.

XI

10 Flamerule, the Year of the Gauntlet

Whale oil lanterns lit the cargo hold. The pale illumination barely lightened the shadows of the men, women, and children shackled in the hold. Jherek looked at them, unprepared for the sight.

Rough iron cuffs held the prisoners at wrists and ankles, connecting to an iron rod that ran the length of the slave ship. Foul odors filled the hold, and the young sailor knew the captives had been forced to sit in their own excrement. They looked at him with fear-filled eyes.

"Don't let us drown," a woman cried out in a hoarse voice. "If the ship is going down, at least give us a chance to save ourselves."

Pain welled up in the young sailor's heart. He'd never seen slaves before. No one should have to face what those people had been through.

"Look out!" a slave yelled.

Jherek sensed a big man stepping from the shadows behind him. The young sailor turned. There was no mercy in Jherek's heart.

The slaver carried a battle-axe in a two handed grip. The lantern's weak illumination glinted off earrings and a gold tooth. The slaver was a mountain of a man, rolling in muscle and fat. He swung the battle-axe with skill, making a short, vicious arc with the double-bitted head. Jherek fended it off, but the slaver followed up with a swipe from the iron-shod butt of the axe that could have crushed the young sailor's skull.

Jherek slipped the hook from his sash as he took two steps back.

"You done crawled into the wrong hole, rabbit," the brute taunted, grinning broadly.

Two other shadows stepped out behind the man, flanking him on either side. One of them carried a spear and the other wielded a short sword and a dagger.

Without a word, Jherek attacked. There was no one else to defend the people in the hold, no one else to set them free. Azla's pirates were shedding blood above so they might all live.

The young sailor swung the cutlass at the axe-wielder's head, expecting him to block it. The slaver followed up with another blow from the butt of his battle-axe. Jherek slammed the curved hook into his opponent's hand, nailing it to the wooden haft and blocking with the meaty part of his forearm.

The slaver shrieked in pain, looking at his impaled hand in disbelief. Before he could move, Jherek stamped on the slaver's foot and ran the top of his head into the slaver's face. Blood gushed from the man's broken nose as he stumbled backward.

Jerking the hook free, Jherek dropped low and slashed across the man's waist, spilling his guts. Even as the man dropped to his knees, the young sailor spun and slashed again, taking the slaver's head nearly from his shoulders.

The spearman came on, thrusting vigorously. The fluted blade cut across Jherek's left shoulder and the spear haft bounced under his chin. He brought the hook down savagely, driving the spear toward the wooden planking. The weapon caught and stopped suddenly, throwing the man who wielded it off-balance.

Before Jherek could attack, the swordsman slashed at him. Only the speed and reflexes Malorrie and Glawinn had trained into him kept the young sailor from getting his head split open.

The spearman drew his weapon back as Jherek parried the long dirk in the swordsman's other hand. Catching the dirk against his cutlass's crosspiece, the young sailor shoved his attacker back, causing him to stumble over the dead man.

Recovering his footing, the spearman thrust again, but Jherek dodged before the edged blade touched him. Blood ran warmly down the young sailor's shoulder. Letting the cutlass lead him, then leading the cutlass, Jherek never presented any undefended openings.

"Get the little wharf rat," the swordsman urged. "You've got the longer weapon."

The spearman feinted, thinking to draw Jherek out, then stabbed at his crotch when he sidestepped. The young sailor parried the spear, then moved quickly inside the man's defense. The slaver tried to bring the butt of his weapon around. Jherek slammed his cutlass through the spear haft, splintering the wood. Before the man could react, the young sailor swept the hook forward, knowing the swordsman was set up behind him.

The hook plunged through the spearman's temple and sliced into his brain, killing him instantly. Even as the lights in the man's eyes dimmed, Jherek released the hook and turned to face the swordsman. He let the swordsman's thrust slice by his face, drawing blood from his cheek, even as he brought the cutlass down in a hard sweep that cracked the man's head open from crown to chin.

He yanked the cutlass from the dead man's skull, not realizing the prisoners were cheering for him until he saw them. Their voices were strong and full.

Sheathing the bloody cutlass in the sash at his waist, Jherek took up the battle-axe dropped by the first man he'd killed. His breath came hard and fast, filled with the sour stench of the slaver's pit. He lifted the battle-axe and brought it down on the long chain that bound the prisoners' cuffs to the iron rod. Sparks flew from the iron.

Prisoners at either end of the rod pulled the two pieces of chain through the manacles. The sound of men fighting and dying on the deck above pierced the hold.

Jherek passed the battle-axe to a large man with broad shoulders and asked, "Do you know how to use this?"

The man smiled, yellow teeth splitting his grimy beard.

"Like I was born with one in my hand, warrior," he answered.

Jherek gathered his weapons. He pulled the hook from the spearman's head, wincing at the gleam of splintered bone in all the blood. He looked at the prisoners, finding them gazing at him expectantly, as if he was supposed to lead them.

"I want no children on the decks above," he ordered. "Man or woman, if you've no fighting experience, stay below with the children. There's little enough space on that deck to begin with. The ship you'll see lashed onto this one, she's a pirate ship flying the Jolly Roger. Don't think that you haven't been saved. Captain Azla of *Black Champion* doesn't tolerate slavers." He paused, his voice thick with the anger he felt. "And neither do I."

"I've heard of Azla," a man said as he helped himself to the short sword. "As pirates go, she's not a bad'n."

"Are there any more weapons in this hold?" Jherek asked.

A woman took a lantern from a peg on the wall and said, "They keep swords and knives back here." She pointed to a small room at the back of the cargo hold.

"Those of you who want to join in fighting for your freedom," Jherek said, "get weapons and come topside. It's not going to be easy."

Jherek turned and dashed back up the steps leading to the main deck. The two armed former slaves followed him.

* * * * *

Pacys floated near the great whale. Generally the creatures were not overly friendly. They had their own agenda and didn't often give time to humans, elves, or anyone else.

How is it that you know me? the old bard asked.

By your heart. Just as the whale song fills all of Serôs, there are those among us who can identify individual heartbeats of any who live below and any who live above. Your heartbeat has been known to my kind for thousands of years. By now, after all you have seen and heard in Serôs, you shouldn't be surprised that you and the Taker are in our histories.

In truth, Pacys wasn't surprised. Every society he'd

encountered in Serôs told tales of his arrival, as well as the Taker's.

What do you want with me?

To give you that which you seek.

Am I here, or am I still among the locathah?

You are safe among the locathah, Taleweaver. Only your mind journeys far at this moment. The locathah chieftain's herbs freed your thoughts. I merely captured them for a moment with my song.

You know I seek the boy, Pacys said.

Jherek. Yes, we know.

His name is Malorrie.

That is the name he gave you, Taleweaver, the whale replied. *He is in hiding, from himself and from the fears that have chased him since childhood. He is not whole.*

Pacys gazed into the great eye and saw the compassion there. *I was told he would not be whole.*

Your voice, your heart, Taleweaver, only these things can heal him.

Where is the boy? he asked.

He is far from here now, but he will be here soon.

Why?

It was foretold. The whales must help him forge his destiny.

Then I should be here.

No, the whale said. *Your time will not be then. You must journey to Myth Nantar. Your destiny lies in that direction . . . for the time being. When everything is as it should be, you will find Jherek.*

Wouldn't it be better if I found him earlier?

It would be easy to write a song in the heat of passion, but that should not be the only time you work on it. Passion and skill must both be applied to make it strong enough to stand in the hearts and minds of those who listen. Time is the glue that binds the two. When the time is right, you will find each other. The eye closed and reopened slowly. *Our time here grows short. My song only transports your thoughts here for a few moments. Like you, I am a bard to my people. It is my duty to record our histories, and to talk to you at this moment.*

You're a bard?

Yes. Who else do you think sang the first songs of Serôs,

*then gave music to the people above and below that they
might spread it across the dry lands?*

There are many stories . . . the bard admitted.

Even now, the whale went on, *my people gather along
the Sharksbane Wall in an attempt to hold back the tide of
sea devils overflowing into the Inner Sea. It is foretold that
we will fail.*

Then why try? Pacys's heart ached to hear the quiet acceptance in the whale's voice.

*Because we must all play our parts. We must all follow
our destinies.*

* * * * *

Topside, Jherek looked at the carnage littering the slave
ship's deck and felt his resolve weaken. Blood ran in
rivulets across the wood, watered down by falling rain.
Black Champion's crew formed a half-circle with Glawinn
as their center. The paladin lunged forward, slamming his
shield into one of the slavers, then running his sword
through the body of a second.

With a cry of warning, unable to attack the men from
the back without letting them know he was there, Jherek
rushed the slaver crew. He caught one man's blade with
the cutlass and stopped another with the hook. Striding
forward, he kicked the first man, then used the cutlass to
slit the throat of the second.

Bodies rolled on the slaver's deck, shifting with the
pitch and yaw of the pirate ship tethered to her. The clang
of metal on metal punctuated the sounds of screamed
curses, prayers, and the wounded and dying. Footing
became treacherous.

Arm aching with effort but never failing, Jherek fought
on. Blood splashed into his face but he distanced himself
from it, from all the death around him. Malorrie had
trained him to think that way, to live past the moment.

Sabyna fought nearby, using twin long knives to turn attacks, then spinning inside an opponent's offense and de-
livering blows herself. She moved as gracefully as a dancer,
sliding through the press of men around her and searching
out opportunities. Skeins floated at her side, wrapped
tightly into a whip that struck out men's eyes or tore their

faces when they threatened its master.

"Fight, you dogs!" Azla screamed, urging her men on. "The first of you who turns tail on me now I'll personally deliver to Umberlee!"

She fought in a two-handed style, her scimitar flashing in her right hand while a long-bladed dirk was held in her left. She blocked a thrust from a half-ogre with her scimitar, then stepped forward and ripped the dirk across the creature's throat.

Incredibly, the slaver crew backed away before the onslaught of the pirates, giving ground steadily as they retreated to the stern castle.

A tall man strode to the front of the stern castle railing, above the trapped slavers. He was deep chested and long-limbed, dressed in crimson and gray clothing, a dark red cloak riding the breeze behind him. Gold and silver gleamed at his wrists, neck, and chest—plain bands with runes carved into them.

"I am Tarmorock Hahn, son of Jakyr Hahn, and I am captain of this ship," he declared. "Who is captain of that floundering pirate?"

The fighting broke off, and the two groups formed lines of demarcation.

Azla stepped forward, and three of her pirates and Jherek stepped with her, keeping a protective ring about her.

"I am Azla, captain of *Black Champion*."

Tarmorock grinned at her, gave her a cocky salute with the jeweled sword in his hand, and said, "You'll not be captain for long from the looks of her."

"I'm standing on my next ship," Azla stated.

"Confidence!" the slaver roared. "Gods, but I do admire that in a woman."

"As captain of a slaver," Azla retorted, "I find you offer little to admire."

"And a cutting tongue as well as good looks. Would that we had met under other circumstances, I'd have offered you a dinner by candlelight."

"It's just as well," Azla said. "Offered aboard a slave ship with the stench you find here, dinner wouldn't have stayed down."

Tarmorock glared at her, stung even more when Azla's crew hurled taunts at him. "I offer you the opportunity to duel for my ship," he said. "Captain to captain. I offer this as a man of honor."

"There's no honor in slavery," Azla said, "and I've no reason to fight you for anything. I've taken out your weapons, lashed my sinking ship to this one to drag about like a stone, killed over half your crew, and freed the slaves from the hold to fight against you as well. There's nothing here for me to fight for. Resist and we'll kill you anyway."

"I offer you honor in battle."

Jherek felt a response stir within him. Azla was correct in her assessment of the situation, but a need rose in him to recognize Tarmorock's challenge. He was barely able to still his tongue.

"I don't need honor," Azla stated. "Honor doesn't have sails nor cargo space. I have your ship in all but name. You offer me nothing I care for."

"Captain," Glawinn said, stepping forward. Blood stained his copper-colored armor and fresh dents and scratches showed. "If you don't mind, I'll stand him to his battle of honor."

"Ah, a true warrior among you," Tarmorock said. "You, sir, are a man of the blade?"

"Till the day I die," Glawinn said.

Pride welled up in Jherek as he watched the knight stand tall in front of the slaver captain.

"No," Azla said. "There'll be no battle for this ship. I've won her, fair and square, and I'll take her if I have to gut you down to the last man."

Tarmorock glanced at Glawinn and said, "Pity. Apparently there's no prize to be won, but what say you to honor itself? Will you be part and party to a bandit's approach to stealing my ship? Become a thief yourself?"

Glawinn's cheeks reddened, but Jherek couldn't tell if it was from anger or embarrassment.

"I'm no thief," the paladin said. "Nor shall I ever be."

"Those are harsh words that drip from your lips," Azla said coldly. "Especially from a man whose livelihood depends on stealing the lives of others."

"And you've never spent a life or three in the pursuit of your own wealth, Captain Azla?" Tarmorock hurried on before she could respond, switching his gaze back to Glawinn. "I was trained in the sword, and conducting myself honorably on the battlefield, long before fate handed me this vocation. You understand this?"

"Yes," Glawinn answered.

"Then you'll fight me?"

"Yes."

Tarmorock grinned. "And if I should win?"

"You'll have all I own," the paladin replied, "and your freedom from this ship."

"There will be no fighting," Azla stated, staring at Glawinn.

The paladin looked at her, gentleness in his eyes. "Lady, I have given leave to your ways though they are not my own, and I have stood in good stead when you needed me. I ask that you give me leave to stand by my own principles in this matter."

"You did the honorable thing by helping rescue the prisoners aboard this ship," Azla told him. "This isn't just about stealing something that didn't belong to you."

"There are times," Glawinn said in a patient voice, "when a man must stand or fall on his own merits, to be weighed and measured by the depth of his heart and the strength of his arm."

"You're risking this for nothing."

"On the contrary," Glawinn stated, "I'm risking this for all that I am." He looked at her. "If I may have your leave."

"Damn you for a fool, knight."

Glawinn spread his bloodstained hands and said, "If only I can be an honorable fool."

Azla waved her men back, clearing the space in front of the stern castle.

Tarmorock descended the stairs and stripped away his crimson cloak. "There is one thing further I'd ask of you." He rolled his bastard sword in his hands, causing it to dance and spin effortlessly. "Even should I lose, I want my men spared. The ones that yet live. I ask only that they be put overboard in lifeboats with provisions. This far out at sea, that's a grim prospect, and I know that, but it's the best I can do for them. They're a motley crew, but they are my responsibility."

"Done," Glawinn replied without hesitation.

The slaver captain glanced at Azla.

The half-elf gave a tight nod. "For the knight's honor, not yours."

"Of course." Tarmorock bowed.

"Do you have any armor?" Glawinn asked.

"No."

"I have an extra set aboard the ship," the paladin offered.

"Thank you, no," Tarmorock replied. "I was trained in the art of the blade without the benefit of cumbersome armor. My father felt I was destined for better things. Through no fault of his own, I managed not to find those things."

"Young warrior," the paladin called.

Jherek hurried over to Glawinn's side.

"This is Jherek of Velen," the paladin said as he began unbuckling his armor. "He will stand as my second."

Fear and pride swelled within the young sailor at the same time. He started helping Glawinn take his armor off and asked, "What am I supposed to do?"

"Take care of my armor," Glawinn said, "see to it that the promises I have made to this man are carried out, and stay with me as I die . . . should it come to that."

* * * * *

Myth Nantar must be open again, Taleweaver, the whale continued, *and made whole once more. You are the only one who can accomplish this. That which is secret must needs be known. Only then will the impenetrable wall that surrounds Myth Nantar be broken and the mythal once again protect those it was designed to protect to promote peace above and below.*

How will I do this? Pacys asked. *I am told the way is impassable.*

You are the Taleweaver, the whale replied. *This is your destiny. It will not be denied. Trust in the songs that are given to you. Now, there is one thing more. Stretch out your hand.*

Without hesitation, Pacys reached out to the whale. A warm tingle filled his hand. When he looked, he saw an ivory orb lying in his palm. It was as smooth as a pearl, no larger than the ball of his thumb, and with a slight translucence.

What is this? the bard asked.

It is your key to Myth Nantar, Taleweaver. This was

created by the whales who first saw Myth Nantar lost to the Dukars, then to the sahuagin. When the mythal hardened and kept all out, the great whale bard of that time created this key, knowing it could only be used by you.

How could he know this?

She, the great whale bard corrected, *knew it the same way you know a song is strong and true, that it will wring joy or tears from its listeners. Do you question your muse, Taleweaver?*

No. Oghma be revered, I am thankful for the inspiration that comes my way.

The key is like a song that comes to you unbidden. The great bard drew upon her skill and magic and forged it, as was her destiny. You haven't yet understood why Myth Nantar is called the City of Destinies. It was created to knit the worlds below and above in harmony, to establish that which all the rest of Toril might follow. Those who live in Serôs know we are all of one. We must live as one if the seas are to survive. That is what we are taught, Taleweaver, and your efforts will help teach others.

Pacys studied the ivory ball in his palm, opening himself to it and feeling the magic inside. It felt very old and powerful, and it drew him to it like steel to a lodestone. The music that filled his heart let him know the talisman was his to use.

He closed his fingers over it, relishing the smooth surface and the confident way it made him feel. He was truly on the right path. The locathah hadn't been the only thing he'd been drawn to here.

Taleweaver, Song Who Brings Bright Rains said gently, *do not be overconfident. Things are written of the future from this point on, but they are more dreams than truths—plans that poke pools of light into the darkness of the waiting uncertainty of the Taker's War. It still remains up to us to find the strength, skills, and heart for victory.*

I know, Pacys replied.

The whale's eye blinked slowly again, as if the great leviathan was tired. For the first time, the old bard got the impression that the creature was immensely old.

It is time for you to go. May Oghma, the Lord of Knowledge, keep you close and watch over you as you bring back that which was lost.

116

And may Oghma grace your song and your skills, Pacys responded.

The sapphire waters grew dark around him, and when he opened his eyes again, he found he was in Khlinat's strong arms. The dwarf peered at him fearfully, holding him as he might a child.

"Are ye back among us then?" Khlinat asked.

"Yes," Pacys replied, finding that his tongue was still a little numb and his voice was hoarse. He was surprised at the weakness he felt, but the whale song still played at the edges of his mind.

Relief showed on the dwarf's face. "Ye were gone so long, I was beginning to fret maybe these folk had kilt ye kindly and out of ignorance but did the job all the same."

Pacys put his hand on the dwarf's shoulder. "I've been a long way, my friend, but we've still leagues to go before I die."

"Ye ain't dying," the dwarf promised. "I done give ye me promise, and I ain't gonna let ye back out of it. And ye ain't been nowhere, because I been with ye the whole time of it. Ye sat right here like some great lump."

Wordlessly, Pacys opened his other hand, revealing the ivory sphere. The polished surface caught the glowcoral light and gleamed.

"I've journeyed," the old bard said. "I've been there and back again."

* * * * *

In minutes, the paladin was stripped down to the sweaty, bloodstained clothes beneath his armor. He looked smaller than usual, and for the first time Jherek noticed that Glawinn's opponent was a head taller, at least twenty pounds heavier, and had a longer reach than him.

"Why are you showing this man honor?" the young sailor asked.

"Because some men show honor despite the circumstances they find themselves in. As I have told you, young warrior, it's so often not how low you may get in life, but how you conduct yourself while you're there. I only pray that you get a clearer understanding of this some day."

Glawinn took a deep breath and the sword the young sailor offered him. He turned to face his opponent and said, "This is as even as I can make it."

"On the contrary," Tarmorock stated, "I fear you make it too easy. I am quite good with the blade."

"We shall see." The paladin saluted smartly with his sword, bringing it down from his forehead and stepping easily into a swordsman's stance. "I am Sir Glawinn, a paladin in the service of Lathander the Morninglord."

Tarmorock bowed slightly, touching his blade to his forehead. "May your god keep you."

"And yours."

The slaver captain sprang into action, launching a volley of attacks, rolling off of each of Glawinn's defenses to launch yet another thrust or slash. Steel rang through the dead silence that washed over the ship.

Jherek found himself holding his breath. Tarmorock was an excellent swordsman. The blades moved almost faster than he could see, and it was only Malorrie's and Glawinn's training that allowed him to pick up every nuance. Instinctively, his body shifted and his hand moved slightly, following the paladin's quick moves.

Years of practice aboard the ship while it rocked at sea should have given Tarmorock the advantage on the heaving deck, but Glawinn's skill and focus with the blade stripped those years of familiarity away, putting the slaver on equal footing with his opponent.

The two combatants stepped forward and back, from side to side. Neither truly seemed able to press an advantage. Long minutes passed. Most sword duels between two men not on a battlefield, Jherek knew from both Malorrie and Glawinn, lasted only seconds at best. Unarmored sword fighting was an art form.

Tarmorock's attack became more loose, but Glawinn's remained tight, his moves compact but fluid. Without warning, Tarmorock lunged, and for once Glawinn's defense wasn't there.

Cold fear knotted Jherek's back as he watched the blade slide toward Glawinn. When the sword stuck through the paladin, the young sailor knew the knight was skewered. The paladin's own blade stabbed deeply into Tarmorock's chest, piercing his heart.

Tarmorock looked down at the blade through his chest in disbelief. His arm dropped and Jherek saw that the captain's blade had missed Glawinn by scant inches though he couldn't see that from behind. Nerveless, Glawinn dropped the sword.

Moving quickly, Glawinn caught the mortally wounded man before he could fall. Tenderly, he held him as he might a brother. Jherek stayed back, wondering what the paladin said to the man he'd just killed, but he didn't try to overhear.

A moment later and Glawinn gently laid the captain to rest on the deck. Reaching into his blouse, the paladin stayed on his knees and pulled out the rosy pink disk that was Lathander's holy symbol. There in the midst of companions and enemies, he prayed for the fallen warrior.

Touched by the moment, wishing he knew of something he could believe in so fiercely, Jherek dropped to his knees beside the paladin and bowed his head as well.

XII

16 Flamerule, the Year of the Gauntlet

"Lady, may I have a moment of your time?" Glawinn asked. He stood with a bottle in his hand in the cramped doorway of Sabyna's cabin.

Surprised, Sabyna looked up from the spellbook she'd been studying. Arthoris, Azla's ship's mage, had given Sabyna two new spells that she believed she was capable of understanding.

"Is something wrong?" She stood up from the small bed. Her heart beat a little faster, and her first thoughts were of Jherek.

"Nothing's wrong," Glawinn told her.

Sabyna placed her spellbook into the bag of holding at her side and Skeins curled around it. Crossing her arms over her breasts, she walked to the window and looked down at the ocean.

The pirate crew stripped what they could from the skeletal hulk that had once been *Black Champion*. With her hold flooded and having her deck partly disassembled and hauled away, the ship listed even more heavily into the ocean, creating increasing drag on the slave ship Azla claimed as her prize. The deck tilted at an incline now and had for the last two days.

Ship's moldings and cleats, the rudder, extra sailcloth, and the remaining rigging were the first items the pirate crew reclaimed. They'd used a block and tackle to take even *Black Champion*'s two good masts to replace the broken ones on the slave ship.

They could not seat the masts while at sea, but after finishing the salvage operation, Azla planned to put into port at Agenais in the Whamite Isles to make the big repairs. Now they were down to taking the long, good planks from *Black Champion*'s corpse.

"What did you want to talk about?" Sabyna asked.

Glawinn hesitated. "The young warrior. I may be overstepping my bounds here, lady, but—"

"No," Sabyna said. "You're way over."

"Perhaps I should go. I thank you for your time, and I ask your forgiveness."

Sabyna pushed out her breath. "Wait." She sensed him standing there, rigidly at attention. "Has Jherek told you what I said to him?"

"No, lady," Glawinn answered, "he's not one to betray confidences. In fact, I think he keeps too many of his own."

"Why did you come?"

"To offer solace and share company." Glawinn held up the dusty bottle. "And to offer a glass of Captain Azla's rather fine port."

Sabyna was surprised. "I didn't know you drank."

"Rarely, lady," the paladin said, "and never in excess. May I enter?"

"Of course." Sabyna went to one of the small cabinets built above the bed and took out two wooden cups. "The service is rather humble."

"But adequate for our purposes. If I may." Glawinn took the cups and poured the dark red wine.

Sabyna returned to the bed and sat, accepting the cup the paladin handed her. "Say what you have to say."

Glawinn sat on the small bench under the window. "If you'll forgive me my indiscretion, lady," he said, "but you can be dreadfully blunt."

"I come from a large family whose lives were spent crowded aboard one ship or another," she explained. "I

121

learned to speak my mind early. Perhaps you're a little sensitive."

"Lathander help me, but I knew this would not be easy," Glawinn said, shifting uncomfortably.

"If it isn't a pleasant task, perhaps it would be better if it were over sooner."

Despite her calm demeanor, Sabyna's heart beat faster than normal. Since she'd talked to Jherek and explained to him how she felt, they'd hardly spoken at all. The young sailor stayed busily engaged with the salvage work.

"It's just that I've become aware you aren't talking to each other."

"Have you talked to him about it?"

"No."

"Why talk to me first?"

"Because he won't listen to me."

"And you think I will?"

Glawinn's eyes turned sorrowful and he said, "Lady, you have no idea what that boy is going through."

"If he would talk to me, I might."

"He doesn't know himself," Glawinn explained. "Even if he did, he can't explain."

"Does he think I'm dense?"

"In his eyes he feels he isn't worthy of you."

"Because he is wanted somewhere for something?" she asked. "I told him that didn't matter."

"Maybe not to you, lady, but it does to him. In his own way, though, I don't think he quite fully understands it. He strives for perfection."

"I've never met a man who didn't have his faults," Sabyna said. "Though, I admit you've come closer than anyone."

"My faults?"

"You're a busybody," Sabyna told him. "I thought paladins knew enough to keep to their own affairs."

The knight blushed. "I beg your forgiveness. I struggled with this decision, and I'd hoped I'd made the right choice."

"You have," she conceded. "If I'd spent another day like this, with no one to talk to, I think I'd have gone out of my mind."

"I thought you talked to Azla."

"She doesn't understand Jherek any more than I do."

Glawinn smiled gently and said, "Probably not."

Sabyna looked away from the paladin. "It's never been like this for me. I've seen handsome men and wealthy men, and men who could turn a woman's head with only a handful of pretty words, but I've never met anyone like Jherek."

"Nor have I."

Tears stung Sabyna's eyes. "I've never pursued a man before. Climbing that rigging to tell him my feelings was one of the hardest things I've ever done."

"But, I wager, not as hard as the climb back down."

"No," she said. "Do you know what he told me?"

Glawinn shook his head. "I can only guess that it was as little as possible."

"Aye . . ." Sabyna didn't trust her voice to speak any further.

"If it helps at all," the paladin stated gently, "I believe he tells you everything he knows."

"There's a lot he won't tell me."

"*Can't* tell you, lady, not won't. There is a difference."

"You defend him very well."

"I didn't come here to help him, lady. I came to help you."

"Me?"

Glawinn nodded in resignation and said, "The Morninglord knows, I can't help him. He won't let me, and his course has already been charted."

"What course?"

"To becoming the kind of man he wants to be," Glawinn said. "The kind of man he has to be."

"Will he be that man?"

Hesitation furrowed Glawinn's brow. "I know not, lady. I've never seen someone come so far, yet have so far to go. I can tell you this: his path will heal him—or it will kill him."

The solemn way the paladin spoke pushed Sabyna's pain away and replaced it with fear.

"And what are we to do?" she asked. "What am I to do?"

"The only thing we can, lady. Give him the freedom to make the decisions he needs must make"

"What if it kills him?" Sabyna asked.

"Then we will bury him, lady, say prayers over him if that is possible, and be grateful for ever having known him."

Jherek strode barefoot across one of the broken beams still above water. *Black Champion* lay mostly under the sea now, her black bulk stretched like a shadow against the green water. Seagulls sat on the spars that made up her ribs and gave plaintive cries.

Rigging on the slave ship popped against the masts where she lay at anchor, heeled over hard to port as she supported *Black Champion*'s corpse. Six others worked the ship with him, seeking more timber to salvage before the sea took her to the bottom.

"Looks like she's been picked clean," Meelat called out.

Meelat was one of the prisoners rescued from the slaver's hold. Though he was scrawny, his narrow shoulders and thin arms were corded with muscle. Scabs showed at his bare ankles and wrists where the iron cuffs had been.

"Aye," Jherek agreed.

He mopped sweat from his face with his forearm, succeeding only in spreading it around. Nothing on him remained dry. He glanced up at the nets the ship's crew used to haul up the last load of timber.

"Comes a time when you gotta let her go," Meelat stated. "She's given up as much for the future of that other ship as she can. Spend much time aboard her?"

"No, but it was a time I'll not easily forget," Jherek replied.

Memory of his conversation with Sabyna in the rigging and of that kiss wouldn't fade no matter how hard he tried to push it to the back of his mind.

Meelat scratched at the scabs on one wrist, pulling them away so that blood flowed. He rinsed the wrist off in the water.

"If there are sharks around," Jherek cautioned, "that might be a foolhardy thing to do. They can smell blood in the water for miles."

Meelat grinned. "If there'd been sharks here, all that noise we been making in the water for days would have already drawn them. Besides, that comely young ship's mage has been keeping a potion in the water to drive away any sharks. Or haven't you noticed?"

Jherek shook his head.

"A pretty girl like that," the grizzled old sailor said, "I was your age, I'd be looking."

"She's a lady," Jherek warned quietly, "and shouldn't be talked about in a cavalier manner."

"Oh, I'm offering no offense, mate." Meelat shrugged. "My manners, maybe they need some brushing up, but a man at sea most of his life, he don't have much chance of that. Does he?"

Turning his attention back to the water, Jherek spotted a conflicting wave below and thought he detected movement.

"That's what I find confusing about you," Meelat continued. "You say you're a sailing man, but your manners put on like you been proper raised."

Studying the water around the bobbing remnant of *Black Champion,* Jherek tried to discern the movement again. Sahuagin prowled the Inner Sea now. Three passing merchanters two days ago had swapped supplies with Azla and offered up warnings concerning staying in one place or alone too long. Reports of attacks on harbors around the Sea of Fallen Stars—from Procampur to Cimbar—were becoming commonplace.

"I was a suspicious man," Meelat said, "I'd be wondering about you. Wondering what a man like you was doing running with pirates."

Jherek gazed at the man silently.

Meelat dropped his eyes. "Not that there's anything wrong with pirates. Been one myself a time or two, but you don't seem the type cut out for it."

"Thank you."

A puzzled expression filled the man's face, but it was quickly replaced by sudden and total fear.

Ripping his knife from its sheath on his thigh, Jherek turned and braced himself, aware that startled shouts had broken out on the slave ship's decks as well.

Less than twenty feet away, a creature broke from the sea and gazed at them. The triangular snake's face twisted slightly in the breeze, bringing one bright orange eye to bear on Jherek, then the other. Fins stuck out on either side of the head like overly large ears, echoed by the ridged fin that ran down its neck for a short distance. After a short space, the fin continued down the creature's back.

Needle-sharp fangs filled the huge mouth and a pink, forked tongue darted out to taste the smells in the air. The gold scales glittered in the sunlight, some of them catching a slightly greenish cast, muted slightly by the water where the rest of the serpent body coiled.

Jherek thought it was beautiful. Four feet of the creature stayed above the waterline, but he judged it to be at least a dozen feet in length. The serpent's body was broader than a dwarf's shoulders at the neck, growing thicker toward the middle, then thinning out to a wide-finned tail.

"Selûne guide us from harm," Meelat whispered hoarsely. "That there's dragon-kin. Some call 'em sea wyrms. Dangerous beasties, lad, so don't do nothing to call attention to yourself."

The sea wyrm lowered its head toward the young sailor, then twisted from side to side again as if taking a closer look.

Jherek felt the ship's hulk bob against a wave and knew that one of the salvagers was moving along the beams behind him. He tightened his grip on the knife and slid his left foot forward.

"You try it," Meelat said, "and that thing will gobble you down where you stand. They're quicker than damn near anything you've ever seen in the water, and most things out."

In the next instant, Jherek got a glimpse of the creature's speed. Dipping its head into the ocean, the sea wyrm flipped its tail and pulled the ear fins in tight against its head. It cut through the water cleanly, gliding twenty feet in the blink of an eye.

The sea wyrm raised its great head from the ocean, water dripping from the edges of its open mouth. It rose from the sea until it could stare into Jherek's eyes with one of its own. The sea dappled it like diamonds.

Hypnotized by the fear that filled him as well as awe, Jherek held the creature's gaze. It was close enough to reach out and touch.

"You have a chance," Meelat stated. "Strike quick, if you can, and put that knife through that thing's eye."

Shifting subtly, Jherek reversed the blade, putting the point down. He stared into the orange eye, wider across than a pie plate. At the distance, he knew he wouldn't miss.

Whether the blade was long enough to reach the serpent's brain was another matter.

The finned head moved closer, tentatively. Brine-flavored breath rushed over Jherek.

"Strike now!" Meelat urged. "That thing's going to have the head from your shoulders like a grape from the vine."

"No," Jherek said.

The forked tongue flicked out at the young sailor, missing him by inches. From the periphery of his vision, he saw the ship's crew armed with bows.

Afraid the pirates would fire at the creature, Jherek slowly sheathed the big knife.

"What are you doing?" Meelat demanded.

"I'm giving us the only chance we have. It's curious—nothing more." Standing steady, Jherek faced the sea wyrm.

The forked tongue flicked again, whispering through the air beside his ear, making light popping noises. The young sailor flinched, then steadied himself again. The forked tongue brushed against his face the next time, feeling wet, tough, and leathery.

The sea wyrm drew back out of reach. Its ear fins popped forward, and its large mouth yawned open. The orange eyes glinted. It hissed, yowling as if in anger.

Arrows sped from the pirate archers. Most of them dropped into the water around the sea wyrm, but three of them bounced from the golden scales.

"Stop!" Jherek commanded.

The sea wyrm turned its attention from the young sailor to the slave ship and back again. Sunlight gleamed from its sharp teeth. It hissed at Jherek again, then dived beneath the water, swimming deep and disappearing almost immediately.

"How did you know it wouldn't attack?" Meelat asked.

Jherek shrugged and said, "I didn't."

"Sails! Sails off the stern!"

Still shaking inside, Jherek turned and gazed back behind the slave ship at the cry from the lookout in the crow's nest. There, against the curve of the ocean's northern horizon, square cut white sails interrupted the line between smooth blue sky and green water. Judging the set of the sails, the young sailor knew the ship was headed for them.

"Where are we?"

On the other side of the gate they'd used to pass from *Tarjana*'s belly, Laaqueel spread her webbed hands and feet, stopping her descent toward the distant ocean floor. From the deep blue color of the sea around them, the malenti priestess judged they were in Serôs's gloom strata, the level of the sea between one hundred fifty and three hundred feet.

"Thuridru," Iakhovas answered without looking at her. He held a gem in his hand that glowed suddenly.

According to her studies of Serôs, Thuridru was a mer-folk city along the Turmish coast. Located north of the Xedran Reefs where the ixitxachitl theocracy claimed the Six Holy Cities, Thuridru held a precarious position. Trapped near the ixitxachitl nation, Thuridru was also the sworn enemy of Voalidru, the capital city of the merfolk of Eadraal.

"The city of rogue merfolk," Laaqueel said.

"What do you know of Thuridru?"

"Little," the malenti admitted.

"Nearly four hundred years ago, there was a territorial skirmish between the mermen and the ixitxachitl nations over kelp beds west of Voalidru. Five war parties from the Clan Kamaar chose to ignore the Laws of Battle that have been in effect since the end of the Ninth War of Serôs and attack the ixitxachitl. As a result, Clan Kamaar was banished from Voalidru and driven out to make their homes in the abandoned caverns left by the defeated ixitxachitl." Iakhovas gazed into the distance with a satisfied look.

"What are we doing here?" Laaqueel asked, expecting to be assaulted for her impertinence.

"Ah, little malenti, your impatience truly knows no bounds."

"I would be more effective as your senior high priestess," she said, "if I knew more of what you were doing."

Iakhovas turned his malevolent gaze on her. Even the incomplete golden sphere in his empty socket gleamed. "This war is mine, and it is progressing exactly as I would have it."

"A small group of reinforcements from Vahaxtyl joined

Tarjana's crew this morning," Laaqueel hurried on, ignoring the threat in Iakhovas's voice. "I overheard them arguing among themselves and their brothers in our fleet. They say that your efforts have grown stagnant, that you no longer hold Sekolah's favor."

"You didn't champion me, or the cause I represent?"

"I wouldn't know what to tell them."

"Instruct them to believe. That's where your power lies. If you believe, they will believe."

Laaqueel let the silence between them build.

"Do not cease believing," Iakhovas warned. "That is the only worth you have to me. If you look to your heart, you know that it is the only worth you have to yourself."

"I know." Laaqueel's throat was tight when she spoke.

Without her belief, she was only a hollow shell. The voice she'd heard in her head created tremendous confusion.

"I'm aware of the surviving princes' efforts to undermine my control," Iakhovas said. "Just as I'm aware that the numbers of We Who Eat coming from the Alamber Sea are not as great as I expected after I shattered the Sharksbane Wall. I also know the Great Whale Bard has drawn a small army of his own to sing a barrier against the passage of more sahuagin."

"Only a few of them fight the magic of the songs," Laaqueel said.

"It will be dealt with, little malenti. In due time." Iakhovas grinned. "For now I conserve my strength and mask my presence. The high mages and the Taleweaver have learned about me. Perhaps they've learned more than they should have—but we will see. Despite everything they have heard, I am more powerful than they can ever possibly imagine."

Laaqueel dropped her gaze from his. Everything he said made sense, and it shamed her that she couldn't see it for herself. She loathed the insecurity that trilled within her, hated the way it took her straight back to the young malenti who knew only fear.

"For now," Iakhovas said, "we must gather our forces. Clan Kamaar will prove providential."

129

XIII

16 Flamerule, the Year of the Gauntlet

Jherek stood on the bobbing husk that remained of *Black Champion* and stared at the approaching ship.

"That's a Cormyrean Freesail from the cut of her," Meelat commented.

The privateers sanctioned by the kingdom of Cormyr were tall-masted brigantines crewed by hard men who took their prizes from the pirates they defeated. Most of the Freesails stayed around Suzail and Marsember, with a few others placed around smaller ports, but some of them took charters as trading vessels.

"She's seen us," Meelat said. "We're showing no colors and tied up as we are to this floundering ship, she'll be coming to investigate."

Jherek called to the rest of the salvage crew. The men climbed off *Black Champion*'s corpse and into longboats with the last of their salvaged timber.

At *Swamp Rose*'s side, Jherek and his crew shoved the planks into the waiting net, then held onto the net's sides as it was hauled up. The boom arm swung over amidships, cascading water across the tilted deck. The young sailor dropped to the deck and trotted back to the stern castle to join Azla.

The pirate captain stood with a spyglass in the ship's bow. "She's coming toward us. What was that thing in the water?"

"Meelat said it was a sea wyrm."

"I thought you were a dead man."

Jherek looked at the approaching ship, noting the ballistae and the number of men apparent on the decks. "She's rigged for war."

"King Azoun may see the release of the sahuagin from behind the Sharksbane Wall as a chance to further his own empire building. I wouldn't put it past Azoun to give the Freesails orders to bring in any suspect ships so they can be pressed into service." At the bottom of the stern castle stairs, Azla strode across the deck. "Tomas," she said, "your axe."

The pirate tossed the single-bitted axe through the air and Azla caught it easily. Pirates emptied the net attached to the boom arm, stacking the salvaged lumber. The ship's mages had magically straightened warped timbers and planks as they'd been recovered.

"All hands on deck," Azla roared.

The command was relayed instantly in loud bellows by the first mate. Men scrambled to the deck.

"Put some sail up on that mast," she said. "I want to be making some kind of speed by the time those Cormyrean dogs get here, and one mast'll have to do."

The pirates mustered out smartly, their ranks actually overfull from taking on men who were slaves only a few days ago.

Azla looked out at where *Black Champion* rolled, nearly submerged beneath the waves. "Umberlee take me for a sentimental fool," she whispered. A tear shone in her eye.

Jherek felt the woman's pain. Azla had lived aboard her ship for years. Since she was rarely on land, the young sailor realized that everything she'd cared about was on that ship.

Abruptly, Azla raised the axe and brought it down again and again, severing the ropes that held the shipwreck to *Swamp Rose*. As the ropes separated, the slave ship righted itself and *Black Champion* drifted further beneath the waves.

Glancing back at the deck, Jherek saw that several of the pirates held their hats in their hands. They'd shed blood aboard that vessel, dreamed quiet dreams, ridden out harsh storms, and learned to become one.

"Don't stand there like a bunch of heartbroken saps," Azla bellowed. "Pay your respects to the lady and move on. We may be fighting for our lives in a few minutes."

She flipped the axe back to the man who'd loaned it to her.

"Begging the cap'n's pardon," a pirate spoke up, "but we ain't got a name for this ship. Unless you want to keep calling her *Swamp Rose*."

"Boatswain," Azla barked, "fetch me a bottle of ale."

When the man hurried back, Azla took the bottle. By then the sails on the surviving mast had latched talons into the wind. The riggings creaked steadily in protest as the ship got underway. The half-elf pirate captain climbed to the top of the forecastle stairs and turned toward her crew.

"The brine took *Black Champion*, but before she went, she helped us win this ship. I'll give this lady a name, but it's up to you to pay the steel and blood it will take to make brave men fear the sound of it, and cowards run from her shadow."

She smashed the bottle against the railing, spewing broken shards and foaming ale over the deck.

"All right," Azla said, "you lump-eared, misbegotten excuses for proper pirates, I give you *Azure Dagger*. Long may she sail!"

Thunderous approval roared up from amidships. Standing there, Jherek felt proud. He turned his gaze to *Azure Dagger*'s stern and watched as the Cormyrean Freesail skimmed the water like a bird of prey.

* * * * *

"This is taking far too long," Pacys grumbled.

He swam at Taranath Reefglamor's side. The Senior High Mage inspected the caravan that assembled in Sylkiir the day after the Sharksbane Wall fell.

Below them, in a small valley behind a sheltering ridge of rock and kelp, the sea elves finished packing supplies onto flat sleds. The sleds were being pulled by narwhals and sea turtles on the journey to Myth Nantar.

The High Mage stopped and floated forty feet above the ocean floor. The incandescence from the sun lit the waters blue.

"Taleweaver," the Senior High Mage stated softly, though not with patience, "this journey will take as long as it will take. If we rush, we risk."

"Senior, I know. Truly I do." Pacys searched for the words to explain the anxiety that filled him. "The music fills me and drives me on," he said, "and I can't help feeling that we're progressing too slowly."

"And if we should fail after we've been given this chance?" Reefglamor eyed the old bard directly. "Who would be left to take up arms in this pursuit?"

"I don't know," Pacys admitted.

Coronal Semphyr, who commanded Aluwand, and Coronal Cormal Ytham, who commanded Sylkiir, both stood against any involvement in Myth Nantar.

Reefglamor clasped Pacys's shoulder tightly in his grip and said, "To most of my people, Myth Nantar is a corpse, better off left entombed by the mythal that surrounds it."

"But the Taker is headed there," the bard reminded him.

"And if you're wrong?" the sea elf asked. "If I and the other mages have left our cities, our people, undefended against the Taker?"

"If you could but feel the power of the songs that fill my heart near to bursting, you would know that what we do is the right thing."

"My friend," Reefglamor said, "I do believe you. That's the only reason we are here now. But even as I believe in you, you must believe in me. We must not just begin this journey, we must finish it as well."

One of the lesser mages swam to a stop nearby and waited patiently. Reefglamor excused himself and swam over to the woman.

"Trouble, friend Pacys?"

The old bard glanced up and saw Khlinat floating in the water only a few feet away. For the first time he noticed how tired and haggard the dwarf looked, then realized the whole caravan probably felt the same way.

With the regular military forces stripped from their ranks, men and women who served and believed in the high mages had volunteered for the journey. Many of them kissed their wives, husbands, and children good-bye on the day they left Sylkiir. No few of them, Pacys felt certain, would never look on their families again. For the first time, he realized the sacrifices they'd made.

"No trouble," Pacys said. "Only my own impatience at how slowly we travel."

"Aye, I been thinking on that meself," the dwarf grumbled, "but there's no way to increase our speed. Them people what's out there making up this ragtag army, they're doing all they can."

"And maybe more than they should be asked."

Pacys looked down at the long line of the caravan. Nearly three hundred sea elves took their breaks while the sleds were secured and the animals were changed out. They sat in small groups and talked. Weariness from the hard travel showed in the stooped shoulders and the lethargy that gripped them.

Glancing around, Pacys spotted a depression in the hillside of the sheltering ridge. It gave a view over the whole caravan. He swam to it and settled on the ledge at the front of the depression. As he took the saceddar from his back, he drew his skills to him, and listened to the music that haunted him all morning. He'd found no words for the music—until now. The music was lively but bittersweet, a tune that would live on.

> Torn from proud history,
> Forged in blood and love,
> Come from the hand and eye and love of Deep Sashelas,
> No longer of the world above.
> They gathered at the behest of the High Mages,
> And descended into Serôs's deepest blue.
> They followed the course of dark prophecy,
> To discover what was right and true.
> They journeyed to far Myth Nantar,
> Still bound in wild and uncertain magic.
> The City of Destinies had a future unclear,
> And a history that had proven tragic.

Pacys played on, finding the words with ease. He let the music fill him and give power to his song. He knew they

134

listened, every conversation brought to a halt by the majesty in his voice. He continued, finding the chorus.

> *We are the Alu'Tel'Quessir,*
> *Our hearts build our home.*
> *Our blood is pure*
> *And our arms are strong.*
> *Together we stand,*
> *And never die alone.*
> *We are the Alu'Tel'Quessir.*
> *We march to right a wrong.*
> *Our bodies may get weary,*
> *But our spirits are filled with song.*

The old bard stopped singing. The rest of the song was yet to be written. Verses would be added as they journeyed, but for now it was all he had.

"Don't worry, friend Pacys," Khlinat said quietly. " 'Twas a good song, strong and true, but mayhap them hearts out yonder aren't ready for something like that."

Pacys nodded, wondering what Reefglamor would have to say about his impromptu performance.

Then, with gentleness at first, the sea elves picked up the chorus, stumbling until a few of them found the meter and rhythm.

> *We are the Alu'Tel'Quessir,*
> *Our hearts build our home.*

More voices joined in, and the song became a thunderous, spirited roar. It was a song of defiance and pride.

Tears spilled from Pacys's eyes, plucked away by the sea around him. It wasn't just their belief he was rekindling and he knew it. The fear and anxiety sapped his strength as well, raked out hollow places within his convictions. Now he filled them up again. His fingers found the notes on the saceddar, pulling the group together until the song filled the valley. Khlinat joined in, adding his deep basso boom.

> *Our blood is pure*
> *And our arms are strong.*

Together we stand,
And never die alone.
We are the Alu'Tel'Quessir . . .

* * * * *

With only one mast in place, even with all the canvas it could support, *Azure Dagger* could not outrun the Cormyrean Freesail. Jherek clung to the railing next to Azla. Glawinn stood beside them.

"They're going to be suspicious of us," Azla declared. "We've obviously been in a fight, and this ship stinks of slavery when you get downwind of her."

Jherek watched as the Cormyrean ship cut through the water to within two hundred yards.

"Steady, young warrior," Glawinn stated softly. "They've yet to prove their intentions as anything other than honorable."

Gradually, the Cormyrean Freesail drew abreast of *Azure Dagger*'s port side. A slim man dressed in maroon with silver trimmings stood at the forecastle railing with a hailing cone in his hands. "Ahoy. This is Captain Sebastyn Tarnar of His Majesty King Azoun IV's ship, *Steadfast*. I'd like to speak to your captain."

Azla accepted the hailing cone one of her men handed over. "This is Azla, captain of the free ship *Azure Dagger*."

"We saw you had some trouble and thought we'd investigate."

"We're fine and sailing under our own power."

"Perhaps not as proudly as you could be," Tarnar replied, "but I'll grant you that. Can we be of any assistance?"

"Thank you," Azla called back, "but no. We're used to managing our own affairs and would rather others would do the same."

"What did for your ship, Captain?"

"We did," Azla answered. "We ran across slavers who thought to add me and my crew to their bounty. By the time we'd settled differences, I'd lost my ship. That was her you saw us cutting loose back there. So we took this ship in her stead."

"I thought I recognized the stench." Tarnar paused, then called, "Where are you headed? Perhaps we could share the wind for a while."

136

"Sometimes it's better to be by yourself than trust someone you don't know."

Tarnar put the hailing cone down and laughed. "You're a feisty one, Captain Azla. I would relish the opportunity to meet you at another time, the Lady willing."

"If chance and tide should allow you your wish, Captain Tarnar, I'll stand you to the first drink."

In the next moment, a wave of unaccustomed vertigo stole through Jherek. He leaned more heavily on the railing, struggling to stay on his feet. Just as suddenly the wind died.

Without warning, a plume of water stood up from the ocean, rising nearly twenty feet tall. In the still air, the twisting plume spun into the form of a man with outstretched arms.

"Jherek of Velen," the plume of water itself seemed to say, "your path lies in a different direction. Leave that ship and join the Cormyreans." The basso voice haunted the waters.

"No," the young sailor whispered.

"There is no choice," the water-being stated. "You are called to follow your own path. Sir Glawinn, warrior of Lathander the Morninglord, you must release the boy. He will no longer be under your guidance."

Jherek looked at Glawinn.

"I don't know what this is before us, young warrior," the paladin said. He stared out at the obviously magical creature. "You can see for yourself the power it wields."

"No." Cold anger and fear battered Jherek but they couldn't overcome the stunned numbness that filled him. His life was his own. He'd forsworn all gods.

Azla approached them, her face hard and chiseled. "This is sorcery," she said as she gazed around the two ships.

Jherek peered through the railing, looking at the eight-foot-high waves that seemed to pass all around them, leaving them in a hollowed bowl in the middle of the Sea of Fallen Stars.

"Young warrior," Glawinn said, "you must go. It is your destiny."

"No," Jherek argued. "This is my curse. I am finally among friends. Now I am being turned from them."

Nothing about this was fair. He looked over his shoulder

and saw Sabyna. The ache in his heart worsened.

"Not a curse, young warrior. I sense this is part of your birthright. You must believe me."

Captain Tarnar shouted across the distance, clearly heard in the still air as he demanded to know what was happening.

A sudden banshee shriek ripped through the air above them, filling the sails hard enough to rip canvas free in places. *Azure Dagger* rocked violently, scattering men across the deck.

"What is going on?" Sabyna demanded as she joined them.

Glawinn looked at her and said, "Lady, he can't stay with us. His path lies in another direction."

Panic touched Sabyna's face for just a moment, but she got control of herself. "If that is true," she said, "I'm going with him."

The banshee wind shrieked again, ripping more canvas free.

"You can't go," Glawinn gasped. "I can't go. No one can go with the young warrior. We each have our parts to play in this tangling of threads."

"No," Sabyna denied quietly. "You have to be wrong."

"My friend, I wish that I was wrong." Glawinn took Jherek's hand tight in his. "Look inside your heart. Tell me if you feel that I am wrong."

Cold and adrift inside himself, Jherek found it hard to concentrate. He closed his eyes and took a deep, shuddering breath, searching within. No voice gave him direction, but he felt a tug eastward, a wanderlust that pushed him to go in that direction.

"There is no place for me here," he croaked as he stared into the paladin's eyes.

"How can you speak so surely?" Sabyna demanded.

Jherek looked up at her, trying not to see the tears that tracked her cheeks. "I can't say, lady."

"You don't have to go," Azla said defiantly. "This is my ship. I say who comes and goes."

Another powerful gust of wind slammed into *Azure Dagger.* Half her canvas ripped free and cracked in the wind. Pirates immediately worked the rigging, dropping the canvas.

"I have no choice," Jherek said. He forced himself to his feet. "What am I supposed to do?"

Glawinn shook his head. "I don't know. Trust the love inside you, Jherek. It is your strength and your belief. You must hold tight to that till you find your anchor and your forgiveness."

"There is no one to forgive me."

The paladin was silent for a moment. "There is one."

"Who?"

"It's not for me to say. When the time is right, you will know. Come. I will help you pack."

"No," Jherek said. "I'll take what I have with me."

"You have gear here," Azla said, "and we have supplies we can spare."

"Nothing." Jherek looked at the still water between the two ships.

"You're going then?" Sabyna asked.

Jherek looked at her, the pain in his heart almost too much to bear. "Lady, perhaps it is better. All I seem capable of doing is bringing you pain, and I am sorry for that. I'm sorry that you are so far from home."

"I am where I need to be," Sabyna said. "I have charted this course as much as you have."

Jherek started to shake his head.

"I'll not tolerate a pig-headed argument," Sabyna warned in a hoarse voice, "and you've no other to offer in this matter."

Before he could stop himself, Jherek took her hand in his and knelt. He pulled her hand gently to his chest above his heart.

"Lady," he said, "I swear that should you ever need me, should there be a way made that I can help you, I will be there."

She tightened her fingers in his shirt. "I know," she whispered.

Jherek turned and hugged Glawinn fiercely.

"Go with Lathander's mercies, young warrior."

Holding tightly onto his control, Jherek stepped in front of Azla. "Captain, requesting permission to disembark."

"Granted," the half-elf pirate captain responded. "May you know nothing but safe waters. If ever you need berth on a ship, my men will know of you."

"Thank you."

Jherek kept himself from looking back at Sabyna. He stepped to the railing and threw himself overboard. Only the certain knowledge that the ship and all aboard her would be sacrificed if he stayed gave him the strength.

He hit the water cleanly, completely submerging. The sea plumed white around him as he passed through it. For a moment he considered diving as deep as he could, until his lungs ran out of air and he couldn't make the surface again, but he didn't.

Whatever drove him from Velen and buried him with the ill luck that pursued him from the time he was born stayed with him. Whatever god, whatever demon, maybe it could make him leave his friends, but it couldn't control him completely.

In Athkatla, he'd given in to that force and to the voice that commanded him and made the trip to Baldur's Gate. After the Ship of the Gods exploded, he gave up. Now, he decided, he would fight that force until he was free of it or it destroyed him.

He surfaced and swam across to *Steadfast*. When he arrived, he pounded on the hull and called, "I need a ladder."

Captain Tarnar gazed down at him with suspicion. "I don't need to be berthing a curse," he shouted down.

Jherek gazed back up at the man, fanning the hurt and anger inside himself until it glowed white-hot. "If you don't take me aboard," Jherek said, "I'm willing to bet you don't make it out of here."

"We'll see about that."

Before Tarnar's words faded away, the water-figure spun quickly and winds whipped the ship, tearing rigging free.

Jherek pushed away from *Steadfast*, treading water until the ship settled again. The coiled rope ladder plopped into the water near the young sailor, and he wasted no time clambering up it. He stood on *Steadfast*'s deck totally drenched, water cascading around his feet.

"What manner of hell chases you, boy?" Tarnar demanded.

"I don't know," Jherek answered, "but there will be an accounting."

No sooner had the young sailor come aboard than the water-figure sank into the ocean and the wind returned, filling *Steadfast*'s sails and shoving them forward again. Tarnar gazed upward, a wary look on his sun-browned features. "You think you can fight *that*?"

"Whoever I see at the other end of this trip," Jherek said, "who is in any way responsible for this will regret ever laying eyes on me."

Glawinn and Sabyna stood at the railing, looking out after him. He stared at them even after they were gone from sight, certain he would never see them again.

The wind flowed over him, bringing the sea's chill to his wet clothes. He ignored the cold, focusing on the hate that he'd finally allowed to take root in his heart.

XIV

21 Flamerule, the Year of the Gauntlet

The ixitxachitl swooped through the sea at Laaqueel with a suddenness that belied its great size. It resembled a manta ray, solid black across the top of its thin body and purple-white underneath. The wing membrane was fully eight feet across, not the largest of its kind the malenti priestess had seen, but close.

She kicked her feet, powering through the water and pulling her trident between her breasts. The lateral lines running through her body echoed the disturbance in the ocean around her. Spinning, one hand flaring out and catching the water in the webbing between her fingers, she avoided the demon ray's barbed tail. One of the Serôsian ixitxachitls' tactics was to snare an intended victim's neck or torso and hold it captive.

Laaqueel popped her retractable finger claws from hiding, raked them across the ixitxachitl's tail, and lopped off a two-foot section.

Blood streamed from the creature's tail stub as it curled its wing membrane and rolled over with deceptive ease.

"Hateful elf!" it cried in its gravelly voice. It sped at her again.

Leveling her trident, Laaqueel sprang at her opponent. The ixitxachitl's mouth opened, over a foot wide and filled with serrated teeth.

She shoved the trident forward, burying the tines in the hard, rubbery flesh between the ixitxachitl's malevolent eyes. The creature's greater bulk propelled her backward, but she swung at the end of the trident safely out of reach of its hungry jaws.

She popped her toe claws and raked her opponent from just behind its mouth all the way to the bleeding tail stump. The creature's entrails spilled into the water in long ropes. The ixitxachitl screamed as death claimed it.

Laaqueel yanked her trident free and raked the surrounding water with her gaze. War raged around her as the ixitxachitls battled sahuagin from the outer and inner seas. Blood filmed the sea the way a surface dweller's smoke choked an enclosed building.

With their greater speed, the sahuagin were making short work of the demon rays.

It feels good to be back in the fray, doesn't it, little malenti?

Laaqueel listened to Iakhovas's voice inside her skull and answered, *Yes.*

In truth, all doubt and fear left her for the moment. There was no uncertainty. She was a priestess serving the will of Sekolah to battle and destroy enemies of the sahuagin.

The ixitxachitls had set up their Six Holy Cities in the Xedran Reefs, south of Thuridru. They ran from just off the coast of Alaghôn on the Turmish coast to the shallows in the mouth of the Vilhon Reach.

A foraging party from the koalinth tribe called the Sea Hulks had been used as bait for the ixitxachitl military party Iakhovas staked out as a target. When the demon ray group attacked, the koalinth foragers fled east, leading their pursuers between the pincer attack of the combined sahuagin and Sea Hulk groups.

Driven before their ambushers, angered and confused—the Laws of Battle had not been adhered to—the ixitxachitls swam east, desperately trying to outrun the death that chased after them.

Her lateral lines warned Laaqueel of the attack coming from behind her. Praying to Sekolah, praying that her failing belief had not yet caused her powers to leave her, she turned and shoved her hand out.

Bright incandescence shot from her hand, causing steaming bubbles to form and dart rapidly for the surface little more than a hundred feet up. The ixitxachitl caught in the blast of power cooked, great blisters rising in a heartbeat, then bursting. The rancid taste of burned fat tainted the water Laaqueel breathed.

To the left, another sahuagin rode an ixitxachitl's back, holding onto the wing membrane with both fists as it took great bites from the screaming creature's back. Its shouts and prayers to Ilxendren, the Great Ray and god of the ixitxachitls, echoed in Laaqueel's ears.

Laaqueel pulled her weapon free and swam on, giving herself over to the chase. It was the closest she'd felt to normal in days.

The meeting with Vhaemas the Bastard had been five days ago. Now Iakhovas hoped to win the support of the Sea Hulk koalinth tribe south of the Xedran Reefs, completing a union of enemies around the ixitxachitls. The malenti priestess was present at only one of the meetings between Iakhovas and the koalinth chief, though she knew Iakhovas met with Dhunnir more times than that.

The fleeing ixitxachitls flexed their wings and skated only a few feet above the ocean surface, gliding over the clumps of coral that gave the Xedran Reefs its name. Sand ballooned out from under their great wings as they swam. Colorful fish darted from in front of them.

Ilkanar, the town the ixitxachitls were from, lay over a mile to the west. The attack was sprung far enough away from the devil ray city that no reinforcements could arrive quickly even if a messenger did get away.

The ixitxachitls swam through a stand of rocks and coral, hoping to escape their pursuers. Instead, they met *Tarjana* rising up from the ocean floor over the rise behind which it had been hidden.

The mudship's deck was filled with more sahuagin wielding crossbows. Even as the ixitxachitls turned to avoid slamming into the massive ship, the crossbow quarrels found their marks.

Iakhovas was among them. Laaqueel swam, watching as Iakhovas's arms became hard-edged with bone and dorsal edges that ran the length of the appendages. His finned arms and legs slashed through the ixitxachitls.

In minutes, the last demon ray had been executed. Sahuagin and koalinth alike made a meal out of their conquered enemies. Laaqueel swam above *Tarjana*'s deck and surveyed the battlefield that stretched for almost a quarter mile. Bodies of sahuagin, ixitxachitl, and koalinth alike littered the water, twisted into inelegant poses.

The survivors moved through the dead with large nets in their wake, gathering them up. Meat was meat, and none of it needed to go to waste.

* * * * *

Jherek was on *Steadfast*'s forecastle deck, whirling the cutlass and hook around him as he moved from attack to defense and back again.

Finished for the moment, standing on quivering legs, his arms trembling from the exertion, the young sailor took a deep breath and looked over the bow at the eastern horizon. *Steadfast* tacked into the wind now, rolling first port then starboard as she plowed through the oncoming waves. The Whamite Isles were two days back and she made for Aglarond.

When his legs were steady again, he stepped over the bow railing and stared along the thirty-foot bowsprit. The wood glistened with salt spray. Ratlines ran down from the forward and mainmasts, helping hold the lanyards square and in place.

Concentrating, anything to keep from thinking about what and whom he'd walked away from thirteen days before, Jherek stepped cautiously and steadily along the bowsprit. The long pole measured nearly a foot across where it buckled into the caravel and narrowed to something less than four inches at the end. Nearly halfway out, the ratlines dropped too low to be any good to him if he fell. Still, he continued, his knees bent as he rode out *Steadfast*'s rise and fall.

Long moments later, he stood within only a few short feet of the bowsprit's end. He reveled in the feel of the wind and the sea's uneven terrain. All around him, he could see nothing but the sea and the sky. He closed his eyes, turning his face up into the wind.

If he lost the anger that filled him, what would be left? The question had haunted him over the last few days. The answer terrified him. Whatever drove him wanted him broken. Perhaps it didn't know how close he already was. Perhaps it would have been satisfied if it had known. He'd even wished for a while that he could break, but he couldn't. He simply didn't know how.

"Jherek."

The call was soft, not meant to startle. The young sailor moved his feet carefully, turning to stare back at the ship. Captain Tarnar stood in the bow, arms folded across his chest.

"It's almost time to come about and tack into the wind the other way. I didn't want to lose you when we re-rigged the canvas."

"Thank you, Captain."

Carefully, Jherek walked back along the bowsprit, then hopped onto the forecastle deck.

Tarnar gazed at him in open speculation and said, "I've never seen a sober man try to do what you just did, and even drunk I never saw it accomplished."

Jherek flushed with embarrassment over drawing unnecessary attention. Since boarding *Steadfast*, he'd been the object of enough of it.

"Most of my crew is convinced that you're cursed, but a few think of you as some kind of holy man. Which of them have it right?"

"I'd say cursed," Jherek replied bitterly. "I don't know."

"Personally, I was thinking you might be blessed."

Jherek glanced at the captain to see if he was joking.

"All these days at sea, and us staring the Alamber in the teeth the most of it, and we've not suffered one sea devil attack. Most ships aren't finding passage that easy."

"The voyage isn't over yet," Jherek said harshly.

"You're not a man to ever see a glass half full, are you?"

"I've had reason not to," Jherek said. "Most days, it's not even been my glass to look at."

Shouts suddenly rang out from the port side of the ship. "Dragon!" a man bawled.

"Where away?" Tarnar demanded, turning and striding to that side of the ship.

"There, Cap'n!" The mate pointed at the sea.

Looking out into the blue-green water, Jherek saw the unmistakable gold scales of the sea wyrm forty yards out. Its serpentine body undulated through the sea, easily pacing the ship, not having to fight the wind.

"What is it?" a man bellowed in consternation.

"Dragon-kin," another man roared back. "Umberlee probably sent the great damned thing to fetch us and pull us under the salt."

A handful of the crew grabbed bows and drew arrows back.

"No!" Jherek ordered even as they loosed. The arrows raced across the intervening distance, but none of them found their mark. "Don't loose any more arrows!"

The young sailor stepped forward and pushed a man to the deck. The crew instantly formed a pocket around Jherek. Knives and cudgels appeared in their hands.

"Demonspawn," one of the men growled. "Shoulda tied an anchor 'round his feet and deep-sixed him!"

Jherek raised the cutlass to defend himself, but—looking into the angry and frightened faces of the men before him—his resolve left him. He knew there was no way he could fight them. They weren't pirates or slavers, nor any black-hearted rogues that he could recognize. They were simply men afraid of what was before them. A warrior didn't fight such men over anything less than honor or to save a life. Jherek couldn't fight them just to save his own life, not when he was the cause of their fear.

The young sailor dropped his cutlass and stood before the crew unarmed. The anger inside him kept his fear away. He waited. He wouldn't run.

"Run him through!" a crewman near the back yelled. "See if his blood's red or if you can read his befouled heritage in his own tripe, by the gods!"

One of the men lashed out with a cruel skinning knife. Jherek turned just enough to avoid the blow.

"Enough!" Tarnar roared. "This is my ship. As long as it remains my ship, nothing will happen aboard her that I don't sanction. That's the way it has always been, and that's how it shall be until I'm not fit to command her." He glared at the men assembled before him. "Is that understood?"

"Aye, Cap'n." The response was quick and came from the mouth of every man. All the oaths were grudgingly given.

"Then get back to work," the captain ordered. "Every mother's son of you."

The crew turned and walked away, grumbling.

Tarnar turned, his eyes wide as he studied Jherek. "By the gods, boy, what is it about you that you'd stare them in the teeth and not raise a hand against them?"

"They didn't deserve my wrath," Jherek answered. "They have no control over my being here."

"They would have killed you if I let them."

"Aye."

Tarnar shook his head in disbelief. "What is that thing doing here?" He pointed at the sea wyrm keeping pace with *Steadfast*.

"I don't know, Captain." Jherek turned to the railing and stared out at the sea wyrm. It disappeared beneath the waves. "I've seen it before. Back on *Azure Dagger*."

"Then it has followed you here," concluded Tarnar.

Jherek made no response to that, but his mind reeled with the implications of the dragon's presence.

"Boy, if something powerful enough to stop the winds and control the waters wanted you dead, it would have drank down the ship and you with it," the captain said. "You're still alive, so I have to ask why."

"I don't know," Jherek said with grim determination, "but whatever it is, it will regret it."

Tarnar shook his head. "A prudent man wouldn't presume to put himself above the gods."

"I'm beyond prudence," Jherek declared. "I will demand an accounting. My life has never been an easy one, and this force—this god if you wish to see it that way—has seen to that. It can kill me, strip the flesh from my bones, but I will not kneel before some heartless thing. I will have my battle, and I will acquit myself with honor."

* * * * *

Sabyna paused at the edge of the narrow, rutted street and watched a wagon pass.

The wagon was loaded with timber the driver was hauling to the sawmill down by the docks. The merry jingle-jangle of the horses' harnesses stood out in sharp counterpoint to the tired plod of the animals. The driver and the three woodchoppers with him looked worn out.

Agenais rumbled with steady business and men. Coin changed hands quickly, and prices marked on goods didn't mean a thing. If no one was interested in something, the price could sometimes be halved. Impromptu auctions went on all around her where there was more than one prospective buyer and a limited supply of goods. The roll of bids, accompanied by oaths and strident voices, remained as steady as the conversations and stories that were told.

Sabyna crossed the street, aware of the men's attentions. Some eyed her discreetly, and others stared at her with openly wolfish hunger.

On the other side of the rutted street, she stepped up onto a boardwalk under a badly listing eave in front of the apothecary's shop. Her boot heels rang hollowly against the wooden surface.

"Hey, little woman," a man called gruffly.

Sabyna kept her eyes forward. From experience she'd learned not to acknowledge speakers in such situations.

The man reached out and wrapped a beefy hand around her wrist. "Hey," he grumbled, "I was talking to you." The man was short of six feet but was as broad as the back end of a barge. He was unshaven and smelled of ale.

Slowly, Sabyna reached out with her free hand for the whip lashed to the big man's belt. She smiled, watching other men come join the first.

"You're lucky," she said in a soft voice.

The man grinned more broadly and asked, "How am I lucky?"

"Despite the mood I'm in and your own bad manners, I'm not going to kill you." Sabyna tapped the whip and said, "Bind."

The whip surged up from the man's side and uncoiled. Before he could do more than let go her wrist and take a step back, the whip wrapped around him, pinning his arms to his sides and trapping his legs together. He yelped in fear and surprise.

Placing a hand in the center of his chest, Sabyna shoved the man into the rutted street. She turned to face his friends, who weren't totally convinced they couldn't take her.

She opened the bag of holding at her side and called, "Skeins."

The raggamoffyn fluttered up through the opening and formed a striking serpentine shape that hovered on the wind. The men backed away at once, terror on their faces.

"Don't," Sabyna said coldly, "let me see you again."

Without another word, the men grabbed their friend from the rutted road and took off.

Releasing a slow, taut breath, Sabyna stepped into the apothecary's shop. Skeins retreated into the bag of holding.

The shop stood small and tidy beneath a swaying ceiling that had seen its best days pass it by. Wheel-shaped candelabras hung from the ceiling. Handmade shelves, added as needed and not with a uniform design in mind, stood against the left and right walls.

Glass bottles of all shapes, sizes, and colors mixed with jars, canisters, and small boxes to cover the shelves. Open vases held sticks of spices and rolled herbs. Cheesecloth pouches of pipeweed sat on barrels.

Some of the herbs had been dried and left in their original shape, lying in jars, in thick clusters, or hanging from strings strung around the room. Other herbs had been ground into meals and powders, grains separated from the chaff.

"Hail and well met, lady."

Fazayl stood behind the battered counter at the end of the shop. Long gray hair hung to his shoulders, but the top of his head was bald. Gray chin whiskers jutted out in disarray. He wore a homespun shirt and worn breeches. A long-stemmed pipe was in one hand, and the rich aroma of cherry blend pipeweed filled the shop.

"Hail and well met." Sabyna crossed to the counter. "You have the herbs and other things I asked for?"

"Aye," the man replied. "That I do."

He reached under the counter and brought out a small wooden box. Inside were a dozen vials, jars, and bottles of different colors. Bundles of herbs and incense sticks took up more space.

Sabyna took the bottles and herbs out one by one, checking each.

"I've gotten some new stock in, lady," Fazayl stated, waving his arm generously around the small shop. "If you'd care to take a look."

"Thank you. I will."

Despite the danger inherent in being in the town of Agenais by herself, Sabyna found she was reluctant to return to *Azure Dagger* so readily. While aboard ship she was consciously aware of Jherek's absence. She left the small box in the apothecary's care and crossed the room to the potions and oils.

Two small children, no more than six or seven, entered the shop amid gales of laughter. Dressed in made-over clothing patched in dozens of places, they pushed and shoved each other in playful sibling rivalry. The children stopped at the counter and peered up at Fazayl.

"And where do you rapscallions think you're off to?" the apothecary demanded.

The children didn't answer, simply peered over the edge of the counter with their big eyes. Dirt stained their wind-reddened cheeks, and they wiggled in excitement.

Smiling, Fazayl reached under the counter and brought out half a dozen hard candies. The children scooped them up, yelled quick thank yous, and scurried for the door. The old man laughed at them, then caught Sabyna looking.

"Bless the children, lady, for they see only the good things in this world."

"Are they your grandchildren?" Sabyna asked.

"No, lady. My boys and my grandchildren live in Chessenta. The Whamites turned out far too small to keep them from roving. Still, most of the children in town know I and the missus can be counted on for a few pieces of sugar candy without too much of a fight."

The shop door opened and two rough-looking men stepped through. Both of them walked with the rolling gait of professional seamen and wore cutlasses instead of long swords.

"Shopkeeper," one of the men roared. "I've got a list of goods here we'll be needing." He reached inside his blouse and took out a scrap of parchment.

"If I can," Fazayl replied. "Some goods are in short supply these days."

The two men swaggered to the counter and gazed around at the shop. One of them looked directly at Sabyna, and the ship's mage recognized him in an instant as one of Vurgrom the Mighty's crew of pirates that had captured her in Baldur's Gate and fled with her down the River Chionthar.

She readied her spells in the event that he recognized her.

After they gave their list to Fazayl, they turned to the barrels where the apothecary kept live fish, salamanders, frogs, and newts that he used to make some of his powders, potions, and oils.

Returning to the counter, still watching the two men, Sabyna quickly paid for her supplies, then shoved them into the bag of holding. Skeins sensed her tension and tried to ease from the bag. She pushed the raggamoffyn back inside, thanked Fazayl, and headed for the door.

Without looking back, she crossed the rutted street that cut through the heart of Agenais and took up a position beside a sail maker's shop. From the alley she had a clear view of the apothecary.

When they left, she followed.

XV

29 Flamerule, the Year of the Gauntlet

"You're an excellent player," the captain said.

Jherek glanced at Captain Tarnar across the inlaid marble chessboard on the small table between them in the captain's quarters. The pieces were done in dark red and white, matching the board, carved in figures of king, queen, priests, horsemen, castles, and kneeling archers.

"You're very gracious," the young sailor responded.

Steadfast cleaved the water as she was named, pulling full into the wind now.

"No," Tarnar replied, "I'm not. I don't like to lose."

He poured another glass of wine for himself, then offered the bottle to Jherek, who politely refused.

The captain had invited Jherek to join him for dinner, and the young sailor had reluctantly accepted. Jherek preferred his own company, but he was loath not to show good manners in light of the situation.

"I find it more disturbing that you beat me three times in a row—" Tarnar paused to sip his wine, "—in light of the fact that you're distracted."

"I'm not—"

"A woman?" the captain asked, interrupting politely.

Jherek didn't reply. To speak of Sabyna so casually would be dishonorable.

"Of course it's a woman," Tarnar said with conviction. His eyes bore into the young sailor's. "The only other interest to so bewitch a man's soul would be an object of greed, and you aren't the type to covet physical goods." The captain started setting up the chess pieces again. "You threw yourself into the sea without so much as a bag packed those days ago."

Jherek set up the pieces on his side of the board, appreciating the smooth feel of them.

"Is it the ship's captain I saw you with?" Tarnar persisted. "The half-elf? Or the young red haired girl that seemed so upset by your leaving?"

"I'd rather not speak of this," Jherek said.

"Nonsense. Men at sea always talk of women," the captain persisted. "First, they speak of their mothers, then of lovers, then of women they've left in different ports. When they start speaking of wives, you'd best start looking for another crewman."

Candles lit the room and filled it with the smoky haze of herbs that eddied out the open windows in the ship's stern. A generous portion of the room was given over to the large bed that extended across the stern a good eight feet. Shelves and closets occupied the remaining space along the wall on either side of the bed.

There was a large rolltop desk that held map scrolls and nautical plotting and marking tools. Ship's journals sat neatly ranked on one side. The current journal occupied the center of the table, open to the entry Tarnar last made. A quill and an inkwell sat nearby.

A shelf on the opposite side of the room from the desk held a row of books. Most of them, Jherek found upon inspection, were treatises regarding the worship of Mystra. Beside the bookshelves was a locked armory that held swords of different makes and styles.

Jherek nodded at the shelves and said, "I've noticed your interest in books."

"The worship of Mystra. Yes." Tarnar swirled the dregs of his wine. "I am a failed priest of her order."

Stunned that the man announced the fact so casually, Jherek opened his mouth to speak but found no words.

The captain grinned. "It's nothing I'm ashamed of," he said. "While I attended the Lady of Mysteries' schools and talked with her priests, I learned a great many things. All of them have helped me become a better man. I begrudge none of the experience, not even when I took myself from the order."

"Why did you?" Jherek asked.

"Because I felt the calling, but I never felt I could devote myself to the priesthood. Not the way I wanted to, wholly and without reservation. So I went to sea, which seemed as wild and as restless as any mysteries I might seek to uncover under Mystra's guidance."

"But your interest remains," Jherek observed. "Why would you keep the books otherwise?"

"Aye," Tarnar replied. "My fascination remains. Mystra is also known as She of the Wild Tides here in the Sea of Fallen Stars. I love her because she seems so much a part of this world, yet above it. Legend has it that during the Time of Troubles she even walked on this plane as a mortal herself."

Jherek remained silent.

"Today I tried to divine something of what lies in your future," Tarnar said.

Shaking his head, Jherek grumbled, "I don't want to know."

"There's not much to tell," Tarnar told him. "I never learned how to divine properly, though I was told by my teachers that I possessed some mean skills at it. I only got two impressions from the attempt. I know that something shapes your future—though you have a choice in that— and that the guiding hand does not belong to Mystra."

"What choice?"

Tarnar ran his finger around the rim of his wineglass and said, "I could not say. Have you any stronger feelings about where we're supposed to go? By the afternoon of the day after tomorrow we'll be at the mouth of the Alamber Sea. Providing the wind stays with us, the trip to Aglarond will not be long."

"No. I have just the steady need to travel east—and even that is not as sharp as it once was."

Even as the young sailor's words faded away, a low, mournful croon echoed inside the captain's quarters.

Drawn by the sound, Jherek excused himself from the table and headed through the door.

Men stood out on the deck, lit by a few lanterns secured in the rigging to warn other ships of their presence and to allow them to see in the dark night. None of the sailors appeared relaxed.

"What in the Nine Hells is that?" one man grumbled.

"It's enough to wake the dead," another volunteered.

"You ask me," a third stated, "that's the cry of someone or something dead. Come to call us on home ourselves."

"Stow that bilge, Klyngir," Tarnar ordered as he followed Jherek up the steps to the stern castle.

"Aye, sir," the sailor snapped.

The mournful moaning continued, just loud enough to be heard over the waves lapping at *Steadfast*'s sides. It echoed on the wind, as if carried a great distance.

Jherek stepped up on *Steadfast*'s stern castle deck. The chill wind snaked icy fingers under his clothing, prickling his skin. His hair whipped about, blown forward from the stern. He scanned the horizon where the star-filled black sky met the rolling, green-black sea.

"I want men circling this ship along the railings," Tarnar roared as he stood overlooking the deck. "Those blasted sea devils are known to be thick in this area."

"Sounds far away, Cap'n," the mate behind the wheel stated.

"I don't want to take any chances," Tarnar snapped.

Steadfast creaked and the rigging popped in the wind, but the ship's noises never covered the mournful moans. Jherek listened to the sounds, finally recognizing them for what they were.

"Whale song," he said.

"Aye, Cap'n, it is," the mate at the wheel said. "I know it now, too."

The cadence of the whale song rode up and down the scale, sounding eerie and menacing.

"I've been told whales can sing the length and breadth of the Inner Sea," the mate said, "but I've never heard anything like this."

"Nor have I," Tarnar agreed. He glanced at Jherek.

"Wherever they are," Jherek said, "that's where we must go."

156

"You're sure?" Tarnar asked.

Men scurried along *Steadfast*'s railing, holding lanterns out over the sides as they scoured the dark water.

"Aye," Jherek replied. The pulling sensation inside him was growing, accompanied by an increased anxiety to get there.

"What direction?"

The young sailor listened, but the mournful moaning seemed to come from everywhere.

"I don't know," Jherek mumbled, frustration chafing at him.

Tarnar approached him and spoke soft enough that his words didn't carry. "Close your eyes, my friend. If this is a message for you, as you believe, it will be made known to you."

Filled with tense doubt, Jherek closed his eyes. The moaning continued to echo around him, faint and distant. He couldn't guess in what direction it truly lay.

He shook his head and said, "It doesn't help."

"That's because you're still listening with your ears," Tarnar said patiently. "Listen with your heart, Jherek, not your head, not your body. Breathe out slowly. Relax."

Jherek exhaled, concentrating on the sound.

"Your heart," Tarnar said, "not your ears. You're still trying to listen with your ears."

"I can't do it," Jherek whispered hoarsely.

"You can," Tarnar told him. "Think of some other place, some other time. Get some distance between here and now. Think of a place you like to go. One that has no bad memories, no pressure."

With difficulty, Jherek imagined Madame Iitaar's house at the top of Widow's Hill in Velen. He remembered the trails he'd raced up and down while working at the shipwright's shop and living with Madame Iitaar.

Breathing out, he recalled the cool breeze that lingered under the apple tree where he'd often stood and watched the ships out in Velen's harbor. He'd spent hours there, hungering after the opportunity to put to sea again. Out in the harbor, he watched *Butterfly* pull out of port, her sails popped full of a favoring wind, knowing that he had Finaren's promise that the next time she sailed he'd be part of her crew.

Whalefriend. The voice in Jherek's mind was rusty with fatigue. *You must come as quickly as you can. Time grows short. The Taker moves more swiftly than our legends foretold. He is already on his way.*

Who are you? Jherek knew the voice wasn't the one that had been with him for the last fourteen years of his life. This wasn't the voice that told him time and time again, "Live, that you may serve."

I am called Song Who Brings Bright Rains.

What do you want?

Only to do that which I have been given to do, Jherek Whalefriend. As we all must. The voice sounded weaker, farther away, like a light growing dim in a long corridor.

You are not the one who has talked to me before.

No. I am but a piece of the tapestry that is your destiny. Another's hand has wrought it.

Who's hand?

That is not for me to say, Jherek Whalefriend. It is not yet the time of choosing. Follow, and may all your songs be strong.

When the communication ended, Jherek opened his eyes. The wind blew cold over the perspiration that covered him. He stared hard into the darkness.

"Do you know the direction?" Tarnar asked.

"East," the young sailor replied. "We need to adjust four points to starboard." He felt the direction like a compass needle.

"Make it so," Tarnar told the mate.

As soon as *Steadfast* came about on her new course, the sensation within Jherek's breast felt a little stronger.

"How far is our destination?" Tarnar asked.

"I don't know."

The captain hesitated, picking up the small lantern near the plotting desk beside the wheel. He glanced at the compass, traced a map with his finger, and said, "If we stay on this course, we're going to end up in the middle of the Alamber Sea."

"When?"

"By the day after tomorrow. That's the very heart of the sea devils' empire. I can't ask these men to go there, and I won't order them to."

"I understand," Jherek replied. "If the time comes that

you're faced with that, I'll go on alone."

Grim-faced, Tarnar folded his map and put it away. "Let's hope it doesn't come to that."

"There is another problem," Jherek said. "I was told we're not the only ones headed this way."

"Told?" For the first time, doubt showed on Tarnar's face. "Who told you this?"

"The whale who sings," Jherek replied.

The young sailor noticed the look the mate swapped with his captain and chose not to respond to it.

"Who else is supposed to be coming?" Tarnar asked.

"The Taker," Jherek said.

Confusion lit Tarnar's face in the glare from the small lantern he held. "Do you know what the Taker is?"

While Azla pursued Vurgrom, mention had been made of the Taker. In fact, some of the people the pirate captain questioned suggested that Vurgrom was somehow in league with this mythological terror.

"A story," the young sailor said. "I've heard a few legends about the Taker."

"And what if this thing is real?"

The possibility seemed overwhelming to Jherek. His life was troubled enough.

"How could the Taker be real?" he asked. "The Taker is a legend. No one has ever seen him."

"If you have spoken to a whale," Tarnar said, "then you know someone must have. Whales never lie."

XVI

2 Eleasias, the Year of the Gauntlet

Follow me more closely, little malenti, Iakhovas ordered as they swam through the currents around Vahaxtyl. *I would not have the princes know we are divided in any way.*

Laaqueel obeyed reluctantly, drawing two feet closer to Iakhovas. The sahuagin princes of Aleaxtis had sent warriors to escort them from *Tarjana*. The great galley sat at anchor above the ruined city. All around them, the whale song echoed.

No one in the sahuagin city seemed happy to see Iakhovas return.

How easily they forget, Iakhovas commented as they swam to the amphitheater. During their absence, the princes ordered the amphitheater cleared so meetings could once again be held there.

Crews of sahuagin women and children still labored to clear the city of debris, but Laaqueel knew the area would never be fit to live in again. Black chunks, shelves, and mountains of cooled lava covered the place where the city had once been. Here and there were pockets, mostly intact, that left a few landmarks to distinguish where proud

Vahaxtyl once stood. Warriors stood guard and foraged for food to feed the populace.

The ringed seats around the amphitheater were only a quarter full but there were still thousands seated. The three surviving sahuagin princes stood in the center of the mosaic of black and gray stones. Fully four dozen guardsmen flanked them, outnumbering the warriors Iakhovas had brought four to one.

Iakhovas sank easily before the princes and stood to his full height.

As the malenti priestess gazed around, she saw that the princes were accompanied by their priestesses as well. Evidently it was hoped that all of their combined power might stand against Iakhovas's might.

Panic sailed through Laaqueel as she looked at the full-blooded sahuagin priestesses. They stood in stark contrast to Laaqueel.

Relax, the feminine voice whispered in her mind. *Make no untoward moves. For now, let Iakhovas have his way.*

Laaqueel glanced at Iakhovas, but his attention was on the princes.

"Honored Ones," Iakhovas addressed them. His voice boomed, carrying easily throughout the amphitheater.

Ruubuuiz, as most senior among the three princes, strode forward. He planted his webbed feet flat on the amphitheater floor and held his trident beside him. The prince wore his best combat harness, adorned with sigils representing Sekolah as well as his own station. Made of soft gold and adorned with finger bones taken from enemies as well as bits of fire coral, his crown gleamed.

"You have journeyed safely," Ruubuuiz stated.

"I have journeyed on a true sahuagin warrior's path," Iakhovas countered with a warning edge in his voice. "I have left broken enemies in my wake, feasted upon them that I might maintain my strength, eaten of my fallen brothers that they might forever stay with me, and created currents that will send all of our enemies cringing in fear."

Ruubuuiz shifted uncertainly.

"I came back here," Iakhovas roared, "to lead the army you were supposed to have readied in my absence. Instead, I find you and your people grubbing around the corpse of this city long after the marrow is gone."

Laaqueel held herself proudly, listening to the words Iakhovas spoke. Confusion vibrated inside her. As Iakhovas had stated, he moved more truly along the currents a sahuagin would, and he gave voice to thoughts only a sahuagin would have. She felt proud and shamed and conflicted all at once. How could he, who Laaqueel knew was not a sahuagin, be better at playing one of her kind than she was?

"Our people were not meant to live as carrion feeders," Iakhovas yelled. "In the days after the destruction of this city, you princes teach your people the way to live their lives. In turn will they teach their children. Now is not the time to be cautious."

"Now is not the time to foolishly throw away the lives of our warriors," Ruubuuiz countered. "We must rebuild, and—"

"While you are rebuilding," Iakhovas accused, "you're going to allow the sea elves and mermen time to rebuild the Sharksbane Wall. You might as well help lay the stones yourself."

"Carefully," Ruubuuiz growled, flaring his fins and puffing up his chest angrily. "Your words here this day will not be forgotten."

"I will have my priestess put them in a singing bundle for you to remember always," Iakhovas declared, referring to the strings of shells, rocks, and knots tied to bone or sinew rings that the sahuagin used as books.

Iakhovas turned to look at the amphitheater seats and called out, "I did not come to Serôs to free you only so you could trap yourselves again. The wall is broken, a world lies in wait out there to feel the caress of your claws and mighty teeth. Are you predators or prey?"

The crowd rose from their seats, clacking their claws against each other, shaking their tridents and spears. They hooted, whistled, and clicked their support of his words. Thousands made the cacophony almost deafening.

Iakhovas turned back to the three princes, strong and tall in triumph.

Maartaaugh stepped forward and gazed at the yelling sahuagin. "Don't be easily swayed by his words," he screamed at them. "Remember the thousands who have left this place already under his guidance, and remember that only hundreds of them have returned—or still may live."

Some of the audience's celebration died away.

"Those who fell in battle fell as true warriors should," Iakhovas rebutted. "With their claws in an enemy's heart or their teeth in an enemy's throat. Through me, they got the chance to die with nobility rather than live out their days behind a sea elf's wall."

Cheering started again, but it wasn't as loud as before. Laaqueel knew it was because there was a lot of truth in Maartaaugh's words. She eyed the other priestesses. Laaqueel knew that if Iakhovas fell out of favor suddenly, or made himself appear the slightest bit weak in the eyes of the sahuagin, the priestesses would kill her first, then turn on him. Their obvious resentment of her spurred her on, overcoming her own reluctance to champion Iakhovas. Her own dignity and self-worth was at risk.

Laaqueel strode forward imperiously, letting her anger bury any hesitation she felt about her actions. Every eye focused on her—she was so different from both the outer sea and Serôsian sahuagin.

"You shame me," she accused the priestesses.

"N'Tel'Quess," one of the priestesses snarled. She touched the holy symbol of Sekolah hanging over her ridged chest and threw out a hand.

Laaqueel braced herself, summoning her own powers. She felt the spell tingle over her body as she clasped the holy symbol hanging between her bare breasts. The tingle went away and the priestess who'd attacked her burst into green flames.

The priestess swam from the others, trying to escape the blaze that consumed her. The water boiled around her, giving off terrible heat that coasted on the currents sweeping over Laaqueel. The malenti priestess watched in quiet shock as white foam from the boiling sea water and green flames consumed the priestess. Seconds later, the priestess's blackened bones drifted to the amphitheater floor. Her flesh was entirely consumed.

Quiet reigned over the amphitheater.

Little malenti, Iakhovas said gently into her mind, *you have their complete and undivided attention.*

Gathering her own composure, Laaqueel saw that it was

true. Wariness gleamed in the black eyes of the priestesses before her.

"You, who are supposed to be the backbone of Sekolah's worship in your tribes, baronies, and kingdom," Laaqueel accused, "choose to be silent about Sekolah's teachings in this time of greatest need."

"Not true," one of the oldest priestesses stated.

Two of the sharks circling overhead under the control of sahuagin warriors broke ranks. Before anyone could say anything in warning, the predators ripped into the Serôsian priestess.

The first shark chewed the priestess's face from her skull in passing while the other disemboweled her. The sharks returned to their positions overhead.

Laaqueel glanced at Iakhovas.

It's no work of mine, little malenti. His human face, when she saw it, even held a trace of suspicious hostility.

Laaqueel had no doubt that he'd taken part in neither attack. It was something else, something divine. She was certain of it. Feeling more confident, she returned her attention to the priestesses.

"If you don't live and teach as the Great Shark would have you," Laaqueel preached, "live in fear of Sekolah's wrath. As always, the weak will be culled from true warriors. So shall it be for the priestesses who stand in the way of the path the Shark God has chosen."

With fierce gazes and open hatred, the priestesses bowed their heads in acknowledgment.

Savage pride burned through Laaqueel. As she took her place at Iakhovas's side, she held her head high.

You've acquitted yourself well, little malenti, Iakhovas sent her, *though I'd like to speak on this matter later, and at greater length. We are still not out of danger here.*

Even that did not dissuade Laaqueel from the joy she felt. Sekolah had defended her, stepping in and destroying the priestesses who challenged her. It was unheard of.

"Warriors make war," Iakhovas roared. "Leaders lead." He spun slowly in the amphitheater, his arms thrust straight out and his claws fully extended. "When I first arrived here, I declared myself as your deliverer, the one who would set you free. I have not done that yet."

Laaqueel glanced at the princes as they conferred

among themselves. They knew where Iakhovas was headed as well as she did. There was nothing they could do to prevent it.

"I tore down the Sharksbane Wall," Iakhovas said. "I opened a path to the outer Serôsian world, to the seas the surface worlders depend on."

Clicks and whistles of agreement echoed around the amphitheater.

"But I failed to truly set you free," Iakhovas went on. "I left, handling errands of my own, taking the first steps to build We Who Eat a conflagration that would end the empires of our enemies, to leave them broken and shattered in our wake. I will not fail you again. I will be the king that you deserve, the one who will make savage warriors of you all in name and in deed."

The shrill sahuagin applause rippled across the amphitheater, growing steadily.

"No!"

The hoarse shout rang over the amphitheater. Laaqueel felt the movement along her lateral lines. She turned and found Maartaaugh striding toward Iakhovas.

"You will not be king here," Maartaaugh swore. "You are not from our sea. You are not of our heritage. You will not usurp our waters."

Silence immediately filled the waters as the sahuagin audience waited to see what would happen. Only the throbbing crescendo of the whale song continued unabated.

"Would you die then, Maartaaugh?" Iakhovas asked. "Would you challenge me and lose your life as Toomaaek did, unable to even fight for your people or the place they deserve in Serôs?"

Maartaaugh slammed the butt of his trident against the inset stones that made up the amphitheater's floor.

"I will not die," the prince said. "Aleaxtis will have one of its own as king."

"I would kill you," Iakhovas stated flatly. "I would rend your flesh from your bones and feed it to those you claim to lead."

"That remains to be seen."

Maartaaugh's courage held him despite the carnage he had seen Iakhovas do.

Laaqueel felt the tension in the water, could feel Maartaaugh's heart beating rapidly through her lateral lines. Surely Sekolah's will would be served now.

"If you wish to dispute my right to the throne," Iakhovas said in a soft, deadly voice, "then I will name the challenge."

Maartaaugh nodded.

Iakhovas swung to the crowd. "In order to prove my worth—to become your king, to take upon myself the right to lead you in your greatest battle—I will slay the Great Whale Bard who even now blocks passage through the Sharksbane Wall."

Excited conversation started up again.

"If I can't do what I say," Iakhovas went on, "then let me die as Sekolah would have me: clawing at the face of an enemy." With noble grace, he spun back around to Maartaaugh. "If you wish, I will give you the honor of trying to slay the Great Whale Bard first."

"No," Maartaaugh replied in a quiet voice.

"Then agree to my terms," Iakhovas said. "If I kill the Great Whale Bard and end the threat of the whale song that attacks this place, you will recognize me as king and serve as my grand champion, to renounce and combat any who would attack or challenge me."

Maartaaugh hesitated only a moment, and Laaqueel knew it was because the warrior tried to find a loophole in Iakhovas's offer.

"I will," the prince answered.

"Good," Iakhovas said.

"When will you attempt this?" Ruubuuiz asked.

"Now," Iakhovas said. "There is a war to be fought, and I will tolerate no waiting."

He turned and leaped away, pausing when he was twenty feet above the amphitheater floor.

Laaqueel swam up beside him, seeing him totally in the sahuagin illusion now. He was a proud warrior, his fins flared out and his chest puffed up, gripping the trident in one fist and his crown seated on his broad head. One eye held a golden gleam.

"I am Iakhovas!" he roared. "I am destined to be your king!"

The sahuagin crowd exploded into movement. They slapped their feet against the stones and whistled and clicked in full support. There were even comments from some that Iakhovas was Daganisoraan, the greatest sahuagin warrior of all, reborn.

"Iakhovas!" some of them began to chant. "Defender and king! Iakhovas!"

"I will bring you victory!" Iakhovas declared. "Meat is meat!"

"Meat is meat!" the crowd roared back.

* * * * *

"It looks like they're waiting for something," Sabyna said.

She kept a low profile on the hill overlooking the stretch of coastline below her.

"Something," Glawinn replied, "or someone."

The paladin lay beside her on the hard, rocky ground. He wore hunter's leather instead of his armor and carried his sword in a plain scabbard.

"They could be waiting for Vurgrom to join them," Azla added. She lay in the tall grass on the other side of the paladin, the spyglass they'd been sharing pulled tight to her eye. "Or perhaps they're putting in to harbor for a few days to join him at a later time."

Irritated at the position they'd been thrust into, Sabyna glared at the pirates. The pirate ship *Brave Wager* rested at anchor in the small, natural harbor. Her sails were furled around her masts, looking for all the world like she was an innocent merchanter taking advantage of a brief respite before sailing dangerous waters again.

Part of the crew maintained lean-tos on the shore under broad-leafed trees. Blackened pits showed where they'd roasted wild pigs and deer they'd brought back from the forest surrounding the harbor. Fishing and crabbing were plentiful as well.

Azla's charts called this island, which lay to the southwest of Agenais, either Zagrus or Kloccbarn, as if the cartographer was unable to chose one name or the other.

After Sabyna returned to *Azure Dagger* and told her story of the men she'd seen at the apothecary's, Azla continued work on the ship. When *Azure Dagger* was fit for sailing a few days later, her replaced masts securely in place and completely outfitted, they'd gone sailing, using the enchanted astrolabe as a guide.

Vurgrom's ship maintained a steady route in the sea way between the Whamite Isles and Turmish, gliding as restlessly as a shark. Even as they prepared to set an intercept course for Maelstrom, one of Azla's crew spotted *Brave Wager* in the distance.

Rather than risk getting caught between the two ships they knew of, and perhaps more, Azla decided to wait *Brave Wager* out and see if they couldn't gather more information on what Vurgrom was doing.

While they'd been in port at Agenais, stories continued flowing in from new arrivals. Sahuagin, koalinth, morkoth, and other sea species continued to raid the surface world nations and take ships. Their goal appeared to be to rid the Sea of Fallen Stars of anything that traveled over the water.

Some of the sea captains even brought news that uneasy alliances between the surface world nations were starting to unravel as realms in turn accused other realms of being involved in the sea-spawned threat. Assassins were rumored to ply their trade on and off the sea. There were still others who insisted the assassins were hired by the different aquatic races.

Trade routes and communication lanes broke down. The Sea of Fallen Stars became a battlefield, something it hadn't been in over four hundred years.

"I've got to get back to my ship," Azla announced. "There's still some trim and other work I want to see to while we're here." She passed the spyglass over to Glawinn, who thanked her for the loan. "Let me know if anything develops."

"I will, lady," the paladin promised.

Sabyna rolled up into a sitting position, still behind the brush and below the ledge so the pirates couldn't see her. She wrapped her arms around her legs and held them tightly. "I'll stay here as well."

Azla nodded. "I'll have two men spell you when it gets dark." She turned and walked away, making her way carefully down the hillside.

Wanting to take advantage of the waning sunlight, Sabyna took out her book of spells and spent time trying to study. Glawinn lay across the ridge, as calm and still as any animal that made its home in the forest. The ship's mage found that irritating.

"Is something wrong, lady?"

"I want to know Jherek is all right." It had been nearly two tendays since she'd last seen him.

"You can look to your own heart for that."

"So you say."

"Trust me, lady. When you feel as drawn to someone as you do to the young warrior, you'll know when something happens to him."

"How do you know?"

"Because it has happened to me."

Startled and embarrassed at her own thoughtlessness, Sabyna glanced up at the paladin. His dark eyes were filled with old pain that time failed to erase.

"I'm sorry," she said.

"As am I." Glawinn returned his attention to the spyglass and said, "Sometimes, in order to love fully and completely, you have to let the other go. When they return, you'll find the bond between you is even stronger."

"I don't know that he will be back. There seems to be so much distance between us."

"Trust," Glawinn urged. "It's all you can do."

"I prefer a much more active solution."

"Then study, lady, that you may get better at your own skills," the paladin suggested. "Wherever you go, however this may turn out between you and the young warrior, you need to be as strong as you can be."

Reluctantly, Sabyna took out her book again and applied herself to her studies. Still, she felt as though she were on the edge of the world, peering down into a bottomless abyss.

"We've not seen the worst of this yet, have we?" she asked.

"No," Glawinn replied softly. "No, lady, I'm afraid we haven't."

* * * * *

Laaqueel stood on *Tarjana*'s deck and stared at the Great Whale Bard. The creature floated in the currents before the broken section of the Sharksbane Wall, flanked by other whales. The great whale was over four hundred feet long from its blunt head to its tail flukes. Gray-blue skin stood out against the blue-green sea so it looked more like a shadow than a solid thing. The whale song continued to echo in shrill squeaks and moans around Hunter's Ridge

He knows you're coming, she told Iakhovas when he joined her.

Of course he does. Iakhovas looked at her and grinned. *Can't you smell the fear on him, little malenti?*

Laaqueel said nothing. She couldn't smell fear from the great whale, but she sensed the anticipation from the sahuagin who ringed the mountains around her. Not far away, Maartaaugh and Ruubuuiz stood together, out of safe crossbow shot from the few sea elves that still manned the makeshift garrison.

Iakhovas held a harpoon in one fist. The thick shaft bore runes etched in black. The metal blade gleamed as though a fresh edge had just been put on it.

Why didn't you challenge Maartaaugh and be done with it? Laaqueel asked. *You could have beaten him easily.*

Little malenti, Iakhovas said patiently, *there is still much you have to learn when it comes to leading warriors. In Waterdeep, though our forces were turned away, we killed many of our enemies, destroyed their boats, and burned their buildings and homes. Though it was a loss in some respects, I taught We Who Eat of the Claarteeros Sea that they could win. They knew before that they could fight the surface world, but never before had they known they could win.*

The whale song continued unabated, throbbing through the water, racing with the currents. It was hard for Laaqueel to stand there and take the whale's abuse. A few of the sahuagin who came from Vahaxtyl to watch succumbed to the whale song's thrall and returned to their city.

Once I gave them that, Iakhovas continued, *Baldur's Gate could not stand against them. The Great Whale Bard will be Serôs' Waterdeep. It will teach these warriors here that anything is possible, and it will give notice to the sea elves and others that would stand in our way.* He grinned, and his golden eye gleamed. *What other creature can sing its death song the length and breadth of the Sea of Fallen Stars?*

170

Iakhovas signaled to one of the sahuagin warriors in *Tarjana*'s stern. The warrior started beating the drum brought up from belowdecks. The basso booms echoed through the water, partially masking the whale song.

The sahuagin warriors aboard the mudship picked up the rhythm, slapping their webbed feet against the deck, creating hollow detonations that amplified the frenetic beat. Within the space of a few heartbeats, the sahuagin warriors along Hunter's Ridge picked up the rhythm as well, slapping their hands and feet against the ocean floor or banging rocks together.

Wish me well, little malenti.

Iakhovas leaped off the mudship. His illusion as a sahuagin warrior for the moment was complete. Not even Laaqueel could tell he was anything else.

He swam strongly, straight for the waiting whales as if propelled by the savage beat of the sahuagin. The long harpoon stayed close at his side.

Just over the broken section of the Sharksbane Wall, unchallenged by the sea elves who knew they were not his targets, Iakhovas halted in the water. He was less than a hundred feet from the Great Whale Bard.

"I am Iakhovas!" he roared. "And I will be your death!"

He swam straight at the great whale like a crossbow bolt.

XVII

2 Eleasias, the Year of the Gauntlet

Confusion consumed Laaqueel's thoughts as she watched Iakhovas close on the Great Whale Bard. The confrontation with the priestesses of Vahaxtyl weighed heavily on her mind. The closest Sekolah came to involving himself in his children's worship of him was when he sent avatars to inspire their blood frenzy, and that almost never happened.

Though she believed Iakhovas when he said he played no part in the matter, she couldn't help questioning whether her defense had come from Sekolah. She couldn't answer why the Shark God would choose to defend a malenti priestess. Malenti birth was only a sign that the sahuagin lived too close to the sea elves, their sworn enemies. There was nothing positive about being a malenti, nothing in their scriptures to suggest that Sekolah would show any kind of special interest.

Her line of thinking pointed her back to Iakhovas. Either he had engineered the priestesses' deaths and gotten away with lying to her, or he was as important to Sekolah's bloody designs as he said he was. Laaqueel's faith was torn in both directions. She was afraid to believe

172

and fool herself, and afraid not to believe and take away the last vestiges of herself she had left, trapped by her own need for understanding.

She stood on *Tarjana*'s deck amid the sahuagin warriors as they kept up the frantic rhythm and watched Iakhovas approach the Great Whale Bard.

The whale song boomed through the water, partially obscured by the throbbing sahuagin beat. The Great Whale Bard shifted only slightly to face his approaching foe.

Taker.

The whale's voice rolled like thunder through Laaqueel's mind. From the way the sahuagin stopped slapping their hands and feet and rocks, the malenti priestess knew they'd all heard it too.

"Death," Iakhovas snarled, not slowing his pace toward the giant creature. The great whale was nearly fifty times bigger than Iakhovas.

There is only belief. High Priestess Ghaataag had told Laaqueel that when the young malenti was first accepted into Sekolah's temple. Belief made a priestess strong, while knowledge took strength away. Never before had Laaqueel so fully understood that insight.

Two killer whales raced for Iakhovas. Their black and white bodies sped through the water, cutting across currents more swiftly even than sahuagin could swim. Iakhovas swam straight for them, never veering from the Great Whale Bard.

At the last moment, Iakhovas shifted, diving below the lead killer whale. He dragged his harpoon's edge along the killer whale's underside, splitting it open and gutting it in a bloody rush that fogged the water. Iakhovas disappeared, lost in the dark red haze.

When he burst through the bloody mist on the other side, the sahuagin warriors broke out in lusty cheers. They slapped the ocean floor with their feet and clapped their hands again, finding the savage rhythm of a raging heart.

Silently, Laaqueel prayed that Sekolah would take Iakhovas from them, prayed that the Shark God would allow the whales their victory, prayed that she would know now if Iakhovas was savior or slayer to her people.

The second killer whale finned around and streaked for Iakhovas again as sharks broke the tethers of their sahuagin masters and dived for the floating corpse of the first. Iakhovas turned once more, quickly overtaken by the killer whale. He dodged it, bumping his chest against his opponent's sleek underbelly. Iakhovas hooked the claws of his free hand into the exposed flesh, followed almost immediately by his foot claws.

Latched onto the killer whale like a barnacle, Iakhovas ripped through its flesh and pierced its heart. Convulsions wracked the killer whale as Iakhovas leaped from it toward the Great Whale Bard.

Other whales surged forward protectively.

Stay back, the Great Whale Bard ordered. *This has already been writ. We have done what we could. Those of you who can escape alive must do so.*

Reluctantly, the other whales ceased moving.

The Time of Tempering has come then, the massive voice proclaimed, *but you will not have everything you seek, Taker.*

"I will!" Iakhovas roared. "It will all be mine again!"

No. For all your plans and machinations, there is one you did not count on, one whom you could not know of.

Laaqueel felt the certainty of the Great Whale Bard's words in her mind.

"You lie!" Iakhovas screamed.

He reached the Great Whale Bard and slashed with his harpoon, driving it deep into the creature's blunt snout. The Great Whale Bard screamed in agony, disrupting the whale song. The other whales tried to continue, but without the Great Whale Bard to lead them and tie their voices together, the mystic enchantment lost most of its power. Laaqueel felt the change. The stomach-twisting nausea left her.

Still roaring in savage rage, Iakhovas dragged the harpoon free, tearing a large wound in the great whale's snout. The creature tried to move to avoid its attacker or to strike back, Laaqueel wasn't sure, but it moved far too slowly to escape Iakhovas's wrath. The harpoon buried into the great whale's flesh again and again, releasing clouds of blood into the water.

Even as she prayed, Laaqueel knew there could be no other end to the battle. With the blood in the water, not all the details of the fight were visible, but the malenti

174

priestess watched as Iakhovas hooked his claws into the Great Whale Bard's side and clambered up to the top of its head.

The frenetic beat of webbed feet against stone and mud continued throbbing through the waters surrounding Hunter's Ridge. None of the elves dared leave their garrisons, and less of them were visible now.

Still hooked into the whale's flesh, Iakhovas pulled himself to the top of the head. He located the great whale's blowhole and shoved himself down inside. The creature continued to swim, but its movements quickly grew weaker. Blood fountained from the blowhole in increasing volume, like smoke from a surface worlder's campfire. The Great Whale Bard screamed in denial and fear. The sound echoed through the sea, and Laaqueel knew that Iakhovas had been right: the Great Whale Bard's death would undoubtedly be heard throughout all of Serôs.

The great whale's tail drooped, no longer moving. Only then did Laaqueel notice that the other whales were in full retreat. Their song had stopped.

The huge corpse turned slowly, like a ship combating an unfavorable wind. Incredibly, the small jaw hinged to the bottom of the huge blunt head opened. Blood spewed out in a violent rush, revealing the massive damage that had been dealt to the creature's insides.

When the currents washed the blood away, Iakhovas stood revealed, levering the jaw open by pushing against the whale's upper jaw. Still holding the Great Whale Bard's jaw open, he screamed defiantly, "I am *Iakhovas!* I am your king!"

The sahuagin warriors screamed with him, defiant and exhilarated.

"Meat is meat!" Iakhovas yelled. "Come eat of the feast I have laid before you!"

The sahuagin surged forward, filling the water as they streamed through the broken section of the Sharksbane Wall. They descended on the Great Whale Bard's corpse like carrion crabs.

Laaqueel stayed on *Tarjana*'s deck. She knew her absence among their ranks wouldn't go unnoticed, but she had no heart to join them. All she felt inside was a curious emptiness.

"All hail King Iakhovas the Deliverer!" one of the sahuagin warriors shouted as the feeding frenzy filled the ocean with blood. The other warriors took up the shout, and the sound filled the currents. They slapped their hands and feet against the whale's corpse, finding the savage rhythm again.

Laaqueel wrapped her hand around the white shark symbol that lay between her breasts and prayed. She found no comfort in an act that used to come so naturally to her.

* * * * *

"Aye, an' there's trouble afoot, friend Pacys."

Drawn from his work on the saceddar, the old bard glanced up at the dwarf. Khlinat's face was grim and hard. The last sweet notes from the saceddar died away.

"What is it?" the bard asked.

Khlinat pointed forward with his bearded chin and said, "It appears we've run afoul of a war party of mermen. They're refusing to let us pass through."

"Why?"

Pacys uncoiled from the flat rock on the sea bottom where he'd been working while the caravan took a brief respite. They'd crossed the outer edges of the Hmur Plateau a couple days back. At present, they were only a few miles east of the Pirate Isles.

"I'm figurin' the merfolk don't exactly take to what looks like a military group paradin' through their land. At least, that's the gist of what I heard afore I decided to come back for ye."

"What does Reefglamor say?" Pacys asked, securing the saceddar to his back.

"A whole lot," the dwarf replied, "but ain't none of it doing him any good. Him and that merman baron are both puffing up like toads. Me, I'm keeping a ready hand for me axe."

The old bard launched himself into the water, and Khlinat followed him. Pacys swam easily, making his way along the caravan line to the front. Undersea mountains around the Pirate Isles made their journey hard even for swimmers. Bands of raiding seawolves and scrags had attacked them during the nights, costing them nearly a dozen warriors before they were turned back. The mountains created too many potential ambush points, but the deeper water toward the center of the Hmur Plateau offered dangers as well. The depths also shortened even the sea elves' undersea vision to but a few feet.

The sea elf rangers among the caravan saw to the care of the narwhals and sea turtles that pulled the flat supply sleds. The warriors formed protective units around the steep hills, stationed in positions that allowed them to see in all directions.

Even with the bright sunlight streaming through the shallows, Pacys didn't see Reefglamor and the mermen until he was a hundred feet away. Twenty warriors floated behind the merman baron with their tridents in their fists.

Reefglamor stood on a small rise in front of the baron, "You must let us pass," he said.

"No." The merman baron studied Pacys as the bard approached. His tone turned derisive. "You even brought humans with you."

"This is not an ordinary human," Reefglamor argued. "This is the Taleweaver. Your people have legends of the Taker . . ."

"Yes."

The baron didn't appear convinced. He was broad and muscled. His long brown hair floated over his shoulders, following the path of the currents that swept over the area. Tattoos covered his arms and chest, and a spiral representing Eadro decorated his right cheek.

"Then you've heard of the Taleweaver, Baron Tallos," Reefglamor persisted.

The baron narrowed his eyes. "Those tales have been twice-told hundreds of times over," he argued. "I choose not to believe in them as much as some of my people do."

"Then your arrogance lends itself to ignorance," Reefglamor accused.

Tallos flicked his tail in irritation and shot a hand out to adjust his momentum. "Swim carefully in these waters, old fins," he warned.

The old sea elf drew himself up to his full height. "I am Taranath Reefglamor, Senior High Mage of Sylkiir."

"I was told who you are," the baron snapped. "Yet you still stand before me on two legs, sea elf, and I tell you that no one not blessed by Eadro with fins and a tail is a true creature of Serôs. Your people migrated here out of their own fear and prejudice. We have always been here."

Rage darkened the High Mage's features. At his side, Pharom Ildacer moved forward. Even as the merman warriors reacted by dropping their tridents toward the sea elves, Reefglamor placed a hand on his friend's chest. Ildacer stopped reluctantly.

"We only want to travel to Myth Nantar," Reefglamor said. "We must see to it that the Taleweaver arrives there safely."

"Not across my lands." Tallos glared at the old bard. "I'll not have a sea elf army moving through my city, or anywhere near it."

"We travel for the good of Serôs," Reefglamor protested. "If we don't stand against the Taker, all of our world may fall."

"The good of Serôs," Tallos echoed. "As I recall, the Alu'Tel'Quessir have long held that as a reason for their attempts to take over all of Serôs. How many have died as your people have tried to force their will on others? The Eleventh Serôs War was fought over the same beliefs. Well, we don't hold forth those beliefs. We don't even presume to know what's best for Serôs. We take care of our own, and life in these waters would be far better if others took care to do the same."

Reefglamor had no reply, visibly stung by the merman's hard tone and words.

"Myth Nantar was another vessel of sea elven conspiracy," Tallos continued. "Better it should remain buried behind the mythal that binds it than to return to this world."

"Prophecy has declared that the City of Destinies is the place where the Taker might be destroyed," Reefglamor said.

"So say you, elf."

"Your people have those prophecies as well."

"Mayhap you'd be surprised how few of my people are willing to trust the Alu'Tel'Quessir these days."

Reefglamor shook his head. "Unrest and strife stir the waters and echo on the currents," he said. "The sahuagin are once more free to roam all of Serôs. Surely you've noticed this."

"I've heard," Tallos answered coldly. "I've also heard that it was the sea elves themselves who shattered the Sharksbane Wall."

"Why in all the seas would we have done that?"

"Because to get to you, the sahuagin must first run through the Hmur Plateau—where the mermen live," the merman accused.

"Your King Vhaemas can't believe that."

"The king," Tallos admitted, "is more reluctant than some, but all are aware that there is no love lost between the sea elves and the merfolk."

"This is bigger than the animosity that lies between our people," Reefglamor said.

"If it were," Tallos countered, "wouldn't Coronal Semphyr or Cormal Ytham have sent you with more troops? Or approached our king first to request passage through our lands?"

"They, too, are blind to the dangers we face."

Tallos regarded the old mage, then said, "If your own people don't believe in you and your journey, why should I?"

"Because it is the truth," Reefglamor said.

"Not my truth."

Without another word, Reefglamor turned and motioned his warriors and fellow mages back.

"What will we do?" Jhanra Merlistar asked.

"We have no choice," Reefglamor answered. "We'll have to go around the plateau, along the western edge."

"That's insane," Ildacer stated harshly. "Those waters are filled with koalinth tribes who would waste no time attacking us. Only fools would swim there."

"The only other choice would be to head to the east and go through the deeper waters there," Reefglamor offered.

"Senior," the chief guardsman said, "I would prefer—"

"As would I," Reefglamor snapped irritably. "We're in agreement that the depths are too dangerous. We will go around to the west. Have someone inform your warriors and the caravan leaders."

Pacys thought about the proposed journey. It would add tendays, perhaps as much as a month to their time. That was just not acceptable. Yet, as he looked at the merman baron's hard face, he knew the decision would stand.

Both the sea elves and the mermen turned suddenly toward the south, their weapons falling naturally into their hands. Pacys prepared himself, wondering what it was they sensed. His eyes revealed nothing but the murky water that took away his vision. All at once the currents swirling around him became a wave that rocked him.

Behind the wave came the death cry of the Great Whale Bard. Hearing it, the old bard knew it belonged to no other. Tears welled in his eyes as he remembered the great creature and the gift it had given so freely while calmly accepting its own fate.

"Taleweaver?" Reefglamor called out, swimming toward him. "What was that?"

"The sahuagin have slain the Great Whale Bard," Pacys replied. "Now there is nothing to hold back the sea devils."

* * * * *

Standing in *Steadfast*'s prow, his cutlass in his hands, Jherek stared at the huge, dark cloud that rode low over the ocean. The ship was ahead of the cloud, only a few miles southwest of Aglarond. The whale song stopped abruptly the day before, but the sense of direction that had dawned in the young sailor's breast remained constant.

He shaded his eyes with his hand. Perspiration cooled him in the sea breeze as his heart resumed a steadier beat. He'd worked himself hard the last hour, concentrating on the cutlass and hook as he went through the exercises Malorrie and Glawinn had shown him. The exertion kept his thoughts reined in, away from the memory of Sabyna and the sweet kiss they'd exchanged.

Tarnar ran up the steps, joining him. "I thought at first it was a cloud," the captain said, "but I'd never seen one settle so close to the sea and be so small. Thought it might be fog, then I thought perhaps it was a sail."

"No," Jherek said, tracking the jerky, fluttering movement visible within the mass now. "Those are birds. Scavengers." Even as he realized it, his stomach lurched and filled with cold acid.

Bringing his spyglass up to his eye, Tarnar swept the sky ahead. "You're right, but I've never seen so many."

Jherek hadn't either. Thousands of seagulls, pelicans,

fisherhawks, and smaller birds skirled through the limited air space above the sea, eagerly seeking an opening. During a voyage on *Butterfly* last year, Finaren had spied a derelict at sea. Upwind of her, Jherek hadn't smelled the carrion stench of the ship until they'd thrown grappling hooks over the railing and prepared to tie on.

Birds had exploded from the decks and broken windows, frightened from the grisly repast they'd helped themselves to. The young sailor had never learned the reason why the crew had killed each other, but there was no doubt that they had. Finaren had guessed that some mage-inspired madness or a curse had overtaken them. No one had lived. For tendays afterward, Jherek remembered the bloated and beak-stripped faces in his nightmares.

"It means there's death waiting up there," the young sailor said hoarsely.

Tarnar didn't bother to disagree.

"Cap'n," the sailor in the crow's nest bellowed. "Got something off the starboard side."

Jherek stepped to the railing, the cutlass still tight in his fist. A sapphire whale, named for the blue flukes it bore, surfaced in the water only a few yards from *Steadfast*. Twenty feet long and easily eight feet in diameter at its thickest part, the sapphire whale could have been a formidable opponent for the caravel. It glided easily just above the water, making no move toward the ship.

"Lady look over us," the sailor in the crow's nest called out, "there are more of 'em out there, Cap'n."

As though appearing from nowhere, the whales rose to the ocean's surface, quickly flanking *Steadfast*'s port and starboard sides.

"They want us to stop," Jherek said.

"They've given us no choice," Tarnar growled. He turned and shouted orders to the first mate to drop their canvas. "The good thing is, if they wanted to, they could have already reduced *Steadfast* to so much kindling. I'm taking this as a good sign."

The caravel drifted to a stop, resting easily against the whales' broad backs. Tarnar gave the order to drop anchor. Crewmen spun the anchor chain on the drum, paying out the length.

Jherek peered across the hundred yards that separated

the ship from the cloud of scavengers working at the water-line. They looked as though they were settling on a small island barely jutting up from the sea.

Tarnar put his spyglass in the sash at his waist and walked cautiously to the railing to peer down at the whales. Porpoises raced through the water around the whales, occasionally leaping up and disappearing beneath the waves again.

"What do they want?" the captain asked.

Jherek shook his head, then a ghostly whisper trickled through his mind. *Jherek, you must come with us.* The voice wasn't the same as the one that had contacted him days ago.

"They want me," the young sailor said.

"How do you know?" Tarnar demanded.

"They just told me."

The captain looked at him as if he'd gone mad.

"You can't hear them?" Jherek asked, amazed that the man could not.

"No."

Jherek, there is not much time remaining. You must accompany us.

Fear and wonderment touched the young sailor's heart. Even days ago when he'd felt the pull and heard the whale song and the voice, he hadn't been as moved. Gazing out at the scavenging birds, he felt the world close in around him.

"Why do they want you?" Tarnar asked.

"I don't know," the young sailor answered.

The sapphire whale swam alongside the caravel, bumping gently up against it. *Steadfast* bobbed in response.

Come, Jherek Whalefriend. Come and learn.

The young sailor peered down into the whale's eye, seeing the intelligence there.

"What are you going to do?" Tarnar asked.

Jherek clung to the railing, squinting against the wind in his face. "We have no choice. I don't think they'll let the ship proceed unless I find out what they want."

Tarnar was quiet for a moment. "If you go into that water, you're taking your life in your own hands."

"Aye." Jherek nodded.

"We're carrying Cormyrean dried pepper seasoning as part of our cargo," Tarnar said. "I can have the men ready the ship and dump a few pepper barrels into the water. It'll burn those whales—chase them away and give us a chance to run. The wind favors us."

"No." Jherek bent and pulled his boots off. "We've come all this way following the whale song. To try to leave without finding out where it led would be a waste of our time."

"Then I'll come with you."

"And leave *Steadfast* without her captain?" Jherek gazed at the man. "What kind of decision would that be?"

Tarnar looked out to sea. "You're talking to a failed priest, Jherek," he said. "If these creatures aren't here for your life, then this has got to be some kind of . . . divine experience. I wouldn't want to miss out on that."

Alone, the voice whispered into Jherek's mind. He repeated the request to the captain.

Tarnar clearly wasn't happy with the stipulation. His face hardened. "Go then, but I'm not going to leave you out here on your own."

"Weigh the risk if it comes to that," Jherek said softly. "One man isn't worth your ship and crew."

"Mystra keep you in her graces." Tarnar offered his arm. Jherek took the captain's hand and shook it. Barefoot now, his dagger sheathed to one leg and the cutlass through the sash at his waist, he stepped over the railing and dropped into the sea. He hit feet first and slid through the blue-green water. From under the surface, where the largest portion of the whale's mass was, the creature looked even bigger.

No fear, the whale urged him, bumping up against him with her rough body. *You are the one to be known as Whale-friend.*

Why?

We will explain what we may. Please, climb on my back and I will save you the swim. The whale sunk lower in the water and came close enough to Jherek that they touched.

Hesitantly, the young sailor hooked his fingers over the sapphire whale's dorsal fin and pulled himself aboard. Jherek didn't look back, concentrating on the birds before him.

The whale swam swiftly, skimming along the ocean's surface while the other whales and dolphins opened the path. As they neared the mass in the sea, the cries of the feathered scavengers reached a crescendo, a vibrant clamoring of hunger and rage. The young sailor recognized the mutilated remains of the largest whale he'd ever seen.

The dead whale floated just below the surface, buoyed up in death. The sea rarely hid her dead unless they went down in ships or the scavengers got to them too quickly. Crabs scuttled across the corpse, hiding in pockets of pink-white flesh as they ate their fill and avoided the larger birds that would have eaten them as well. Fish of all sizes and colors darted about at the waterline, and Jherek knew there would be even more working the dead whale's underbelly.

An overwhelming sense of loss filled the young sailor as he surveyed the carnage. Fresh in death, the whale would float for a few days before the sea dragged it back down. Even then, it would be a long time before it was stripped down to its bones.

The sapphire whale closed on the corpse, nudging up against it tenderly. Crabs, fish, and birds fled from that small area.

This was Song Who Brings Bright Rains.

Jherek recognized the name. "What happened?"

The Taker slew him.

"Why?"

Because the whales joined together in song in an attempt to block the sahuagin from entering Serôs.

Jherek remained silent for a long moment, hardly able to think in the cacophony of sounds that filled the air. Fish bumped up against his feet and ankles in the water.

"Why have I been brought here?"

Because your coming was foretold in our legends. Song Who Brings Bright Rains had a gift he was meant to give you.

"Why?" Jherek tried desperately to understand, but he couldn't find a foundation.

You are the Whalefriend, the sapphire whale replied as if that answered everything.

"I don't understand."

We are here to help you understand, but you must claim the gift Song Who Brings Bright Rains had for you.

"Where?"

It is on the body. The Taker never suspected it was there.

184

The magic that guards it is very strong.

"All my life," Jherek said numbly, "I have heard a voice in my head at times. Was it one of your people?"

No, Whalefriend, that was another.

"Who?"

That is not for us to say. We only have our part. If you live, you will one day know all. That is all we know. Go. Get the gift that has been held for you. You have far to travel, and there is much danger for you to face.

The whale's muscles rippled along its back. Taking the hint, Jherek lifted himself from the water and stood on the animal's back. Even walking barefoot was tricky. The whale's hide was slick. His stomach cringed as he stepped onto the great whale's carcass.

The corpse's buoyancy caused it to bob under his feet. Water rushed in and swirled over his ankles, mixing with the bright red blood. Birds took wing before him, revealing even more of the ravaged flesh. The young sailor steeled his mind and made himself go forward when everything in him wanted to turn back to *Steadfast.*

"What is my destiny?" Jherek asked.

You are to be the Whalefriend.

Jherek kept going, feeling the greasy flesh twist and turn beneath his feet.

"What am I supposed to do?"

You will be a friend to our people. In times of need, you will champion us.

Jherek tried to imagine anything the whales would need him to champion for and couldn't. Anything that could kill the creature he now walked on would be far too powerful for him to combat.

You have only just begun your revelations, Jherek Whale-friend. You do not yet know what you will be.

"Then tell me."

I cannot.

For a moment, the young sailor faltered. Was this going to be another false trail? Another game played by the voice that had haunted him? Or had he been lured to his death this time?

Look to your heart for strength and you will find it, Jherek Whalefriend. You have always been much stronger than you have thought. This is one of the things Song Who

Brings Bright Rains has always told us of you.

"How did he know?"

With quiet determination, Jherek resumed his search. The sheer savagery that had torn the great whale continued unabated, and the young sailor knew the sahuagin had eaten their fill of the whale when the Taker had slain it.

He has always known. The whale bard that trained him told him, and the story came from the whale bard before him.

"They knew about *me*?" Jherek couldn't believe it.

They knew someone would come, the sapphire whale replied, *and they knew you would be recognized when the time came.*

Jherek struggled with what he was being told even as he skidded and slipped across the great whale's corpse.

"How could they know?"

The whale bards of Serôs have always been powerful in the ways of knowing. We choose to remain apart from most of those who live below and above because most ignore us. In times past, we have been ostracized for being harbingers, and even the surface folk hunted us for the ambergris. You are a sailor, Jherek Whalefriend, and you have ties to the sea. You can feel in your heart the twists and turns of wind and sea. How can you know these things?

Some of the larger birds challenged Jherek as he advanced. The young sailor drew his cutlass and used the flat of the blade to knock the more aggressive ones aside. He didn't want to kill them. The birds served a purpose in disposing of the body.

"Where is this thing I am supposed to find?"

You are looking for it. You will never find it that way. Close your eyes and feel *for it as you felt for the whale song.*

Doubt gnawed at Jherek's thoughts. He felt as though he was in a dream, that he might wake up at any moment to find himself in a hammock aboard *Steadfast.* If he'd really believed what was going on, what he was taking part in, he didn't know how he would have reacted. The numbness inside allowed him to remain focused.

The young sailor stopped and closed his eyes. It was hard to concentrate with all the angry cries of the birds around him.

Feel with your heart, Jherek Whalefriend. Your heart

will always guide you if you listen to it.

Growing frantic with frustration, Jherek tried to relax. The birds distracted him, but the feel of the dead, rubbery flesh underfoot distracted him more. Still, with everything that had happened, how could he walk away?

He felt it. The small tugging pulled at the center of his chest. He concentrated on the sensation and slowly opened his eyes. Following the tug, he shoved his way through the large, ungainly birds, shooing them into the air.

Only a few feet farther on, he dropped to his knees, knowing whatever he searched for was below him. Water occupied pockets torn from the whale's flesh, mixed with ropes of congealed blood. A few hermit crabs occupied the small pools, drawing back tightly into their borrowed shells at his approach.

"It's inside the body," the young sailor rasped.

Yes, the whale replied. *That is where Song Who Brings Bright Rains carried it, as did the whale bards before him. You must cut it out.*

Jherek surveyed the dead flesh, knowing the whale was long past any suffering. He raised the cutlass and prepared himself to drive it down into the corpse. His hands shook with the effort, then he lowered the blade.

"I can't."

The birds shrilled angrily all around him, fluttering through the air above. Feathers flew as the scavengers battled each other for access.

Place your hand on the spot where the gift is, the sapphire whale encouraged. *Perhaps there is another way. The tie between it and you is very strong.*

Hesitantly, given strength by the numbness and desire within him, Jherek placed his hand over the spot where he believed the gift to be. Vibrations tingled against his palm. For a moment he believed it was only the ocean rocking the great carcass.

Iridescent tendrils shot up from the whale flesh and encircled Jherek's left wrist. Panicked, he tried to yank his arm back. On the third attempt, the tendrils still crawling around his forearm, a silvery mass of red, crimson, scarlet, yellow, and pink tore free of the whale's body.

Do not fear, the sapphire whale encouraged. *This is the gift—nothing more.*

Unable to get away from the wriggling rainbow-colored mass shifting along his arm, Jherek stared at it. His reflection in the polished sheen stared back at him. The mass smoothed out, becoming a thick bracer that covered him from his wrist almost to his elbow. A protective cuff flared out over the back of his hand to his knuckles. The colors twisted in stripes, each leading to the other. Instead of feeling cold and heavy, the bracer felt warm and light, like another coat of skin though it was nearly an inch thick.

"What is this?" he asked.

Designs surfaced on the rainbow bracer, distinct whorls and loops that looked like nothing the young sailor had ever seen.

It is your gift, Jherek Whalefriend. A gift that makes you one of our pod, a gift that will protect you in your direst need, and it is a weapon that will serve you against the Taker. It is also the first step you must take on the path to your destiny.

Turning his attention from the shiny bracer to the sapphire whale, Jherek demanded, "What destiny?"

Again, it is not for me to say.

"I won't accept that," Jherek declared.

He pulled at the bracer, managing to get a finger down inside the tight fit along his arm. Even then he thought the bracer only allowed him to do that so he wouldn't hurt himself. As he continued to dig, the bracer turned liquid under his questing finger—for just a heartbeat—and he pulled through. The bracer flowed back together almost instantly and was solid once more.

You have no choice.

"I will always have a choice," Jherek said.

You came here. You are the one, the sapphire whale told him. *You are the Taker's Bane. Every choice you make will be right for you and for your destiny. There is no wrong way for you to go. You have only to accept the power and responsibility that will be yours.*

"And if I don't?"

That will be your choice, and it will be the right one.

Jherek looked around at the dead whale and the scavengers covering it. The birds grew bolder, hissing and crying out as they closed on him. He beat them away with the flat of his blade.

188

"I don't understand," Jherek said. "I won't accept anything without understanding it first."

You have accepted the bracer, and it has accepted you.

Jherek barely restrained his angry frustration. "There was no acceptance," he claimed. "It attached itself to me."

If it had not been time, if you had not been right, that would not have happened. Only the One may wear Iridea's Tear.

Jherek held up his arm and the sunlight glinted off the rainbow bracer.

"Is this thing alive?" he asked.

No, but it will serve to help keep you living. It will shield you and be a weapon. As you become accustomed to it, you will find that you can shape it to fit your needs. Now be silent, for we must finish the Binding.

The sapphire whale lifted its true voice in song, an ululating chorus that echoed over the water. The other whales joined in and the prickly sensation of an approaching storm blanketed the area.

Questions flooded Jherek's frenzied mind, but before he could ask the first one, blinding pain flared along his left arm where the bracer touched him. Unable to stand, he dropped to his knees, certain that someone had set his arm on fire.

He howled in agony and crawled toward the edge of the whale's carcass, scaring birds from his path. As the song continued, he reached the edge of the corpse and thrust his arm into the seawater, sure the wound he was undoubtedly suffering would kill him—or cost him his arm at the very least.

After what seemed an interminable time, the pain lessened, then went away.

Jherek drew his arm from the water expecting it to be burned clear through the flesh down to the bone. Instead, his arm seemed perfectly healthy, as if nothing had ever happened. Even the multi-colored bracer was gone.

Not gone, the sapphire whale corrected. *The Binding has been completed. You and Iridea's Tear will never be separated as long as life remains within you.*

Still on his knees, the young sailor held his bare arm up for the whale to see. Water droplets clung to his skin.

Iridea's Tear will be your badge, Jherek Whalefriend. In

189

time, you will come to be known by it. But there will be times that you won't want to be known at all. The Binding allows this to happen. Think of the bracer upon your arm.

Jherek didn't want to, but once the thought was in his mind he couldn't help remembering the image.

Crimson, scarlet, yellow, and pink strands erupted from his skin. The strands quickly wove themselves into the bracelet, again running from his wrist to his elbow, the iridescent surface showing no fractures or lines.

The bracer can be easily hidden again when you wish.

Jherek willed the bracer to go away, but it remained upon his arm.

There is much you have to learn, the sapphire whale said. *We will take time to teach you until you are ready to become.*

"Become what?" Jherek persisted.

That which you are destined to be. Nothing more, nothing less.

XVIII

8 Eleasias, the Year of the Gauntlet

"To me!"

Laaqueel heard Iakhovas's thundering battle cry over the din of war even as she twisted from the path of an attacking ixitxachitl. The malenti priestess swept the barbed net from her hip and threw it at her attacker as it spun gracefully around in the ocean.

The weighted net flared out and enveloped the ixitxachitl, sinking barbed hooks into the creature's flesh. It screamed in rage and pain. Even as the net tangled its wings, Laaqueel drove her trident deep into its body. The ixitxachitl shuddered through its death throes.

"Most Sacred One, let me be of assistance."

Turning, Laaqueel found one of the sahuagin warriors from the outer seas swimming toward her, his movements already registering on her lateral lines. Bleeding from several wounds inflicted by the ixitxachitl fangs, the sahuagin warrior offered her another net. Bits of flesh clung to the coral and steel barbs woven into the strands.

"I will strip the net from this one," the warrior offered. "King Iakhovas will have need of you. The demon rays are attempting to rally their forces."

Laaqueel accepted the net and swam for Iakhovas. She gazed around the ocean floor, studying the buildings that comprised the ixitxachitl community of Ilkanar. Ageadren was the closest ixitxachitl city, but Ilkanar was an outpost town. The tallest structure in the community was the temple, built of coral and stones by the locathah, merrow, and koalinth slaves the ixitxachitls kept.

Iakhovas stood at the forefront of the invading sahuagin forces, ripping apart his foes with trident and claws. Corpses littered the city, including ixitxachitls and the slaves who hadn't quickly chosen sides. Iakhovas's wrath was unforgiving. As the invading army rolled through the resistance put up by the demon rays, the slaves scattered in full revolt, driven before sahuagin who would kill them if they tried to flee.

The oceans' currents darkened with blood.

Even as she drifted down and took her place at Iakhovas's side, he glanced up at her. Gold gleamed in his eye socket.

"Ah, little malenti, come to join the celebration?" he said, holding a bloody chunk of dead ixitxachitl out to her.

"I came to fight at your side."

A cruel smile twisted his lips in both his human and sahuagin guises as they flickered back and forth in Laaqueel's vision.

"As you can see," he said, "there are many who believe in me these days—many ready to fight at my side. I searched for believers, little malenti, and they have found me."

Feeling the spongy surface below the layer of sand at her feet, Laaqueel drove her trident down. Blood spewed up and the ixitxachitl crouched in hiding there flapped in pain. The malenti priestess slit its belly with a talon and watched it swim away to die.

Sharks and sahuagin finned by overhead, chasing all that fled before them that weren't of their kind. It was a whirling maelstrom of slaughter, a true vision of sahuagin power and savagery the like of which Laaqueel had never seen before. By rights, by her heritage, she should have been in bliss—or in a blood frenzy as so many of her brethren were—but she wasn't.

"What about you, little malenti?" Iakhovas asked. "Why do you fight?"

"I live to serve you," she answered. Fear filled her as she gazed at him, knowing he had the power to see through her and the lies she told.

"But do you believe?" Iakhovas asked. "Do you believe in me, or do you fight only to save your own life?"

Laaqueel gazed around them, aware of the fighting taking place. Sahuagin invaded buildings on either side of the thoroughfare, yanking ixitxachitls out and putting them to death where they found them. The slaves died as well. There was no rescue.

Even though the temple stood in the city, very few ixitxachitl priests stood against them. The sahuagin priestesses fought them spell for spell and emerged victorious even if they had to swim over the bodies of those who'd gone before them.

"I believe," Laaqueel replied, "as best as I am able."

She waited, thinking he was going to strike her down where she stood. Over the past few days, he'd been distant from her while plotting his intricate conspiracies.

"In Sekolah or in me?" he asked.

"In my eyes," Laaqueel answered, "you and the Shark God are equal. How could I believe in Sekolah's teaching if I didn't believe in you?"

If the Shark God had cared at all about what she did or thought, the malenti knew she'd have been struck down in that moment for the words of sacrilege she spoke. Instead, she prepared herself for the blow she fully expected from Iakhovas.

He gazed at her for a long time, as if the battle raging around them didn't exist. A disemboweled ixitxachitl drifted by them. Iakhovas angrily swept it away. His living eye showed malignant black as he surveyed her.

"You have changed, little malenti."

"We are all changed."

"I have grown and become more powerful."

"And I have become less so?" Laaqueel asked.

"No, it's not that . . ." Iakhovas waved the sahuagin warriors behind them onward. He paused to glance briefly at the carnage that was reaped in his name, grinning broadly enough to reveal the fangs that filled his sahuagin mouth as well as his human one. "It's just that I've never seen you without vision."

"I don't understand," Laaqueel responded.

"When I first met you all those years ago," Iakhovas said, "when I first saw you, I saw the hunger for power within you. It filled every fiber of your being, little malenti, a force so wild and powerful that for a moment I was afraid— tempted to kill you outright instead of using you."

Laaqueel stood in the middle of the battle waiting patiently. There was nothing she could say. Emptiness swallowed her emotions save for a trace of fear that kept her reactions on the edge.

"I thought I could control that hunger," Iakhovas went on, "so I let you live. In mastering you, though you may not see it that way, I shaped and strengthened that hunger in you."

Shame swept through the malenti priestess because she knew Iakhovas spoke the truth.

"I remember the way you stood up to King Huaanton after we brought Waterdeep to its knees." Iakhovas closed his fist, and it was at once human and sahuagin. "It was something you would have never done had I not entered your life."

Screams punctuated his words.

"I know," Laaqueel said, only because she knew some response was necessary.

"You would have tried to kill him for going against Sekolah's will."

"Yes."

"Then, only a few days ago, two priestesses who would have done harm to you were struck down before you."

Laaqueel knew that was a sore point for Iakhovas. Even though he'd questioned her at length about it, she'd been able to offer no reason why that had happened. That she had no explanation also undermined her own confidence. She didn't know why she couldn't believe Sekolah had acted on her behalf, but she didn't.

"At this point, little malenti," Iakhovas said, "I would think that your hunger would be about to consume you, that you'd want to stretch your talons and see how deeply you could cut into the world."

Laaqueel eyed him levelly and said, "To cut any deeper in this world I'd have to step from your shadow, and that would be dangerous."

For a moment Iakhovas held her gaze, then he tilted back his head and laughed. The deep, roaring bellow echoed through the ixitxachitl outpost, riding on the swirling currents that followed the path of the battle.

"Ah, little malenti, in truth, I had not thought about that. You think you have risen as far as you can go?"

"Yes," Laaqueel answered without hesitation. It was the truth.

"Then you truly have no vision," Iakhovas stated. "Before I am done, I will rule Toril. I will conquer its oceans and coastal lands, then I will find a way into the tender heart of the surface world. I will become the greatest emperor Faerûn—and beyond—has ever known."

"And will you be needing an empress?" Laaqueel challenged.

Iakhovas grinned cruelly. "No, little malenti."

"Then what am I supposed to envision for myself?"

Iakhovas was silent for a time. "Perhaps you are right. I miss the way you were, but should I see those hungry lights in your eyes again, I'll know to guard my back."

Laaqueel crossed her arms over her breasts and asked, "Do you fear me then?"

Cold anger froze Iakhovas's features. "You go too far," he warned.

"Yet you think I don't go far enough."

"Don't ever make that mistake."

Laaqueel shook her head. "What you saw in my eyes when we met wasn't just a hunger for power," she told him, "it was desperation. When I feel desperate, I've found I can do almost anything I need to do."

"And do you feel desperate now, little malenti?"

"No," she said quietly, again telling the truth. "For now, I only feel hollow."

"Perhaps," Iakhovas admitted, "that is a good thing. I will work to instill that hunger in you again, though. I want you to be all that you might be, Most Sacred One."

Laaqueel didn't know what to say. She sensed truth in his words, and that he cared about her in his own way.

"Come," he said after a time. "We have a war to win."

He leaped up and swam through the water, heading for the thick of the diminishing battle.

With nothing else to do, Laaqueel followed.

"To me!" Iakhovas cried with savage glee as he descended on the last rallying point of the ixitxachitl at Ilkanar. With all the priestesses around, he used his magic without fear, making sure no one could trace the efforts back to him.

The ixitxachitls holed up in the temple, holding their own at the doors and windows. Sahuagin clung to the stone walls with their claws, slashing savagely at any demon ray that stayed in the open too long.

Iakhovas battled through ixitxachitls that had been luckless enough to be caught out in the open. His attention riveted on the temple for a moment. Gold gleamed in his scarred eye socket and a thin green ray, almost lost in the swirling blue-green of the sea, stabbed toward the temple.

Without warning, the temple tower's base glowed green. In the next instant the glowing section of the tower turned to fine black dust. Shorn of part of its mooring, the tower fell to the ocean bed. It stretched out far enough to crush two more buildings, then threw a cloud of sand into the water. The hollow thump echoed, followed immediately by the clattering of stones as the temple went to pieces.

Laaqueel stared in disbelief. The ruined tower had killed not only most of the ixitxachitls hiding inside, but a large number of the sahuagin who'd been clinging to the walls.

The tower's destruction signaled the end of the battle. Dozens of demon rays remained, but they fled for their lives, only making the sahuagin and sharks chase them farther to kill them.

"To me!" Iakhovas cried, holding his trident triumphantly overhead. "I have brought you yet another triumph, as I promised."

"Long live King Iakhovas the Deliverer!" someone yelled.

The rest of the sahuagin quickly took up the cry. They slapped their feet against the silt-covered streets of the fallen ixitxachitl outpost, slammed their tridents against the stone walls of the buildings holding only dead and dying, and gave voice to clicks and whistles pledging their support.

Laaqueel kept her silence and her distance. Only she

knew the truth of the beast the sahuagin had clutched to their breasts.

"Long live King Iakhovas the Deliverer!"

* * * * *

Jherek flexed his left hand and gazed at the brown skin of his arm, then he closed his hand and visualized the multi-colored bracer covering it. In the space of a heartbeat, the magic armor leaped through his skin and wrapped around his arm in a blur of color. It sparkled in the sun that shone down on *Steadfast's* deck.

"Do you feel it?" Tarnar asked. The captain stood across from Jherek, sword in his fist.

"No," Jherek replied.

In the seven days that had passed since recovering the Great Whale Bard's gift, not a minute had gone by that the young sailor hadn't thought about Iridea's Tear.

"No extra weight?" the Cormyrean Freesail captain asked.

"No."

"Not even now, when it is manifested upon your arm?"

Jherek shook his head. "It's like it's a part of me," he said. "It's no more noticeable than the hair on my arm."

The caravel stood at anchor at a small cove south of Altumbel. They'd been met by a dozen caravan wagons manned by warriors who swore allegiance to the Simbul, the queen of Aglarond. *Steadfast's* cargo was parceled out among the wagons even as the caravel's crew took on the goods the caravan had carried overland from Velprintalar, the closest thing to a port city Aglarond had.

Pirate activities in the eastern waters north of Aglarond had increased. Having no regular standing navy and only a small, desperate army, the Simbul had made arrangements with the merchants in Cormyr to avoid the waters with the overland caravan and make the exchange along the southern coast. It wasn't a tactic that would last long, but trapped as Aglarond was between Altumbel and Thay, the realm still needed the glass, iron, and food the merchant ships brought to trade for lumber, gems, and copper.

The southern coastline of Aglarond was harsh and

uneven. Cliffs overlooked the Alamber Sea, broken only by the treacherous trails the wagoneers had used to descend to the rocky shore. Trees grew almost out to the sea's edge, kept at bay only by the saltwater that drenched the ground.

Foresters manned the wagons. All of them were hard-eyed men with the gruff manners of warriors constantly marching off to battle. They bore scars and memories, and their songs at night held sadness for things lost as well as hope for a brighter tomorrow.

Some of the wagons bore coast boats that many of the surrounding pirates feared. Though the coast boats were open, equipped only with lateen sails, oars, and poles, a group of them could grapple and board ocean-going vessels to kill pirate crews. According to Tarnar, they'd done that several times in the past.

For the last two days, only a ghost of a wind had threaded along the rocky coast, not enough to allow them to put out to sea. Jherek had spent most of that time with the captain.

"It's a wonderful thing you've been given, Jherek," Tarnar said.

"But I ask myself why." The question had plagued Jherek's mind constantly.

"Sometimes," Tarnar said softly, "things are meant to be accepted, not understood. So we practice, and the whales talk to you here, giving you what information they have. What follows will follow."

"I want to be back with my friends."

Tarnar grinned and said, "Good. Maybe that is a step in the right direction." He lifted his sword. "Prepare yourself."

Jherek squared off with the man, falling easily into combat stance. Though Tarnar wasn't as powerful a swordsman as Glawinn or Malorrie were, there were things the young sailor picked up from the captain. Malorrie and Glawinn had concentrated on raw power, complemented with quick, decisive strokes. Tarnar, however, moved from bold attack into feints that had upon occasion left Jherek open.

The young sailor watched his opponent's eyes, waiting for the captain's opening move. Tarnar slashed at Jherek's left arm. Jherek raised his arm and took the blow on the bracer, trusting it completely. Sparks flashed from the iridescent surface, but the bracer showed no signs of ill use.

Thrusting with his cutlass, Jherek came close to Tarnar's face but the captain parried the thrust with his dirk. Steel rasped. Jherek blocked again, this time causing the bracer to form a two-foot diameter buckler that he used to press up against his opponent. Even as they disengaged, he caused the bracer to form into a hook like the one he normally used. Each change was coming with less conscious thought now. The young sailor settled into the combat, trying not to think of Sabyna, Glawinn, Azla, or the pirate crew he'd come to know and care about.

Tarnar's crew had finally come around to him as well, after he'd walked upon the Great Whale Bard's body and retrieved the bracer. Over the days they'd spent traveling to meet the caravan in Aglarond, the crew seemed to accept him as one of their own. Tarnar had commented on that as well, stating that the young sailor had a natural affinity for drawing men to him.

Finally, after hammering away at Jherek's defenses for almost an hour, Tarnar called for a break. They drank sweet water the Aglarondans brought in wooden casks, and poured some over their heads to cool down in the murky summer heat.

"Never," the captain stated, "have I seen someone adjust so quickly to a new weapon."

"My teacher, Malorrie," Jherek explained, "schooled me in all manner of weapons."

Tarnar shook his head, spraying droplets to the wooden deck. "It's more than that, my friend. You are a true, natural born warrior."

Embarrassment flamed Jherek's cheeks and the back of his neck. He willed the bracer away, feeling only a tingle as it sank back inside his arm. "Perhaps I have an advantage with the bracer that we hadn't counted on."

"You mean that it enhances your skill?" Tarnar shook his head. "Even if that were so, it would perhaps only guide your arm, it wouldn't move the rest of your body or make you a better swordsman. I've seen people fight with magical—"

Jherek.

Responding to the quiet call inside his mind, the young sailor walked to the railing and peered down to find Swims Truly, the sapphire whale, in the water beside the caravel. Tarnar studied him intently, aware that Jherek could hear a voice he himself could not.

You will be leaving with the tide, Jherek Whalefriend, Swims Truly told him. *The wind will be with you then.*

"Where am I supposed to go?" Jherek asked.

Where you are supposed to go, of course.

"I want to rejoin my friends," Jherek said. "I still have to find the disk of Lathander that I caused to be lost."

Then, should you find your way there, that is where you should be.

Irritation stung Jherek. The whales' cryptic announcements contained truth, but what truth wasn't always apparent.

"How do I find them?"

As you may, Jherek Whalefriend.

"I don't know how."

Yes you do. Listen with your heart, just as you listened with it when you found Song Who Brings Bright Rains. Search inside yourself. The bond between you and your love is the most constant thing in your life. The ability to love and seek out love is your most whalelike trait, Jherek.

Jherek was suddenly glad Tarnar couldn't hear the whale's thoughts.

"I don't think I can do that."

Swims Truly twitched a fin in a gesture Jherek had come to learn signaled irritation. *You have not yet tried. How can you know what you can do and not do?*

Chastened, Jherek remained silent.

Close your eyes and let me guide your thoughts.

The young sailor closed his eyes, ignoring the inquiring look Tarnar gave him.

You have a gift, Jherek Whalefriend, Swims Truly said, *that comes from what you are, what you will be. Born upon the seas of Toril, destined to spend your life there, it has been seen to that you will always have a sense of where you are and in what direction people or objects lie from you.*

Jherek waited, trying to understand, trying simply to believe.

Paint the picture of your beloved in your mind. Open it

to the special tie that will forever bind you to her.

Doubt clouded the young sailor's mind that such a thing existed.

You think too much, Swims Truly chided. *Build her face in your mind, remember her scent, then reach for her.*

Tentatively, afraid of failing, Jherek did as the whale suggested. He imagined Sabyna as he'd first met her, the wind blowing through her copper-colored hair. He imagined the lilac scent that she favored, then felt a familiar tugging within his breast. Another image of Sabyna, when she'd come to him in *Black Champion*'s rigging and dug her fingers in his shirt, filled his mind. It hurt him, remembering how he'd told her he couldn't give her his love. The feeling in his chest dimmed.

No. Do not doubt your love for this female, Jherek Whalefriend. Your doubts are in truth your greatest enemy. Try again.

Forcing himself to remain calm, Jherek built Sabyna's face in his mind again. He saw her smiling and his heart swelled within him. The tug in his chest returned, stronger than ever. He reached for her, knowing for sure in what direction Sabyna was: west, and a long distance away.

The love is true, Swims Truly said quietly. *You feel the connection strongly. It is how our kind finds our mates.*

"I can't—" Jherek started to protest.

Hush, Swims Truly instructed. *Jherek Whalefriend, no matter how much you doubt, you can never be other than what you were born and guided to be. Perhaps you can delay these things, but you can never make them go away. Whether you wish it or not, whether you feel entitled to it or not, at this time you love the female and she loves you.*

Abruptly, a wind came up from the east, flowing over *Steadfast* and rattling her rigging. Even with his eyes open now, Jherek could feel the tug urging him in Sabyna's direction. He closed his eyes again, imagining her and drinking her image in. He reached for her, calling her name.

The image sharpened and he saw her in one of the small rooms aboard *Azure Dagger*. She sat on a chair in front of Arthoris, the ship's mage. Her head turned and her eyes searched for him.

"Jherek," she called. A feeling of dread, of loss and confused pain, clung to her.

Startled, the young sailor lost his concentration. He dropped to his knees, suddenly weakened.

You put too much of yourself into the seeking. You must be wary of this.

Jherek gasped, gazing down at the sapphire whale. "She's in danger."

Of course, Swims Truly said. *All of Serôs is in danger. Your love follows the currents to the greatest danger of all.*

Anxiety filled the young sailor. "I should never have left her side," he said.

There was no choice. To be what you need to be, you had to come to these waters. If you had stayed with her, she would have been lost for certain. As you would have been, and all of Serôs as well. Now you are closer to being what you need to be so that most will be saved.

"Will she be saved?"

That remains to be writ, Jherek Whalefriend. We can see but a few currents from this point on, and all of those are not clear, nor without risk. Much death lies ahead for all of Serôs. No one may save them all. Perhaps, you will not even save yourself. If you do not complete yourself, you may not have even that chance.

"What do I need to do?"

Accept. Begin there and the rest will follow. May Oghma, Lord of Knowledge and Bards, keep you within his sight.

Without another word, Swims Truly dived deeply into the blue-green water and disappeared.

"Should we sail?" Tarnar asked. "Or do you yet have business with the whales?"

"No," Jherek said. "It's time for us to go."

He stared west, wishing he could be with Sabyna at that moment, facing whatever danger waited for her.

"Where do we sail?"

"West," the young sailor answered. "As fast as we are able."

XIX

6 Eleint, the Year of the Gauntlet

"He hates you, my liege," Tu'uua'col said, "even though you are his father."

He swam easily at King Vhaemas's side through the palace in Voalidru. As usual, even though he'd been the king's advisor and trusted friend for years, all the other court personnel stayed away from him.

The merman king's face turned bitter, and his eyes wouldn't meet his friend's. Broadened by the sea and battle, a little more than eight feet long from head to tail, the old king's frame remained heavily muscled despite his sixty-eight years. His gold crown, inset with precious gems and rare bits of coral, held back his white hair. Scars decorated his arms and torso. Pink-ridged flesh scored the left side of his face from a koalinth attack years past.

"My blood is in him," King Vhaemas argued.

"And you denied it."

"Because I had to," the merman monarch replied.

"Yet you loved his mother."

Vhaemas put out a webbed hand and stopped his forward motion through the palace hallway. The nearest pages and court attendees scattered. Though he was one of the most favored kings in the history of the Serôsian merfolk, his temper was legendary.

"A nation," the king said, "cannot be compromised by a young man's indiscretion without proper perspective."

Tu'uua'col knew the king wasn't referring to his own illegitimate son, but to his own past mistakes.

"Your son does not see himself as an indiscretion, my liege, and I think he would take grave umbrage at your own insistence upon calling him that."

"He would not form an alliance with Iakhovas of the sahuagin."

"My sources suggest he already has."

"They're wrong," the merking snapped.

"Remember when your own court of advisors denied that you had made me one of them? Denied, in fact, the friendship that exists between us?" Tu'uua'col sighed heavily, hating the turbulence that formed between him and his friend.

The court rejected him for a number of reasons, and most of them still hadn't changed their minds. First and foremost among their complaints was that he was not a merman. He was a shalarin.

Tu'uua'col stood not quite six feet tall but seemed much taller due to the dorsal fin that started between his full black eyes and jutted up nearly a foot above his head before running all the way down his back to his buttocks. The jadelike sheen of his smooth, scaleless skin further set him apart from the warmer colors of the merfolk and their scaled tails. His gill slits were along his collarbone and ribcage.

All the merfolk knew him as a wizard, and a teacher of the royal princelings. That he had the ear of not only King Vhaemas but the royal offspring as well was enough to unnerve most of the other advisors. If the royal court at Voalidru had known he was a Blue Dukar of the Order of Kupav and interested in the protection of Myth Nantar, assassination attempts might have been the order of the day.

"They do not know you as I know you," Vhaemas stated irritably. "They think of you simply as a wild-tider."

The merman nickname came from the prophecy of Selana, the mermaid who rose to prominence after the Tenth Serôs War and the fall of Hmurrath, the merfolk empire. The mermaid predicted that the merfolk would one day ally with the shalarin. The wild tide referred to the magical force that brought the shalarin from their homes in the Sea of Corynactis, whose exact location had never been decided.

"Yet they will not listen," Tu'uua'col pointed out. "Sometimes the plainest of truths are the hardest to believe. They require acceptance rather than recognition."

Vhaemas shook his head wearily. "These are difficult currents we face, my old friend."

"That is why we must recognize and quickly deal with the dangers that surround us."

"Including Thuridru's king."

"Yes, my liege."

In all the years that they'd known each other, Tu'uua'col had never heard Vhaemas refer to his bastard child by the Kamaar clan as his son.

Vhaemas scoured the palace corridor with a jaundiced eye. As capital of the Eadraal empire, Voalidru was beauty itself, sculpted from the sea. The merman builders had combined stones dug from the ocean's floor with quarried rock lost in shipwrecks. The royal buildings were wide and generous, sporting shells and coral decorations in myriad colors and shapes.

"The ixitxachitl cities of Ageadren and Orildren, as well as their outposts, have fallen to the sahuagin. I have heard that Thuridru was instrumental in destroying Orildren and the outer temples."

"But to join with the sahuagin?" Vhaemas questioned. "Why?"

Tu'uua'col was silent for a moment, weighing his words. "Perhaps, the enemy of my enemy is my friend. Thuridru has no alliances in Voalidru and remains trapped between the demon rays and the morkoth, who also attacked the ixitxachitls with the sahuagin."

"The Taker is not to be believed. In our legends he only looks toward his own interests."

"I think that is true," the shalarin Blue Dukar replied. "Still, Thuridru's ruler is willing to set aside merman histories and beliefs in order to forge his own future. He is openly ambitious. This alliance is the only one open to him. At worst, he gets some of the ixitxachitl lands. At best . . ."

Tu'uua'col shrugged. "Perhaps he even thinks to have a hand in humbling all of Eadraal."

"What would you suggest I do?"

Vhaemas started forward again, following the bend of the hallway to a balcony. The royal palace was built on the lower foothills of Mount Teakal. The vantage point allowed it to overlook Voalidru below.

Most of the citizens of Voalidru lived in stone houses and caves, though some of the merfolk took up residence in ships that had come to rest on the ocean floor. Once, centuries ago, a great naval battle had been fought along the coast of Chondath between the coastal and inland city-states during the Rotting War. Many of the ships had sunk around the Whamite Isles and drifted down to the Lesser Hmur Plateau.

Tu'uua'col hesitated, knowing the advice he was prepared to give wouldn't be well received. "I think you should take the first step in allying the merfolk with the sea elves and the shalarin. I have learned of a caravan journeying toward Myth Nantar. Locathah I have talked to have told me of them. They tell me the Taleweaver is with them."

Vhaemas's answer came immediately. "Never! I would rather cut my own throat than trust the accursed sea elves."

The Blue Dukar maintained his silence. Vhaemas could not be argued with on certain matters, and the Alu'Tel'Quessir was one of those.

"If they had the means and the power, they would take all of Serôs for themselves," Vhaemas said.

"But they don't. The Taker, however, has an army of sahuagin, morkoth, and koalinth at his beck and call that are already invading lands that can be used as staging arenas to attack Eadraal."

"Even with all of those, there are not enough to conquer these waters," the merking declared.

"We have not seen everything the Taker has planned. If you add Thuridru, you increase the threat even more."

"I refuse to believe that is possible," the king said.

"Perhaps the ixitxachitl felt the same way."

Tu'uua'col waited, remembering his friendship with the merman and all the years they'd shared between them. It was a lot to risk, and all on the next few words he had to say. "Denial is no defense, my liege."

Vhaemas did not look at him, drifting quietly in the current with his hands on the balcony railing. "Leave me for a time, Col," he said finally. "I need to think on things."

"Of course, my liege."

Pain shot through the Dukar's heart. He couldn't remember when he'd last been dismissed from the king's side so abruptly. He bowed his head and swam away, frustrated and embarrassed.

Pride, foolish, ill-afforded, and dangerous, was a sword pointed at the heart of the kingdom, and Vhaemas couldn't see it. But then, the Blue Dukar supposed, neither could anyone else. Though the High Mages journeyed from the sea elf waters, there were no ambassadors seeking a meeting with the merfolk or the shalarin. Nor were the shalarin seeking audiences to combine their forces.

He wandered alone and aloof from the other palace dwellers and those who had business within the walls. He knew the other advisors talked about what was going on in the Xedran Reefs, but none of them would take the tack he did. They believed themselves inviolate.

Sahuagin raiding parties had spread throughout Serôs, attacking coastal lands and ships, and more continued to come from the Alamber Sea, making the waters between there and the Xedran Reefs dangerously close to impossible.

Still, Tu'uua'col knew it would take even more before all parties involved would admit the extent of the peril that existed. It remained to be seen how much would have to be lost before they realized it.

* * * * *

Li'aya'su moved down the long line of shalarin eggs that incubated in the mud of the warm sea cavern of the Aya clan in Es'rath. As one of the provider caste among the shalarin, she was the Heart of her people. Unlike those of the servant or ruler castes, she'd been able to choose what she would work at. Her immediate decision had been caring for the hatcheries.

The cavern followed a twisting tunnel, widened by artificial means to more easily accommodate the eggs. It was twenty feet wide and almost that high.

Her glance roved over the eggs as she turned them in their nest of warm mud. She and three other providers were responsible for caring for and turning the six hundred eggs under their care.

Passing down the line, she turned each egg carefully, aware that her actions were necessary to keep her race healthy in this home they'd found away from home. Even though Li'aya'su had been born in Es'rath and had not been out of the deep waters her people called home, she still felt she was a visitor to Serôs. These waters were not her home, and she'd been told that since birth. One day the shalarin would be allowed to go back home, but until that time, she promised herself to make the best of it.

She studied the shells as she moved among them. The rough, dark brown shells would one day add to the ranks of the protector caste. Rust colored shells with striated surfaces signified new members for the scholar caste while the smooth, black shells would give birth to the seeker caste. The seekers swam forever among the currents and searched for meaning beyond the shalarin. The light brown whorled shells belonged to the provider class, and most of the eggs here were that color.

Working quickly and methodically, enjoying the nature of the work as well as the work itself, Li'aya'su touched each unborn child with love and prayed to Ri'daa'trisha, the Waverider, who was known as Trishina in Serôs, for the goddess's blessing on each. It was a simple task, but she had been doing it since she had been a girl forty years ago.

Screams broke her reverie.

Startled, Li'aya'su turned from the eggs and swam back toward the hatchery's entrance. Li'ola'des, another of the providers, stood at the entrance and gazed fearfully out.

"What is it?" Li'aya'su asked, joining her.

"The sahuagin," the other provider replied in disbelief. "They have come here to Es'rath."

Cold fear hammered the elder provider as she looked out over the shalarin city. She had heard about the war that raged the length and breadth of Serôs, but she had hoped her people lived too deeply for the sahuagin to bother.

Hundreds of the vicious sahuagin swam from above, engaging the shalarin protectors at once. Though the protectors fought bravely, there simply weren't enough of them. The protectors stood as the Hand of the shalarin, taught the ways of war and battle from the time they were newly hatched.

The providers and scholars couldn't help much even in their own defense. A warrior was a warrior and a provider was a provider. According to caste thinking and training, one could not be the other.

Long minutes after the battle began, Li'aya'su heard their battle cry. "Long live King Iakhovas the Deliverer! Meat is meat!"

Horrified, the shalarin provider watched as the sahuagin not only killed her people, but ate them as well. Blood tainted the water in a way she had never seen before.

A group of sahuagin swam toward the hatchery, clicking and whistling in savage glee.

Not knowing what else to do, Li'aya'su stepped forward, intending to somehow protect the hatchery and the defenseless unborn that lay within the cavern.

The sahuagin didn't pause at all. The lead warrior lowered his trident. Li'aya'su felt the impact of the weapon piercing her chest, but surprisingly she didn't feel any pain. The sahuagin's powerful legs drove her backward through the water. She slammed against the wall behind her, feeling the rock tear her skin but again there was no pain.

"Please," she gasped, feeling the incredible pressure squeezing the life from her. Her gill slits flared open in a vain attempt to breathe. "Please don't harm the children."

She lifted her hand in supplication. One of the sahuagin raked his claws against Li'ola'des's neck, ripping her throat out. The provider died without a sound.

Holding the trident to keep her pressed back against the wall, the sahuagin grinned at her and growled, "Meat is meat."

His great head snapped forward suddenly and his jaws opened to crunch down on Li'aya'su's wrist. When he pulled away, he took her hand with him, chewing it between bared fangs.

"No mercy, finhead."

THE THREAT FROM THE SEA

Peering through a cloud of her own life's blood, Li'aya'su watched helplessly as the sahuagin ravaged the hatchery. They lifted the blessed eggs that nurtured the future of the shalarin race and ate them, one after the other. Pieces of broken shell littered the gentle currents that helped keep the cavern warm. The sea devils' terrible roars and laughter filled the cavern even as the shalarin provider's life was spent.

XX

3 Marpenoth, the Year of the Gauntlet

"The sahuagin destroyed the Ola, Aya, and Yea clan hatcheries at Es'rath over a month ago."

Pacys felt the horror and helplessness of the tale the locathah female told him. She called herself Tyhlly. Music tugged at the old bard's fingers, sending them quietly questing along the saceddar's gems. Though he didn't touch the inset gems, the notes filled his mind along with the images.

He sat on the ocean floor on a rise that overlooked the valley the sea elf caravan had come through only moments before. Taranath Reefglamor had ordered a brief respite until the scouts returned. The three older High Mages—including Yrlimn Tidark who had remained to himself studying ancient texts written on specially treated sharkskins—and the three new High Mages, sat with the bard and Khlinat. They talked with the locathah who'd come looking for Pacys.

During their long trip around the Pirate Isles, the locathah had maintained contact with the sea elf caravan. Most particularly, they'd maintain contact with Pacys, bringing him stories from all around Serôs.

Despite the sea elves' initial resentment of the locathah habitually seeking them out, the High Mages had recognized their value and even commented on their valor and loyalty. During some of the skirmishes they'd had with groups of koalinth, the locathah had even pitched in and fought.

Though they maintained contact with mages back in Sylkiir who routinely monitored Serôs through crystal balls, there was much the sea elves missed. The locathah, however, were everywhere.

"Didn't the shalarin fight back?" High Mage Ildacer asked.

The locathah turned her attention to the sea elf and said, "Yes, Lord High Mage." Tyhlly's deference to Ildacer was obvious, reflecting the locathah attitude toward the Alu'Tel'Quessir. "They fought, and they died. Over a thousand of the unhatched shalarin died as well."

"A thousand innocent deaths," Reefglamor whispered in a hoarse voice.

Pacys studied the Senior High Mage. During the long months of travel, the journey had marked Reefglamor with fatigue.

"If the merfolk had let us travel across the Hmur Plateau instead of having to go around it, mayhap we could have prevented those deaths."

"Better that you had not," Tyhlly stated.

"How can you say that?" the Senior High Mage demanded.

The locathah blinked her huge eyes and hesitated.

"I'm sure," Pacys interjected gently, "that she meant no harm by the statement."

"No harm, Lord Senior," Tyhlly said. "No harm intended at all. I give my life to Eadro and to improving our world in ways that will benefit all. I would not wish such a terrible thing on anyone." She paused. "I only meant that since the deaths at the hatcheries and the attacks on Es'rath, the shalarin now openly take up arms against the sahuagin. You have more potential allies in your quest."

"Aye," Khlinat growled. "She's got the right of it there."

"Why would the Taker attack the shalarin?" Ildacer asked. "He's already engaged a host of enemies above and below the sea."

212

No one seemed to have an answer. Pacys let his fingers wander across the saceddar, listening to the notes in his mind. Excitement filled him—he knew the fabled city of Myth Nantar was only a short distance away—but doubt lingered with him, too. So far there had been no word of Jherek, the boy he felt certain was the hero Narros had told him about. He prayed to Oghma for guidance regularly, but there had been no definite course set other than the one he now followed.

Tyhlly broke the silence after a time. "There is a simple reason why he attacks the shalarin," she said.

"What?" Jhanra Merlistar asked.

"To take away further avenues you have open to you in the war against him," Tyhlly answered.   -

"What do you mean?" Ildacer asked.

"The Taker seeks to keep the races of Serôs divided." Though the locathah spoke softly, Pacys knew she had the attention of everyone there. "The merfolk wouldn't let you cross the Hmur Plateau to get here. The Taker's attack on Es'rath and occupation of parts of the Xedran Reefs has assured that their paranoia has increased. The elves of the Dragon Reach have erected battlements to keep out those potentially hostile to them."

Pacys knew it was true from the conversations he'd had with Reefglamor. The Dragon Reach sea elves stayed on guard against sahuagin attack, as well as hostilities from the nearby coastal lands.

"How do you know this?" Ildacer demanded.

The locathah ranger pointed at the dolphins that had accompanied her. "The whales sing of it, and we are friendly with the whales."

"What would you have them do?" Ildacer asked sarcastically. "Lay down arms and let the sahuagin death tide wash over them?"

"No," Tyhlly answered. "Freedom is precious—something that should never be easily given up. A bigger foe may threaten you or imprison you for a time, but you should always be looking for your first chance at freedom. My people learned this long ago, and at great cost."

Pacys's fingers stroked the keys, echoing the locathah's words.

"Now that the shalarin are put on guard," Tyhlly went

213

on, "how do you think they would feel about another race invading their lands?"

"They wouldn't tolerate it," Jhanra said. "They would fight against anyone who wasn't one of them."

Tyhlly nodded, turning her head from one side to the other to fix her other eye on the young High Mage. "Exactly. You do see."

"I don't," Talor Vurtalis grumbled.

Unlike the other two newly made High Mages, Vurtalis wore his selu'kiira gem openly on his forehead. Over the months-long journey, Pacys had learned the choice was in direct opposition to elven tradition and propriety.

"The Taker has allied himself with the morkoth," Tyhlly said. "If he joins with them again and marches on Eadraal, successfully forcing the mermen from the Lesser Hmur Plateau and Myth Nantar, where will they retreat to?"

"Possibly the shalarin lands," Reefglamor said.

Pacys saw understanding light the Senior High Mage's eyes.

"And, after the attack on the hatcheries," the locathah asked, "what would the shalarin do?"

"They would attack. Vhaemas's army and his people would be cut down from both sides." Reefglamor's answer was sobering. He stared at the locathah with new respect. "You have quite an understanding of war."

The locathah ranger spread her hands. "It is just that we have been involved with them for so long, Lord Senior. We have come to understand war, and we have come to understand that unity often means our freedom. In times past, when the locathah were taken as slaves, we were particularly vulnerable when we fought among ourselves. We have learned from those experiences and vowed never to make them again. Working together, we understand that we are stronger than we would be if we stood alone." She hesitated, then added, "Some of our leaders, as well as the whales, feel that is something the other races of Serôs would do well to learn."

An uncomfortable silence followed her words.

Tyhlly rounded her shoulders self-consciously, making herself more vulnerable. "Forgive me if I have trespassed in my zeal to spread the news I have learned," she said.

"There's no need to apologize," Reefglamor assured her.

"You have spoken fairly. Sometimes the truth is a hard thing to hear."

"Thank you, Lord Senior."

"Perhaps we should be thinking about a unity of some sort," Reefglamor suggested.

"With the mermen?" Ildacer scoffed. "They wouldn't even let us travel across their lands. An alliance will be out of the question."

"I take it you are not in favor of it?" Jhanra asked.

Ildacer's answer was immediate. "Of course not. With all the wars between us, how could anyone entertain such an idea?"

"In some of those wars," Reefglamor said, "the Alu'Tel'Quessir and the merfolk were allies, not enemies."

"That was a long time ago."

"Currents change," the Senior High Mage replied. "Things are not as they once were."

"Aye," Khlinat put in. "Dwarves are known for their warrin' ways. Don't know if ye get much stories about us down here, but I can tell ye that nothing sets a dwarf afire with passion the way a good battle can. Different communities battled orcs and goblins for caves where gems were mined and a dwarf could live if he had a mind to. They also fought one another for the same things. Now ye take a dwarf down to a tavern and him blowing the suds off a fresh mug and a human or elf get physical with him, why any other dwarf in the place would be the first to stand up for him if he got into more than he could handle."

"But if it was an elf or a half-orc in trouble, these dwarven feelings you praise so highly wouldn't be quite so ready, would they?" Ildacer asked sarcastically.

"Now there's a funny thought," Khlinat said without taking offense. "I seen mates on a ship, crew that had been together through some stormy weather and buckle to buckle against pirates what had tried to reeve them of their cargo—and they was a mixed bag, the lot of 'em. Aboard ship, they had their problems, but the cap'n set 'em straight. Mayhap on occasion they'd take an unkind hand with each other once they reached shore, but when it come to taverns and local roustabouts laying hands on 'em, why ye'd have thought they was long-lost brothers the way they took up for one another."

Everyone looked at the dwarf, who appeared suddenly as though he'd rather be elsewhere.

Finally Reefglamor broke the silence. "I've never heard you speak so much."

"I have me moments," Khlinat replied gruffly.

"Thank Deep Sashelas that you do, Khlinat. Your words ring true and I shall have to think upon them."

"I'm just saying there ain't no grand and perfect solution to how folks are to get along with one another," the dwarf said. "Neighbors ought to pay attention to who's in the neighborhood before they start picking fights with one another."

"The mermen will never listen," Ildacer argued. "You know how proud and haughty they are."

Reefglamor glanced at his second-in-command. "How very like the Alu'Tel'Quessir they are, you mean?"

"No, that's not what I meant to . . ."

Reefglamor sighed and looked out over Mount Halaath standing tall to the northwest. After circling under the Whamite Isles, the caravan had fixed on it and marched straight toward it. The City of Destinies lay between them and Mount Halaath.

"Senior, what I am saying is that we might be swayed by Khlinat's words while sitting here so far from our own homes, feeling perhaps a little lost and friendless, but King Vhaemas and his people are not going to feel the same. This place is the source of their strength. Even with the morkoth and koalinth adding to the ranks of the sahuagin, the Taker can't possibly hope to overrun all of Eadraal."

"From what I have pieced together," Pacys said. "The Taker only wants his eye."

"Have you found out what that is?" Jhanra asked.

Pacys strummed the saceddar. "Not yet. All that I am sure of at the moment is that it is some device the Taker had in his possession when Umberlee struck him down."

"Even so, to get the eye from Myth Nantar, the Taker will have to march through Eadraal," Reefglamor said. "As much as King Vhaemas hates the City of Destinies and all that it stands for, he won't see the Taker free to ravage it."

"Again," Ildacer said, "the Taker will have to raise up an army the like of which has never before been seen."

"And you have assurances," Reefglamor asked quietly, "that the Taker cannot accomplish this?"

"No, Senior."

"Good," Reefglamor responded. "So far the Taker has succeeded at everything he's attempted to do. We have no proof that we've set him back in any way at all."

"Except for the Great Whale Bard," Tidark commented in his whispering rasp. The High Mage was much older even than Reefglamor and usually given to his studies, not spending much time in the company of others.

Pacys knew it was true, but he didn't know what the whale bard had made his sacrifice for.

"We have every reason to believe that when the time comes," Reefglamor said, "the Taker will find the means to raise the army he needs to invade Eadraal."

The thought sobered all of the High Mages, Pacys noticed with satisfaction. The hardships of the journey, the turning away they'd experienced at the hands of the mermen, had tempered all of them.

A group of sea elf warriors approached from the north. Morgan Ildacer, young cousin to Pharom Ildacer and captain of the High Mages' guard from Sylkiir, came to a stop in the water. He bowed his head, his arms crossed at the wrist, and waited to be recognized.

"Captain," Reefglamor said, "your report."

"Our scouts have returned with good news, Senior High Mage Reefglamor. The way to Myth Nantar is clear."

"What of the merman guards?"

"If we move quickly enough, Senior," Morgan Ildacer said, "we'll be able to gain the city within the hour. Vhaemas's warriors seem to be concentrated to the south, prepared to defend their borders against the morkoth and koalinth. They're searching for groups much larger than ours."

"Very well," Reefglamor said. "Give the order, and let's get moving. Better this were done sooner than later."

"There are others of my kind in the area," the locathah ranger stated. "We can cover your backs in the event you are discovered. There are hiding places around here that not even the mermen know of."

"That won't be—" Morgan Ildacer started before Reefglamor cut him off with a raised hand.

217

"That would be very kind of you," the Senior High Mage said.

Tyhlly stretched to her full height and bowed, then turned her attention to Pacys. "Your gods be with you, Lorekeeper, for you shall soon be sorely tried."

"My thanks to you," the old bard said. He spread his hand and touched palm to palm with the locathah ranger. "May Eadro give you only pleasant and free currents."

She leaped up and was gone in seconds, disappearing into the darkness of the sea.

Turning to face Mount Halaath, Pacys strained to pierce the gloom that lay ahead. He made out the glimmering blue glow of the Great Barrier that sealed Myth Nantar off from the rest of the world.

He'd come so close to one of his goals. Now it only remained to be seen how things would play out.

* * * * *

Laaqueel stood on the sandy, rocky western shore of Graubunden, the largest of the Whamite Isles, and peered out at *Maelstrom* at anchor in the shallow waters. The pirate ship's sails were furled around the masts, and crew filled her decks.

Iakhovas stood beside the malenti, an imposing figure amid the sahuagin warriors he'd brought with him. The sahuagin lay in the shallow waters to prevent their scales from drying out. Though he had barely talked to her in fully two months, concerned with all the battles and alliances he'd made, Iakhovas had commanded her presence for the day.

Attention, little malenti, Iakhovas spoke into her mind. *You are about to see the first culmination of my labors here in the Inner Sea.*

Laaqueel turned her gaze to him.

Iakhovas smiled. He looked human at the moment, though she knew the sahuagin perceived him as one of their own.

Your astonishment astounds me, little malenti. Surely you didn't think I came here to conquer this place and never return to the outer seas.

The crew in *Maelstrom*'s longboat rowed into the beach

with consternation showing on their faces. They'd been waiting since early morning, the malenti priestess gathered from Iakhovas's comments, after arriving in the night. When they gained the beach, the crew bailed out and pulled the longboat up onto the sand.

Vurgrom stepped from the boat and approached Iakhovas. The pirate tried to act courageous, as if he wasn't standing in the midst of a hundred sahuagin warriors, but his nervous gaze and white-knuckled hand on the haft of his battle-axe gave his uneasiness away.

"Lord Iakhovas," the burly pirate rumbled in greeting.

"Captain Vurgrom," Iakhovas acknowledged. "Are you prepared to finish your part in this bit of business?"

"More than ready," Vurgrom replied. "Carrying that disk around without knowing what it does is getting to be worrisome."

"I know what it is," Iakhovas stated, but offered no explanation. "You have the map?"

Vurgrom patted his shirt over his heart. "Aye."

"March inland," Iakhovas ordered. "Follow the markings on the map and be in position three days from now."

Vurgrom hesitated, then asked, "What then?"

Iakhovas glared at him. "Wait."

The big pirate's face purpled, and for a moment Laaqueel thought he might actually speak out angrily. The malenti priestess thought that would have been interesting to see. Evidently Iakhovas needed the man or he would have done whatever needed doing himself.

In the end, Vurgrom lacked the nerve to stand up to Iakhovas. "As you say," the pirate said, "Lord Iakhovas."

"What of the kegs I asked you to prepare?" Iakhovas demanded.

"All of my ships have been outfitted with them, lord."

For a tenday and more, Iakhovas had commanded sahuagin groups to hole up in caves with air pockets so they could make the poison their people used. Laaqueel was versed in it as a priestess. Usually the sahuagin used the poisons on their weapons, coating them every few days as they had need. Iakhovas had come up with a new design.

Once the lethal poison had been rendered in powder form, it had been packed in thin glass shells, then placed in weighted wooden kegs that would sink to the ocean floor.

By design, the thin glass shells collapsed under the pressure of the depths at three hundred to four hundred feet. The poison quickly diluted into the water, killing anything that breathed it. The effect might only last a few minutes, though, before currents would sweep it away.

Iakhovas had told the malenti priestess he planned to use the kegs to completely destroy Myth Nantar once their initial attack was finished. Laaqueel had seen the effects of the poison kegs and feared them. Once the poison was released into the water, there was no way to escape it.

With no further word, Iakhovas strode into the water and disappeared under the incoming waves. The only sound was the lapping of the waves against the shoreline.

Laaqueel followed woodenly, aware of the pirates' leering stares at her nudity. None of them dared offer any comment. Underwater, she swam quickly and fell into pace a little behind Iakhovas. He swam effortlessly, totally at home in the sea. The sahuagin warriors flanked them. Scouts immediately flared out to watch for the mermen guards that swam through the area.

The malenti priestess scoured the ocean floor. She knew from Iakhovas's statements that the sea elf caravan from Sylkiir should be in the area as well.

They are further to the north, little malenti, Iakhovas told her. *They believe their mission has met with success. They won't know any different until it is much too late.*

What will happen then?

His tone, even in her mind, was mocking. *I succeed, of course, and they'll find that their precious legends have ultimately betrayed them.*

* * * * *

High in *Azure Dagger*'s rigging, Sabyna studied Vurgrom and his pirates through her spyglass. The last of the sahuagin had disappeared into the sea some minutes ago, but the pirates didn't rush back to their vessel.

"Blessed Tymora," Azla said quietly at Sabyna's side, "those damned sea devils must not have swam under us. I thought we were lucky the first time they showed up and we weren't seen."

Arthoris had woven an invisibility spell that covered *Azure Dagger*, but there were drawbacks to the maneuver. Even though they couldn't be seen, the ship still made its usual noises, and those carried across the ocean. If they'd been too close to *Maelstrom* the crew would have heard the sounds and recognized them. They'd quietly dropped anchor during the night when *Maelstrom* was nearly a thousand yards away.

When they'd seen the sahuagin surface along the shoreline, they hadn't dared hope their good fortune would last. If one sahuagin warrior swam under *Azure Dagger* the ship would be sensed in the water or possibly seen against the sky.

Another drawback was that the ship's crew couldn't see each other or the ship. Despite being unseen, it was also a lot like being blind except that Sabyna could see the ocean and the island. Movement was done cautiously and only as necessary. Unaccustomed to moving about in the rigging, Glawinn remained below.

The longboat was rowed back to *Maelstrom* while Vurgrom and five pirates remained ashore. Sabyna wasn't close enough to see the pirate captain's expression, but she judged from the way he kicked rocks and gestured at his men that he wasn't happy. It was in direct contrast to the timid way he'd acted around Iakhovas.

Sabyna watched as provisions were lowered over *Maelstrom*'s side in a cargo net.

"Shore expedition," Azla said. "Maybe we're going to finally do something other than wallow around."

"Aye," Sabyna agreed.

In the months they'd followed Vurgrom and *Maelstrom*, they'd never had a proper opportunity to overtake the ship and board her. Even with the new crew that the voyages had given Azla time to whip into shape, Vurgrom's pirates outnumbered them two to one.

In frustration, Azla had limited herself to spying on the captain, hoping for a lucky break. During part of those times, Vurgrom had sailed with other ships under his command.

They'd become separated from *Maelstrom* three times during those months. Once they'd rescued a crew that had been attacked by sahuagin and barely escaped with their lives and lost a tenday getting the sailors to a safe port. Another time one of the freak storms that ravaged the coastal lands upon occasion had spun them into its clutches, then left them in a lull that lasted four days. Then, while in Ilighôn, the island port city in the Vilhon Reach, they'd nearly gotten Vurgrom in an ambush while he conducted a trade for unknown items. They lost him again, but each time the enchanted astrolabe had brought them back to Vurgrom.

All of it had added up to the certainty that Vurgrom had an assignment in the area that he hadn't yet finished. Now, perhaps the time had come. Though they'd seen the pirate captain with sahuagin one other time, they'd never seen him act so contrite.

"That sahuagin he talked to must have been Iakhovas," Azla said.

"That was no sahuagin," Sabyna said. "Vurgrom talked to a man. Very tall, with a beard and dark hair."

"I saw no men there other than Vurgrom and his pirates. You must mean the elf woman."

"No," Sabyna said deliberately. "I saw what I saw."

"They say the Taker is very powerful," Azla replied after a moment. "Perhaps one of the guises we saw was only an illusion."

"Perhaps both were."

During their travels, they'd added to the lore they'd heard about the Taker. They'd also learned about the war going on under the waves they sailed upon. Several times they'd sailed through small islands of dead morkoth, ixitxachitl, mermen, sahuagin, and koalinth being savaged by birds, crabs, and fish.

"We've seen enough," Azla declared. "If we're to keep up with them, we need to get to shore ourselves."

"Go on," Sabyna said. "I'll follow you down after you reach the deck."

She waited, clinging to the rigging as *Azure Dagger* heeled over repeatedly at the end of her tether. When slack returned to the rigging, she knew Azla had reached the deck. The ship's mage clambered down easily but paid more attention than normal to her efforts.

Once on the deck, she went forward, one arm before her and walking slowly so she wouldn't run into an unwary rewman. She ascended the steps leading to the forecastle and called, "Glawinn?"

"Here, lady."

Judging where the paladin was from the sound of his voice, Sabyna went over to the railing. "You've seen?"

"Yes. Captain Azla and I were just discussing when we should attempt moving the ship. Or whether we should just try swimming for the shore."

"We have the small boat," Azla said from nearby, "but here is the risk that we'll be seen once we leave the spell Arthoris has around the ship."

"We should wait," Sabyna said. "Vurgrom is moving a lot of supplies. He isn't planning on living off the land. I think he'll be easy enough to find."

"Then we wait till after dark and pick up his trail?" Azla asked.

"Yes," Glawinn said. "He won't get so far ahead of us that we can't catch him soon enough. If he's stocking supplies, what he is going to do isn't going to happen too soon."

"I'll see to our own supplies," Azla stated. "We're going in stripped down. I want to be able to move quickly if the need arises."

"Agreed," Glawinn said.

Sabyna listened to the half-elf's footsteps recede from the railing.

"Lady?" the paladin asked.

"Aye."

"You're quiet."

"I'm thinking."

"About the young warrior?"

Sabyna hesitated. Upon occasion she and the paladin had talked of Jherek, but those talks had never brought much in the way of satisfaction. She couldn't help thinking that he might be dead and she'd never know, but the feeling Glawinn had told her would come if that were so never did.

"Do you still feel him close to you?" Glawinn asked.

"Not now, but earlier this morning. I could have sworn I heard him say my name on the wind again. It was foolishness, brought on by too much anxiety and too little sleep."

"And, mayhap, love?"

223

She hesitated. "I don't know anymore, Glawinn. The way I feel has changed."

"Don't you still miss him?"

"Aye, but not like I did."

"That's a good thing, though, lady. There's only so much pain a heart can bear."

"I don't know. Not missing him so much scares me."

"Why?"

She smiled at herself, then realized Glawinn couldn't see the expression. "When I was younger, just coming into my teens, I fell in love with one of the sailors on a ship my father worked on. He was seven or eight years older than I was, and he was so beautiful. I wanted him so badly to love me—to just notice me—but I was Ship's Mage Truesail's daughter, and the crew knew to leave me alone. My father was very protective then."

"So this love went unrequited?"

"Not entirely. I followed him around like a guppy staying with its school. He couldn't ignore me, but he didn't say anything. My mother noticed. She talked to my father. My mother is the only one who has the ability to convince my father to change his mind. She persuaded him to let me eat eveningfeast with the sailor."

"Did the sailor live up to your expectations, lady?"

Sabyna laughed at the memory, but there was a bit of sadness in the effort as well. "No. It was horrible. We sat there at that little table across from each other and had absolutely nothing to talk about." She laughed again. "Well, I had nothing to talk about. All he did was talk about the things he'd done, the women he'd seen, and how he'd be captain of a Waterdhavian Watch warship someday.

"That was an infatuation, Glawinn. How am I to know this isn't?"

"I know love when I see it, lady."

She suddenly wished she could see the warrior's face. "How do you know it's love?" she asked.

"Close your eyes, lady, and imagine his face in your mind."

Sabyna pictured Jherek in her mind, as she'd first seen him aboard *Breezerunner*, then again as he'd fought for her when Vurgrom kidnapped them in Baldur's Gate. All the memories she had of him, of the way his chest had felt beneath her fingers, the way his lips had felt and tasted against hers, tumbled through her mind.

She seemed to see him again. His light brown hair twisted in the wind and a green-blue sea spread out behind him. White sailcloth fluttered overhead. There was a cut on his face, running vertically over his right cheekbone, half-healed and slightly red from inflammation.

Jherek?

Aye, lady. His lips moved, as though he spoke, but she couldn't understand any of his words.

Sabyna's heart swelled within her breast and ached so fiercely she thought she'd die. Then the connection blurred for a moment.

Come to me! she called.

He spoke again, smiling through the sadness in his pale gray eyes. She couldn't hear him this time either, but she read his lips. *As you wish.*

Opening her eyes, Sabyna remained somewhat confused. She couldn't see her own hands in front of her body due to the invisibility spell.

"Lady?" Glawinn asked.

"I'm all right."

"I called for you but you didn't answer."

"It was like I could talk to him, Glawinn," Sabyna said. "He felt closer than he'd been those times before."

"Maybe he is."

"I don't know whether to wish that was so or not."

"Why?"

"I hate not knowing if he's all right," Sabyna answered honestly, "and I don't like missing him—but we're so uncomfortable around each other."

"I know."

"I just don't see that changing."

"It won't," Glawinn said after a short time. "Not until the young warrior himself changes. But tell me, lady, when you imagined him, how did it feel?"

Sabyna thought about her answer. There were so many things she could say. "I like thinking about him."

"Then accept that as it is for now, lady."

"It's not that easy."

"No."

Sudden irritation at the paladin dawned in Sabyna, and

her mind seized on something he'd said. "How did you know about my brother? I never mentioned it to you."

"Jherek told me," Glawinn said.

"Why?"

The silence drew out between them and Sabyna wished she could see the man's face.

"I would rather the young warrior tell you that."

"Is that part of the secret he won't tell me?" she asked. "How could it be?"

"Lady, as I said—"

"He's not here for me to ask him myself."

Sabyna grew more frustrated. If not for Arthoris's invisibility spell she could pin the paladin down with her gaze.

"The things I was told were told to me in confidence."

"Glawinn, I will have the truth. From you or from him, I will know what you both hide. I'm too deeply involved in this not to know." Sabyna made her voice harder. "Tell me, Glawinn. What is it about my brother's death that so concerns Jherek?"

XXI

3 Marpenoth, the Year of the Gauntlet

Myth Nantar.

Even the name evoked magic and a sense of incredible history.

From the moment he saw the sea elven city in the shallows of the Lesser Hmur Plateau, Pacys was at a loss for words. Thankfully, music came to his fingers. Still a quarter mile from the City of Destinies, the bard stopped swimming and settled on the foothills of Mount Halaath.

" 'Tis a pretty thing, isn't it?" Khlinat, who swam to the bard's side, asked.

"Yes," Pacys whispered.

Around them, the sea elf caravan came to a stop along the foothills. From the behavior of most of the warriors, it was the first time they'd seen the city as well.

The pale blue glow of the ancient mythal illuminated Myth Nantar against the dark black of the sea. The City of Destinies sat on a tableland that rose up from the ocean floor above the Lower Hmur Plateau, three hundred and seventy feet below the surface.

During the centuries of its isolation, coral had invaded Myth Nantar. Thick clumps of aqua-colored cryscoral grew in crystalline plate formations and clung to the exteriors of the ancient buildings. Pale blue ice coral dominated the upper reaches of the city, strung together in knobby clusters that reminded Pacys of spiderwebs draped over the upper reaches of the mythal. Bright patches of glowcoral had set up colonies throughout the city, creating shadows that twisted and turned in the currents.

"By Marthammor Duin, the Finder of Trails," Khlinat whispered solemnly, "never had I dreamed I would ever see such a sight as this."

Pacys drank in all the sights, letting his fingers pluck notes from the saceddar. The music he wrung from the instrument was bittersweet memories mixed with the sharp euphoria of hope and dreams yet unfulfilled. Tears came to the old bard's eyes as the song possessed him.

> Elven city, pale and cold,
> Shaped by hands strong and bold,
> Vessel and shaper of destiny,
> Care-taker and leader of unity,
> Lost Myth Nantar lay wrapped in her own shroud,
> Broken but unbent, humbled yet proud.
> Promise of life had not deserted her,
> As proven by those who sought succor.

The words and the notes flowed around Mount Halaath, and there were none among the sea elves who weren't touched by the emotion stirred by the old bard's song. After a short time for reflection and prayer from the clerics among them, who asked for guiding and blessing from Deep Sashelas, Reefglamor gave the order to swim to Myth Nantar.

The warriors went first, flanking the High Mages on all sides.

Pacys gazed at the city as the caravan closed on it. He heard the haunting singing that came from somewhere among the city's empty buildings. Some of the Alu'Tel' Quessir's legends had it that the city was now haunted by the ghosts of those who'd been slain during the sahuagin invasion of the Tenth Serôs War.

As he got closer, the old bard was able to make out the four quarters of the city and identify them from the maps he'd seen. The Elves' Quarter—a place of libraries and villas—lay in the northeastern corner of the city, covered over by the thick layers of aqua-colored cryscoral. What had been the Trade Quarter lay to the south of the Elves' Quarter. The Alu'Tel'Quessir histories had it that markets and entertainment had once ruled there, powered by the merchants who traded with those above and below. Now tiger-coral reefs grew rampant, closing most of the buildings from sight. The Law Quarter—the now-deserted seat of the sea elf government—occupied the southwestern corner of Myth Nantar. Tiger-coral grew from the roofs of the tallest buildings in Myth Nantar, making them even taller.

The least devastated area of the City of Destinies was the Dukar Quarter. Lucent coral street lamps lined the surprisingly clear streets. Pacys easily recognized the Dukarn Academy by the arrangement of four rectangular buildings facing the octagonal Paragon's College. Crafted of opulent pearl, the Palace of Ienaron stood nestled up against Mount Halaath along Maalirn's Walk and picked up the glow from the lucent coral climbing the mountain. The Keep of Seven Spires stood two stories tall, then branched into seven four-story towers all made of green marble.

At the center of the City of Destinies, where Maalirn's Walk, Chamal Avenue, the Street of Ser-Ukcal, and the Promenade of Kupav all came together, the Fire Fountain shot twisting yellow and orange flames into the sea. It burned hot enough to actually warm the currents within the mythal. Pacys had read that the flames had burned more than nine hundred years. Three Gates' Reef got its name from the arches over the three roads that exited the city. Maalirn's Walk ended at Mount Halaath.

The city's illumination made everything seem normal despite the crusty coral growth spread throughout the streets and buildings. The Great Barrier was invisible to the naked eye save as an occasional shimmering in the water. It looked as though Pacys could swim right into the city.

He saw the first of the advance warriors colliding with the Great Barrier. They drew back at once in stunned disbelief, then tested their tridents against the mythal's might. The impacts rang like steel on stone.

Pacys and Khlinat joined Reefglamor as the Senior High Mage swam toward the Great Barrier. The glow from the lucent coral washed the color from Reefglamor, lending him an ethereal pallor. Together, they sank toward Myth Nantar.

"It's a beautiful place," Pacys said.

"It was," Reefglamor said, his eyes sweeping the city. "It is my fervent wish that before I die I should be able to swim these streets, to touch the things that my ancestors once touched."

"Perhaps you shall."

Pacys stretched his toes down, fully expecting to touch the solid surface at any moment. Instead, he was surprised to find himself sliding on through where the Great Barrier should have been.

"Pacys!" Khlinat's startled yelp followed the metallic thunk the dwarf's peg made when it crashed against the Great Barrier. He made a quick grab for the old bard's hand but missed. "Marthammor Duin take me for a—"

The rest of the dwarf's expletive was cut off. Looking up through the shimmering haze that separated him from the sea elves and the dwarf, Pacys realized that he was on the other side of the Great Barrier.

More of the sea elf warriors descended on the protective shielding and tried to force their way through with their weapons. Pacys never even heard their efforts through the shimmering haze. The old bard swam upward but found the way blocked. He put his hands against the Great Barrier and tried to will himself through.

Instead, the barrier remained firm.

"You can't get out, Taleweaver," a deep voice rumbled.

Slowly, sliding his staff free of the harness that held it across his back, Pacys twisted it, flaring the foot-long blades open at either end.

"There are things you must be shown, things you must learn."

Above Pacys, the Great Barrier darkened, shutting out the view to the outside world. At the same time an impossibly large shadow stepped from the buildings below. The old bard recognized him immediately as a storm giant. The green skin, dark green hair and beard, and glittering emerald eyes gave room for no mistake. He stood something less than thirty feet tall with huge shoulders and a broad chest. In true Serôsian custom, the storm giant wore no clothes, though anklets, bracelets, and rings adorned his forearms, ankles, and fingers.

"Who are you?" Pacys asked, remaining near the top of the Great Barrier above the storm giant. Even as he looked at the huge warrior, the old bard could sense that there was a glamor around him. Skilled as he was, Pacys could almost see past it.

The giant smiled. "I am Qos, a Green Dukar. I am the Grand Savant of the Fifth Order and Paragon of the Maalirni Order. I have been waiting for you. There is much work ahead of us."

* * * * *

Floating well back of Iakhovas, Laaqueel watched as he reached inside his cloak and pulled something free. She felt the crackle of magic in the air as Iakhovas spoke strong words of power. The singsong cadence filled the currents ten miles north of Naulys, one of the chief cities of the merman empire below the western shores of the Whamite Isles. He spread the items he'd taken from his cloak into the water. Gold gleamed from his artificial eye. Bright purple sparkles danced from his palm when he opened his hand.

The malenti priestess recoiled from the new onslaught of magic that sped through the water. The purple sparkles spun and danced like tiny reef fishes evading a predator, whirling out in broader patterns around Iakhovas. At the center of the orbiting purple flashes, Iakhovas continued speaking words Laaqueel didn't understand.

When he was finished, the purple specks slowed, then floated calmly toward the surface. They also started to grow, stretching out into masses of leafy vines, floating against the currents under their own power.

Laaqueel watched them, aware of the eerie litany coming from the plant masses.

Whatever the spell, Iakhovas had been working on it for most of the last two days, devoting every moment and all of his energy to it.

Raiding by the sahuagin continued, gaining added momentum from the Sea Hulk koalinth tribe and the morkoth. Even with those allies, and the Thuridru mermen waiting in the wings, they weren't strong enough to take on Eadraal and the mermen of the Hmur Plateau.

She held her place and awaited him.

"It's done," he said.

Laaqueel nodded.

Only a little surprise showed in Iakhovas's dark eye. "You have no questions, little malenti?"

"I have learned," she replied, "that you only answer when you choose to."

Iakhovas regarded her with open disappointment. "I miss the zeal in you, little malenti, and I'm surprised by my own feelings in that regard." He glanced back in the direction of the masses of purple-leafed vines floating toward the surface and said, "Those are very old plants. They haven't been seen on Toril for thousands of years. No one in these waters has ever seen anything like them."

Laaqueel believed him. The eerie litany the plants voiced grew louder, pulling more strongly at her conscious mind with a bewitching attraction. She glanced up, noticing the first of the plants had reached the ocean's surface and still headed toward the southeast where the Whamite Isles lay.

"Even so," the malenti priestess said, "you lack the army you need to invade the merman empire. The longer we wait here, the greater the chance of our discovery. In time, even the bitterest of enemies in Serôs will join against you if you keep sending the sahuagin against them. Once joined, they will attempt to hunt you down."

Iakhovas laughed. "Little malenti, they have to join forces, otherwise everything I've done is for naught."

"I don't understand." If the worlds above and below the Sea of Fallen Stars joined forces, sahuagin lives would be forfeit.

"Only by their joining forces may the Great Barrier surrounding Myth Nantar be dropped," Iakhovas said. "I can't get through the Great Barrier alone, and I need access to the City of Destinies." He stared after the plants. "As for an army, little malenti, I'll be raising one of those soon now and it will be unlike anything you've ever faced before. That I promise you."

Laaqueel glanced up at the plants continuing to spread across the ocean's surface. She recognized them as a form of kelp she'd not seen before. The singsong litany grew stronger and stronger still.

"Let's go, little malenti," Iakhovas growled. "In your present state of fatigue and apathy, you might succumb to the kelpies' ensorcelment in spite of the protection I lend you."

It was true and she knew it. She hadn't prayed to Sekolah in days and only stayed awake because sleep would not come to her. Wordlessly, she followed him back through the shimmering gate he'd opened to bring them here.

Whatever Iakhovas had planned next, she knew the resistance in Serôs was growing. Sahuagin warriors had reported being attacked by shalarin east of the Whamite Isles, and there were even reports of morkoth battling morkoth along the eastern fringes of the Arcanum of Olleth. The surface world's response was the most sluggish, but even they were going on the offensive now.

Only the mermen of Eadraal had failed to attack, and their presence in the center of the Hmur Plateau prevented shalarin armies from marching against the sahuagin in the Xedran Reefs. Even the ixitxachitls couldn't be controlled now. Raiding parties of demon rays swept through the sahuagin rearguard in the two fallen ixitxachitl cities. The ixitxachitls weren't able to secure the cities, but losses were mounting, dividing the standing sahuagin army there.

On top of that, the surviving sahuagin princes from Vahaxtyl had started to foment rebellion due to the high losses among their warriors. Even Prince T'Kalah was cautiously hoarding his warriors instead of spending them as Iakhovas demanded. Iakhovas, though he knew of the resistance within his troops, ignored the situation.

Laaqueel knew that the sahuagin presence along the western reaches of Serôs was balanced on a knife's edge. Nothing could be completely controlled—especially if Iakhovas continued concentrating on his own missions instead of taking care of the armies he marshaled.

Taking on the merman empire in Eadraal wasn't something he should try to do. Laaqueel felt certain it would be the breaking point of the war. Yet, if the mermen couldn't stand against Iakhovas, the malenti priestess knew their defeat would demoralize the rest of Serôs.

She just didn't see how Iakhovas planned to raise a fresh army even with his mysterious kelpie.

Patience, the soft feminine voice whispered in her mind. *The time is near for all things. You have allies you've not yet seen, and the Taker doesn't know as much as he believes he does.*

Surprisingly, Laaqueel took a little comfort in the words. Ahead of her, Iakhovas disappeared into the gate that would take them back to *Tarjana.* She followed.

* * * * *

Sabyna lay low in the scrub brush that dotted the hilly interior country north of Agenais. Her breath stirred the red dust next to her cheek and a trail of black ants marched across her left hand. She held a dagger in her right.

Ahead, three of Vurgrom's pirates stood guard at the mouth of the cave the pirate captain and the rest of his group had entered nearly an hour before. Evening fast approached, stretching long shadows to the east while the red sun sank into a mass of purple clouds in the west.

"Lady."

The whisper almost startled Sabyna into movement. If she hadn't recognized Glawinn's soft voice she thought she might have screamed. She glanced down toward her feet and saw the paladin standing there.

"Aye, and—by Selûne's sweet grace—don't scare me like that again," she whispered hoarsely.

"I'm sorry," Glawinn said. Despite the plate mail the paladin wore, he moved almost as soundlessly as a shadow. "Azla and I have found another cave entrance that leads down to where Vurgrom and his men are."

"What are they doing?"

"It looks like they're waiting, lady."

"For what?"

"I couldn't say. I came back for you so that you could join us. Whatever Vurgrom is here to do, this is the place he's going to do it."

Sabyna waited until the three pirates standing guard

234

were talking again and not looking in her direction before she eased down the hillside, taking care not to disturb the brush. When they were safely out of sight, Glawinn offered his hand and helped her up.

The paladin took the lead, following the small ditch that zigzagged behind the rocky knoll where the cave was. Agenais lay to the south, not quite five miles away, about the same distance it was to the cover where *Azure Dagger* lay waiting, hidden from *Maelstrom*'s crew. From the way Azla had it figured, they stood near the heart of the island.

She trotted after Glawinn, avoiding the loose rock spills that had tumbled down into the ditch. The center of the island tended to be rockier than the outer edge. Loose limestone shale rose in pockets or showed in the parched, cracked land of the interior.

The limestone was a natural filter and removed the salt from the ocean in the numerous pockets and caves that formed in the island's heart. Rainfall added to the local water supply, trapped in natural and artificed cisterns. The limestone foundation also provided for the honeycomb effect of caves under the island. These caves were once the lair of brigands, who had been rooted out centuries before.

Her muscles ached from fatigue, short hours of sleep while they shared guard duty at night, and sleeping on the hard ground. Azla had decided that only the three of them would attempt to get close to Vurgrom's pirates. A dozen pirates from *Azure Dagger* waited at a hidden campsite half a mile away, providing them a position to fall back to if they were discovered.

Glawinn stopped ahead and pulled at a clump of brush that covered a narrow slash in the earth forming the knoll. It wasn't quite opposite the cave Vurgrom had entered, but Sabyna didn't think it missed by much.

The paladin turned sideways and fit himself inside. The slash extended up through the knoll, almost to the top, and allowed a narrow crack of the waning sunlight into the passage.

The ground was treacherous with loose rock and pebbles. Nearly forty feet into the passage, they lost the sunlight, and the air around them turned cool. Condensation chill to the touch glistened on the rocky walls and ceiling.

The passageway continued to go down and bear slightly to the left. Long minutes later, Glawinn waved her to slow down even more. They moved cautiously, deeper into the knoll.

Sabyna's hand trailed across the cracked surface of the passageway, feeling the jutting shale. The rock edges were sharp enough to cut if a person accidentally ran into them in the dark. Luckily, there was enough natural light coming from ahead to illuminate the passageway.

Azla, dressed in black chain mail and dark clothing, crouched on a narrow ledge ahead. She glanced at them briefly, a hand holding her scimitar across her knees, then returned her attention to the scene playing out before her. She wore a short bow and a quiver of arrows across her back. A spear rested on the stone floor at her side.

Glawinn touched a forefinger to his lip in caution as he hunkered down beside the pirate queen. He placed his shield against the wall at his side.

Sabyna crept closer, dropping to her knees between them to peer down into the cave below.

"Aye, and she was a feisty one," Vurgrom was saying. He sat on an ale cask in the center of a ring of seventeen pirates clustered around a campfire that poured oily black smoke against the cave ceiling thirty feet above. The cave looked at least three times that wide. He drank deeply and noisily from a tin mug, then wiped the ale foam from his lips. He touched a jagged scar on the top of his bald head.

"I had her," he said, "holding her down on the duke's own dining table and him crying for his life in the corner, preparing to take care of my business, and she reaches back for this damned great copper cook's pot. Next thing I know, the wench brains me with it."

The pirates laughed at their leader's story, but Sabyna noticed they waited until Vurgrom himself started laughing first.

"Like to split my head open, she did. If the wench had been swinging a slaughterman's mallet instead of that damned pot, why I'd a' been holding my own brains in."

"Bet you really gave her what-for then," one of the pirates stated.

"By the Bitch Queen's locked knees, are ye daft, man?"

Vurgrom roared. "Wench liked to killed me. Had blood a-seeping down into my face and me three sheets to the wind and truly not knowing how bad a shape I was in. I took up a carving knife from a nearby roast bird set for the duke's own table and shoved it through her heart. I was done, she had no complaints."

Gales of cruel, ribald laughter ripped through the cave.

Sabyna shuddered, involuntarily remembering her own brother's death at the hands of Bloody Falkane. She glanced around the cave, wondering what had brought the pirates there. Other than the long and tall stalactites and stalagmites, a few patches of lichen that glowed soft blue and green, and a few threads of streams running across the stone floor, there appeared to be nothing of interest in the cave.

A shimmering haze formed only a few feet from the group of pirates. The grim-visaged man Sabyna had seen four days ago leading the sahuagin pack that met Vurgrom stepped through the haze, followed by the elf woman who had been there as well.

"Vurgrom," the grim man said.

"Lord Iakhovas." Vurgrom handed the tin cup to the pirate beside him and stood. "As you see, we stand ready. As we agreed."

"Do you have the pearl disk?"

Vurgrom reached inside his blouse and took a cloth bag from around his neck. He loosened the drawstrings and poured the pearl and inlaid gold disk into his hand, then tossed it to Iakhovas.

Azla quietly slipped the bow from her shoulder and nocked an arrow to the string, aiming at Iakhovas. Sabyna wasn't sure that such a move was wise, but she kept her own counsel, readying her spells. Glawinn took up his shield and found a new grip on his broadsword. He kissed the rosy pink quartz disk that hung at his neck and whispered Lathander's name.

"No!" Anger flashed in Iakhovas's voice. He gestured at the thrown disk as the inlaid gold flashed the campfire light. It froze in mid-tumble, then glided back to Vurgrom, who caught it gingerly. Iakhovas's scarred face twisted, and the tattooing showed even blacker in the shadows. "I will not touch that thing!"

"Beg your pardon, milord," Vurgrom said, turning the disk over in his fingers in open wonder. "I didn't know."

Iakhovas walked to the cave wall to his right. "Did you ever manage to find out what this disk was, Vurgrom?"

"No, milord."

"But you tried?"

Vurgrom hesitated only a moment. "Spent good gold on it, milord." He shrugged. "Maybe cut a few throats of them that demanded payment and them not telling me any more than I already knew."

"It's a key." Iakhovas drew back his fist and pummeled the rock wall.

Stone split and splintered more easily than Sabyna would have thought. She breathed shallowly, waiting for Azla to release the bowstring.

"To what, milord?"

"I don't know," Iakhovas said as he hit the wall again, deepening the crack he'd started. He gestured to Vurgrom, who walked forward and thrust Lathander's talisman into the hole.

The talisman rattled a few times, the sound echoing clearly in the cavern, letting Sabyna know the crack Iakhovas had created reached far deeper than she'd have thought.

"I only know that it contains power I can use when I destroy it," Iakhovas said.

A ruby ray jumped from one of Iakhovas's eyes. The sound of a powerful detonation deafened everyone in the cave.

Sabyna might have cried out in pain. She wasn't sure. In the next moment the ground quavered and rumbled, twisting and turning like a storm at sea. Despite her familiarity with rolling waves, she stumbled and would have fallen had Glawinn not steadied her.

Below, the pirates spread out and drew their weapons, crying out to their gods and cursing. Vurgrom bellowed and pulled up his battle-axe, but whatever he was trying to say was lost in the tremendous *cra-ack!* that suddenly filled the cavern.

A chasm opened in the floor, spreading quickly from a hand's-span to several feet. Stalactites fell from the ceiling, one of them crashing through a pirate's shoulder and driving him to the ground. Blood pooled around the man as he quivered and died.

Iakhovas strode through the falling debris untouched, keeping his feet with apparent ease even though the earth shifted dramatically under him. The elf who had arrived with him didn't fare so well. She fell and rolled toward the chasm's edge. Moving with inhuman speed, Iakhovas reached down and caught the elf woman, lifting her effortlessly.

At that moment, Azla released the bowstring.

* * * * *

Kellym Drayspout walked his rounds through Agenais's docks out of habit. He carried a heavy crossbow at full cock in his scarred and gnarled hand. The chain mail he wore had seen better days but remained serviceable. He was a stout man with a bigger belly than he cared to admit, and gray hair that showed how many years had passed him, but he was a warrior few would want to confront. His lined and scarred face threw fear into most folks he had stern words with.

The docks seemed less well lighted than he'd ever seen them, but he didn't pay it any real mind. Quiet was a good thing. The carousing and drinking that went on more nights than not meant a long shift.

More ships than ever anchored in the shallows around the port. Almost all were shattered and broken husks, some of which would never move again, just be plucked apart to salvage other ships.

Drayspout's feet thumped against the creaking wooden dock as he made the corner that led down to Verril's Tavern. He'd stood in at the tavern enough that the locals, and the sailors that had been in Agenais any length of time, knew better than to cause any problems on his shift. Verril proved generous with the tapped ale kegs in return. It had proven a good arrangement.

The still, black water in the harbor was as smooth as polished glass. Ships' rigging slapped against masts. Over all of it he heard a melodic tune almost hypnotic in its intensity. The tune was enough, he'd discovered, to raise the hackles at the back of his neck.

Instead of merely trusting the way tonight, he'd found himself raising his lantern on more than a few occasions to strip away the shadows and make sure some foul thing wasn't crouched there waiting for him. His nervousness made him angry.

Being a guard wasn't a new job for Drayspout. He'd been a mercenary along the Dragon Coast for Lady Nettel Thalavar of the Thalavar trading family in Westgate for twenty years, until a bandit's blade had nearly found his heart a few years ago. He wasn't quite as quick as he had been, and he figured he'd had enough of it.

He'd been too well known on the Dragon Coast to retire there. Bandits he'd slain often had kin who didn't believe in forgiveness. In fact, some of the rogues' bands had even put a price on his head.

So he'd come to the Whamite Isles to spend his last years. He'd even met a widow who owned a bakery and had three teenaged children he could almost tolerate. He'd surprised himself by settling so easily into the sort of domestic life he'd never expected to have.

That life meant yelling at those damned kids every day, occasionally helping out in the bakery, and a few free pints of an evening down at Verril's between rattling merchants' doors and seeing to it nobody broke into a warehouse or shop too easily. The ships provided their own security.

Come early morning, he could count on snuggling for a little while with that widow before they started the sweetbreads and cakes she sold for morningfeast.

He cursed the damnable haunting tune that lay heavily over the dock area as he stepped onto the boardwalk running in front of Verril's Tavern. The building was a rundown affair cobbled together from leftover ship's lumber that had been, upon lean times, stripped back off and sold to vessels seeking materials to make repairs.

Drayspout stepped through the single batwing door that hadn't yet been auctioned off to a quartermaster in need of lumber. He stared at the empty tables and chairs that filled the small room, not believing what he saw.

The pale, oil lantern light pooled weakly in the room, and the smell of burning milk and meat from the untended chowder kettle hanging over the fireplace stunk the place up. The dice cups Verril used for wagering with his patrons, slipping in the special set he kept up his sleeve when he need to, sat on the stained bar. The painting of naked sea elves frolicking around Deep Sashelas hung on the wall behind the bar. Waves lapped noisily under the wooden floor and echoed hollowly through the room, striking a counterpoint to the melody that streamed in from outside.

Drayspout's unease grew by leaps and bounds. Maybe the sailors might take a quiet night to rest up, but there was never a night when Verril's went empty.

"Dray."

The hackles returned to Drayspout's neck. Everyone in Agenais who knew him called him Dray, but the whisper that called his name almost unnerved him. He was certain he knew the voice, but he couldn't place it.

He lifted the crossbow and placed the butt against his hip so he could fire it one-handed. Turning, he gazed back through the tavern's entrance, the view partially obscured by the batwing door. Usually there was some ship's crew working by lantern light to repair their vessels and he thought one of them might have called out to him.

There was no one. The docks stood totally empty.

"Dray."

A figure rose up from the black water beyond the boardwalk. Raising his lantern so the beam fell over the boardwalk, Drayspout recognized the figure at once. "Whik?"

It was his wife's oldest son. Whik stood as tall as Drayspout and was only fifteen. He still lacked a man's growth and strength, but he had a temper that had earned him the back of his stepfather's hand on occasion. He was pale and blond like his mother.

"What the hell are you doing in that water, boy?" Drayspout growled. It wasn't the first time Whik had slipped out of the house at night. Drayspout had caught him before. "You'll catch your death and break your ma's heart."

Whik made no reply.

Irritated that the boy may have seen him acting nervous, Drayspout strode toward him and raised his voice. "You got water in your ears, boy? I asked you a question."

When Drayspout reached the boardwalk, Whik fell backward, letting the water close over him.

Thinking something was wrong, Drayspout hurried to the boardwalk's edge and raised the lantern again. The light played over the water, lighting the pallid oval of the boy's face gazing up at him. Whik made no move to swim, slowly easing more deeply into the dark water. The haunting melody seemed louder than ever.

Dropping to his knees, Drayspout laid the crossbow aside and placed the lantern nearby so he could see Whik. He plunged his arm and shoulder into the water, feeling the chill, and reached for the boy. With his face less than two feet from Whik's, Drayspout noticed how dead the boy's eyes looked. Living around the Sea of Fallen Stars all his life as he had, the old warrior knew what a man looked like who'd succumbed to Umberlee's endless embrace.

Whik was dead. Sure as Tymora hated two-headed coins, the boy was never coming home to his mother again after this night.

Even as Drayspout started to withdraw his arm, the dead boy lunged at him, coming up out of the water with a leering half-wit's grin. He roped an arm behind his stepfather's head, grabbing Drayspout's wrist with his other hand. He pulled the old warrior down into the water with him.

As they sank deeper into the harbor, Drayspout fought against the dead thing that held him. The boy's corpse was as cold as the water. The old warrior tried to fight his way loose, but his hands kept sliding off the dead thing's wet, flaccid skin.

Still clinging to Drayspout, the corpse lunged forward and sank sharp teeth into the old warrior's throat. As his life drained out of him, clouding the water the lantern light shined through, Drayspout saw dozens of other pallid faces surrounding him. He recognized many of them as regulars at Verril's.

All of them were dead, their open eyes staring at him with dulled intelligence. They floated easily, wreathed in the kelpie-beds that sang the eerie music and held them like favored lovers.

Even as his final moment of life fled, Drayspout watched as other citizens of Agenais—men, women, and children he could have passed on the streets—plummeted into the water and didn't even try to save themselves from drowning.

Something evil had come for Agenais, Drayspout realized, and it wasn't going to rest until it had them all.

XXII

7 Marpenoth, the Year of the Gauntlet

Azla's arrow sped true, flashing through the rolling fog
of dust that billowed up from the chasm that had opened
in the cavern floor.

Iakhovas turned, fixing the ledge with his harsh gaze.
Quicker than the eye could see, he snatched the arrow from
the air, stopping it only inches from his heart. He snapped
the thick shaft in his hand.

"You've been followed, Vurgrom!" he roared, dropping
the broken arrow and pointing at the ledge.

Sabyna opened her bag of holding and released Skeins.
The raggamoffyn surged into the dust-laden air and set up
in its familiar serpentine shape. A pirate pulled a heavy
crossbow to his shoulder and fired. The ship's mage dodged
back, doubting she could get clear in the narrow passageway.

Glawinn was there, shoving his shield out. The crossbow
bolt slammed into it. "Easy, lady," the paladin warned.

Coolly, Azla nocked another arrow and let it fly. The
pirate with the crossbow looked down at the feathered
shaft that stuck out of his chest.

"Get them!" Vurgrom bellowed.

As the earthquake continued, five pirates managed to get to their feet and race toward the ledge. More debris dropped from the cavern roof, pummeling one of the pirates to the ground.

Sabyna took a pinch of sand and rose petals from her bag of holding, crushed them together, and spoke. A light green haze spiraled from her closed hand as the sand and rose petals were consumed by the spell. The haze sped toward the rushing pirates, wrapping around them. All four dropped, asleep before they hit the ground.

Iakhovas pointed over the heads of the other pirates who had regrouped and started toward the ledge. A lightning bolt lanced across the distance.

Glawinn swept Sabyna back with one arm and stood to block the streamer of crackling energy. The detonation rolled thunder through the cavern and blew the paladin off his feet, knocking him back ten feet over the ship's mage's head.

Sabyna started toward the warrior's sprawled form, knowing in her heart he had to be dead. The colorful image of the scarlet hawk on his shield hung in tatters of peeling paint. She knelt beside Glawinn, who lay loosely, his eyes open and staring blankly.

"Glawinn . . ." she said.

The paladin's chest gave a convulsive heave as he sucked in a sudden breath. He groaned and levered himself up, picking up his shield.

"By Lathander's blessed eyes," he managed to say, "the magic in this shield is stronger than I thought."

He slipped the shield over his arm, coughed raggedly, and got to his feet with difficulty.

Face tight, Azla slipped her bow over her shoulder and turned to them. She drew her scimitar and said, "We can't stay here."

"Agreed," Glawinn agreed. He took a fresh grip on his broadsword.

Azla took the lead as they raced back toward the other end of the passageway. Night had descended since Sabyna had entered the cave, and she didn't see the opening she'd come through earlier until skeletal arms suddenly thrust through it.

The skeleton stepped into the passageway, moving jerkily and holding a rusty short sword in its bony fist. The ivory grin showed missing front teeth and black hunger burned in its eye sockets. More skeletons filed in behind it.

Glawinn moved in front of Azla, sliding his sword into its sheath, and thrusting forward his hand, palm out. "By the grace of the Morninglord," he said, "get you back, hellspawn."

The skeletons acted as if they'd hit a brick wall. Most of the creatures stopped their advance, but a few in the rear didn't. They were held back by the ones in front. Bones clacked as they collided with each other. Their jaws snapped open and shut in anger, but they turned and walked slowly back out the passageway, fighting with the others that hadn't been affected by the paladin's power.

Even turned away as they were, the skeletons moved too slowly to clear the passageway before Vurgrom's pirates overtook them. Sabyna glanced back toward the ledge as the first of the men scrambled up. The ship's mage ordered Skeins to attack.

The raggamoffyn swirled into action, wrapping itself around the man and possessing him. The pirate turned to attack the next man, swinging his cutlass at his comrade's head.

The pirate ducked and skewered the possessed man through the stomach. Blood drenched the raggamoffyn, staining it crimson.

Azla's scimitar flashed as she closed on the pirate while he freed his weapon from his possessed comrade. He stepped back, holding his slashed throat, and lost his footing over the ledge.

"This way," Azla called, turning to the right and following a narrow ledge that ran around the upper part of the cavern.

"After you, lady," Glawinn said.

Sabyna called Skeins to her and drew a pair of throwing knives. She followed Azla into the darkness. The light from the pirates' campfire was barely enough to illuminate the way, leaving long, dark shadows draped over the cavern walls and floor. Tremors still shook the cavern, causing minor avalanches around them.

Azla turned left and headed through an opening. Sabyna was at her heels, aware that the surviving pirates had climbed up onto the ledge and were after them. The passageway ran only a short distance before opening to another cave.

A shaft of blue moonlight spewed through the crack in the cave twenty-five feet up. The light showed thick stalagmites and stalactites that had formed columns around a pool of water on the other side of the cave. Bones littered the floor. Farther back, three figures huddled against the wall on the other side of the pool.

"Help us!" a woman's voice called out. She moved toward them, revealing the length of iron chain attached to the spike driven into the wall. A small boy cried helplessly, his arms wrapped around the woman. The third figure was a young man who'd picked up large rocks in both hands.

Sabyna noted the ragged clothing the three wore, as well as the obvious lack of nourishment, but she couldn't figure out what they were doing there. Sabyna didn't know if they could save themselves, much less free the prisoners. The crack in the roof, obviously created by the tremors, was the only way out of the cave.

"The columns," Glawinn said. "It's our only chance."

Sprinting across the room, Sabyna looked at the woman and the small child and asked, "Who are you?"

Glawinn and Azla slid into position behind two of the columns. The half-elf took up her bow again and put a shaft through the neck of the first pirate in the cave from less than fifteen paces. The man fell back, mortally wounded and drowning in his own blood. It gave the other pirates pause.

"Prisoners." The woman's face was grime-streaked, her hair knotted. Half-healed scratches covered her arms, neck, and shoulders. "A tribe of koalinth took our ship maybe a tenday ago. They brought us here." She glanced at the pile of bones by the pool. "There were nine of us once."

"How did they get you here?"

"An underground river," the woman replied. "It leads from the pool out to the sea. They brought us here so the sahuagin wouldn't take us away from them. Koalinth are able to breathe fresh water. This cave was a convenient place to keep their larder."

Azla loosed another arrow but missed her target as the pirates invaded the cave. They quickly fanned out and took cover behind boulders and other stalagmites. Vurgrom came in last, bawling orders at his men to attack. With Glawinn ready to face them, none of the pirates appeared too eager.

Iakhovas strode into the room with the elf woman behind him. One of his eyes blazed.

"I want them dead," he ordered. He pointed, spoke, and three of the columns near the pool shattered as if struck by a battering ram.

Sabyna dropped beside the woman and grabbed her chain in both hands. She pulled fiercely but the spike didn't budge.

"Don't leave us here," the woman begged. "Please."

"I won't," Sabyna promised. She slipped one of her daggers behind the spike's head and tried to lever it from the wall, putting all of her back into the effort.

"At them, you scurvy dogs!" Vurgrom ordered.

Glancing over her shoulder, Sabyna saw Glawinn whirl suddenly and engage a pirate. The paladin blocked the pirate's thrust with his soot-stained shield, then cleaved the man's head in twain. Glawinn kicked the dead man from his blade, sending the body sprawling in the middle of the open.

"Have at you, then," the paladin challenged. "By Lathander's swift justice, here you'll find a warrior tried and true."

Iakhovas raised a hand.

"No," a calm voice called through the shadows.

Recognizing the voice, not believing that she'd truly heard it, Sabyna looked up from pulling on the knife and spotted him standing in the opening leading to the last cave.

Jherek stood in the doorway, the cutlass level before him, the gaze in his eyes defiant. The cut Sabyna had seen on his face was really there, and the ship's mage knew that the times she'd felt he'd spoken her name hadn't been her imagination after all.

The young sailor wore breeches tucked into calf-high boots and a white shirt with belled sleeves. Blood streaked the shirt, proof that he'd come in through the cave's main entrance.

"You should have struck me from behind, boy," Iakhovas

rasped, then he smiled. "But you couldn't do that, could you?"

Jherek threw himself forward, revealing the other men behind him. A lightning bolt shot from Iakhovas's finger and struck Jherek in the chest. The young sailor flew back out of the cave, slamming into two men behind him and disappearing over the ledge.

"No!" Sabyna yelled.

The knife blade snapped, and she fell, sliding across the rough stone floor toward the pool. As she started to push herself up, a face surfaced in the water. It was dark green and topped by coarse black hair. Pointed ears framed its head. The mouth was a broad, lipless slash filled with sharp fangs that gleamed in the moonlight.

The koalinth reached for Sabyna even as three other heads surfaced.

* * * * *

"You closed the Great Barrier around Myth Nantar?" Pacys was astounded at Qos's announcement.

The old bard sat on top of the coral in the courtyard south of the Maalirn College. Over the four days they'd talked, the storm giant seemed most comfortable there. Though he'd studied his host in detail, the old bard still hadn't managed to pierce the guise the Green Dukar wore, nor managed to find out why he wore it.

"I had no choice," Qos replied in his great, booming voice. "Myth Nantar represents the promise all Dukars made to each other and all of Serôs. When those we sought to protect and guide turned on each other during the Tenth Serôs War, I could stand it no longer. None of the Serôsian races deserved something as grand as this city and its promise."

"The Dukars have faced problems before," Pacys replied. His fingers idly strummed the saceddar, coaxing the tune he'd decided would best represent the storm giant.

"Yes," Qos said. The giant paced, looking at the tall, tiger-coral covered buildings in the Law Quarter. "For nearly eight thousand years, the Dukars held positions of influence. Within five hundred years of our alliance with the sea elves of Aryselmalyr and our triumph over the koalinth, nearly five thousand years of peace ensued." He closed his hand into a fist. "Can you imagine what those years must have been like?"

Pacys let his fingers roll over the saceddar, playing by instinct. "I can try."

"During that time we built Myth Nantar and we created the Dukarn Academy. We did not know it then, but the Aryselmalyr sea elves planned to exact a price for letting us build there.

"The Dukars were told to swear fealty to the elven empire and the Coronal at Coryselmal."

Qos clasped his hands behind his back and continued to pace. Being twenty-six feet tall, the giant's strides were impressive to the bard.

"The elves began fighting among themselves and began trying to expand their empires," Qos said. "The merfolk objected, and rightfully so. However, their first order of the day was to battle their way to Myth Nantar and claim it as theirs. The enmity between the elves of Coryselmal and Aryselmalyr escalated events. The Dukars stepped in, hoping to end it. Instead, the Dukars of Nantari who had sworn allegiance to Aryselmalyr warred against the other orders."

Pacys listened to the sad weariness in the storm giant's voice. Qos hadn't lived during those times but it was easy to see that he had taken the history to heart. The old bard made the giant's sadness and fatigue a part of the music, blending it so that it spoke eloquently.

"Never had anyone thought that Dukar hands would be raised against each other," Qos continued. "They lived to promote peace and harmony throughout Serôs and all races, believing that Serôs could only prosper."

"It was a grand dream," Pacys commented.

"It wasn't supposed to be a dream." Fire sounded in the storm giant's words. "That was the destiny of the Dukars, and why they founded their academies here in the City of Destinies. During that war, the merrow and the koalinth banded together to create the Horde of the Bloodtide, and mages aligned with Coronal Essyl created the Emerald Eye, which has been a bane in Serôs ever since. Also, our first new order among the Dukars, the Order of Nantari, was destroyed."

A school of fish swam in front of Pacys, creating a haze for a moment. He watched their gentle undulations, felt the miniature currents break against his body. His fingers moved a little more swiftly, adding in the motion that complemented the mood he sought to create.

"When the shalarin arrived after that and we allied with them, we made powerful friends," Qos said. "They easily took to the Dukar ways. Prosperity followed our orders again for a time, then a coronal was assassinated and the Dukars were blamed. The sea elves began striking out at the Dukar orders. In response, forty of the more aggressive of our order removed their normal colors and dressed in purple, calling themselves the Purple Order of Pamas, and began a limited war of their own."

"But things didn't end there," Pacys said.

"No. War continued to be a way of life here, and everywhere it went, the Dukars could be found in it. Finally, after the Ninth Serôs War, the Dukars helped draft the Laws of Battle, hoping it would stem the tide of violence that seemed unstoppable in this world. When that failed, when the Dukars could no longer believe, they left Myth Nantar."

"And without the Dukars to protect it, the City of Destinies fell to the sahuagin."

"Yes." Sadness almost quenched the angry, molten fires in Qos's emerald eyes. "After I joined the Dukars, I came to Myth Nantar." He gestured with one hand, taking in the expanse of the city. "I saw most of what you see here, and my heart could not bear it."

Pacys looked at the storm giant, seeing past the towering foe to the gentle spirit beneath. He coaxed that image with his song, building it note by note.

"So I chose to close Myth Nantar from those who'd deserted her."

Pacys knew the storm giant hadn't kept everyone who'd journeyed to the City of Destinies away. Dozens had slipped in past the Great Barrier over the years when Qos had deemed them worthy.

"Why did you let me in?" the old bard asked. It was a question he hadn't dared ask the first few days. Qos had obviously known he was coming but hadn't been too much in favor of his presence.

"If it had been my choice," the storm giant said, "I wouldn't have."

Pacys silently accepted that, his fingers never betraying the musical weave he worked on.

"The Great Whale Bard was my friend," Qos went on. "He chose you. I chose to honor both his request and his memory."

"What am I supposed to do?"

"What you normally do, bard. Tell the tale of what goes on around you." The storm giant gestured at the surrounding city. "This is history in the making. The legend of the Taker is true. If we don't remove him from Serôs, he will destroy everything."

"Everything?"

"The rebirth of Myth Nantar. A second beginning, one that will be of even more import to those below and above." Qos turned and pointed back to the Dukarn Academy off the Promenade of Kupav. "The weapon we need to accomplish that is there."

"What is it?" Pacys stopped playing for a moment and turned to look. It was the first anything had been said of a weapon.

"The Great Gate," Qos said. "Once it's activated, it will pull the Taker and his army through it and exile him from Serôs."

"Where will he go?"

"It won't matter. Anywhere but here." Qos locked his emerald eyes on the bard's and said, "Song That Brings Bright Waters believed that you were the Taleweaver, the one destined to touch the heart of the young hero who would slay the Ravager."

"How am I supposed to accomplish that?"

Qos shook his head. "These are legends, bard. As familiar with them as you are, you should know that legends never tell everything."

"My song will," Pacys declared. "When it's ready, and when I sing it, the listener will know all." He stretched, adjusting himself on the coral. "When will you open the Great Barrier?"

"As soon as Serôsian races can come to an alliance."

"I believe the sea elves would be interested," Pacys said. "As well as the shalarin, but the mermen remain adamant about staying apart."

"They won't," Qos said, "once Voalidru falls."

"I've overheard the sea elf warriors talking about that. The locathah keep information coming to us. The warriors believe the Taker has stretched his alliances too thin and that he doesn't have the power to challenge Eadraal at this point."

"The Taker is mustering his next army even as we speak."

A cold chill raced through the old bard. "How?"

Qos held up his right hand. Green coral suddenly emerged from his palm and flattened, covering his huge hand.

"The Taker has surrounded the Whamite Isles," Qos told him, "with an evil and ancient kelpie that sings its listeners to their deaths. He wracks the islands with massive earthquakes that will drive the people to the shore so they can hear the kelpie songs. Few, if any, will survive. When enough have died, the Taker will call the victims back as drowned ones in his service."

Horror filled Pacys, stilling his fingers. He gazed at Qos's palm where images formed. He saw the pallid figures hanging from kelpie beds in the black water, their arms and legs limp, their dead eyes red and blank, mouths hanging open. A few of them were drowning even as he watched, thrashing slightly as their lives left them.

"No," the old bard cried hoarsely. "We can't let this happen."

"It already has," Qos stated. "It must happen to make way for the only chance Serôs has at peace."

Unable to look away, Pacys watched as more people dropped into the black water, immediately tended to by the kelpie beds. No matter how great his skill nor the fact that Oghma himself had set his present course before him, he would never be able to capture the abomination being played out before his eyes.

* * * * *

Blasted by the lightning bolt that should have killed him, Jherek hit the ground hard, so hard that the breath was driven from his lungs and he almost blacked out. He clung to his senses, though, thinking of Sabyna, Glawinn, and Azla trapped like rats in the cave. Rolling over on his side, he felt blood trickle down the side of his face.

The journey that had taken only days before had extended to two restless months. A sahuagin attack had cost them their rudder. Replacing the rudder had taken tendays after *Steadfast* had finally made a friendly port. Despite the time, the pull in his chest had brought him to Sabyna without fail, never once wavering.

As he got to his feet, the young sailor noticed the lightning bolt fading in the high sheen of the bracer on his left arm. The bracer had somehow protected him from the magical assault.

Black spots whirled in his vision as he gazed around the main cavern. Two of Tarnar's sailors—the two he'd been thrown into—were down, alive but unconscious. Jherek looked for his cutlass but didn't see it. The sounds of battle and the screams of dying men continued above.

He started to take one of the sailors' cutlasses, but impulse drew his eyes to the chasm in the center of the cavern. Looking down over the edge, he spotted a man-made entrance cut in the left side six feet below him. Before he knew quite what he was doing, feeling pulled to get back to Sabyna's side, he hung over the ledge, staring down into a pit that looked fathoms deep. Thankfully, the chasm walls provided finger and toeholds.

When he looked into the opening, he saw the sword hanging on the wall at the other end of what looked like a man-sized pink pearl box. Glancing at the other side of the chasm, he noticed what appeared to be the other side to the pink pearl room. The sword's steel glistened with a lambent pink light.

Ignoring the reluctance that filled him, Jherek clambered into the room. It stood to reason that if a sword had been hidden as cleverly as this one, it had to be a powerful weapon. The question of whether the sword was good or evil only touched his mind fleetingly. As powerful as the mage in the other room was, Jherek needed a powerful weapon.

Wrapping his hand around the sword hilt, Jherek felt a small tingle run through his arm. He almost released the sword, but the tingle was gone before he did. He thrust the blade through his sash and climbed the chasm wall again, then he jumped up the ledge and ran back to the second cave.

Tarnar looked at him with a surprised smile and said, "I thought you were dead."

"Iridea's Tear saved me." Jherek drew the sword from his waist, surprised that the blade was a curved cutlass and not the long sword he'd thought it was. The blade still held the pink glow.

Two of *Steadfast*'s crew lay dead inside the second cavern.

Peering into the shadows, Jherek saw Sabyna and Glawinn battling koalinths rising from the pool. Vurgrom's men took advantage of the situation and rushed forward.

Azla stepped from behind a column, batted aside the pirate's clumsy attack, then slid her scimitar across the man's stomach, spilling his guts. Still on the move, the pirate queen engaged her next attacker. Steel gleamed as it moved, then she sank the dirk in her left hand between the man's ribs, stiffening him up at once.

Lifting his arm, Jherek willed the bracer into a shield, then stepped into the cavern. One of the pirates rushed at him. The young sailor stepped sideways at the last moment, letting the pirate's overhead swing go past him, then he slammed the shield into his attacker with all his weight behind it.

The pirate hit the wall and sagged, dazed by the impact. Before he recovered, Jherek knocked the man's blade from his hand.

Tarnar stepped up and grabbed the pirate by the shirt, yanking him into a stumbling run and passing him back to one of his men.

"I've got him," the captain growled.

"Don't kill him if you don't have to," Jherek said.

"In that, my friend," Tarnar said, "we are in agreement."

Vurgrom bellowed orders from hiding but didn't make a move to engage Jherek as the young sailor moved forward.

Iakhovas stood his ground, glancing at Jherek with real curiosity. "Who are you, boy?"

Jherek shook his head, peering over the shield and hoping it would hold against any further magic. "I'm no one," he said.

"What are you doing here?"

Jherek thought he detected suspicion in the dark mage's tattooed face and mismatched eyes. "Let my friends go," Jherek demanded.

"I don't know you, do I?" Iakhovas asked.

"I'm only going to ask you once."

The man's eyes narrowed and he said, "Boy, I've eaten creatures bigger than you."

Without warning, Jherek stepped forward. It bothered him that the mage didn't draw the sword at his side, but if he didn't have to kill the man he wouldn't. He swung the sword, surprised at how balanced it felt, like it was a weightless extension of his body.

Incredibly, Iakhovas grabbed the sword with his hand, stopping the swing, but from the pained expression on the mage's face, it was a surprise for both of them. He lifted his hand, gazing with ill-concealed astonishment at the blood that spilled from around his closed hand.

"Who *are* you?" the mage demanded.

Before Jherek had time to answer, Vurgrom bellowed and rushed from hiding. He barreled across the short distance and slammed into the young sailor with his considerable bulk.

Already sore from his earlier fall, Jherek couldn't keep his feet, but he did keep his grip on the cutlass. It felt as if his arm was being torn from its socket before the blade slid free of the mage's hand.

"Going to kill you now, boy!" Vurgrom roared as he came down on top of Jherek. "I remember you from Baldur's Gate. I should have killed you then."

Willing Iridea's Tear from shield to dagger, a handle forming in his hand, Jherek shoved it toward Vurgrom's face. The fat pirate captain's eyes rounded as he stared at the multi-colored blade. Taking advantage of the man's shifting weight, the young sailor levered his forearm under his opponent's jaw hard enough to make his teeth clack, then rolled out from under him.

Jherek willed the bracer into a hook, the handle fitting easily between his fingers. Vurgrom got to his feet at the same time as the young sailor, taking up his battle-axe in both hands. Iakhovas was still visible over the pirate captain's shoulder, his attention torn between his bleeding hand and Jherek.

255

Reversing the battle-axe so the hammer end of it was forward, Vurgrom swung at the young sailor. Jherek dodged, barely escaping the speeding weapon. The blunt head smashed against the wall, cracking rock loose and driving stone splinters into Jherek's face and left shoulder.

Lining up behind his blade, Jherek gave himself over to it, relishing the feel and movement. He whipped it forward, forcing Vurgrom into a defensive posture. The bigger man managed to block the sword strikes, but only just.

Another pirate stepped from hiding at Jherek's side, coming too quickly for the young sailor to bring the cutlass around. Jherek dropped, falling backward, watching the pirate's sword flash by only inches from his face. The young sailor kicked upward, rolling on his back and right shoulder to get the necessary height, aware that Vurgrom was renewing his attack.

Jherek's foot connected with the pirate's sword arm elbow hard enough to crack bone. He continued the roll to escape Vurgrom's battle-axe. More stone splinters sprayed against his back, then he was on his feet in a squatting position, ready to spring upward.

Vurgrom already had the battle-axe back and was swinging the blade at him, intending to cleave him between wind and water. Staying low, Jherek drove forward, firing off his bent legs and planting his left shoulder and neck at knee level.

Vurgrom squalled in surprise and toppled.

As the big man fell, Jherek rose to his knees and struck again, snaring the battle-axe's haft with the hook. He brought the cutlass down hard and sheared the head from the haft. A small blue light flared as the weapon came apart.

Vurgrom raised the haft in defense as Jherek stood and swung again. The cutlass blade sliced through the thick axe haft as if it were made of paper. With uncanny precision, somehow knowing he could trust the sword, the young sailor brought it to a stop less than two inches from Vurgrom's face.

"Surrender," Jherek told him, "and I'll not kill you."

"You broke my axe," Vurgrom said in disbelief. "That axe was enchanted. It's never been broken before—never failed me."

256

Jherek twisted the tip of the cutlass, emphasizing his point.

"Fight me hand-to-hand," Vurgrom roared. "Give me a true man's challenge."

Breathing hard, perspiration and blood covering him, Jherek replied, "If there were time, and if there were honor in it, I would, but there's no time, and the only honor at risk would be my own."

Jherek glanced at the mage, already willing the bracer into a shield again.

"Pray to your gods, whelp," Iakhovas said in a cold, hard voice, "that you never meet me again."

Jherek wasn't planning on it, but he didn't say anything. He also didn't break eye contact. If any of his friends had been hurt, it would have been a different matter.

Iakhovas turned, gestured, then walked into what appeared to be a solid wall, the elf woman at his heels.

When the mage had gone, Jherek left Vurgrom with one of Tarnar's men holding a sword to his throat. Tarnar's sailors flooded into the cave. Their captain cowed, the surviving members of Vurgrom's pirates surrendered easily enough.

Jherek sprinted to the pool where koalinth battled his friends, Tarnar at his heels. Two of the creatures lay dead, silent testimony to Glawinn's skill. The paladin was on the floor, his sword locked against a koalinth's spear and his shield holding the creature's savage jaws from his face.

Changing the shield back to a hook, Jherek hooked the koalinth's shoulder from behind and yanked the monster off the paladin. The young sailor kicked the sea hobgoblin in the face, driving it back into the pool. He offered the paladin a hand up.

"Hail and well met, young warrior," Glawinn greeted him in a strained voice.

"Hail and well met," Jherek replied.

"The helping hand was appreciated," the paladin said with a crooked smile, "but I'd just gotten him where I wanted him."

Glawinn's sword flashed, engaging another koalinth's trident. He shoved the tines aside, then slid back through and slashed across the creature's stomach, mortally wounding it.

Jherek shifted the hook back to a bracer and swung his arm out to slap aside another koalinth's spear. The young sailor chopped the cutlass into the koalinth's neck, nearly beheading it. He stepped around the falling corpse, moving toward Sabyna.

When he saw her, the copper tresses framing her face, Jherek felt as though he'd been hit in the heart with Vurgrom's great hammer. Eighty-three days they'd been apart, and not one of them had passed that he didn't think of her with both longing and trepidation.

Now she was there before him, bent over in a knife-fighter's stance, a blade in each hand, battling for her life against a koalinth. The creature struck with its spear but Sabyna turned it to one side and darted in to score a wound on her attacker's arm. The wound wasn't life threatening, but it bled heavily.

The koalinth howled in pain, then shoved its head open, the massive jaws aiming to bite her head.

Jherek thrust the cutlass forward, not willing to attack the creature from behind. The blade settled between the creature's jaws and it snapped its fangs on steel instead of flesh.

"Lady," Jherek said softly as the koalinth withdrew, "I am here."

Sabyna glanced at him and said, "You're alive."

"Aye."

Jherek stepped between her and the koalinth as another joined it. Despite the stench of wet leather, the closed-in stink of the cave, and the smell of blood, he caught the scent of the lilac fragrance she wore. Just one breath steeled his arm in spite of the beating he'd taken and the fatigue of racing across five miles of rugged terrain to reach the cave. He felt calm and centered.

"I thought you were dead," Sabyna said.

Jherek batted away a spear thrust, riposting and slicing the koalinth on the forehead so that blood ran down into its eyes.

"As I feared you might be before I returned," he told her.

"I wasn't sure you cared about that—even cared enough to come back from wherever you'd gone."

Her words hurt Jherek more grievously than any wound he'd received. He grabbed the next spear thrust in his free hand, held the haft, and stepped forward to pierce the koalinth's breast with the cutlass.

He yanked his blade free and turned to her, full of anger and pain. He kept his words as calm as he could, not understanding how she could doubt him.

"Please, lady," he said, "I have told you I would lay my life down for you. I would never desert you in troubled waters without seeing you home."

"You've told me that," Sabyna agreed, "but there's much you haven't told me."

Jherek gratefully turned back to face the koalinth he'd wounded.

"Perhaps we could talk about this another time," he said.

He parried a spear, knocking sparks from the weapon.

"Do you swear?" Sabyna pressed, stepping up beside him to engage another koalinth.

Her knives flashed as she blocked the spear thrust, then one of the blades flew from her hand, burying itself in her opponent's throat. Crimson sprayed over her and Jherek.

Jherek hesitated, blocking the spear twice more, then stepping in as he formed the bracer into a dagger and punched it through the wounded koalinth's heart. Even as the creature fell, another shouldered up to take its place.

"Promise me," Sabyna said.

"Lady, please."

Jherek tried to turn the koalinth's attack, but it was too savage, too fierce. It drove him back as he tried to find an opening.

"I will not be denied, Jherek," Sabyna said.

"Now," the young sailor said, thrusting and breaking his opponent's attack, "is not the time."

"Your secret, whatever it is," Sabyna said, "is holding both of us back. Neither of us can be happy until we know where we stand."

"Lady, I care deeply for you."

The conversation and the emotion that went with it distracted Jherek. He missed a parry and watched as the spear streaked toward his chest. He managed to turn at the last moment, letting the iron point graze his ribs. He willed the bracer into a hook and tore out the koalinth's throat before it was able to withdraw.

"Pretty words," Sabyna said. "Jherek, I wouldn't ask this if I knew you weren't confused, scared, and hurting, too."

He faced her, his chest heaving from emotion and exertion, and said, "Lady, I have never known any other way."

He was only dimly aware that the last of the koalinth were being beaten back by Glawinn, Azla, Tarnar, and the sailors from *Steadfast*. Skeins had claimed one of the koalinths, wrapping the creature and using it against the others.

"I have never known pain like this," Sabyna replied. "Never known confusion like this. My world was far simpler before I knew you."

Jherek was silent for a moment as the sounds of the battle died down. His voice was quiet, barely above a whisper when he said, "Lady, I'd never known my world was as small as it was before I knew you."

"If you feel that way," Sabyna asked in frustration, "then why have you put up all these walls?"

"Walls are a part of my life, lady."

"I won't have them in mine."

Sabyna gazed at him fiercely. The fact that he'd pushed her into such a position shamed Jherek. His heart ached and a lump that he could scarce swallow filled his throat.

"What is there to risk?" she demanded.

"The friendship that we have between us."

"But it could be more."

That she'd voiced the possibility of something more both embarrassed and terrified Jherek even more than getting hit with the lightning bolt only moments ago.

"Lady," he said, "I have treasured every moment of it, and if that friendship was all that would ever exist between us—ever could exist—I would be happy."

"Jherek," Sabyna's voice was thick with emotion, "it's been hard these last—what, nearly three months—never knowing if you were alive or dead. I truly don't know the depth of my emotions for you. I'm not sure if I'd know true love, but I do know that I've never felt this way about anyone before. Even as tense as things have been between us since we arrived in the Sea of Fallen Stars, I still remember the meals we shared aboard *Breezerunner*."

"Aye," he said.

"That was the reality that could exist for us, Jherek, but we'll never know unless whatever shuts the door on that possibility is revealed. If I could, I would tear it down with my own hands."

"You don't know what it is you ask."

Her eyes were sad. "Maybe you can live with what we have and never know anything more than that, but I can't. I can't limit myself the way you do. I'm not that strong."

"Lady, you're one of the strongest people I've ever met. Please don't think you're weak because of me."

"Then trust me, Jherek. Whatever it is you're hiding, trust me with it."

Tears welled in the young sailor's eyes and the pain in his throat and chest was almost unbearable. He tried to speak but couldn't.

Sabyna lowered her voice, and it was as if there were only the two of them in the world. "You believe in love, Jherek. I heard you say it, and I saw the strength of your conviction bind a spell that was very powerful. That wouldn't have happened if you didn't mean it. As you believe in love, believe in my love for you." Tears ran down her cheeks, tracking the blood and dirt on her face. "Tell me what holds us apart."

Jherek spoke the words he knew would doom him to unhappiness for the rest of his life. "As you wish."

XXIII

8 Marpenoth, the Year of the Gauntlet

"Are you going to tell her then, young warrior?"

Jherek gazed at his hands as he toweled himself off once more. He'd never seen them shake that way. Except, perhaps, for the night he'd chosen to leave his father's ship and leap into the sea, not knowing if he would live.

He glanced up at Glawinn and said, "I promised her."

The paladin nodded slowly. "There's a case to be made for the fact that she coerced you."

They were in the warrior's quarters aboard *Azure Dagger*. Returning to Azla's ship in the dark with Vurgrom and his pirates as prisoners—and with the weakened prisoners the koalinth had held as livestock—had taken hours.

During that time Sabyna had concerned herself with the prisoners they'd rescued from the koalinth and given Jherek time to think. Unfortunately, all he'd been able to think on was this moment. When they'd reached the ship, he'd begged off time to bathe and tend his wounds, hoping the words he needed would come to him.

He'd drawn a bucket of fresh water from the ship's stores instead of bathing in the salt, wanting to be at his best even though he felt everything was going to end at its worst. He'd washed with lye soap, then groomed himself as best as he could, borrowing Glawinn's shaving kit to scrape the sparse stubble from his chin like he was a man in danger of raising a beard. When he was finished with the task, with his hands shaking the way they were, he guessed that he'd drawn more blood than Vurgrom and the koalinth had.

"As much as I don't wish this, " Jherek said, "I know she needs—and deserves—to know."

"And you? Could you love her from afar if it comes to that?"

Jherek looked at his friend and mentor. "Aye," he said, "without hesitation."

"Ah, but you've got Lathander's heart in you, young warrior." Glawinn's voice turned husky and his eyes shone brightly. "Then you will never lose her, no matter how this goes."

"And her?"

Glawinn shook his head. "I cannot speak for the lady, young warrior. The thing that crosses the two of you is strong. It's not just her, it's you, too. She'll look at you and think of her brother, but you'll look at her and think of your father."

"No."

"You will, and you need to face that."

"My father will not be a part of my life forever," Jherek objected.

"No," Glawinn responded. "I don't think he will, but for a while longer yet, he will be."

Jherek folded the towel and looked around for his clothes. They weren't on the bunk bed where he'd left them when he'd gone to bathe in the crew's head.

"I took the liberty of seeing to your breeches," Glawinn said, taking them from the built-in chest of drawers. "I washed them while you were tending yourself, then dried them in the ship's galley."

Jherek took the breeches, amazed at how clean they were. He'd never gotten real clothes while on *Black Champion* or *Azure Dagger*, and the things he'd traded for while on *Steadfast* remained aboard her on the other side of the Whamite Isles. Azla sailed *Azure Dagger* around to the south of the island, intending to stop briefly at Agenais to replenish the ship's stores before returning Tarnar and his crew to their ship.

"Thank you," Jherek said.

"I knew you'd want to look your best. Here are your socks."

Jherek took them and pulled the pants on, then his socks and boots.

"I'm afraid there was nothing that could be done about the shirt," Glawinn said, kneeling and taking his kit from under his bed. He opened the kit and pulled out a sky-blue shirt with white ruffles and belled sleeves. "I thought perhaps you could wear one of mine. The breadth of our shoulders are about the same."

"That's far too fine."

Jherek loved the look of the shirt but he couldn't imagine himself wearing something like that. Velen had been a simple sailors' town and he'd established early in his relationship with Madame Iitaar that he wouldn't accept charity. She'd accepted that, but she'd also cared for his clothing.

"Perhaps something else?" Jherek asked.

Glawinn didn't look in the kit. "There's nothing else." He held the shirt up and said, "Unless you're prepared to walk out there with your father's tattoo showing for all to see, I'd suggest accepting the loan."

Reluctantly, Jherek took the shirt. It felt incredibly smooth.

"Silk, young warrior, as smooth as a caress from Sune Firehair herself." Glawinn smiled. "That shirt has seen me through many a difficult situation."

"You wore this in battle?"

"In King Azoun's courts, where the pecking order is oft determined by dress. Put it on."

Jherek pulled the shirt on, amazed at the feel of it.

Glawinn took a mirror from his kit and hung it on a peg on the wall. "Let's have a look at you."

Feeling very self-conscious, the young sailor glanced at the mirror. The image he saw surprised him. His tanned face and pale gray eyes stood out against the sky-blue shirt. Sun streaks colored his light brown hair. The scar on his cheek lent him a roguish air. His gaze was

264

direct, challenging. The past months had been hard, and they'd hardened him with it.

The look was all too familiar and disturbing. He turned from the mirror.

"What's wrong?" Glawinn asked.

"For the first time," Jherek said in a thick voice, "I see my father's face in mine."

Glawinn was silent for a moment, then he stepped behind the young sailor and held his shoulders. Gently but firmly, the warrior turned him back to the mirror and said, "Look deep."

Jherek did, captivated by the unacceptable resemblance he now noticed. It was something about the set of his eyes, the square of his jaw. Maybe more, but at least those things.

"Young warrior," Glawinn said, peering into the mirror over Jherek's shoulder and still clasping him tightly, "you may find your father's likeness in your features, but you'll never find your father's ways in your heart."

Jherek nodded as if he accepted that, but he knew he didn't.

"Thank you for the loan of the shirt," he said. "I should be going. We agreed to meet on the forecastle. This time of morning, it's the most private place on the ship."

He took his sash from his bed and wrapped it around his hips, then shoved the newly acquired cutlass through it. At first he'd felt guilty about taking the weapon, but it had come from the destruction of Lathander's disk, so he felt he owed it to the priests at Baldur's Gate to take it to them.

"There is one other thing." Glawinn took a small bottle from his kit. "Cologne. Hold out your hands." He pulled the cork stopper from the bottle and poured. "Rub your hands together and slap it onto your face."

Jherek did, finding that it stung the cut on his cheek, but it had a pleasant, if bold, fragrance. "You make me feel like I'm suiting up for a battle."

"All true affairs of the heart between two people who have the trials between them that you two have *are* battles, young warrior. Too often, in the right circumstances, a man's—and a woman's—dress is a weapon."

"I've got to go."

Glawinn put his hands on Jherek's shoulders again and said, "Wear your heart on your sleeve that she may know your mind truly. All the worries, all the fear, as well as all the love. When you are done, should you need me, I will be here in this room." He leaned forward and kissed Jherek lightly on the forehead. "Should I ever be blessed with a son, young warrior, nothing would please me greater than to see him turn out like you. May Lathander bless you."

The lump returned to Jherek's throat. It was all he could do to nod and walk through the door. He took the stairs from the nearly empty cargo hold that still stank of slavery and walked up on deck.

Morning tinted the eastern sky a rosy pink peering through wheat-colored clouds. Sabyna Truesail stood in the middle of it on the forecastle deck, peering east, in the direction *Azure Dagger* was headed.

Jherek gazed at her with longing. Though the rising sun behind her reduced her to a silhouette, he could picture every line and every rounded curve of her. No matter what happened from this moment on, he knew he'd never forget that sight.

He crossed the deck hurriedly and went up the steps to the forecastle.

"Lady, I'm sorry I kept you waiting."

She turned at his voice, and surprise lighted her eyes.

"So it would appear well worth the wait," she said. "Had I known, I'd have dressed accordingly."

She wore dark green breeches and a white shirt with her sleeves rolled to mid-forearm. She'd bathed and combed her hair, and the scent of lilacs was gentle around her. Jherek thought he'd never seen a lovelier woman in all his life.

"It's the shirt," he said lamely. "Glawinn loaned it to me."

"He has good taste."

"I'll tell him you thought so." Jherek paused, wondering how to continue. How did you tell someone you cared about that your father killed her brother?

"Jherek, about last night," Sabyna said, "I was perhaps out of line."

"Does that mean you've changed your mind about talking?" Instead of feeling relieved, Jherek was anxious, wanting to be done with the secret he kept. It was confusing.

"No, we're going to talk," she said adamantly. "I meant it when I said I can't go on like this, but I think perhaps I could have waited for a better time or spoken somewhat less harshly."

"You did what you had to do, lady. I claim no foul there."

"Good, because I'm not leaving here without knowing your heart."

Jherek took a deep breath and said, "You know my heart, lady. It's my past you're unaware of." He paused, uncertain of where to begin.

"You said you were wanted," Sabyna said. "For what?"

"For things I never did, lady. I'm innocent of any crime, but I had the misfortune to be born the son of a bad man."

"No man is responsible for the mistakes his father has made."

"You may not feel that way after you hear the whole story." With a trembling hand, Jherek unfastened his sleeve, his eyes on Sabyna. "When I was twelve, I ran away from my father, from all the things that he did."

"That was a very brave thing to do."

Jherek forced himself to roll the sleeve up. "But I found running away didn't rescue me from my father's heritage." Rolling over his arm, he showed her the tattoo of the flaming skull masked in chains.

Sabyna's face drained of color and her eyes filled with cold, hard tears. She wrapped her arms across her breasts and glared at him. "That's the mark of Bloody Falkane," she whispered.

Jherek nodded slowly and said, "Bloody Falkane—the man who killed your brother—is my father, lady."

Sabyna turned from him and walked woodenly to the prow railing.

Not knowing what else to do, Jherek followed after her. He stayed back, wishing he could comfort her. Why did it have to be her brother? But he knew that wasn't a fair question. There were a number of families who'd lost brothers and fathers, and other family to the notorious crew of *Bunyip* and Bloody Falkane. It was only his ill luck that numbered Sabyna's family among their victims.

He stood quietly waiting. He had no words. All he could do was try to figure out how a day that was starting so beautifully could be so bad already.

"Anything," Sabyna croaked hoarsely as she turned around to face him with a face wet with tears and wracked with pain. "I was prepared for anything but that."

Jherek nodded but couldn't get a word past the lump in his throat. He looked at the deck between his feet and tried to think. Even if he could speak, what would he say?

Sabyna's startled scream ripped through the morning.

Looking up, Jherek saw two pallid gray arms seize the pretty ship's mage from behind. They wrapped around Sabyna's body and yanked her from the deck. The young sailor caught a glimpse of the gray corpse that had climbed up the ship's prow as it fell back into the water. Two more corpses pulled themselves up the ship's prow as well, throwing their arms over the railing.

"Boarders!" Jherek yelled as loudly as he could.

He ripped the sword from his sash, knowing he was in danger of losing Sabyna. *Azure Dagger* had all sails out and was running with the wind. He sprinted toward the port railing and threw himself over.

The Sea of Fallen Stars sparkled blue-green for an instant, and he heard other sailors aboard *Azure Dagger* take up the warning cry.

"Boarders! Boarders!"

"Boarders my arse! Them are sea zombies straight from Umberlee's—"

Jherek hit the water cleanly, following the line of the cutlass. Foam churned white around him as he dived. Turning in the water, he floated, using his empty hand to turn himself around.

Dozens of bodies floated in the sea, all of them pallid gray and bloated from drowning. A hundred and more walked the sea floor, followed by schools of fish and crabs that feasted on their dead flesh.

An eerie, haunting melody suddenly filled the water. Jherek felt a tingle run through his whole body and a warm lassitude started to creep in on him. He pushed the music away, remembering that Sabyna was down there somewhere.

A heartbeat later, the young sailor spotted her, still

pulled along by the drowned one that held her less than forty feet away. Jherek kicked his feet and took off after her. Even with the cutlass in one hand and wearing boots, he overtook the sea zombie in seconds. His muscles screamed silent protests after the beating they'd taken the night before.

Other sea zombies noticed the young sailor and swam for him. Two of them were male, but the third had been a little girl no more than ten.

Sabyna struggled against her captor who held her with its arm locked under her throat.

Jherek's optimism flagged. Zombies of any type could prove incredibly hard to kill. They had to be chopped literally to pieces or have the necromancer's spell that created them broken.

Sabyna's eyes widened when she saw him.

Fisting the drowned one's chin with his free hand from behind, Jherek twisted with all his strength. The drowned one's spine cracked as the head came fully halfway around. Still, the creature didn't release its hold on Sabyna.

The young sailor shoved the cutlass forward, preparing to cut the thing's water-rotted arm from it. As soon as the sword touched the drowned one, electricity sparked the length of the blade. The zombie convulsed, its limbs flaring out and the seaweed-tangled hair on its head standing straight up. Great boils erupted on the dead flesh, causing a sudden eruption of blue-purple cuttle worms three inches long and as thick as a man's finger.

Jherek waved the worms from his face, knowing he was safe because they didn't like live flesh. He glanced up, seeing Sabyna swimming for the surface. Before she made it, long vines from a kelp bed snaked out for her, curling around her and pulling her in.

For the first time Jherek realized the hypnotic melody came from the purple-leafed kelp beds. He swam toward her, watching as other zombies closed in on her.

What felt like iron bars wrapped around his ankles and dragged him down. He plummeted toward the ocean floor like he'd been tied to an anchor. Glancing down, he saw that a large man with eye sockets picked clean by a hermit crab still curled up inside one of them had grabbed him.

The man's waterlogged weight was enough to drag them both to the bottom.

Jherek shoved his cutlass into the man's face, hoping whatever magic filled the blade hadn't exhausted itself. The zombie's limbs and hair popped straight out and the flesh boiled. Lungs near to bursting, the young sailor swam after Sabyna.

A pair of drowned ones reached her first, digging into the kelp bed with her. Sabyna fought against them, but their teeth dug into her right thigh and left side. Blood stained the water.

"No!" Jherek shouted, causing an eruption of air bubbles from his mouth.

He shoved the cutlass into the creature biting on Sabyna's thigh. Jherek watched as the magic in the blade destroyed the undead thing, then he attacked the one worrying at Sabyna's side, destroying it as well. Sabyna's movements showed definite weakness.

Jherek sawed at the vines holding her to the kelp, cutting her free. Her wounds bled freely. He hooked an arm around her waist and swam for the surface, knowing even if he made it there was no way they could reach *Azure Dagger* or out-swim the rest of the drowned ones.

Another zombie swam at them from above, giving Jherek no time to dodge away. With no warning, a rush of golden scales intercepted the drowned one, snatching it up in a huge mouth and crunching it to pieces.

Even with only that brief glance, Jherek knew it was the sea wyrm that he'd first seen when they'd salvaged *Black Champion*. The creature had followed *Steadfast* all the way to Aglarond and back, but he thought it had been left on the other side of the island with *Steadfast*. Somehow it had known where he was and made its way to him.

Jherek watched the sea wyrm constrict in the water, flipping its body around so that its fins caught the currents in such a way that it turned back around on itself like a corkscrew. The fins on its head flared out as it regarded Jherek. Then another zombie seized its attention less than ten feet away. The sea wyrm streaked there and bit the dead woman in half. Both halves remained active for a time, arms and legs moving desperately but without an ability to control their direction as they dropped slowly to the sea floor.

A moment later, Jherek brought Sabyna to the surface. She looked into his eyes, coughing and gasping. He glanced down at the wounds in her side and leg, knowing he had to put pressure on them to stop the bleeding. Furthermore, if there were any sharks in the water, the blood scent was sure to bring them.

"Go," she gasped hoarsely. "I'm getting cold, Jherek. I don't think I can swim."

"I'm not going to leave you," he said.

"By yourself you might have a chance."

"No, lady." The young sailor gazed down at the sea wyrm still darting through the water below. It struck like lightning, destroying zombie after zombie that swam toward Jherek and Sabyna. He locked eyes with the creature and said, "Help me."

The sea wyrm curled in on itself, then exploded into motion. It streaked through the water like an arrow, surfacing almost casually beside Jherek. Cautiously, it folded the fins down around its head and stretched its muzzle forward.

Not daring to believe, yet knowing it was somehow true, Jherek placed his hand on the sea wyrm's broad head. The scales felt slippery and solid and a buzzing filled his palm. After a moment, the sea wyrm wrapped its coils around Jherek and Sabyna. The young sailor moved quickly, aware of the sea zombie heads that broke the surface around them.

He pushed Sabyna onto the sea wyrm's neck behind its head where the dorsal fin was missing. He slid on behind her, wrapping his arms around her and his legs around the creature's thick torso.

The sea wyrm lifted its head clear of the ocean, gazing back at Jherek expectantly.

"The ship," the young sailor said, hoping he wasn't wrong.

The sea wyrm's body undulated and sent them speeding through the water. Jherek held Sabyna tightly. The creature easily avoided the bobbing zombie heads that gnashed their jaws in frustration and reached for them as they passed. The sea wyrm swam unerringly for *Azure*

271

Dagger, overtaking it with ease.

As he got closer, Sabyna became dead weight in Jherek's arms. Spray from the sea wyrm staying so close to the surface blew back over them. It was cold and salty and stung his nose and eyes. The young sailor watched a vein throb slowly on the side of the ship's mage's neck and took heart in that. As long as she lived, there was hope.

Azure Dagger's crew pointed at the sea wyrm as it swam along the port side. Two men hung from the prow, cutting away the net the drowned ones had used to set their trap and catch the fast-moving caravel. Once it had caught onto the prow, they'd climbed it to attempt boarding the ship.

Glawinn and Azla stood at the port side railing. The pirate queen ordered a longboat put over the side. It was a dangerous move. If it got too low and hit the water, it could be pushed back to smash a hole in the hull. Glawinn and two other sailors manned the boat as it swayed unsteadily down from the cargo arm.

The sea wyrm swam for the longboat, getting alongside it as if it was an everyday thing. It lifted its neck from the water and put Jherek and Sabyna closer to the longboat. Holding Sabyna in his arms, Jherek passed her up to the paladin.

"I've got her, young warrior," the paladin said. "Climb on up."

Glawinn sat cautiously, holding Sabyna tenderly. He inspected her wounds.

Jherek caught hold of the longboat and pulled himself inside. He gazed back down at the sea wyrm, still not believing what had happened. The creature looked back up at him and flared its head fins again.

"Thank you," the young sailor said.

The sea wyrm gave a trumpeting call, then dived beneath the waves.

Jherek turned his attention to Sabyna.

* * * * *

Pacys swam across the Dukar Quarter in Myth Nantar as fast as he could. His heart still pounded from the dream that had awakened him. He'd slept in the Dukar Academy room Qos had offered him. The seaweed bed had proven surprisingly comfortable and, despite his excitement, when he'd lain down, he'd had no problem sleeping. Until this morning.

He stopped at the coral in the courtyard near Maalirn's Walk where he and Qos usually met. The storm giant was already there, or perhaps the Green Dukar Paragon had never left.

Pacys tried to keep his voice calm. "Grand Savant Qos."

The storm giant looked up.

"I have to go," the old bard said.

"No—there are things not yet done."

Pacys felt frantic. "You've got to understand, this is about the boy, Jherek."

"The one you believe to be the hero of your song?" Qos nodded. "I know."

"The girl he loves—"

"—lies dying," Qos said. "Truly, Master Pacys, I do know these things. I keep watch over a lot of currents at this time. I also know a huge army of drowned ones marches on Eadraal."

"I must go to the boy. He's on the verge of giving up."

"Your place is here," the storm giant said, his voice holding a note of warning. "There are parts that have to be played yet, and you need to be ready to play yours. You could be called upon to open the Great Barrier. When that time comes, we'll have little time."

"You can open the Great Barrier."

Qos's emerald eyes blazed with angry impatience and he said, "If I could open the Great Barrier, you wouldn't be here."

The revelation stunned Pacys into silence for a moment.

"You can't open the Great Barrier?"

"No," the giant said.

"Why?"

"Because it was my decision to close it," Qos answered. "I can allow others in, but I can't return Myth Nantar to Serôs. The prophecies about the Taker creating a reunion of the peoples of Serôs must come to pass first. That's the price I paid for salvaging what was left of the City of Destinies. If events don't go as I hope, if you aren't able to open the Great Barrier, Myth Nantar may never rise again."

Pacys stood mute, feeling the pressure of the depths above him for the first time since he'd descended into Serôs.

"That's why the boy must wait," Qos said patiently. "Everything must come in its own time."

"He may break before I reach him," Pacys said. "He's that close to hopelessness."

"Master Pacys, we all are. We must each hold to our individual strengths just a little longer."

* * * * *

"Is she going to be all right?" Jherek asked.

He stared at Sabyna's limp form lying on the bed in her private quarters aboard *Azure Dagger*. She looked so small and pale.

Sabyna's wounds had been cleaned and tended, but they were inflamed and leaked pus. Glawinn had attempted to cure them with his paladin's ability, and Arthoris had tried a healing potion. In both instances some of Sabyna's strength and color had returned for a short time only to dwindle away again. She hadn't regained consciousness.

"I don't know, young warrior," Glawinn said. Kneeling by the bed, he took a compress from a small water pitcher, folded it, and tenderly laid it over her head. "The bite of the undead can be toxic, carrying diseases even advanced healers know little of. Her fate is in stronger hands than we have aboard this ship."

"We'll find a priest when we put into Agenais," Jherek said. "Everything will be all right then, won't it?"

Glawinn hesitated, then said, "Mayhap." He took the compress from her head and wet it again. "The main thing is to keep her fever down, give her body a chance to heal itself. Even then, the battle she fights is a draining one."

Jherek felt so helpless and empty inside. "It's my fault," he said hoarsely. "If I had not loved her, she would not have been cursed by my ill luck."

"No," Glawinn said gruffly. "I'll have none of that kind of talk in here. The girl may not be in her right mind now, but I've seen people like this come back and know every word that was spoken around them. If you're going to stay here with her, you're going to speak positively. Do you understand me?"

Jherek met the older man's gaze and said, "Help me, Glawinn, I can't be this strong."

Glawinn put the compress back on Sabyna's head. "Yes you can, young warrior," he said. "You'll be as strong as you need to be, whether to hang on or let go. You'll see it done because that's how you are. It's the only way you can be."

Jherek clenched his hands into fists, hating the helpless feeling that filled him. "What do I need to do? Tell me and I swear it will be done."

"Believe."

"In what?"

"I can't tell you."

Jherek looked at the small, pale form on the bed and begged, "Give me something to believe in."

"I can't. You'll have to find it within yourself."

Jherek knelt there beside the bed and searched his heart. He reached out to Ilmater the Crying God, the god he'd rejected months ago. He prayed the way he used to, but there was no comfort.

Sabyna's breathing remained ragged.

* * * * *

"Everyone's dead," Azla announced, looking through the spyglass she held.

Jherek stood beside her, raking Agenais with a spyglass as well. The port city's streets remained empty. Even the ships in the harbor were untended.

"Now we know where the drowned ones came from," Tarnar said. "I have to worry about my ship."

"The kelpies seem to have attacked the civilized areas first," Azla said. "Since you weren't anchored near a port, maybe they've survived."

"If they didn't decide to come looking for me."

"By the end of the day," Azla said, "you'll know."

Resolutely, Jherek kept the spyglass trained on the shore. Azla had ordered the helmsman to keep *Azure Dagger* far enough away from the evil kelpie beds that the haunting melody they sang was barely audible. There was no hope in his heart, but he wasn't ready to go back to the small room where Sabyna lay just yet. He wasn't helpful there and the rasp of her strained breathing tortured him. At least here he could search for someone who could help her.

"Survivors!" the pirate in the crow's nest shouted. "Survivors starboard!"

Reflexively, Jherek swung his gaze around and spotted the small boatload of people a quarter of a mile or more out to sea.

Azla gave orders to pick them up and the crew hung the sails. Silently, Jherek hoped one of them would be a priest or a healer. Unfortunately, priests had proven extremely susceptible to the call of the kelpie beds.

XXIV

14 Marpenoth, the Year of the Gauntlet

Laaqueel swam above the army advancing northeast to Voalidru, lost in her own thoughts and fears. The two previous merman cities had fallen after a considerable amount of bloodshed.

The sea zombies Iakhovas had raised from the shallows around the Whamite Isles had proven to be the turning point of the sweep through Eadraal's holdings. Despite their fierceness and their familiarity with the terrain, even the strong-willed merman warriors had given ground. The once-dead were harder to kill the second time around.

The malenti priestess also knew that, as large as the army was, it was also extremely vulnerable—not from external forces, but from internal pressures. T'Kalah and the other sahuagin princes grew steadily more displeased with Iakhovas's decisions.

What had once been jealousy over the crown turned now to unrest with how the war progressed. That feeling was spreading through the sahuagin of both the inner and outer seas as they marched to the very eye of the storm between all the nations of Serôs. If they chose to unify, they could attack the sahuagin from three sides. Only the retreat back to the Xedran Reefs seemed secure.

Adding the legions of undead from the Whamite Isles had been strategically the best move to increase the army's strength, but the sahuagin didn't believe Sekolah had anything to do with the sudden appearance of the sea zombies. Scouts that had ventured too close to the kelpie beds had succumbed to the ancient magic as well, becoming undead themselves. Those were the hardest of all to bear, and Laaqueel had destroyed them as soon as she'd discovered them.

If it hadn't been for Laaqueel, the sahuagin wouldn't have been put back to take care of the flanks, away from the undead. The koalinth saw the sea zombies as flesh-and-blood battering rams that softened up the merman defenses so they could roll over them more easily.

She gazed down through the murky water, watching the drowned ones swim through the currents toward Voalidru as Iakhovas had commanded them. They looked like a school of scavenger fish hugging the sea floor along the shallows.

"Little malenti, you think too much. Your thoughts cause doubt instead of hope."

Startled, Laaqueel looked up in time to see Iakhovas glide into position beside her.

"There's much to think about," she said, then glanced back and saw *Tarjana* in the distance.

"On the contrary, the time for thinking is almost over. Voalidru will be mine within hours."

"Perhaps, but the merfolk will continue to fight to win it back."

"I'm not intending to hold it," Iakhovas said. "It will only be a staging area for the attack on Myth Nantar."

"Then what happens?" Laaqueel asked because she knew it was expected. She no longer really cared, but Iakhovas enjoyed taunting her.

"Then the High Mages save the world," Iakhovas replied, "just the way their legends say they will—but not before I get what I came for."

Laaqueel studied him, noting how confident he was of himself. His manner was so sahuagin it hurt, yet he talked casually of defeat while hinting that everything was going as he'd planned.

"How can you be so sure Myth Nantar won't prove your undoing?" she asked.

"Because I know how those people think. They care more for their precious City of Destinies than anything else. The whole idea of unity in Serôs is based around Myth Nantar."

"But it didn't work," Laaqueel protested. "I've read some of their histories. In the end, Myth Nantar failed because they fought over it as well."

"As it might fail again. But for now, they'll believe, and they'll attempt to save it and themselves. You'll see. Every step of this war has been carefully orchestrated. None have been born, little malenti, who will ever get the best of me."

Laaqueel was silent for a moment, knowing he wouldn't like what she next had to say. She didn't pause out of fear for herself; there was none of that left. She let the pause add weight to her words and glanced at Iakhovas to see his reaction.

"You hadn't planned on the boy in the cave, had you?"

With a mocking smile, his golden eye gleaming, Iakhovas gazed at her.

"No," he admitted, "I hadn't. He was a surprise engineered by someone else."

"Who?"

"I don't know, nor do I care. He is no threat to me. He is too lost in his own pain to look past that."

"His sword cut you when you thought it wouldn't."

"There's not much that can now," Iakhovas said. "I am almost whole."

"But he did."

"It's no matter. Don't irritate me, little malenti. I've got victories to arrange and a war to lose."

In the next instant he faded from the water.

Laaqueel assumed he'd teleported back to *Tarjana*. The fact that he no longer bothered to hide his magic bothered her as well. She reached up to touch the white shark symbol between her breasts and tried to feel the connection to the Shark God she'd once had.

It wasn't there. Still, the powers granted by her love and devotion to Sekolah worked. When a priestess truly lost her faith, those went away as well. How was it then, she wondered, that she could doubt so much yet still retain them?

279

She had no answers and nowhere to turn. So she swam, heading to Voalidru because there was nowhere else to go.

* * * * *

"Lady, I do hope that Glawinn was right and that you can hear me," Jherek whispered.

He took a fresh compress from the water pitcher by Sabyna's bed and placed it across her fevered brow. Even the paladin's daily attempts to heal her and Arthoris's attentions with his waning supply of healing potions didn't stave off the infections that wracked her body. She enjoyed a brief respite from the fevers, but the bite marks deepened, turning black around the edges, drawing in the flesh around them as they consumed her. Both of the wounds were the size of one of his hands now. It had been seven days and still she had not regained consciousness.

Azla had ordered *Azure Dagger* to sail north but they lingered still around the Whamite Isles. At present the nearby seas were filled with drowned ones, morkoth, koalinth, and sahuagin. Once they'd even been turned back by a merman patrol claiming the waters as something called "Eadraal's."

The young sailor ministered to Sabyna with care. Tears filled his eyes as he listened to her harsh breathing and his hands shook as he touched her hot flesh. Over the days he'd cared for her, he'd found he talked incessantly. He'd told her of his life aboard *Bunyip* and in Velen, of Madame Iitaar and Malorrie, and of the mysterious voice that had led him this far by speaking the cryptic, *Live, that you may serve.* And he'd talked of her; what she'd shown him, what she'd come to mean to him.

In the quiet moments of the long nights when he'd sat by her bed working to keep her fever down, he couldn't help recalling how her face had looked before the drowned one had grabbed her and dragged her into the sea. Had she been about to forgive him, or about to condemn him? He didn't know and the waiting was unbearable—only second to knowing whether she would ever awaken.

"I love you, lady," Jherek whispered.

He told her that several times a day, hoping that she might seize onto it and return to them. That was the declaration she'd challenged him for, but he felt it wasn't enough to truly turn her from the dark path she walked into the shadowlands. Still, he told her because she'd asked and because he did love her and wanted her to know even if she was taken from him.

A knock sounded at the door, then Glawinn's voice said, "Young warrior."

Jherek brushed his eyes free of tears and cleared his throat. "Aye."

"May I enter?"

"Aye."

Glawinn entered the room carrying a plate of food. He didn't ask if she'd awakened, and Jherek was grateful for that. If Sabyna opened her eyes, the young sailor didn't doubt that everyone on the ship would know.

"I brought you something to eat," the paladin said.

"I'm not hungry."

Glawinn put the plate on the chest of drawers against the wall and asked, "When was your last meal?"

"Not long ago," Jherek answered, applying a fresh compress to Sabyna's fevered forehead.

"Not long for a camel, perhaps," Glawinn replied. "I know you've not eaten in two days. It will do no good for you to get sick as well."

"I won't get sick. I haven't so far."

"When was the last time you slept?"

Jherek looked at the man's eyes and said, "I don't remember."

"This isn't healthy. Others can care for her."

"I know," the young sailor whispered, "but I would rather."

For a moment he was afraid Glawinn would argue with him, then the paladin got down beside the bed on his knees and prayed to Lathander, asking for the Morninglord's guidance and succor.

Jherek joined him on his knees but couldn't join in the prayer. No gods were interested in him. He was cursed by the fates, and now that curse had spread to Sabyna. He only wished that he might die soon after she did. He truly believed he wouldn't be able to live after that.

* * * * *

Before the battle was joined at Voalidru, Laaqueel sensed that Vhaemas the Bastard's loyalties would not stay with Iakhovas. She saw the pained look in the eyes of Thuridru's ruler as they marshaled the skirmish lines just south of the merman capital. His father hadn't abandoned the city as the regular citizens had, and stood proudly among the army he'd assembled.

Vhaemas the Bastard held Thuridru's forces to the west, awaiting Iakhovas's signal. The drowned ones marched in first, shoving the front line of the mermen back and opening holes that the koalinth rushed to fill. The killing went on in the lowlands for more than an hour before the merman line really began to cave. Still, the warriors didn't run, staying in and doing battle as the drowned ones and koalinth ground them down. Bodies floated in the water, drawing marine scavengers that weren't too afraid of the combatants.

Iakhovas rode *Tarjana*'s forecastle deck as the mudship bore down on King Vhaemas's waiting forces in the second wave of battle. Laaqueel stood beside him. They hadn't talked since earlier in the day, and she was comfortable with that.

Sahuagin packed the deck around them, armed with heavy crossbows.

King Vhaemas controlled his army from a rock shelf, relaying orders through his commanders. Even as *Tarjana* raced for him, the merman king held his ground, staring back at Iakhovas.

The line of attacking koalinth hammered into the mermen at the same time Iakhovas gave the order to fire the crossbows. The heavy quarrels took down rows of merman warriors.

Iakhovas leaped over the mudship's side and swam toward the merman king. The sahuagin followed him, advancing rapidly on the royal guard.

Having no heart for the battle, Laaqueel still followed and defended herself as she needed to.

Flanked by one of his daughters, Vhaemas swam to meet Iakhovas. The merman king had been in his share of battles while holding Eadraal together, and it showed in his ability as he engaged Iakhovas.

A merman wearing Voalidru's colors attacked Laaqueel.

Distanced from the danger, the malenti priestess battled flawlessly, turning the other man's trident then using her finger talons to open his throat. Survival still took precedence over the absence of fear.

When she glanced back at Iakhovas, she wasn't surprised to see Vhaemas the Bastard had joined his father in battling Iakhovas. Merman king, son, and daughter all swarmed on Iakhovas, who barely held his own against their combined might.

The koalinth and merman warriors spread out, battling around the four of them.

Little malenti, to me.

Laaqueel felt the black quill next to her heart quiver demandingly. She gutted the latest merman warrior that had engaged her and swam toward Iakhovas.

The trident Iakhovas used was magical in nature. Through it, he'd been able to affect the outcome of past battles, affecting the luck that his army had. It had been one of the many items his searchers had found for him around the Sea of Fallen Stars.

Waiting for a chance to reach his side, Laaqueel darted in and engaged Vhaemas while his son and daughter sped toward Iakhovas. Vhaemas the Bastard caught Iakhovas's trident in his own even as his half-sister, Princess Jian, swam in with her sword.

Jian swung the sword as she passed, breaking the trident haft with a thundering crack that rolled over the hills. When the broken trident fell away, Vhaemas the Bastard pulled his own back and rammed it at Iakhovas.

"No!" Iakhovas shouted in rage.

His shape blurred, becoming the thing Laaqueel remembered from the cave near Coryselmal. Fins appeared on Iakhovas's head and face, arms and legs, back and chest. If she hadn't already seen the form before, the malenti priestess knew she would have thought it was a trick of the sediment and sand swirling around Iakhovas.

Before Vhaemas the Bastard could shove his trident tines through his opponent's head, Iakhovas grabbed it with superhuman speed and shoved the weapon to one side. He rammed the broken haft of his own trident through the bastard king's torso. Iakhovas continued to push until his talons reached Vhaemas's abdomen. He ripped out the merman's entrails and strung them through the water. Vhaemas the Bastard struggled only briefly before going limp.

Still in motion, Iakhovas pursued Jian, who turned to confront him. The mermaid warrior lashed out with her sword, scoring a slash across Iakhovas's chest. Iakhovas kept going, driving himself at the mermaid and receiving another wound to his arm.

Vhaemas redoubled his efforts against Laaqueel, driving her back so that he could disengage. He swam through the water, stopping only long enough to pick up the end of Iakhovas's broken trident. Still in motion, the merman king slammed the mystic trident into Iakhovas's back, burying the points deeply.

Roaring in pain and rage, Iakhovas batted Jian's sword aside and seized her head in an impossibly huge hand covered in sharp edges. Holding her head, he raked the long fin from his other arm across her midsection, ripping her into halves—one belonging to a beautiful girl and the other to a fish.

King Vhaemas tugged at the trident tines imbedded in Iakhovas's back, trying to free them. Iakhovas whirled, closing his massive fist and hammering the merman king on the head. Partially senseless, Vhaemas tried to retreat but couldn't move away fast enough. Iakhovas made a fist and brought it down on top of the king's crown.

Before the dazed merman king could move or defend himself, Iakhovas dived at him, grabbing him around the throat. Blood and sand misted the water around the two combatants, obscuring the view as the battle raged around them.

Laaqueel kicked out, flicking her toe claws out and gutting the merman warrior who swam at her. She whirled and brought up the barbed net hanging at her side, whipping it out to drape over another merman warrior she narrowly avoided. She gloried in the battle, embracing the thought of death because then there could be no more doubts. A smile twisted the corners of her mouth, and she felt more alive than she had in days.

Little malenti, you've come back into your own.

The malenti priestess didn't bother to reply. The exhilaration she felt was only temporary, and she knew it. As the merman warrior fought the net, the barbs buried themselves in his flesh. She choked up on the trident haft and raked the tine across another merman's face, taking out his eyes.

NO!

The female voice echoed in Laaqueel's head, driving her to her knees in the loose sand. The malenti priestess put her hands to her temples, willing away the pain and the vertigo.

This is not your path, Laaqueel. Not anymore.

"Stop!" the malenti priestess pleaded, gazing out at the battle before her. "This is what I was born and bred for. This is Sekolah's purpose for me."

Little malenti, are you hurt?

Laaqueel looked at Iakhovas. "I am all right."

"Then get up. There's a battle to be won here before we lose the war."

Iakhovas held the unconscious merman king by the throat. King Vhaemas's head bled profusely, bits of gold and bone glinting amid savaged flesh. Iakhovas's blow had driven the crown into the merman king's head.

Staving off the vertigo and uncertainty, Laaqueel picked up her trident, taking the fight to the merman warriors.

I will not allow you to take the lives of these people, the feminine voice stated.

"I am sahuagin." Laaqueel engaged the nearest merman, thrusting her trident at his face.

No.

Laaqueel's trident thrust stopped short. The merman warrior moved to take advantage of his luck. As he thrust, though, a wild current sprang up from below him and pulled him away.

Nor will I allow you to be harmed. Not unless you make me.

"Then strike me down if you can." Laaqueel gazed around the depths. "Come out of hiding. I will fight you. My life has not been my own, and I'll spend it gladly."

I come to give you your life, Laaqueel.

"How?" As the malenti priestess looked around, she noticed that none of the merman warriors even seemed to know she was there, as if she'd suddenly become invisible.

There is another path you must take that is better suited to your nature.

"I am sahuagin."

You do not have to be.

"It is all I have ever wanted to be."

Then you should raise your standards, Laaqueel.

"Sekolah gave me life and gave me the strength to kill in his name. It is enough."

And Sekolah let you be placed in the power of the Taker.

Laaqueel had no reply.

Yes, you know him for who he is, and you know the kind of destruction he's brought to this world. If he should return to the Sword Coast, it will only be the same. And Iakhovas no longer needs you. You know that.

"The Great Shark gives me power to serve his will."

Sekolah gives you power to kill in his name.

"Yes."

You could have more.

"I only want to be sahuagin."

You're not. You have never fit in with your people, Laaqueel, and you know you never will.

"I can."

No. You live a lie now, and you know it. As long as you remain in Iakhovas's grace you will be protected, but should you fall, you will be killed and rent. Meat is meat. I can give you more than that.

"Why should you?" Laaqueel shouted. "What am I to you?"

You are strong, Laaqueel. The times coming after the Twelfth Serôs War will not be easy. I have use for that strength.

"So I could serve you instead of Iakhovas?" Laaqueel shook her head. "No."

When the time comes, you will live or die as you choose, but if you kill any of those under my protection, you will know my wrath as you have known my benevolence.

"And should they attack me?"

They won't. You are under my protection, and they will know it. Iakhovas remains your only true enemy, but one is coming who has the power to deal with him.

"The boy in the cave?" Laaqueel couldn't believe it. Though the human had put up a good fight against the koalinth in the cave, he couldn't challenge the savage deathbringer that was Iakhovas.

Yes.

"He's too weak."

Not once the Taleweaver brings him into his belief. Wait, Laaqueel, wait and see if I don't have more to offer than you've ever known.

Emotion ripped through Laaqueel as she felt the voice fade from her mind. Uncertainty and doubt plagued her, and her faith wasn't there to shore her up. She prayed to Sekolah, but she felt the words were only empty effort.

"I am *Iakhovas!*"

Turning, Laaqueel watched as Iakhovas swam into the midst of the battlefield. He looked every inch a proud sahuagin warrior-king. His voice boomed, gaining the attention of the warriors around him.

"Your king has fallen," Iakhovas roared in triumph, "and I have killed his children."

He threw the merman king down to the torn bodies of Princess Jian and Vhaemas the Bastard.

"I am death—unstoppable and merciless. Oppose me and die!"

As Laaqueel looked across the war-torn sea floor, she saw the wave of defeat sweep over the surviving warriors of Eadraal. The Thuridru mermen screamed in triumph. The malenti priestess felt the arrival of a thundering presence hammering against her lateral lines. She looked to the east, in the direction from which the shifting currents came.

Whales materialized out of the deep blue-green depths. Half a dozen four-hundred-foot-long humpbacked whales swam in the lead, trailed by dozens of smaller ones. They stampeded over the battlefield, scattering both armies.

Iakhovas hung in the sea, staring at them.

An auburn-haired mermaid swam with them, flashing between the two lead humpbacks.

"Arina."

Several of the mermen near Laaqueel spoke the name, and she assumed it belonged to the young woman with the whales.

The whales broke before Iakhovas, swimming under him, knocking the nearby warriors around in whirlwind currents that drew sand up from the ocean floor in massive clouds.

After the whales passed, Laaqueel noticed that King

Vhaemas's body was gone, evidently taken up by one or more of the great creatures. The morale of the mermen disappeared with the merman king, and they began disengaging where they could and falling back.

Iakhovas evidently wasn't going to give them an easy retreat. He issued orders at once to begin the pursuit. It was going to be a bitter death march back to Voalidru.

* * * * *

Tu'uua'col swam through the clutch of rocks and settled gently on the ocean floor behind Prince Mirol as he prayed to Eadro.

Built lean and angular, Mirol didn't look like a warrior, or the newly named heir to the throne of Eadraal. King Vhaemas had awakened only once after the whales and Princess Arina had transported him to Naulys, the merman city west of Voalidru. During that time he named Mirol as his successor, then slipped back into the coma that held him still.

Tu'uua'col hadn't accompanied King Vhaemas during the Battle of Voalidru. The prejudices the merman warriors had against him because he was shalarin ran too deep. Still, he had not allowed himself to be put on the sidelines as the Taker's army closed on Naulys. His place, for the moment, was at the prince's side. Quietly, the Green Dukar put his hand on Mirol's shoulder.

Unhurried, Mirol finished his prayer to Eadro, asking for deliverance in this time of need. He flipped his tail and turned to face his advisor.

"Our scouts have spotted the Taker's advance guard," Tu'uua'col said.

"How soon will they be here?"

"Within minutes."

"And their numbers?"

"As at Voalidru," Tu'uua'col answered.

"Do you think we can hold them from Naulys?"

The Dukar hesitated. Mirol had remained very true to his calling as a priest until his father had handed him the reins of leadership. As a result, the boy didn't know much about the ways of war and warriors.

"No, my prince. Not without a miracle."

Mirol showed him a brave smile and said, "Exactly what I was praying for. Now let's see if Eadro can deliver."

He took up the trident that had been his father's and swam to the front of the line.

The land around Naulys was hilly, rife with coral reefs. They'd used those reefs to set up ballistae that had been salvaged from surface world ships. The Taker's army came on, the drowned ones at the lead.

Tu'uua'col watched as the first rows of warriors clashed. Priests of Eadro, summoned by Mirol, worked to turn the undead, chanting praises to Eadro. Many of the drowned ones were turned away, leaving the koalinth to bear the brunt of the first attack while their own ranks were broken by the zombies' retreat.

For a moment, confused by the retreating zombies, the koalinth gave ground in the face of the vengeful assault by the merman warriors of three conquered cities who'd managed to join Naulys's defenders. The sheer numbers of the koalinth turned the tide yet again. The merman warriors were slowly driven back.

Tu'uua'col watched, desperately seeking some way out of the situation though he knew there wasn't one. The Taker had planned too well, and the priests had not turned all of the drowned ones. He gazed at the Taker's flagship floating above and behind the koalinth, then noticed the fluttering movement that came in from the north.

The winged shapes sped through the water without warning, and they came by the thousands. They descended on the staggered line of koalinth without mercy.

"What is that?" Mirol asked. He peered into the deeper reaches of the sea.

"Ixitxachitl," Tu'uua'col answered, feeling somewhat better. "Apparently, they decided to join in and retaliate against the Taker."

"It's a miracle," Mirol said quietly.

Tu'uua'col didn't agree, thinking it was more like the demon rays taking advantage of the diversion the mermen provided. As he watched the ixitxachitls swoop in on the koalinth, the Dukar thought the real miracle would be if the demon rays didn't turn on them next.

The merman warriors pressed to the forefront, cutting down koalinth as chance presented itself.

"Col," Mirol asked, "do you think there's a chance to form an alliance at Myth Nantar to stand against the Taker?"

"Yes," the Dukar replied quickly.

Excitement flared within him. The merman cities held the largest population in the immediate area around Myth Nantar. If they took a step to form an alliance he was certain the other races would agree.

"I would like you to start on this immediately after this battle is finished," Mirol said. "Provided we both yet live. I will go with you."

"Of course, Prince Mirol."

Tu'uua'col turned to watch the battle as the koalinth continued to retreat before the savagery of the ixitxachitl. If Myth Nantar rose again, as was alluded to in some of the legends, the Dukars would also rise once more.

* * * * *

Nine days later, Pacys stood close to the Great Barrier. Senior High Mage Reefglamor and the other High Mages of Sylkiir stood there with the others who agreed to the Nantarn Alliance. After nearly a tenday of hammering out the details, the old bard knew them all. While they'd bickered and argued among themselves, he'd written, adding their songs to the epic that came so readily now to his lips.

The Taker's army had been turned at Naulys, leaving the city intact, though Voalidru was still heavily occupied at the moment. Scouts had also determined that Iakhovas was pulling together reserves from the sahuagin raiding parties and guiding even more of the drowned ones that continued the occupation of the Whamite Isles.

With arms as thick as oak trees crossed over his huge chest, Qos faced the Great Barrier beside the old bard. When he'd first put in his appearance there had been many who had known him.

"Know you this," Qos said in his booming voice, "as we begin this alliance. If any of you who represent your nations and people are not truthful, the Great Barrier will know and it will not open. Only the true interest of saving all of Serôs, of seeing Serôs once again healthy and whole, will allow the barrier to unlock the City of Destinies."

The faces on the other side of the Great Barrier regarded him solemnly.

"Myth Nantar holds her secrets jealously these days," Qos went on. "She has been betrayed, the ideals she was founded on corrupted. Blood of those who were to make this city their home has run in her streets and scarred the mythal that surrounds it. The Weave will have to be honored and respected for now and for always." He paused. "Else we may lose great Myth Nantar forever."

The rulers and representatives of the world below, the High Mages, and Khlinat all stared through the barrier.

"We will begin," Qos said. "Step forward, place your hand against the Great Barrier, and speak your name."

The crowd hesitated for a moment, then Reefglamor strode forward and pushed his hand to the invisible wall.

"I am Senior High Mage Taranath Reefglamor of Sylkiir, and I am here to see that the City of Destinies is reopened."

Pacys closed his eyes, listening to the vibration the sea elf's voice started within the Great Barrier. The other High Mages followed suit and Pacys listened intently to the changes in the vibration.

"Princess Arina of Eadraal."

"Prince Mirol of Eadraal."

"Tribune Akkys of Vuuvax."

The triton Akkys stood aloof, as all his kind did. He was slightly built compared to the mermen, but everyone in Serôs knew not to judge the tritons lightly. They were savage fighters. He wore his shoulder-length blue hair tied back and carried a tapal, the signature weapon of his race, which curved in the middle like a fishhook and seemed to be made of all sharp edges.

Pacys knew that the Vuuvax was of the avenging protectorate within the triton race. His people had undertaken the job of bringing the Great Whale Bard's killer to justice. The triton slapped the Great Barrier forcefully, changing the pitch of the vibration.

"Dukar Gayar," a thin voice said, "Grand Savant of the Third Order and Paragon of the Kupavi Order."

The morkoth had been a surprise but Qos had vouched for him. His touch was soft, hardly changing the vibration at all.

"Lashyrr Maerdrymm, Grand Savant of the First Order and Paragon of the Numosi Order."

Pacys recognized her as a baelnorn, a once-dead elf returned to life as a guardian for others. Her body had transformed into living pearl upon her acceptance of her destiny. She was pale blue and ivory, and could have been mistaken for an elegant statue. Her hand slapped flatly against the barrier, changing the vibration's pitch more than anyone.

"Keros the Wanderer, of . . . Serôs."

Though the young triton Keros showed hesitation, his voice was strong and clear. The young triton had come to Myth Nantar for reasons of his own and stayed away from the others of his kind.

"Roaoum, subchief of the Tiger Coral tribe."

The locathah's voice was soft and carefully measured. Over the last days he had a habit of not speaking unless he truly had something to say. He and Prince Mirol had been friends for a number of years.

"Khlinat Ironeater," the dwarf said, putting his callused palm against the Great Barrier as well. He stared through the barrier at Pacys. "By Marthammor Duin, I'll stand with ye long as me heart beats and I got me good leg under me."

The roll of names continued until there was only one to go.

"Dukar Peacekeeper Tu'uua'col of Eadraal. I swear my allegiance for I have dreamed of this day for many years." The shalarin Dukar slapped his palm against the Great Barrier.

Pacys listened to the vibration running through the structure. His ear was trained by long years in his craft, gifted by the passion that existed within his heart and had never faltered, and guided by the need in him to be the best he could be.

He opened his mouth and sang, holding the one note at perfect pitch, feeling it resonate within his body as the Great Barrier reacted to it. He continued, lifting his arms at his side so that he could put all of himself into it.

Like a bubble bursting and vanishing within the space of a heartbeat, the Great Barrier shattered.

And the outside world rushed in over Myth Nantar once again, leaving it vulnerable to its greatest enemy.

XXV

27 Marpenoth, the Year of the Gauntlet

"Are ye sure we'll find the swabbie here?" Khlinat Iron-eater asked. He sat in the saddle of a seahorse they'd borrowed from the sea elves, and shaded his eyes against the morning sun with one hand. "That ship has surely seen some better days, I'm thinking."

Seated on a seahorse as well, Pacys nodded, feeling his heart race as he neared the boy he'd searched for. The hero's song played in his head, making his fingers itch for the yarting slung across his back in a waterproof bag.

"He's here," Pacys assured the dwarf.

A guard of twenty sea elf warriors rode with them as the seahorses cut across the ocean's surface. The ship's crew had already seen them and hurried across the decks to get into defensive positions.

"Well, and they're surely promising a heated welcoming if we're the wrong 'uns," Khlinat said.

"We're not."

Pacys guided his mount toward the ship, the seahorse straining only a little to catch up to it. When he drew abreast of the caravel, he found himself looking up at half a dozen bowmen with only tattered mercy and trust left in their souls.

"State your business and be quick about it," a woman dressed in black ordered from the railing.

"I'm here to see Jherek," Pacys called up.

"How do you know him?"

"I'm Pacys the Bard. I'm a friend."

The woman glanced at the sea elves. "We haven't seen too many friends lately," she said, "and damn few of them promise to come from under the sea."

"Lady—" Pacys began.

"Captain." The woman's voice was unrelenting.

"As you will, Captain. As Oghma is my patron, I'm only here in Jherek's best interest." Pacys kept his voice loud to be heard over the slap of the waves breaking against the ship's bow and the whip-crack of the canvas pulling tight in the rigging. "I know that he's wasting away, unable to control the darkness trying to consume his soul. I promise you, if you don't let me come aboard and speak to him, you're going to lose him. We'll all lose him."

A bearded warrior stepped forward and said, "Let him come aboard, Captain. He's speaking the truth."

The ship's captain hesitated.

"I'd know if he was lying," the warrior said.

The captain nodded to her crew. They put away their bows and dropped a cargo net over the side, leaving it caught up at the top.

"Climb on," the captain said. "We'll pull you up."

* * * * *

Jherek sat beside Sabyna's bed, his forearms resting heavily on his bent knees, his forehead pressed against them. He held her hand, not daring to let it go, afraid she might drift away from him in her sleep.

Glawinn continued using his power on her daily, but there were no healing potions left. Now, every day, the ship's mage lost ground. Her wounds festered, growing larger, taking her away from him a piece at a time.

The young sailor was ragged and unkempt. Not an hour passed that he didn't feel pain—hers as well as his. He ignored the knock on the door, not wanting to deal with

Glawinn trying to get him to eat or leave. If he had kept his distance from Sabyna, she would have been fine, but he'd returned.

"Young warrior," Glawinn spoke softly, "someone has come to see you."

"No." Jherek knew he was being petulant, but he'd had enough of looking at other people.

"Jherek."

The musical voice captured the young sailor's attention, striking a chord deep within him. He found it immediately uncomfortable. "Go away."

"I can't. I've waited all my life to meet you."

Shamed by his own lack of manners, knowing Glawinn wouldn't think well of him either, Jherek pushed himself to his feet and opened the door. It took him a moment to recognize the two men standing beside Glawinn. He'd met both of them the night Iakhovas and the pirates attacked Baldur's Gate.

"Hail and well met," the old man said.

His clothes were wet, almost dripping, and he smelled of the sea. He offered his hand.

"You're the bard," Jherek said, his tired mind wandering through all the memories. He clasped the old man's arm.

The bard bowed and said, "Pacys."

The resonance continued in Jherek but he still didn't understand where it came from.

"Hail and well met, swabbie," the dwarf greeted him good-naturedly.

"Khlinat."

Seeing the dwarf sailor standing there brought the beginnings of a smile to Jherek's lips. He took Khlinat's arm and felt the powerful grip.

"Hear tell ye've been betwixt some proper demons' brews since these old eyes last seen ye."

Jherek nodded quietly and glanced back at Sabyna. "It's been far harder than anything I could have imagined."

"This is the one who holds your heart?" the old bard asked.

Pacys glided into the room, in motion before Jherek even knew it. He stood by her bed and trailed his fingers across her feverish brow.

Jherek didn't know how to respond. Sabyna never had

the chance to let him know her mind after he'd revealed who he was.

"The look in your eyes is all the answer I need," Pacys said softly. "The love you share is a powerful thing."

Tears clouded Jherek's vision but he didn't let them fall. He spoke through a too-tight throat. "As it turns out, I wasn't the man she thought I was."

"On the contrary, my boy," the old bard said, "it's you who aren't the man you think you are."

"Can you help her?" Jherek had put off the question because he'd been afraid of the answer.

Sadly, Pacys shook his head. "No. The young lady lies beyond any help I might give her."

Jherek tried to will himself into a state of numbness but couldn't. The resonance within him that the bard's presence elicited wound him up inside.

"You should go," Jherek said.

"I can't. I was sent here to find you and to help you."

Jherek shook his head. "The only way you can help me is to help her."

"You don't know all there is yet."

The old man took the waterproof bag from his shoulder and opened it. He sat on the floor of the small cabin.

"What are you doing?" Jherek demanded.

Pacys's practiced fingers brushed the strings lightly. He twisted the knobs at the end of the instrument, adjusting the string tension. When he brushed the strings again, creating a mellow note that seemed to fill the room with light and warmth, he smiled and said, "Blessed Oghma, after being under the sea for so long and not able to practice, I thought I might have lost the gift."

"You have to go," Jherek said sternly, unable to believe the audacity of the bard.

Pacys effortlessly played a tune. It was soft and quiet, melding the gentleness of a stream running over smooth rocks and the sight of the wind through winter's bare tree branches.

"Music is a balm," the old bard said. "Let me play to her that I might ease her mind for a while."

"You said you couldn't help her."

"I can't, but I can ease the pain she suffers from."

Pacys nodded toward the unconscious woman. His

fingers whispered across the strings, coaxing soothing notes that filled the room. Turning, Jherek saw that Sabyna's face appeared more relaxed than it had in days.

"Will that be all right then?" Pacys asked.

"Aye."

Jherek returned to the bed and took a fresh compress from the pitcher, then gently wiped Sabyna's face. He sat, the resonance within his chest unfaltering.

"She's very pretty," the old bard said.

"Aye." Jherek slumped forward, trying to find a way to be comfortable.

"I'd like to hear how you met her."

"It's a long story."

The old bard smiled and said, "Actually, those are my favorite kind."

At first, Jherek wasn't going to speak, but there was something about the music that loosened his tongue. It changed subtly, though he couldn't point to exactly what the change was. So he began with how he met Sabyna on *Breezerunner*. Of course, that meant dredging up everything that happened at Velen. Pacys asked how Jherek happened to be there, which meant explaining about Bloody Falkane.

He also mentioned the voice that haunted him all his life and the cryptic message it gave him: Live, that you may serve. As the music played, he realized that there were only the three of them in the room. He couldn't remember when the others left. He didn't remember ever talking so much in his life.

Even when Jherek finished speaking, Pacys continued playing. The tune was different from when he started hours ago. Khlinat brought a plate of food, but the old bard turned it away, as did the young sailor. When Pacys finally stopped playing only the sound of Sabyna's ragged breathing filled the room. The weight of it almost broke Jherek.

"It seems," the old bard said, showing no signs of discomfort after sitting on the floor for hours, "that you have searched everywhere you might for help for the young lady except one."

"What?"

The old bard's hazel eyes flickered with reflections from

the lantern hanging on the wall.

"All your life," the bard told him, "you've had a benefactor who has looked out for you."

"The voice?"

"Yes."

"I never knew who that was."

"Perhaps it's time to ask."

Jherek put another compress on Sabyna's fevered brow and said, "I did ask."

"When you were on *Black Champion,* following Vurgrom."

"Aye. I asked, and I got no answer."

"Perhaps that wasn't the time. Perhaps you were supposed to wait a while longer."

"Why?"

The old bard shrugged. "I don't know how these things work, my boy," he said. "Faith in the gods is like a good song. You must wait to have everything revealed. You can try to force it to happen, but a song, and that faith, has its own time and place."

"But I had a faith."

"You could have already been spoken for at the time you sought out the Crying God."

"Spoken for?" Jherek echoed incredulously. "By a god?"

"Priests are called to serve their gods," the old bard said softly. "That call is undeniable. I've had friends who were good bards and artists who worked with passion at their craft only to be called into service of one of the gods."

The young sailor changed the compress again, thinking hard. Everything he thought forced him to the same conclusion. "I'm no priest."

"No, I never thought you were." Pacys began playing again, and this time the tune was a little faster, more uplifting than calming. "Remember in Baldur's Gate when Khlinat lay wounded? It seemed as if the wound might even prove fatal. Yet, you laid your hands on him and he was healed."

"It was the necklace he wore."

"No," Pacys said. "I've handled magical things in my time. That necklace holds no magic."

"It could have been used up saving his life. He even believed it saved him."

"Khlinat doesn't believe that now," Pacys said softly.

The whole idea confused Jherek. "You think I somehow saved him?"

"Yes." Pacys found another chord, and the resonance within the young sailor's chest felt stronger, more sure. "Why did Malorrie teach you?"

"I don't know."

"You said that someone pointed him in your direction."

"Aye." Jherek felt as though the room was closing in on him.

"And Madame Iitaar, whom you respect and love, told you there was a destiny ahead of you."

Jherek sat quietly and still, wanting only to deny everything the old bard said.

"Look at your whole life, my boy. Have you ever raised a hand against another with malice in your heart?"

Jherek thought back to the bar fight in Athkatla. "Aye. Against Aysel from *Breezerunner*'s crew."

"The man who insulted Sabyna's honor?" Pacys smiled. "Why, Jherek, I could expect nothing less from such as you."

"Such as me? What do you think I am?"

Pacys shook his head. "It's not what I think," he said. "When you needed the astrolabe from the diviner at the Pirate Isles and you were asked what you believed in, what was your answer?"

"Love," Jherek whispered, looking at Sabyna and feeling like he was about to fall apart. He grew angry with the bard for speaking in such a circumspect way.

"How can you believe in love after the way you were brought up?"

"Because it was shown to me by Madame Iitaar and Malorrie, then by old Finaren, captain of *Butterfly*."

"A phantom with a geas laid on him?" Pacys asked. "A lonely widow woman who could use a strong back and a pair of hands around her house to fix it up? A ship's captain who let you go once it was discovered you were one of Bloody Falkane's claimed? What could these people know of love? How can you trust their motives?"

Jherek shook his head. "Say what you will, but they loved me when no one else did."

"And you gave them love back."

"Aye," the young sailor said, "all that I had. Only to be driven from them."

"For a reason," Pacys said softly. "There were things you had to learn." He glanced at Sabyna and said, "Perhaps a new love to be found."

"Only to have those taken from me because I was cursed the day I was born?"

"I've seen the love Glawinn has for you," Pacys said. "The man has laid his life on the line for you."

"He was only serving Lathander, who guided him to help save the disk I pridefully took in Baldur's Gate."

"You were meant to have that disk."

"I didn't have it, and it was used to kill all those people on the Whamite Isles."

"Perhaps they were forfeit anyway," Pacys said. "So the best was done that could be, and the disk saw you to that sword."

"It's not mine."

"Yet I've been told no hand may comfortably hold it but yours."

Jherek couldn't argue; it was true. Others in Azla's crew tried to hold the sword but none of them could do it, or even wanted to, for any length of time.

"The Great Whale Bard sought you out and gave you a gift."

Jherek looked at the old bard and said, "All these things you say are true, but I can't make any sense of them."

"They were a path, my boy," Pacys said softly. "A path that led you here, to this time and this place."

"To do what?"

"What you were born to do. Battle the Taker."

Jherek couldn't help it; he laughed. The sound was bitter and insane and rude, but he couldn't help himself. Fatigue and pain had broken down his self-discipline, made it impossible to keep all those feelings to himself.

"It is your fate," Pacys said. "Even the whales told you so."

"Don't you see?" Jherek asked. "It's a mistake. Another part of that ill luck that has followed me. It's just my misfortune, and yours, that you're here wasting your time when you should be with this hero you're looking for."

"You've already faced the Taker once," Pacys said, "in the caverns. You wounded him, survived his attempt to kill you with the buckler given to you by the Great Whale Bard. Iakhovas is the Taker."

"He was just a mage."

"No."

The firm denial shook Jherek, brought him back under control a little. He sobered and looked at the bard. "What you're saying is impossible," he insisted.

"What I'm saying," Pacys stated, "could be no other way. You are the champion that these times call for."

"I'm a sailor."

"And more."

Jherek shook his head.

"It's true," Pacys said. "Every step you took, every decision you made, has brought you to here and now."

"I've brought only bad luck to everyone I know," Jherek said. "Madame Iitaar probably lost business in Velen after it was found out that she was harboring one of Bloody Falkane's pirates. Finaren probably lost work as well."

"You don't know that," Pacys said. "Even if it's true, you could change all that by becoming what you're meant to be."

"And what is that?"

Pacys eyed him again and stopped playing. "Ask."

"I have asked."

"Not me."

"Then who?"

"The voice that has been with you all those years."

Jherek shook his head and felt empty inside. "I've not heard it in months."

"And you think it is gone?"

"Aye. Don't you see? Even if what you were saying was somehow true, I've already broken faith with the voice."

"Ask," Pacys said gently.

"How can you be so certain?"

"How can you be so *uncertain*?"

Jherek looked at the bard incredulously. "Have you not listened to what I've told you?"

"Oh yes. Even better, it seems, than you have. Ask."

"I have asked."

"Ask now."

301

"If the voice cared whether Sabyna lived or died, it wouldn't have allowed her to be infected by the bite of the drowned ones."

"And you would never have had a reason to search so deeply within yourself these past few days. Ask, Jherek. The truth is the tonic you need."

Anger gripped the young sailor. The old bard dangled false hope like fat fruit hanging on the vine. "Fine," he said. "And after I do, I want you to leave."

Pacys ignored Jherek's anger, keeping his voice soft. "Ask, Jherek." The old bard put the yarting down, then rolled to his knees. "Ask properly, and with respect, as you would ask one of those you love."

Seeing the old bard's belief brought stinging tears to Jherek's eyes. How could anyone believe what the man said after everything he'd been told. Why did the bard's words have to ring so true? Angry with himself, so scared of the final denial he was about to experience, he rolled to his knees. He faced the bard and brought his hands together in supplication. The young sailor was surprised at how his hands shook. He looked around the room for some inspiration, not knowing where to begin. *Azure Dagger's* gentle sway as she sailed rocked him.

"I don't know how to begin."

"Live," Pacys said, "that you may serve."

"I live," Jherek said, the words coming somehow naturally to his lips, "how may I serve?"

The great voice that answered filled the cabin. Even the lantern light seemed brighter.

I am here.

Jherek saw the old bard's eyes widen and knew he heard the words, too.

"You are back," the young sailor said.

My son, I have never left you. On every step of your journey, I have been with you. When your heart faltered, I gave you the strength to carry on.

"Why?"

Because I have chosen you.

"For what?"

To be my champion. To work in my name. To live by living and serve by serving.

"Why me?"

I have looked into your heart, my son, and found it to be one of the truest I have seen. You love with all the length and depth and breadth of your soul, never holding back any of yourself, never letting your fear that you might be hurt stand in your way.

"I would not listen to you."

Pride is not a bad thing when tempered properly, my son. You did not yet know me when you turned away.

"Why didn't you tell me more?"

You were not ready. You had enough things in your life that you still held to that you could not have accepted, could not have believed.

Jherek didn't understand that. "I had nothing," he maintained. "I'd been driven from my home, never had family. Nothing."

You had no belief. You would not have listened to me. Now, there is nothing else for you to cling to. Before you would have rejected the destiny that is yours.

"Now I have no choice?" Anger boiled up in Jherek. The shaking hands before him turned into fists. "You would try to enslave me?"

"Jherek," Pacys warned softly.

"No," Jherek said to the old bard in a harsh voice, "this is not your affair. I'll speak as I wish."

I would not enslave you, my son, the great voice said. *You could never live under those conditions, and I would never ask. Your doubts in yourself would have kept you from turning to me and allowing me to give you the gifts I have for you.*

Jherek trembled, sensing the truth behind the words. "I'm sorry. I should not have spoken in such an ill fashion."

The voice spoke, and Jherek felt he could hear the smile in the words. *My son, you are going to be one of the very best. I knew it was so when I saved your life as a boy.*

"Who are you?" Jherek whispered, not as afraid of the answer as he had been back in Velen when he'd first contemplated it.

I am the spring, dawn, birth, and renewal, my son. I am beginnings and hidden potential. I am conception, vitality, youth, and self-perfection. Know that I am Lathander, called the Morninglord. And you, my son, are one of my chosen champions.

"Glawinn," Jherek croaked, "does he know?"

He has suspicions, but he does not know. That has not been his to know until you tell him.

Jherek glanced at Sabyna, hardly daring to ask for what was on his mind. "What of Sabyna? She is my heart. I could not live knowing I had caused her life to be taken."

That was no fault of your own.

"She believed in me when I couldn't believe in myself."

She saw the goodness in you, and the potential.

"Must—" Jherek's voice broke and tears streamed down his face. "Must I lose her? I would ask you for her life, Lathander, and pledge mine in its place. Save her and do with me what you will."

No, my son. I would never bargain over a champion. You will serve me only if your heart wills it.

"But you could save her."

Yes. And you would look to me as though you forever owed her life to me. I will not have that.

"So I'm to watch her die?"

My son, you have the power to save her. As you saved Khlinat, and as you have saved yourself upon occasion in the past. Trust in yourself, Jherek. Trust in the love you have for her, and in your own ability to do what must be done.

Slowly, Jherek reached for Sabyna. He remembered how Glawinn came into her room and laid his hands upon the ship's mage, but it didn't seem right that he do so. "I don't know how," he said.

Love her, my son. That is your greatest gift. But you must give and receive it. You cannot lock yourself away from it.

Trembling, his face covered in tears, so afraid that he would be somehow found wanting, Jherek laid his hands on Sabyna's face. He willed her to be well, pictured her in his mind hale and whole, saw her with the smile on her lips that he knew so well.

Power coursed through his hands, filling them with heat. He knew it wasn't enough. Tenderly, he leaned forward, pressed his lips to hers, and kissed her. He remembered how she'd been in the rigging the day she kissed him. The love and the hunger crashed down over him, threatening to sweep him away.

Sabyna kissed back, her lips soft against his.

Jherek opened his eyes to find her staring back at him. He tried to back away, knowing the question of his birth still lay between them, embarrassed by what she must think of him to find him there, obviously taking advantage of her weakness.

"Lady," he said breathlessly, "I know this must appear unseemly, but I swear I only had—"

"Shut up," she ordered. She wrapped her arms around his neck and held him tightly, then covered his mouth with hers and kissed him deeply. "Hold me, Jherek, and don't let me go."

The young sailor wrapped his arms around her, pulling her to him fiercely. Somewhere in there, the old bard had the decency to leave.

* * * * *

"Are you sure you want to do that, young warrior?"

Glawinn's quiet words startled Jherek from his reverie. He stood on *Azure Dagger*'s stern castle, the wind blowing through his hair. Late morning tinged the eastern sky pink, but the rest of it was pure cerulean. Bright white doves winged overhead, and the young sailor chose to take that as an omen.

"Aye," Jherek replied. "I can see no other way of it."

"This thing you're undertaking," Glawinn said, "it's no easy thing."

"Would you talk me out of it?" Jherek asked.

Glawinn shook his head.

"I would see it done, then, if you're willing."

"Young warrior," Glawinn said in a voice that was suddenly hoarse with emotion as tears glittered in his eyes, "if you only knew the honor you show me."

Jherek reached for him, his own eyes tearing even as he smiled fiercely. The young sailor pulled the man to him in a bear hug that was returned full measure.

"I only show what you have shown me," Jherek told him.

Azure Dagger lay at anchor with only the small wind blowing over her, so the song from Pacys's yarting was audible from one end of the ship to the other.

Jherek gathered himself, standing on the stern castle

in borrowed clothes, his sword thrust through the sash at his waist. He gazed at Sabyna, who stood with the small crowd around Pacys at the other end of the stern castle.

During the last two days, the ship's mage had made a complete recovery. No scars remained to mark the drowned ones' bites. She wore a dress that Azla loaned her. Even the old-timers among the pirate crew were surprised to learn the half-elf captain owned a dress, though they all had a care not to say anything of the kind in her presence. Khlinat stood beside her, his chest puffed up proudly. Captain Tarnar of *Steadfast* was there as well, unable to cross the dangerous seas yet. He wore vestments that bore Mystra's mark. The crews of both ships stood on their decks, *Steadfast* within easy hailing distance.

Jherek hadn't known so many would be interested, but Azla declared the proceeding as an official event and her pirates even cleaned up a bit for it. The young sailor glanced at the audience and felt self-conscious.

"I didn't know so many people would be here," he said to Glawinn.

"Young warrior, the word spread quickly last night when you asked for this. Those people out there, once they learned of it, they would have it no other way. This is not something that is often witnessed."

"It was only you and I," Jherek pointed out. "And I told only Sabyna."

Glawinn shrugged, grinning. "And I told only the bard because he needed to know for the tale he weaves. So, we have two suspects. Choose one."

Jherek couldn't keep the smile from his face. "No."

"Then, perhaps we should begin."

"Aye."

Excitement and anxiety hummed inside Jherek and he had second thoughts about his own worthiness. Quietly, he shoved those aside and gazed at Sabyna. He knew she was proof that Lathander had found him deserving, even if he couldn't yet see it himself.

"Kneel, Jherek of Velen," Glawinn ordered.

Quietly, Jherek knelt, placing his hands before him, palms pressed together. He bent his head forward in benediction.

"You have been blessed by Lathander," Glawinn said,

"to be among those who would defend the Morninglord's name and His wishes. How say you?"

Jherek marshaled his courage, hoping to overcome his nervousness. Surprisingly, his voice sounded strong and clear over the gentle wind. "I, Jherek of Velen, do hereby pledge to honor the strictures of this sacred heritage and promise by my faith to be loyal to Lathander, maintaining my devotion against all persons without deception or forethought. Further, I vow to promote and uphold the principles of fealty, courtesy, honesty, valor, and honor, and to solemnly and faithfully follow the edicts of the Morninglord."

"May your heart be forever true to Lathander's cause to hold compassion for those who will need your help and to hold righteous anger for those who have been trespassed against," Glawinn said. "May your arm be forever strong in the Morninglord's service."

Jherek listened to the silence around him and felt more complete than he ever had. By Lathander's sacred covenant, this was where he should be. His heart swelled inside his chest as he awaited Glawinn's next words.

"For the Morninglord's glory and in my true and unwavering service to him, I name you Sir Jherek, paladin in the service of Lathander."

Jherek felt Glawinn's sword touch both his shoulders.

"Arise, Sir Jherek, and be whole of heart and spirit to show Lathander's great love for you."

The crowd aboard *Azure Dagger* clapped, and the pirates hooted and hollered their support. Rising on shaking legs, Jherek stood, looking up at the blue sky above.

"Thank you," he said to the sky," for finding me and freeing me."

My son, the deep voice said, *you were never lost, and you have freed yourself. Take your shirt off.*

Jherek hesitated for only a moment, then did as he was asked. As he stripped the shirt away, he noticed the clapping and hollering quieted, until the ship was silent once more. He was conscious of the tattoo—a flaming skull masked in chains—that showed so plainly on his arm.

No one, the deep voice boomed, startling the people on the ship and letting Jherek know he wasn't the only one who could hear the words now, *may mark one of my own.*

A pink incandescence flared to life in the middle of the flaming skull, burning brightly. Jherek watched, surprised there was no pain, only a tingling feeling. When the incandescence passed, only unmarked flesh remained behind.

Jherek held his arms out at his sides, staring at the clear skin through tear-blurred eyes that spilled over his cheeks.

The stain of your father's heritage is gone, my son. Live free of it.

XXVI

30 Marpenoth, the Year of the Gauntlet

"Why would Lathander be involved in any of this?" Qos asked.

Pacys swam beside Qos as the storm giant looked over the preparations being made to the Great Gate beside the Dukars' Academy.

"For several reasons," the bard answered.

Mermen, shalarin, sea elves, locathah, tritons, and even some of the men from *Azure Dagger* and *Steadfast*—both ships now at anchor above—labored to clear the great plaza. They chopped down coral reefs and carried them away. The humans used all manner of potions and magical devices to reach Myth Nantar, but once there, the mythal surrounding the City of Destinies allowed them to stay, breathing the water as if it were air.

"What reasons?" the giant asked.

"The Morninglord is the god of beginnings," the old bard said, letting his fingers stray across the gems inset in the saceddar. "There have been several beginnings involved in the legend of the Taker."

"Those legends have been around for thousands of years, as has this city. There are no beginnings there."

"Lathander is also the god of renewal. Just as you hoped to open Myth Nantar so that Serôs might again unite, the Morninglord wanted to see that happen. He has been working toward this end for a long time as well, else how would Jherek be here now?"

"The young paladin truly holds great promise," Qos said. "I've looked at many young men and women in my years at the academy, but the potential in him is strong."

"Jherek is another beginning," Pacys said. He'd talked to the young paladin himself after Sabyna's recovery, and Jherek told him some of what the Morninglord had revealed to him. "Not only does Lathander believe that Jherek will be one of the finest warriors to serve in his name, but Jherek will also be the first paladin to be based upon and in the seas of Toril."

"I have heard of 'seaguards,' " Qos said, "Paladins who ride upon ships and protect them for their lieges."

"Yes," Pacys agreed, "but none of them have understood the sea as Jherek will. You've only begun to see the promise in him."

"If the Taker doesn't destroy him."

Pacys studied Jherek among the crews seeking to clear the debris from the Great Gate. He didn't say anything.

"I'm sorry, Taleweaver," Qos said after a moment. "I know that is never far from your mind. Nor, probably, from the young man's."

"No."

"I'm still adjusting to the fact that Myth Nantar is once more open and no longer truly under my safekeeping."

"It will be all right."

"I hope." Qos let out a long breath. "And how goes it for you, Taleweaver? I have listened to your music, and it sounds good to these ears. I've even heard parts of your songs being sung in the Resonant Horn Inn. The song you wrote for the Alu'Tel'Quessir during their long trek seems popular."

Pacys smiled, letting his pride grow. "Give me time, my friend, all who have participated in these efforts will have their part of the song."

"But at the heart of it will be the story of Iakhovas and that young paladin."

"Yes. I'm still working on that. It is going to be the best thing I've ever written."

"Provided your young hero survives," Qos said.

* * * * *

"The merfolk lead us into a trap," Laaqueel said.

She stood beside Iakhovas on *Tarjana*'s deck, watching as the mermen battled sahuagin and the few remaining drowned ones. Only a few koalinth remained among them after the ixitxachitls' attack during the assault on Naulys.

"Of course they do," Iakhovas said. "They seek to slow us and let Myth Nantar prepare to meet us."

Laaqueel had seen that the city had been opened through the images in the crystal brain coral. Iakhovas peered through the crystal almost incessantly. She'd had no contact with the female voice that spoke with her at the Battle of Voalidru. She also hadn't had to fight for her life since then.

And since that battle, she hadn't once prayed to Sekolah.

"Then we're going to go into the trap?" Laaqueel asked.

Iakhovas smiled confidently. "I wouldn't miss it, little malenti."

* * * * *

"Are you afraid?" Sabyna asked.

Jherek cracked open a crab leg and dug out the tender meat inside. He sat with Sabyna on one of the benches on Maalirn's Walk near the Fire Fountain. The flames blazed up in spite of the water, and cooks used the heat to prepare meals for the humans who weren't used to eating uncooked seafood. They'd been in Myth Nantar now for five days.

"Aye," he told her without hesitation. "By all the stories I've been told of the Taker, by all the legends that Pacys has seen fit to tell me, he's a fearsome creature. I'd be a fool not to be afraid."

"You don't have to fight him."

Jherek was silent for a moment, then said, "Aye, but I do, lady. It's as Lathander would have me do, and there are those who believe I might be the only chance there is to end his menace for all time."

311

"You mean Pacys and Glawinn believe that."

"Aye."

"One wants to sing about you, Jherek, and the other believes in heroes."

"Do you find me so hard to believe in, lady?"

Sabyna shook her head, the anger in her features softening. "No," she admitted, "I believe in you, Jherek, but I'm afraid for you, too."

"It only shows you have good sense."

"How can you joke about this?"

"Lady, forgive me. I'm not joking. I just don't want to burden you—or myself."

"What if I asked you not to do this?" Sabyna asked. "What if I asked you not to stand and fight with these people?"

Jherek was silent for a moment, looking into her copper-colored eyes. "Would you?" he asked finally.

She looked away from him. "Selûne help a misguided fool," she said, "I should never have brought this up."

"Would you ask me?" Jherek asked quietly. "Now I need to know."

"If I was going to ask you, I already would have," she told him. "I know what your answer would be anyway. It just seems so unfair that we have this between us and we stand on the brink of losing it all."

Jherek took her hand in his, squeezing it lightly. "Lady, I prefer to think that we stand on the brink of having more than I'd ever dreamed."

Tears glittered in her eyes, and he could tell she searched for something to say. "I'm sorry I even thought about asking you this, Jherek. It's a streak of selfishness in me that I'm not proud of."

"It's good to know the things you want."

She smiled through her tears. "I know I want you."

"As I want you, lady." He lifted her fingers to his lips and kissed them softly. "Neither of us knows what the future may bring, and I've had enough of living in the past. I will take what I can get."

"I know."

"As for fighting the Taker, I won't be going into that battle alone. Glawinn will be there, as well as a host of warriors who have spent their lives in battle."

"I don't know why it has to be you."

"Nor do I, lady. I only know that I won't walk away from this. All my life I've looked for something to believe in. Lathander is teaching me to believe in myself. No one caused me to be the way I am. I walk the path I do because I chose to walk it. I stayed with the people I did because I wanted to, not because I had to. Looking back as Lathander has bade me, I realize now that I had more choice in those matters than I thought I did. I stepped away from my father in search of becoming what was in me, not because of what I wanted but because I couldn't accept what was there. If I walked away from this, I couldn't accept myself. I wouldn't feel as though I deserved you."

"I wouldn't judge you harshly for walking away from this."

Jherek nodded. "I know."

"I love you."

Her hand trailed gently across his face, briefly touching the water-softened scab that covered the slash on his cheek.

"As I love you." Jherek touched her face with the back of his hand, wiping away the tears he found there. "I could not love you so much did I not love honor, lady. It is all I know to be, and I would die before I betrayed that honor or my love for you."

"I know," she said hoarsely, holding his head between her hands. "I know. One does not come without the price of the other. For either of us."

She pulled him closer and wrapped her arms around his waist. Jherek put his arms over her shoulders and held her tightly.

* * * * *

"Die, huu-mannn!"

Jherek lifted the cutlass and blocked the sea devil's trident thrust. He willed Iridea's Tear into a hook, reaching out quickly and tearing the throat from his opponent. He pushed the dying sahuagin away, almost bowled over by the next sea devil pushing up from behind.

The young paladin stood with other defenders of Myth Nantar at Chamal Gate. The Taker's final attack came after

313

the triton offensive of the fifth of Uktar—only a couple days before—had split his forces. According to the tritons who'd reported to Qos, fully half his remaining army of sahuagin had turned and swam back to the Alamber Sea.

The sound of steel against coral filled the area, ringing more stridently than Jherek was used to. Over it all he heard Pacys singing. The bard's song rang true within him, making him feel stronger and more confident. Iakhovas's army still outnumbered the Myth Nantarn defenders nearly two to one, even after the tritons' victory.

Fighting undersea wasn't like fighting on a ship's deck, Jherek discovered. Underwater, the sahuagin could come at him from above as well as ahead and behind—and they didn't have any sense of honor. Nor did they abide by the Laws of Battle he'd heard so many of the Serôsians lived and died by.

"Fall back and regroup!" Morgan Ildacer shouted, waving his troops back. The High Mages had named the sea elf captain to head up one of the defensive units.

The young paladin fell back with the rest of his group. He swam with the others, finding it easier to battle in the mythal that covered the city than he expected. His moves in the water came more naturally since he didn't have to hold his breath. Somehow his sense of balance seemed more sure as well.

A sahuagin thrust a spear at him from the right while another yanked its weapon from a mortally wounded sea elf.

Jherek swung the enchanted sword and chopped the trident head off, leaving the sahuagin with only the shaft in its hands. Once under water he'd found the sword swung as easily as if he stood on dry land, the blade not slowed at all.

The sahuagin seemed startled, then angrily threw the useless shaft away and spread the claws of both its hands. The second sahuagin approached in a flash, its fins pushing at the water.

Jherek willed the bracer into a two-foot shield and set himself as well as he could. He pulled the shield in against his body at the last minute. Like the sword, the bracer—in any shape he willed it into—had no water drag at all.

The trident slammed against the shield then deflected

harmlessly over Jherek's shoulder. The sahuagin shoved a hand out with its finger webs spread to slow and turn. Jherek uncoiled his arm and lashed out with the shield. The razor-sharp edge, thinner and more solid than the finest steel, sliced through the sea devil's stomach, disemboweling it at once.

Still moving, Jherek swept the shield in, catching the water now because he willed it to, and lifted himself from the first sahuagin's path. He brought the sword down and nearly severed his opponent's neck.

Before he could recover, one of the few koalinth survivors caught him with a spear thrust in the chest. The silverweave mail shirt he wore prevented the blade from slicing through his chest, but the impact knocked him backward, slamming the breath from his lungs.

The young paladin went with the motion, flipping backward and reaching out to the water element of the mythal, letting it buoy him up. He'd discovered within the mythal that he could treat the city as if it were two-dimensional, like a city on dry land, or three-dimensional as if he were underwater.

Jherek kicked his feet and twisted as he willed the bracer into a hook. When the koalinth shot over him, the young paladin flicked the hook and caught the marine hobgoblin in the leg. He used the creature's momentum to pull him faster, angling his body so he came up behind the koalinth.

The young paladin reversed his sword as he swung toward the koalinth. Though the creature's back was toward him, he couldn't strike. He switched the bracer to a dagger and readied himself as the koalinth turned toward him, lashing out with its spear. Jherek blocked the spear with the dagger, then drove his sword through his opponent's heart.

Even as the koalinth died, Jherek changed the bracer back to a shield as a dozen sahuagin leveled their crossbows and fired. The short, heavy quarrels flashed across the distance and thudded against the shield. One of the sea elves a few feet away didn't fare so well and took a quarrel through the throat.

In the next moment a Dukar stepped forward and formed a fireball in one hand. He threw the swirling

315

flames at the mass of sahuagin. They had only a moment to attempt escape before the fireball detonated with a thunderous crack that left only burned and torn bodies behind.

Blood filled the water around Jherek and created a salty taste to the water he breathed. It was like nothing he'd ever experienced.

The sea elves kept falling back, having no choice as their numbers dwindled. Jherek caught sight of the House of the Waves on his left, then it was lost to the sahuagin forces as well. He lifted his sword and kept fighting, knowing the battle was continuing on a number of fronts.

* * * * *

"Pull those damned sails!" Azla roared as she ran across the decks, keeping her quarry always in sight. "Bring her about!"

Sabyna stood beside Arthoris on *Azure Dagger*'s forecastle. Skeins floated at her side, riding the wind. Sabyna's attention was torn between helping Arthoris with his spells and with worrying about Jherek. She wished she could have stayed with him in the City of Destinies, but with the attack coming from the surface, they both knew she would be of more use there.

Twenty pirate vessels sailed the sea above Myth Nantar. The crews worked to dispose of Vurgrom's poisoned kegs. The pirate had told them about the kegs after being taken prisoner. He bargained for his own freedom by telling. Jherek, in turn, informed the Myth Nantarn defenders.

Mermen and locathah swam under the water with nets, trying to catch as many of the barrels as they could.

Azure Dagger and *Steadfast* harried the pirate ships. In the beginning they'd thought there would have been a chance to prevent some of the sabotage, but with twenty ships against them, it was only a matter of time until they were captured or sunk.

After Captain Tarnar of *Steadfast* found out about the poisoned kegs, he'd sent a patchwork crew under his first officer south to Ilighôn in the hopes of reaching Corymrean Freesails that might be using the port city as a staging point. So far none of the hoped-for reinforcements had arrived.

As Arthoris prepared his next spell, a pirate ship closed on *Azure Dagger*, running broadside to her. Ballista crews worked to crank their deadly devices around and take aim.

Sabyna invoked one of the new spells Arthoris had taught her, knowing that the ship's mage was vulnerable on the forecastle. She inscribed the mystic symbol in the air, and it glowed briefly before disappearing.

"Very good," Arthoris said as he pulled on a leather glove that looked like it was equipped with brass knuckles.

"If Selûne guided me well enough," Sabyna said.

Arthoris spoke a command word and held his glove-covered, clenched hand before him. A huge, disembodied hand appeared in the air before him. It measured five feet across at the knuckles.

"Deck crew—stand by to repel boarders!" Azla called, taking her place at the starboard railing. Pirates sprang to her side. "Ballista crews—fire at will!"

Under Arthoris's control, the disembodied fist flew across the water, ignoring the ship that paced them, and hammered the mainmast. Three hits later, the mast cracked and sheared off. Sinking the ships wasn't a good idea. The kegs would sink with them, and there were no guarantees the poison would drift far enough away not to hurt anyone. As soon as the mast crumpled, Arthoris moved the magic hand on to the next ship, attacking the rudder there.

Archers targeted the mage, who stood out against the rest of the crew as he gestured. Arrows sped from their bows, few of them getting anywhere close to Sabyna or Arthoris. Only a handful struck the invisible shield Sabyna had raised in front of them. They dropped to the deck, spent.

Grappling lines tossed from the pirate ship landed over *Azure Dagger*'s railing but were quickly cut away by the ship's crew. Her own ballistae fired, clearing the pirate decks.

The fore ballista on the pirate vessel cut loose. The huge shaft came straight at Arthoris and Sabyna, then splintered against the magic shield. The impact, however, was enough to send both mages to their knees. Arthoris lost control of the disembodied hand, and it faded away.

Less than thirty feet away, Vurgrom's pirate crew linked up.

"Stand ready," Azla yelled.

Her crew raised their shields and their weapons.

The other ship's crew all leaped together, using magic to span the distance to *Azure Dagger*.

"Haul!" Azla commanded. "Haul, damn you, if you would live!"

Men at either end of the caravel's main deck pulled ropes and ran up a cargo net that spanned the distance across the main deck. The enspelled pirates thudded into the cargo net, caught off guard. Before they could slash their way through the net, Azla's crew attacked them with swords, daggers, and bows. Up against the cargo net as they were, it was like stabbing fish in a barrel.

Sabyna helped Arthoris to his feet, peering out at the water. They hadn't stopped many of Vurgrom's pirates from dumping their deadly cargo, but she hoped they'd slowed them enough that the undersea rescue teams could gather most of the falling kegs before they descended to Myth Nantar.

"Now there's a welcome sight," Arthoris said.

Turning south, Sabyna looked out over the horizon and saw the sails from at least five tall ships running with the wind. All of them flew the colors of Cormyrean Freesails.

"Let's hope they're not too late," Sabyna said grimly.

* * * * *

Hurry, little malenti. There's not much time.

Laaqueel swam after Iakhovas high above Myth Nantar. She glanced at the gates leading into the city, realizing that few of the koalinth had actually penetrated the city itself, proof that the mythal that protected against such creatures still worked.

The maps Iakhovas had drawn of the area from stories they'd gathered were very accurate. She saw Chamal Avenue to the left, noting the fighting going on there, all of it garishly lit by the Fire Fountain.

Iakhovas swam boldly, using his claws against any Myth Nantarn defenders who made it through his defenses. Over a hundred sharks swam with him as a living wall of protection, all under the control of the headband he wore. The sharks acted like battering rams, barreling through would-be defenders or ripping arms and legs off in their cruel mouths as they passed.

The sea elf rangers and mages of the city tried battling the possessed creatures as well, but they were too tightly packed and controlled to be turned away. A shalarin Dukar slashed through them, arching his body and gliding gracefully toward Iakhovas while using the sharks themselves as cover.

Laaqueel spotted the shalarin and almost shouted a warning. Her first instinct was self-preservation, and she knew without Iakhovas she would never escape the city. *Tarjana* waited outside the city, hidden behind a reef and the magic spell woven by Iakhovas. Before she could get past her hesitation, the shalarin Dukar cut through the sharks and engaged Iakhovas.

The shalarin's hand glowed white and changed shapes, becoming trident tines that flashed out for Iakhovas. Reacting immediately, Iakhovas shifted his arm into the edged weapon Laaqueel had seen before as he engaged the Dukar. The sharks changed courses, swirling around their master to deflect other potential attackers.

The Dukar thrust the trident hand out but Iakhovas blocked it effortlessly and slashed the shalarin's arm off with his own altered limb. Before the shalarin recovered, Iakhovas slashed again and decapitated his opponent. A shark glided by and snatched the tumbling head from the water, swallowing it whole.

Iakhovas turned at once and streaked for the collapsed ruin surrounding a circle of green and blue marble with coral mosaics that created a picture of a beautiful mermaid. Her hair, arms, and tail flukes each pointed to the seven carved coral arches set around the circle. Beneath her tail was the word AMTOLA, which Laaqueel recognized from her studies. Translated, it meant "traveler."

The malenti priestess wasn't sure what the mosaic represented. The information Iakhovas gave her regarding Myth Nantar's history and geography was limited.

Shooting from the protection of the sharks, Iakhovas swam down to the ruins. He dropped to one of the coral arches as a squad of mermen raced for him from above. Iakhovas flung one hand out, blue fire shooting from his fingertips. A moment later a huge web uncoiled across the seven arches in front of the approaching mermen. Unable to stop, they slammed into the webbing. Sharks finned that way at once, attacking the easy prey.

Iakhovas moved to the nearest coral arch, a smile on his dark face. He hammered one side of the arch with his fist, breaking a section of it into pieces that floated through the water. He caught one of the coral chunks and crushed it in his hand, brushing the flakes away.

"See, little malenti?" Iakhovas showed her what was in his palm.

Laaqueel floated closer and saw the tiny jade gem carefully set into a dark red fire opal no bigger than her thumb. "What is it?" she asked.

"My eye, little malenti," Iakhovas laughed. "The eye that Umberlee took from me. The eye I made to make me more powerful than ever. Until the Great Barrier around this place was shattered, I could not reach it—but with it, little malenti, with it I shall be invincible!"

Currents swept against Laaqueel, pushed by the mermen trying to escape the web and the savaging sharks. She glanced up to see other mermen, sea elves, and locathah working desperately to free their comrades from the death trap.

"Stand ready, little malenti."

Iakhovas formed a fireball in his hand and threw it into the web. The strands caught fire, burning the trapped victims and those rescuers who were too close. Laaqueel dodged the falling bodies and the flaming web ropes.

"Now, little malenti!"

Iakhovas leaped up from the mosaic. Laaqueel followed, wanting to be free of all the enemies surrounding her. When she'd first entered Myth Nantar, even with an army twice the number of the defenders, she'd felt little chance of emerging from the battle alive. Now that Iakhovas possessed his prize, the slim hope that she might yet live entered her thoughts. Even so, she had no idea what she would do next.

She watched as a keg dropped on top of a nearby coral-encrusted building. A vaporous sediment billowed out from holes cut in the keg's sides, and the purplish hue looked immediately familiar. The sediment spread quickly, enveloping a group of sahuagin battling a clutch of tritons. Within seconds all of them were dying, gripped in the paroxysms of the sahuagin poison.

More kegs drifted down around the city with the same effect. The poison spread quickly so it didn't last long, and its killing radius extended no more than twenty feet. Glancing up, straining her eyes, Laaqueel saw huge nets manned by mermen and locathah already burdened with dozens more kegs. Their effort spared Myth Nantar a lot of damage.

Laaqueel halted for a moment, still stunned even after everything she'd seen that Iakhovas would so willingly sacrifice the sahuagin. She knew if the kegs were present that Vurgrom's pirates must be on the surface. She doubted that would prove an effective escape route, but she had no idea of any other he had in mind.

"Live or die, little malenti," Iakhovas called as he swam toward the surface.

She hesitated, not knowing which would be better.

Live, the feminine voice called out. *Live, that you may serve.*

Reluctantly, fearfully, Laaqueel swam.

*   *   *   *   *

Pacys stood atop the Colossus of Dukar. His fingers effortlessly found the saceddar's gemstones, and the notes rang out as pure as dwarven steel.

At ninety feet tall, the statue was the tallest structure in Myth Nantar. The old bard stood on its head and sang, pouring his heart into the ballad he'd written for the defenders of the City of Destinies. Carved from lucent coral, the statue glowed brightly, providing nearly a third of the light filling the city. The statue held a tapal high in its right hand and stood straddling the entrance to a most revered tomb.

From his vantage point, Pacys could view the battle clearly. Qos, the High Mages of Sylkiir, and the Dukars led by Tu'uua'col stood in a circle around the Great Gate west of the Dukars' Academy.

The mosaic plaza that held the Great Gate was almost two hundred feet across. The mages around the perimeter all glowed lambent blue-green from the ancient, eldritch forces they controlled. They continued their spell even though their defenders were swiftly falling to sahuagin tridents.

Drawn by the powers that connected him to the story that he told, blessed by Oghma, the old bard was able to see the main players in the battle as if he stood next to them. When he focused on them, he even heard their words.

His attention was drawn to Iakhovas as the Taker swam for the surface. Jherek remained low in the city, battling from building to building as the sahuagin and drowned ones continued pressing toward the center. Khlinat and a handful of sea elf guards stood watch over the old bard.

Pacys sang, giving voice to the words and the music that filled him. Never before had he felt the strength and confidence of a performance the way he did now. He knew his music affected the valiant men who battled below, adding strength to their flagging bodies and courage to their hearts in the face of a superior enemy.

" 'Ware now, friend Pacys!" Khlinat roared.

The bard ducked as the dwarf sailed overhead astride a sahuagin nearly three times his size. One hand axe was buried in the sea devil's neck and Khlinat held the other back, ready to strike. The sahuagin flailed with a handful of claws, narrowly missing the dwarf's face. Khlinat put the hand-axe blade through the sea devil's skull.

A burst of magic that suddenly flooded from the mythal staggered Pacys. With his senses fully open and receptive, he was overly attentive to such things. He turned back to the Great Gate plaza and watched as the sahuagin struck within the ranks of the High Mages and Dukars, driving their defenders back before them. The claws of the sea devils pierced the bodies of the magic-users.

At the same time, a yellow-green comet roared from the Great Gate mosaic and streaked for the surface. The comet's tail stretched from the comet's head to the mosaic, maintaining contact. The yellow-green glare washed over the City of Destinies, stripping away all other colors.

Qos roared and drew the huge two-handed sword he carried. Twice as tall as his attackers, he swept the blade through the sahuagin in a glittering arc, shearing them limb from limb. The Dukars that survived the initial attack summoned weapons from their bodies and battled desperately.

Even from as far away as he was, Pacys could see that Tanarath Reefglamor was among the fallen, a sahuagin's trident shoved through his heart. Still, the old bard's voice didn't falter, remaining steady and true.

The yellow-green comet struck the ocean's surface above and exploded into bright embers that whirled in the air. Several of them struck pirate ships, reducing them to rubble in heartbeats. The embers whirled faster, coming closer and closer together. The ocean's surface whirled in the opposite direction of the embers, creating a swirl of white-capped peaks that abruptly inverted and stabbed down deeply into the Sea of Fallen Stars.

Even though he wore one of the mystic gems that all the Myth Nantarn defenders wore to spare them from the effects of the Great Gate, Pacys felt the pull of the huge whirlpool that suddenly formed and reached from the Great Gate to the ocean's surface. The eldritch energies lighted the whirlpool from the inside, throwing out yellow-green light like it was a giant lamp. He watched as the swirling waterspout around the pirate vessels broadened to a thousand feet and more, sucking them down into the deep trough that opened.

The ships turned sideways and tumbled down into the waterspout. The vessels that went prow or stern first stayed level even though they followed the circular motion of the whirlpool, but the ships that went down sideways rolled over and shattered, filling the whirlpool with deadly debris that slammed into the other ships.

"Blessed Oghma," the old bard whispered, stunned.

From everything Qos, the Dukars, and the High Mages had talked about, he was certain no one expected this. The Great Gate had never been opened before, it was intended as a desperate, final effort against invaders.

The sahuagin, drowned ones, and koalinth barred from the city by the mythal were drawn into the whirlpool as well. The ships, whole and broken, smashed into them, killing dozens in a sweep. The mythal was all that prevented the city itself from being pulled into the whirlpool.

Pacys caught sight of *Azure Dagger* as the caravel was yanked into the whirlpool as well. No one thought to give the two ships any defense against the whirlpool. No one believed it would reach so far. Miraculously, *Azure Dagger* went into the whirlpool prow first, followed by *Steadfast*. Three Cormyrean Freesails followed next.

Though filled with horror and hurt, Pacys's pain was nowhere near that of another's.

* * * * *

"No!" Jherek screamed in disbelief.

Azure Dagger seemed to sail straight into the whirlpool's jaws.

Within seconds, the first of the ships and the sahuagin reached the eye of the whirlpool at the Great Gate and disappeared, thrown half a world away—for all anyone knew. The only thing the High Mages and Qos agreed on was that the Great Gate took all in it far from Serôs.

Something shoved the young paladin from behind. Angry, he turned, only to find the golden sea wyrm floating there. It coiled and flexed, struggling against the whirlpool's pull. For the first time, he understood the creature's attraction to him; why it mysteriously followed him to Aglarond and back, and why it helped him rescue Sabyna from the drowned ones.

Azure Dagger plummeted toward the whirlpool's eye as Jherek reached for the sea wyrm and pulled himself up onto the creature's back. He slapped it on the neck gratefully and urged it forward. The sea wyrm darted forward like an arrow. Jherek ripped the necklace with the whirlpool gem from his neck and threw it away, feeling the pull of the gate at once.

"Jherek!"

Knowing the voice, the young paladin glanced ahead, spotting the bard atop the statue.

"I must know the end of the story," Pacys shouted.

Jherek hesitated for an instant as the sea wyrm closed the distance to the old bard. Doing what he planned was without question dangerous, but he knew Pacys was as driven by his part in the events as he was. He willed the bracer back into its resting form and reached for Pacys's hand.

Though the force of the contact must have almost ripped the bard's arm from his shoulder, Pacys didn't say a word. The old bard twisted himself expertly in the water until he sat behind Jherek.

The sea wyrm jerked suddenly.

Glancing back, Jherek saw that Khlinat had managed to grab the creature's tail. The dwarf held on fiercely.

"Leave him," the young paladin told the sea wyrm.

In response, the dragon-kin curled the dwarf protectively in its tail.

Jherek watched *Azure Dagger* plunge toward the whirlpool's eye. Two masts hung in broken shards, wrapped in sailcloth. The sea wyrm reached the outer edge of the whirlpool and they were sucked inside.

* * * * *

Sabyna gazed up in disbelief at the swirling wall of green-blue water that surrounded her. *Azure Dagger* stabbed straight down into the maelstrom. The roaring water made conversation impossible. The ship's mage thought she might be screaming, but she'd have never known.

She lost her footing on the deck as the caravel tilted forward even more. As she fell toward the prow, aware of the tangled rigging and the broken mast ahead, Sabyna angled her body and managed to seize the rigging with one hand. She swung under it and prayed that her fingers wouldn't be pulled off.

She was hit from behind, and when she spun to see what had happened, she found herself face to face with a pirate who'd been hanged in the rigging. The bloated face and protruding tongue let her know it was too late to cut him away.

The caravel hit the bottom of the whirlpool and the world went away.

* * * * *

Laying low along the sea wyrm's neck, the old bard's arms wrapped tight around his waist and with Khlinat in tow, Jherek guided his mount through the swirling wall of water into the center of the whirlpool. For a moment they hung motionless in the raging roar of the ocean, then they fell toward the bottom of the whirlpool. The sea wyrm convulsed, then poked its head down.

Jherek locked his legs around his mount and leaned back, forcing himself to stay on its back through sheer willpower. They hit the bottom of the whirlpool, followed immediately by a moment of blackness, then crashed through a tumbling seascape.

Pirate ships lay scattered along the ocean floor, smashed, broken, and driven into the mud and sand. Ships crashed into the reef, became buried in broken coral strands, and hopelessly tangled in each others' rigging.

The sea wyrm flared its fins and angled its head, bringing them up from the steep dive only a few feet short of the ocean floor. It turned its head and twisted its body, rolling neatly around the coral reef, then it angled toward the surface.

Away from Myth Nantar's mythal, Jherek suddenly found he couldn't breathe without drowning. Though Pacys wore some kind of bracelet that allowed him to move underwater with ease, Khlinat was in the same shape as Jherek. Somehow the dragon-kin knew that.

Ahead, *Azure Dagger* and four other ships that survived the wild ride rose toward the surface, buoyed by the air in their cargo holds.

Jherek knew the ships probably wouldn't last even if they reached the surface. Though there was still some air in their holds, the structures were weakened beyond repair and would be taking on water rapidly. Quick crews might man the bilge pumps and keep themselves afloat for a time, but that assumed any crew was left.

"There is the Taker," Pacys said, still able to talk thanks to the bracelet he wore.

Jherek spotted the big sahuagin ahead. Only the Taker didn't resemble a sahuagin any more. He looked human as he fumbled with an object in his hands. A pale female elf holding a trident swam close behind him.

In the next instant, the sea wyrm broke the surface and

Jherek drew in a long breath. Glancing over his shoulder, he saw that the sea wyrm had raised Khlinat to the surface as well, holding the dwarf in its curled tail.

Turning, Jherek watched *Azure Dagger*'s stern clear the surface first, revealing the broken stern mast. Then the crow's nest bucked up, wavering with the sea's motion.

The young paladin headed for the caravel by tugging on the sea wyrm's forward fin. The creature raced across the ocean surface.

Frantically, Jherek searched *Azure Dagger*'s deck.

"Jherek, here!"

Drawn by her voice, the young paladin spotted Sabyna crawling down from the twisted remnants of the foremast rigging where a corpse hung. He guided the sea wyrm to the caravel.

Azla stood up, coughing and gagging in the stern, then took a deep breath and started bellowing orders to her crew. *Azure Dagger* listed heavily in the sea, nearly half of her below the waterline.

"Look," Pacys said softly. "The Taker."

Jherek turned in time to see Iakhovas pull up from the sea, grabbing hold of *Azure Dagger*'s stern. The helmsman turned on the man, swinging a cutlass.

Iakhovas blocked the blade with his bare arm and the steel broke with a sharp ping. The Taker shoved his arm against the man, thrusting a sharp-edged fin through the helmsman's chest in a spray of blood.

Striding to the railing, Iakhovas roared, "Get off my ship or die!"

* * * * *

Laaqueel tasted the salt in the water around her and knew she was home. She gazed through the deep blue-green sea and tried to sense in what direction the sahuagin kingdom of Alkyraan in the Claarteeros Sea lay.

And should you go back there, the female voice asked, *what do you think will be waiting for you?*

"Leave me alone," Laaqueel demanded.

A hero's homecoming? A grateful return for the Most Sacred One? And what happens when some of the sahuagin in these waters return there as well with stories of the way Iakhovas has betrayed them? What if Iakhovas himself returns there intending to control the kingdom he won while he plots war with the rest of Toril?

"No."

Those are his plans, Laaqueel. You cannot deny that.

The malenti priestess cowered in the water, wishing there was some way to be free.

You can be free.

"By giving myself to you?"

I will teach you to live free, Laaqueel. I will show you things you've longed for all your life and have never been able to name. You've changed too much now to go back to what you were.

"No."

Yes.

Laaqueel floated in the water, watching as sahuagin and pirate continued the war they'd begun in Serôs. Some of the sahuagin wore the bluer colors of the Inner Sea.

"Who are you?"

I am Eldath, called the Green Goddess and the Quiet One. The Twelfth Serôs War has destroyed much of the harmony my priests and priestesses have wrought over the last years. This is necessary, though, to promote the greater harmony we've striven for throughout the Inner Sea.

"Why have you come to me?"

During your association with the Taker, Laaqueel, you have changed and grown. I see much promise in you. Like you, Serôs will have to change and grow. There are noble malenti in Serôs who have no ties with the sahuagin. I would introduce you to them.

Laaqueel adjusted her air bladder and floated effortlessly, torn between what she hoped for and what she knew to be true. Home could never be home again unless Iakhovas was there to enforce her privileges. She would give up more than she would gain.

Little malenti, Iakhovas called, *to me. There is a ship I want, and we'll need a crew to get it to Skaug where we may begin planning anew.*

Skaug was the pirate capital of the Nelanther Isles, a place Iakhovas had taken Laaqueel before. She hesitated.

Little malenti!

The quill next to Laaqueel's heart twitched in warning. She started up to the surface, tracking the bond between her and Iakhovas.

* * * * *

Placing a hand on the sea wyrm's back, Jherek vaulted to *Azure Dagger*'s tilted deck. Azla ran up the stern castle steps toward Iakhovas, her scimitar in her fist. The Taker grinned cruelly at her and a ruby beam leaped out from his golden eye.

The beam touched Azla and blasted her in a shower of sparks. She flew back over the railing to the main deck, her blouse afire and the stench of ozone in the air.

Jherek broke stride, thinking to go to Azla's side.

"Go, young warrior," Glawinn thundered.

The paladin lurched across the broken deck, dragging his right leg heavily at his side. His left arm was curled up tightly by his chest, blood streaming from a wound marked by a wooden shard protruding from it.

Jherek ran up the stern castle stairs, watching as Iakhovas swung on him with the mystic eye. The young paladin leaped, taking advantage of the tilted deck, arching his body in mid-air and flipping to land on the stern castle only a few feet from Iakhovas.

Though he hadn't fought a mage before, he knew from stories that their power relied on being able to cast spells, and spells took time. He intended to give Iakhovas none. He willed Iridea's Tear into a two-foot shield and advanced on the Taker.

"You're the boy from the cave," Iakhovas said. He grinned and took a step back as he drew the sword at his side.

"I am Jherek, a paladin in the service of Lathander, the Morninglord. If you would surrender, I would allow it." The young paladin didn't expect the man would, but the opportunity had to be offered.

Cruel lights glinted in Iakhovas's real eye as well as the golden one that sat in the scarred socket. His runic tattoos made his face seem even darker. He laughed loudly.

"And you would kill me otherwise, boy?"

"Aye, and praise Lathander for giving me the strength."

The words still sounded strange to Jherek's ears, but in his heart they felt right and true.

Iakhovas drew himself up to his full height of nearly eight feet and drew the sword at his hip.

"I *invented* swordplay, boy. Edged steel . . . sharp as a shark's tooth . . . shaped like a fin. Who else but me could create that?"

The great sword came around much quicker than Jherek anticipated. The young paladin stepped back and ducked, letting the blade go harmlessly by. Even as he started to set himself, Iakhovas brought the blade back at Jherek's knees faster than any human could have done.

Leaping over the blade, Jherek flipped and came down on his feet. He lifted the shield just in time to keep the blade from cleaving his skull. He parried with his cutlass, scoring a deep cut on his opponent's arm.

Iakhovas scowled and took a step back. A violet ray shot at Jherek from the Taker's golden eye.

Reacting instantly, the young paladin raised his shield, which absorbed the ray and threw it back into Iakhovas's face, staggering him. The young paladin immediately went on the offensive again, driving Iakhovas back. He thrust and parried, then lunged and slashed, moving steadily into the bigger man. Blood from Iakhovas's wound dripped on the ship's deck and left burned stigmata.

"You cannot kill me, boy," Iakhovas shouted. "I will not allow myself to die. Even Umberlee tried to kill me and failed. Who are you to challenge me who would be a god?"

"I am a strong right arm of Lathander," Jherek replied, burying the cutlass in the railing then ripping it free and diving back. He blocked Iakhovas's return blow with his shield this time and slashed his opponent across the chest. "I am a beginning, chosen by the Morninglord."

"Chosen to die," Iakhovas taunted.

"No," Jherek said, "chosen to live."

Jherek thrust and swung and parried. His blade moved even faster, picking up the pace in spite of all the battles he'd been in this day.

Iakhovas's scowl deepened as he was forced back. Steel rang on steel, and for the first time Jherek realized some of the surviving sahuagin were attacking *Azure Dagger*.

330

Her crew defended her, aided by the sea wyrm. Pacys fought on the deck, his staff whirling as he chopped into the sea devils that fought to board. Khlinat was at the old bard's side, his axes whirling madly.

Taking advantage of the young paladin's distraction, Iakhovas stepped forward suddenly and chanced a side-arm blow straight for Jherek's head. Jherek barely got his cutlass around to block the sword, but he was driven stumbling backward, off-balance.

Iakhovas came at him, snarling and with bloodlust in his eye. He raised the great sword two-handed and brought it down.

Jherek turned quickly, barely escaping the blow that shattered the navigator's table behind him. He rolled to his feet, willing the bracer into a hook as he ducked under Iakhovas's backhanded blow. He caught the blade in the hook, stopping it short and pulling the Taker off balance. Turning in, knowing the chance he was taking, the young paladin brought the cutlass crashing down on the trapped blade.

Harsh green light exploded on impact, and electricity filled the air. Steel shattered, falling in two pieces, leaving only an inch or two sticking out from the hilt.

Iakhovas stepped back in surprise, but a crafty smile lit his scarred and tattooed features.

"You haven't seen all there is to me, boy," Iakhovas said.

He turned and sprinted for the stern railing, leaping over it in a long, flat dive.

Jherek followed the movement, but stopped at the rail, amazed at what he saw.

By the time Iakhovas hit the water, he was no longer anything human. A manlike form went down, but a ninety-foot great white shark surfaced. Scars and tattooing showed around a golden eye. It sped out to sea and gradually went down, leaving only the triangular dorsal fin—as big as a house—sticking out of the water.

Sahuagin swarmed up the stern, and Jherek spent a few moments riposting their attacks and killing them. As he kicked the corpses back into the water, he noticed the triangular fin streaking for *Azure Dagger*.

"Hold on!" he roared in warning.

In the next instant, the huge shark slammed into the

caravel. Timbers cracked and gave way as the predator hammered through the hull.

"Abandon ship, damn it!"

Jherek turned and saw Azla up and about. Wounds still covered her, but evidently Glawinn had healed the worst of it. She was mobile, but hurting greatly.

"Get the boats over the side and get into them!" she shouted. "We're taking on water like a sieve!"

Glancing back out to sea, Jherek watched the massive predator come around for another pass.

* * * * *

Laaqueel watched Iakhovas in awe as he transformed into the great shark.

Not a shark, Eldath corrected. *Iakhovas is a megalodon, a prehistoric creature and perhaps the first such of his kind.*

"But he once walked with gods," Laaqueel said, watching as Iakhovas sped toward the ship.

With Umberlee, yes, and possibly even with Sekolah.

"He was never one of Sekolah's chosen?"

No. He's an aberration, a thing whose time is well gone.

Iakhovas turned from attacking the ship and fixed her with his real eye. *Little malenti,* his voice sounded in her head, *you are slow to come when I command.*

You must make a choice, Eldath said, *here and now. Will you stay as an outcast with the sahuagin and keep Iakhovas as your master, or will you take what I offer?*

* * * * *

"Brace yourselves!" Jherek yelled as he grabbed the stern railing.

Iakhovas rammed *Azure Dagger* again, splitting the hull even more. As the huge predator pulled away this time, the young paladin felt the caravel listing, taking on water. He glanced over his shoulder as the vessel sank to its midsection. The crew routed the attacking sahuagin. The sea wyrm raised its golden finned head from the sea and returned Jherek's gaze.

"I need you," Jherek said.

The sea wyrm dived without hesitation and swam to the stern section. Out in the distance, Iakhovas came around for another pass. Jherek was certain this attack would leave the stricken vessel in tatters and the crew vulnerable to that great mouth filled with serrated teeth.

"Jherek!" Sabyna called from behind him.

"Lady," the young paladin said. "You need to get in one of the boats and row for shore." He pointed toward the low, green-forested hill that could be seen in the distance.

"What are you going to do?"

Jherek gave her a smile and answered, "All that I may, lady. I can do naught else."

Sabyna took her kerchief from her hair and quickly tied it around his arm. "I would not stop you from doing as Lathander has directed, but you heed my words well." Her voice cracked with emotion and a sheen was in her eyes. "You finish what you have been given to do, and you come back to me in one piece."

Jherek's heart soared, pushing aside even the fear and insecurity that thrummed inside him. He took her face in his hands and kissed her deeply.

"As you wish, lady," he said, then threw himself from the stern castle in a dive that took him straight at the approaching shark.

Curving up toward the surface, watching the huge predator bearing down on him and suddenly realizing how vulnerable he was when the shark could swallow him and the sea wyrm whole, Jherek grabbed hold of the dragon-kin's dorsal fin and pulled himself up on its back.

The bond between Jherek and the sea wyrm was strong. He guided it with his knees as he willed the bracer into a shield. He held his sword in his hand as they sped toward their foe.

Ninety feet of silent, sudden death sped at the young paladin. Jherek sat his mount, holding on tightly, gambling that the bracer's power would see him through. The sea wyrm didn't falter as it finned toward Iakhovas.

Holding on tightly to the grip inside the shield, Jherek narrowly avoided the black, cavernous mouth ringed by serrated teeth and smashed the shield into the huge predator's snout. The impact hurled him dozens of feet from the sea wyrm and almost knocked him out, but the shield absorbed the brunt of the blow.

Iakhovas, incredibly, seemed staggered.

"You'll die for that boy," he said as he turned in the water.

The sea wyrm swam to Jherek's side in a flash of golden light. Fighting the disorientation that gripped him, the young paladin tried to mount again.

Iakhovas's snout was bloodied. His golden eye gleamed.

Jherek tried to pull up onto the sea wyrm but missed. He concentrated, keeping his grip as the dragon-kin pulled him backward. The great predator bore down on him.

* * * * *

Laaqueel swam toward the young warrior trying to pull up onto the sea wyrm. When she reached him, she pushed him up onto his mount and turned to face Iakhovas.

Little malenti, what do you think you're doing?

Laaqueel made no reply. There was none to make. In the next few heartbeats, she'd live or die. She summoned her powers, intending to crush Iakhovas if she could.

Where she'd once felt all the gifts Sekolah had given her, there was only emptiness.

Your belief in the Shark God is gone, Eldath said. *As goes the belief, so goes the power. There is no other way.*

Helplessly, Laaqueel watched as Iakhovas rushed toward her.

Die, traitorous bitch!

Laaqueel felt the quill stir next to her heart, then it, too, was gone. Before she could move, though, Iakhovas was on her.

* * * * *

Transfixed with horror, Jherek watched as the huge shark overtook the elf woman and swallowed her in a single gulp. Jherek urged the sea wyrm up, feeling the need for air burn his lungs. They surfaced and Jherek grabbed a couple deep breaths before they plunged back beneath the waves. He heeled the sea wyrm around, going directly at Iakhovas again.

"I won't miss this time, boy."

Jherek tightened his grip on his shield as they sped toward their opponent. This time he directed the sea wyrm down, at the same time striking up with the shield. He held the shield edge on, slicing deeply into Iakhovas's side, feeling the hard muscle and rough skin slide along his forearm. The cut, nearly a foot deep and almost the length of the body, bled profusely.

Iakhovas screamed in pain.

Kneeing the sea wyrm, Jherek turned back around, intending to pursue Iakhovas if he fled. Instead, the Taker came at him again, the great slash along his body flaring wide. Behind Iakhovas came dozens of sharks, drawn by the blood spoor Iakhovas trailed.

The young paladin willed the bracer into a hook. The sea wyrm went high this time, turning at the last moment and going over the predator's head. Jherek leaned down and buried the hook in the muscle above the Taker's good eye. He held on and let himself be dragged from his mount. He straddled the great shark's head as best he could, then reversed his sword as Iakhovas dived deep.

"I'll take you down, landling," the Taker said. "So far down you'll never make the surface again before your lungs burst."

Fiercely, despite the fear that rattled inside him, certain he was doing Lathander's will and saving the life of the woman he loved, Jherek hung on. He knew if he turned loose and the sea wyrm couldn't get back to him in time, Iakhovas would eat him as well. He couldn't outswim the Taker.

Jherek leaned forward, using the hook to brace himself, and drove the sword into Iakhovas's good eye, plunging it deep.

Iakhovas screamed in pain, and the shrill squeal echoed through the sea. Blood streamed from the ruined eye, but the Taker still did not give up.

Noticing how the golden eye glowed more brightly and remembering how his sword seemed to surprise his foe when it cut him, Jherek pulled the sword free. He steadied himself, pushing the need to breathe from his mind. He rammed the sword down into Iakhovas's eye.

The resulting explosion blew Jherek from the huge predator's back. Dazed, he struck out at a shark that got too near him, turning the animal away from him. He looked down, seeing that the destruction of the magical eye had blown the Taker's head almost completely away. In Jherek's hand, though, the sword was miraculously still whole and unmarked.

Remembering the elf woman, Jherek dived after the sinking carcass, spots whirling madly in his vision as his lungs ached for air. The sea wyrm came up to him just as he reached Iakhovas's ruined head.

Jherek peered into the cavern of torn flesh and spotted the elf woman. He climbed into the Taker's ruined maw and cradled the woman in his arms, taking her up from the blood and gore that filled what was left of the creature, covered in it himself from his passage. For a moment, the young paladin believed the elf was dead. The great teeth had torn her body in several places.

The gills on the side of her neck feathered, and she opened her eyes and looked up at him.

Jherek's whole body ached. If they hadn't been in the water, he didn't think he'd have the strength to lift her. He turned and started toward the grievous wound where the Taker's head had been, but his legs failed him. His lungs were on the verge of bursting.

The sea wyrm batted furiously at the sharks that came for the fallen giant, keeping them free of the wound. Still, it wouldn't be long before the sharks overpowered even it.

Out of breath, spots swimming before his eyes, refusing to believe that he could fail now, Jherek sagged, struggling to keep his mouth closed, struggling to keep from taking a breath.

The woman in his arms took his face in her hands and pulled his mouth to hers. At first, he resisted, but even her weak strength was greater than what waned within him. She held her mouth on his and opened her lips. The gills on the side of her neck flexed and she blew air against his closed mouth. Bubbles raced for the surface.

Understanding, Jherek opened his mouth and received the breath of life she pushed into his lungs. He drank deeply from what she had to give, then stood again and pushed them out into the ocean.

He caught hold of the sea wyrm and pulled them onto it, holding the woman in his arms as she held onto his face.

Gazing at the Taker's corpse, watching it settle slowly into the black depths of the sea, the young paladin saw the sharks feeding at the raw meat and knew in hours it would be gone.

Epílogue

The Sea of Swords
7 Uktar, the Year of the Gauntlet

"Jherek!"

The young paladin glanced up, hearing the sound distorted by the water.

Pacys swam down for him, protected by the magic bracelet. He stopped when he saw Jherek was on his way up, then swam alongside.

When they reached the surface, Jherek breathed deeply and shook the water from his eyes. He was facing east, toward the green lands he saw along the coast. Morning had only lately come, filling the sky with pinks, oranges, yellows, and reds.

"I saw the end," Pacys said excitedly. "I witnessed your battle with the Taker and your triumph. Blessed Oghma, I will have my song and my name will be known throughout Faerûn. There will not be a shore you ever touch, Jherek, that will not know your story."

"Aye," Jherek said, embarrassed, "but make sure you don't make my part too big, old bard. I played such a small part in everything, and I have never been a hero."

The woman in the young paladin's arms hacked and shifted weakly.

For the first time, Jherek noticed the shark's tooth embedded between her breasts near her heart. He sluiced water over her, washing away the clotted hunks of meat from the Taker's corpse.

The woman smiled weakly as she peered down at the tooth. "Even in death," she rasped, "he has managed to kill me."

"Her name is Laaqueel," Pacys said quietly. "The mermen learned of her at the Battle of Voalidru. She served the Taker."

"Not in the end," Jherek replied, washing the blood from his hands and slipping the cutlass through his sash. "In the end she stood for what was good and right."

"It's better this way," she whispered. "I am finished."

Her eyes glazed slightly.

"No," Jherek promised, drawing on the powers Lathander had seen fit to give him.

He prayed to his newfound god who watched over him for so many years, waiting until it was time to reap the harvest, and he asked for the Morninglord's blessing.

The young paladin put his hands on the woman's breast, cupping the embedded shark's tooth. As he continued to pray, golden light gleamed from his palms. The tooth shattered and fell away. Blood gushed from the wound, but he placed a hand over it and continued praying. When the golden gleam dimmed, he scooped water over her chest, washing the blood away, and revealed only whole, unblemished skin.

"No," Jherek repeated. "You'll not die this day, lady." He helped her sit, seeing the amazement on her features. "Lathander is a god of beginnings, not endings."

Laaqueel slipped from his grasp and slid into the water. She broke eye contact.

"Gratitude is not something I was brought up to believe in. My people have always taken what they wanted, and it was a weaker being's ill luck to have it taken from them." She glanced back at Jherek and added, "But I thank you for my life. There are new currents in it that I would follow."

"I wish you well in them," Jherek said, "and I thank you for saving my life."

Without another word, Laaqueel dropped under the ocean and out of sight.

"Jherek!"

Twisting, the young paladin spotted Sabyna standing on a ship's forecastle beside Glawinn. Jherek urged the sea wyrm forward and it cut across the ocean through the shattered remains of other ships, the longboats filled with pirate survivors, corpses, and the sharks that fed on them.

Khlinat threw a cargo net over the side and called, "Pipe aboard, swabbie. We done found us a ship that a gaggle of pirates didn't have the guts to keep once we decided we liked the look of 'er." The dwarf was splattered in blood, but not much of it looked like his. He offered a hand as Jherek climbed aboard. "Ye done for that bad 'un, yeah?"

Jherek nodded and glanced at the ship. The stern mast was broken, the rigging was in tangles, and most of the canvas was gone.

"Aye," Khlinat bellowed, "she ain't no pretty 'un, swabbie, I'll grant ye that, but she's tight as a duck's arse and she's got some promise."

"There's also a pretty impressive cargo below," Azla said. She stepped up from the hold, limping only a little. "No matter where we're at, we're not going to be broke. We'll find a port and get this ship fixed up."

"Then where, Captain?" Jherek asked. "Back to the Sea of Fallen Stars?"

Azla hesitated, then smiled a little. "I don't know," she said. "I'm beginning to think I've been around you and Glawinn too long. The life of a pirate doesn't hold quite the allure it once did."

"And maybe you've taken a better look at yourself," Glawinn said, cradling his injured arm as he approached. "Maybe you aren't as uncaring or disbelieving as you think you are."

"Back off, Sir Knight," Azla said with only a trace of humor. "I'm quite capable of finding my own way. Without your help."

Glawinn turned his gaze on Jherek and asked, "What about you, young warrior? Where are you bound?"

Jherek looked at Sabyna, then took her into his arms, enjoying the warm feel of her.

"Home," he said, looking into her eyes. "I want to see

Madame Iitaar and Malorrie again, and make sure old Finaren and *Butterfly* are still hale and whole."

Glawinn softened his voice. "Not all of your troubles are over, young warrior. Your father and his crew still roam the waters along the Sword Coast."

Sabyna gazed into Jherek's eyes with her copper-colored ones. "Whatever his troubles may be," she promised, "great or small, he'll never have to face them alone."

"Lady," Jherek began, "you don't know the kind of trouble—"

The ship's mage placed her hand over his mouth. "No," she bade him, "no arguments. There's been enough of those. I mean what I say, Jherek, and I ask only that you love me in turn. Without restraint, without remorse. With all of your heart." Tears glittered in her eyes, but she was smiling.

Jherek held her to him tightly, smelling the lilacs in spite of the brine that clung to her. He grinned at the dawning sun in the eastern sky and said, "As you wish, lady."

The Cormyr Saga
Death of the Dragon
Ed Greenwood and Troy Denning

The saga of the kingdom of Cormyr comes to an epic conclusion in this new story. Besieged by evil from without and treachery from within, Cormyr's King Azoun must sacrifice everything for his beloved land.

Available August 2000

Beyond the High Road
Troy Denning

Dire prophecies come to life, and the usually stable kingdom of Cormyr is plunged into chaos.

And don't miss . . .
Cormyr: A Novel
Ed Greenwood and Jeff Grubb
The novel that started it all.

Sembia
The Halls of Stormweather
A new FORGOTTEN REALMS series

In the mean streets of Selgaunt everything has a price, and even the wealthiest families will do anything to survive. The cast of characters: the capable but embattled patriarch of the Uskevren family, a young woman who is more than just a maid, the son who carries a horrifying curse, a wife with past as long as it is dark, a servant with more secrets than his master could ever guess, and much more.

Seven talented authors introduce the FORGOTTEN REALMS to a new generation of fans. Featuring novellas by Ed Greenwood, Clayton Emery, Richard Lee Byers, Voronica Whitney-Robinson, Dave Gross, Lisa Smedman, and Paul Kemp.

Available July 2000

Sembia
Shadow's Witness
Paul Kemp

Erevis Cale must battle ghosts from his own dark past if he is to save the family he dearly loves. The first full-length novel in this exciting new series—your gateway to the FORGOTTEN REALMS !

Available November 2000

R.A. Salvatore
Servant of the Shard

The exciting climax of the story of the Crystal Shard

In 1988 R.A. Salvatore burst onto the fantasy scene with a novel about a powerful magical artifact—the Crystal Shard. Now, more than a decade later, he brings the story of the Shard to its shattering conclusion.

From the dark, twisted streets of Calimport to the lofty passes of the Snowflake Mountains, from flashing swords to sizzling spells, this is R.A. Salvatore at his best.

Available October 2000

Enter the magical land of the Flanaess, world of adventure!

GREYHAWK is the setting of the role-playing game
DUNGEONS & DRAGONS. Each of these novels is based on a classic
D&D adventure module.

Against the Giants
Ru Emerson

A village burns while its attackers flee into the night. Enraged, the king
of Keoland orders an aging warrior to lead a band of adventurers on a
retaliatory strike. As they prepare to enter the heart of the monsters'
lair, each knows only the bravest will survive.

White Plume Mountain
Paul Kidd

A ranger, a faerie, and a sentient hell hound pelt with a penchant for
pyromania. These three companions must enter the most trap-laden,
monster-infested place this side of Acererak's tomb: White Plume
Mountain.

Descent into the Depths of the Earth
Paul Kidd

Fresh from their encounter with White Plume Mountain, the Justicar
and Escalla depart for the town of Hommlet. But life around a faerie is
never exactly . . . stable. Before he knows it, to save her life the Justicar
is on his way into the depths of the earth to fight hobgoblins, drow,
and the queen of the demonweb pits.

Available June 2000

Expedition to the Barrier Peaks
Roland J. Green

Amid a range of forbidding mountains broods a secret from out of
the skies. Now a daring band of explorers must discover the truth
that hides among the Barrier Peaks.

Available November 2000